The Sons of Anubis

The Sons of Anubis

A Novel

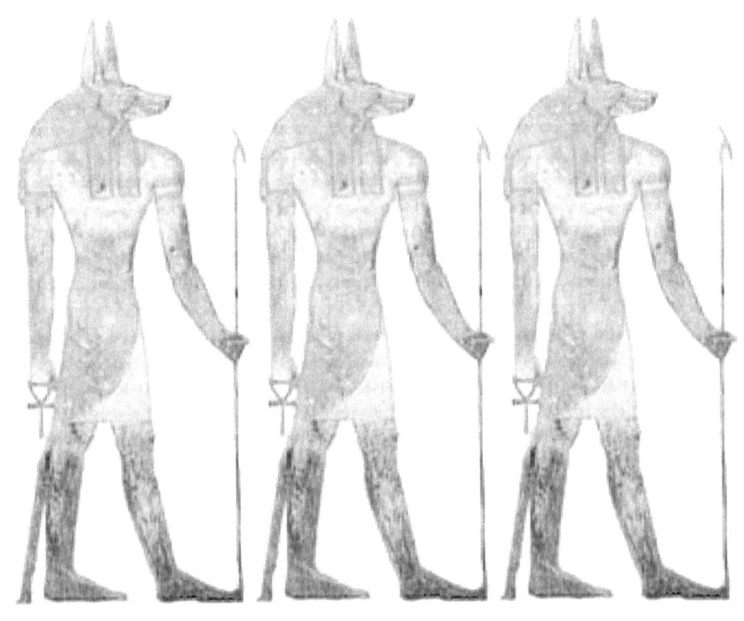

Anthony Myron Clark

First paperback edition October 2020

ISBN 978-1-7358469-0-3 (paperback)
ISBN 978-1-7358469-2-7 (hardcover)
ISBN 978-1-7358469-1-0 (ebook)

Dedication

To my father and mother, for all their support in my life, including their encouragement of my hobbies and youthful enjoyments. Especially to my father, who once commented out of the blue, "Have you ever tried to get published?" When I responded that I had not, he asked "Why not? You should try."

This set me on the path of completing the first of my stories, which has been a great adventure. I often wish I had spent more time with my father talking about writing while he was alive.

Hence, to my father, Ronald K. Clark, and my mother, Edwina J. Clark, I dedicate this book.

PROLOGUE

S ILVER EYES HAD *watched the approach of the blue Nissan Pathfinder. Hidden in the shadows across the street, undetected, the entire mansion front could be seen from a safe vantage point as the five Americans had driven up. Their arrival was shortly after the Isha'a, the last call to prayer. A cool breeze brought their scents across the desert air.*

Two men in the front were obviously armed and armored with Kevlar vests and M4 machine guns. The three passengers in the back, though dressed in matching sand-colored attire, were not so obviously armed with their smaller M9 handguns hidden in fanny packs. When they had arrived and stepped from the vehicle, the way they moved and held their hands betrayed their weapons.

The silver eyes honed in on the two in the front. Both men held a confidence and certainty in their purpose. The passenger side guardian seemed the calmer of the two, with a sense of energy teaming within him; however, the driver seemed by far the colder in purpose. The driver would be the dangerous one; a man who would not hesitate to pull the trigger of the weapons he held, and most certainly would be deadly accurate.

They had arrived and entered the house of Colonel Khalil just after sunset to enjoy his hospitality and dinner. The moon was rising, although the night was still dark. This hunt would be on tonight as an ill omen hung in the air. The hunter settled back into the shadows, watching and waiting.

Chapter 1

Silver Eyes at Night

IT WAS JUST past nine p.m. when the Nissan Pathfinder pulled away from the Colonel's house, driving through the dark streets of Kuwait City. The Navy Chief in the driver's seat kept an eye on the road while his officer, Lieutenant Commander Liam Brand swept the surrounding streets. The two in the front wore Navy desert battle dress uniforms, with weapons and body armor. The three riders in the back wore civilian attire, complete with fanny packs to hide their service weapons.

Before the Pathfinder had pulled around the block, one of the three in the back seat started up. NCIS Special Agent Enrique Chavez griped at the Chief, "Keep it on all fours and avoid the potholes. I've just experienced enough pain for one evening. God, why the hell are we here? This is a waste of NCIS manpower."

Brand shook his head as he heard Chief Gunner's Mate Dean Prim exhale and cast him a sidelong glance. Brand and his Chief had been assigned what should have been an enviable task providing security for the NCIS Special

Agents in Kuwait. Special Agent Chavez had made their assignment a nightmare.

Philip Ross sat in the center behind them as the Senior Agent in Charge. He was a small, bald man, and pleasant to work with; however, he remained silent when Chavez started to rant, which was quite often. Brand could imagine Ross closing his eyes for the ride back, choosing to sleep through the half-hour drive as opposed to listening to the coming tirade.

The smallest of the three, Special Agent Arianna Minos, sat behind Prim. She was just over five feet in height with long, dark hair pulled into a tight bun for the evening. She had wrapped on a hijab headscarf when they were arriving earlier, but upon climbing back into their vehicle, had removed it. Of the agents, she was the junior and had arrived in Kuwait less than two weeks prior. Although still getting her feet under her, Brand found her to be highly intelligent, as she had already demonstrated the ability to understand the workings of the Middle Eastern methods.

"I would think you'd welcome the opportunity to build U.S.-host nation relations, while we get to work on an actual case." Minos mused.

Chavez looked to her and grumbled dismissively, "Wait until you understand these rag-heads better. They are lazy with their inshallah: God willing my ass. It's probably one of their goat lovers out there committing these crimes. Not a U.S. soldier or a Navy issue."

Brand sighed and kept his eyes on the side of the road. Colonel Jassim Khalil Al Azzaan was an extremely educated and charismatic Kuwaiti officer, having spent many years abroad in both the United Kingdom and United States. He was a leading support of U.S. forces in the Middle East and specifically Kuwait. Colonel Khalil had insisted on NCIS visiting and discussing with him a concern of, as he had stressed, "utmost importance." Although the five had enjoyed dinner, Brand and Prim had been directed out of the room by Chavez, insisting they were not Special Agents and should wait in the car.

For an instant, Brand caught a flash of what appeared to be silver eyes from a dark alley and then the Pathfinder was past. Looking back over his shoulder, he had a sense of being followed and consciously shifted his M4, fingering the weapon to semi-automatic.

"What's up, sir?" Prim asked, his eyes still locked on the road before them although now more alert. One hand slid down to release the lock on his drop holster to free up his M9, although while driving it would be a struggle to pull the weapon.

"Don't know. I'm just getting a funny feeling. I possibly saw infrared goggles. Drive faster."

Brand saw a dark form shoot from the shadows ahead, streaking towards his side of the Pathfinder. It was large and moving fast. He tried to react, lifting his M4 and barking a course order across the jeep. Prim gunned the engine and the light four-by-four lurched forward; however, before

Brand was able to pull the trigger, the vaguely human form slammed into the side of the vehicle. For a sickening moment, the Pathfinder shook violently as it stood up on edge and rolled, skidding forward and sliding into the corner of a building.

Brand fell into Prim and tried to scramble to his knees, pushing off the Chief and lifting his weapon towards the passenger door. A dark snout peered over the door and the M4 fired a burst, scoring a hit as a spout of blood sprayed the interior and the creature howled, disappearing in the dark.

In the back seat, the three NCIS lay jumbled together. Chavez shouted curses at the Chief for poor driving. The heavier agent pushed Ross, who hung limp from his seatbelt, and attempted to unbuckle his own belt.

Without further warning, the vehicle shook again and continued its roll, landing on its roof. Brand and Prim fell side-by-side, and swung their weapons towards either side; Brand's M4 and Prim with his M9 Beretta handgun. Chavez continued to berate the Chief, falling on his back with his legs jacked in the air. As he realized both Brand and Prim were bearing arms, he turned his anger on the discharge of the M4, screaming. As his volume began to rise, the passenger door tore from its hinges and a large, dark snout snapped around Chavez's throat, instantly silencing him.

"Fuck!" Prim cursed, scrambling back from the horrific scene. He leveled his M9 towards the back seat.

"No!" Brand shouted, watching Chavez's body drag from the back. "Outside!"

He pushed across the ceiling and out the passenger side front door. He struggled to his feet and tried to gather his surroundings, swinging the muzzle of the M4 in a path to find Chavez.

Yards away, a scene unfolded that froze him in his tracks. A man-sized creature hunkered over Chavez, dark of skin and fur. Where a face should have been was an elongated snout, similar to a canine, with long, thin ears and long, sharp teeth. Yellow eyes glared across the short distance as it growled, its jaws clenched tightly about Chavez's throat.

Its body was vaguely man-like, with slightly longer arms. Its legs bent oddly like the hind legs of a dog, with longer padded paws vice feet and the joint of the ankle higher on the leg. Its fingers ended in larger and longer digits, with thicker, sharper nails more akin to large claws. The entire body seemed covered in a thin, black fur.

From the far side of the car, he heard a scream and found himself yanked out of his daze. Lifting the muzzle of his M4, he pulled the trigger and fired a burst. Incredulously, the creature moved before the rounds struck and disappeared further into the dark, leaving behind the corpse of Chavez. The screams around the vehicle intensified and he spun.

At his feet he saw Prim crawling from the passenger window. Checking his M4, he moved along the edge of the overturned Pathfinder to the fender and tracked around the surroundings with the sight of his weapon. As he came around the rear of the vehicle, he saw Minos being dragged across the street into an alley between two buildings, barely catching a glimpse of a second, dark creature.

Prim was at his side, M9 in a double grip. "Where?"

"Stay with Ross. Call for help." Brand ordered, heading across the street. As he ran he knew Prim would be pulling larger firepower hidden in the back of the Pathfinder.

Ahead down the alley Brand could hear the screams of Minos with deep snarls muffled beneath her cries. And then a loud roar that threatened to freeze him in his tracks a second time echoed through the neighborhood.

Brand surged forward, picking up speed as he hurtled around a corner and barely had to the presence of mind to stop short as the alley opened into a broad, dark courtyard, dimly lit by the rising moon and a few building lights. With M4 leveled at his shoulder and finger loosely on the trigger, he stepped into the courtyard.

Minos lay prone under the paw of one of the creatures. It bent down over her, salivating jaws snarling across the expanse. The creature glanced above to either side, almost nervous, and then Brand felt the trap sprung as a second beast fell from above, snapping powerful jaws onto his left shoulder. He felt searing pain as the Kevlar did its duty, yet the SAPI plate shattered under the intense pressure exerted by the jaws and sharp teeth.

Rolling with the assault, Brand released his M4 and slid one hand to his K-Bar, pulling the lethal blade while delivering a hard elbow to the creature that was now attached to his back. Brand controlled the roll enough to land on top, and delivered a second hard elbow down into the creature. Immensely powerful claws raked at his back and legs as his assailant tore at him with all four limbs, and he could feel hot breath from the jaws that attempted to tear through his armor.

Shifting his grip, he slid the K-bar straight back, and felt the blade penetrate deep to the hilt. A loud yelp rang in his ear and he delivered yet another hard elbow, followed by the steel heal of his boot straight up the leg of the creature and into its groin. He was rewarded by a less emphatic wince and felt the tearing limbs shift, grabbing him and forcing a roll. As they tumbled, he struggled around, and half turned into the creature he fought. He drove the K-Bar in again, yet felt the powerful muzzle grinding down through the Kevlar and SAPI plates into his collarbone, tearing through skin.

A blur of silver slammed into the creature on top of him, and he felt it lifted and born away. Momentarily stunned, he attempted to collect himself before rolling away from the ferocious struggle of black and silver fur that took place across the courtyard.

Brand scurried for his M4 and took up a defensive position with his back against a wall and his barrel directed at the creatures.

What was already a surreal scene suddenly erupted as a huge silver creature drove into the two darker ones. A savage fight tore across the expanse as the larger creature, similar to the darker two, chased them down. Where the first two were dark black, the third was silver and grey, and his relentless attack drove them to the ground and away from Minos and Brand.

Brand watched, uncertain of what to do. His M4 followed the three combatants as they raced around the courtyard, the larger one dogging the other two. The huge silver beast split the smaller of the two open with one swipe of its massive paw across its throat, nearly severing its head clean and sending a spurt of blood across the courtyard and the prone NCIS agent. With an angry bark, it turned upon the first of its dark foe. The darker creature tried to back down, reaching out defensively and almost submissively. Its paws were pushed aside and massive, powerful jaws clamped down upon its throat.

Brand heard a short gurgled yelp before a loud snap, and the silver creature stood tall, shaking its victim in its mighty maw like a rag doll. With one final violent action, it tossed the corpse away and took a moment to glare around, looking first to the two corpses, then to the buildings and above, and finally to Minos and Brand.

Silver eyes locked on Brand. The Navy officer stood fixed in place. Slowly, he lowered his M4, not certain of what would happen next. He felt his pulse hammering in his ears, threatening to explode his heart from his chest. He was acutely aware of the pain in his collar and shoulder where his body armor had saved his life but he knew the bones were bruised and he was bleeding. For a brief moment, silence reigned, and the two simply stared at one another.

From the center of the courtyard, Minos moaned. Both creature and Brand looked down to her as she moved a leg. Blood covered much of her torso, some of it hers and a good deal of it belonging to the creatures that had been torn open above her.

Brand slung his rifle and started towards her. The huge silver creature swung its massive snout towards him, blood on its lips and teeth from its recent kill. Brand stopped and slowly lifted his hands, palms up and wide, and after a moment resumed slowly moving towards Minos, never taking his eyes from the eyes of the creature.

He was almost at her side when the creature turned towards the alley at Brand's back and snarled. He heard Prim swearing and a sudden steady course of gunfire erupted from behind, whizzing past. The silver creature spun away as its side and chest opened up in a spray of blood, pierced by a dozen rounds.

Time froze.

Brand swung, shouting orders under the din of the automatic weapon. Prim stood with an M16 firing fully automatic intent upon emptying the clip of forty rounds into the creature. Before he could take a few steps to intervene, he saw the creature gaining it's footing and then drop out of the path of fire in a blur of speed. It shifted into the shadows and circled around the courtyard towards Prim, apparently enraged but otherwise unscathed by the attack.

Without thinking, Brand threw himself between the two and felt himself driven by an inhuman force that bore him down upon Prim and the three fell in a rolling, snarling ball of bodies. He wrapped himself around Prim, attempting to protect his chief from the savage beast. He felt blood falling everywhere and realized it was seeping through his torn Kevlar. His skin burned around his collar and shredded shoulder, yet he held onto Prim and tried to pull both himself and his chief away from the creature.

The creature lifted both men up and threw them like dolls. For a second, Brand felt himself airborne and flipping head over heals. The impact with the wall across the courtyard took his breath away and he crumpled into oblivion.

....

Brand woke with throbbing pain throughout his skull, the pain almost blinding. Prim knelt over him beside their disabled Pathfinder. Colonel Khalil directed a host of his men in securing the area.

Brand attempted to sit up but felt a wave of nausea rush through him. His shoulder and neck ached like they were on fire beneath the skin and he grimaced.

"Oh, so you feel like joining us again, do you?" Prim mocked, although his voice was not as steady as Brand was used to.

"Minos?" He voiced his one word question.

"She's here. I pulled both of your heavy asses back here from the alley. And let me tell you, you need to run more. Jeese you're heavy." The chief snubbed out one cigarette and lit a second. "Hell, at least she wasn't half as heavy as you. But typical officer, taking a nap when there's work."

Brand could tell Prim was attempting to keep it together. The chief normally didn't speak this much in public.

Colonel Khalil heard him talking and turned to see Brand's eyes open. He approached and knelt. "Commander. How are your wounds?" Colonel Khalil was a middle-aged man with sharp, handsome features and short-cut black hair. A well-groomed thin mustache completed the picture of this proper Middle Eastern military officer.

Brand attempted to lift his arm and pain ignited his shoulder. The bones were definitely bruised, but he doubted broken. His right hand slid up under his uniform and the torn Kevlar vest to feel warm, sticky blood congealed all around his lacerated skin. It burned and seemed to be seeping deeper into his chest. Pain echoed in his skull causing waves of nausea to flood his stomach.

"I'll live. My pride is worse off than I am." He lied. "Do we have a medic on the way? How are Ross and Minos? And where is Chavez's body?"

Colonel Khalil pointed to his men who stood around the still unconscious Ross and a woman in black burqa knelt by Minos. "Special Agent Ross seems to have suffered a concussion from the accident. He has yet to awake. One of the women of my house is tending to your female.

She seems to have bled somewhat considerably and is in shock. The third is missing and we cannot find him."

Prim leaned in and whispered. "Gone when I dragged you back. Ross was still in the car. I dialed up the Colonel and they were here in minutes."

Colonel Khalil continued. "I've contacted your Army and they should be arriving soon. An ambulance to take you to Arifjan was requested."

"I'm good. Make sure Ross and Minos are in it." He pushed himself to his feet and felt the world spin. Reaching out, he caught himself on the overturned vehicle and tried to steady himself.

Prim was at his side and grabbed his arm. "Sir, you'd better take a knee. That . . . um . . . well, we got thrown pretty hard when we . . . well . . . fell. You may have hit the wall pretty hard."

Brand looked at Prim and realized although both men had seen what they had seen; the Chief had neglected to inform the Colonel of the actual events. From the look in the Chief's eyes, Brand realized Prim did not want to divulge the information. Brand nodded and politely brushed the helping hand away.

"As you constantly remind me, Gunner, I have a pretty hard head. I'm sure I'll be fine. Now unless you have a better idea, I think we need to find our missing special agent. Did he just walk away?"

Colonel Khalil shook his head and looked to the sky. "No, my friends. I do not believe your special agent was able to walk away on this evening. The blood in the streets and the drag marks leading away would indicate otherwise."

"Do the marks lead far?" He found his M4 and took it up.

"Sir, I'm not too certain we're up to this right now." Brand realized his Gunner still held the M16 firmly gripped and kept glancing around nervously. "Army is on its way. We'll have more men here soon."

Colonel Khalil smiled and patted the Chief on his shoulder. "I have plenty of men in the streets right now. We will find your Agent Chavez."

"Oh . . . I'm certain, Colonel." The Chief added hastily. "But I meant the Commander should wait for the medics to make sure he's ok too."

"I agree. Stay here with your charges, Commander Brand. My men will find Agent Chavez. We will bring him back." The Colonel nodded and turned towards his men, leaving the two alone.

"Gunner, what the fuck just happened?" Brand whispered, sitting back and sliding to the road against the Pathfinder.

"I have no effing idea, sir. I haven't had enough coffee for this bullshit."

"Did I really see what I think? Were those . . . ?"

Prim took one final long drag on his cigarette and snubbed it out before lighting a new one. "This isn't a SyFy movie. I don't know what the fuck I saw. I must have hit my head when we flipped."

"How the hell did we flip? You didn't hit anything. We got hit, and I saw it. It was a dark black thing, and big. Like a bull mastiff running on two legs." His head was beginning to clear a bit. "So what happened in the alley? Last thing I remember I felt like a chew toy being thrown by a Rottweiler."

"You hit the wall hard." Prim took another long drag, watching the Kuwaiti soldiers continue to look around the area. "I thought you were dead. You hit harder than the Pathfinder when it flipped."

Brand closed his eyes and took a deep breath. He tried to envision the scene.

"I shot it, sir. I shot it a whole lot of times, and it just fucking jumps out of the way. And runs. I think it was mad. And I know you jumped in the way to save me, but why the hell didn't you just shoot it?"

Brand shook his head and sighed. "I don't know. It wasn't trying to kill me. It actually saved me."

"What?" The Chief asked incredulously.

"I know. It doesn't make sense. They were trying to kill us. They did kill Chavez, I'm sure of it. But the two I saw in the alley, they were on me. And I wasn't doing well. Thing nearly bit through my armor." He touched his shoulder again and winced. "And then that one showed up. The big white one."

"It killed the other two. It kept them off of us and saved Minos. And it looked right at me. It could have killed me, and you for that matter. You hit it full auto and it simply rolled out from it and charged. How the hell are you untouched?"

"I don't know. Maybe I didn't have enough meat on my bones." They laughed. "After you hit the wall, the thing turned on me and swatted my gun away. I thought I was dog food, but it just growled at me. Put its face real close to mine and growled. I could feel its breath." He took another long puff from his cigarette.

After a moment of silence, he looked directly into Brand's eyes and spoke. "It shook its head and just walked away, dragging the two dead things with it like they were nothing. And I can't be sure . . . but I think it kept watching us until the Colonel showed up with his men. I just felt it, like it was making sure we were safe or something."

"What the hell do we say? Who's gonna believe this? I don't believe this, sir. Its just bullshit."

Brand shook his head and looked around at the Kuwaiti soldiers. "I don't know Gunner. But do you notice? None of the Kuwaiti soldiers are actually leaving the immediate area. They keep looking around and coming back to the immediate site here. And no one is at the windows of their houses. This is a neighborhood. You'd think they'd come outside to see the commotion."

Prim nodded, blowing smoke. "Yeah, I saw that. These fuckers know what's up and they aren't saying. Like the training says, follow the locals. Well the locals are in hiding, and so should we be. Once the medics arrive, we leave with them. And we get you checked."

"No! Just get me back to my bunk. I need to rest and think." His shoulder ached and his head spun. He needed time to think. "This doesn't make sense."

"Well, sir. While you're thinking, come up with what you're going to tell the chain. We have to tell them something, and I don't want a psych eval."

"Normally I'd say the truth, Chief. But . . ." He let his words trail off and they waited for the Army.

An Army ambulance pulled around the corner and came straight to Colonel Khalil followed by four HUMVEES full of soldiers. The soldiers poured out and immediately set up a perimeter, while the Colonel guided the ambulance to the Pathfinder. The medics set upon the two NCIS agents. One corpsman knelt beside Brand and set a large medical triage bag down.

"I'm Sergeant Wise, Sir. Where's the blood from?"

Brand held out his arms and glanced around his torn and bloody uniform. "Not mine, sergeant. I'm fine. Just thrown around a bit. I may need a tetanus shot, though. Lord knows what kind of disease or filth I've got on me."

"Bullshit. He's being obstinate. He hit his head and was unconscious. I think he has a concussion." Prim spoke up. "You'll be able to tell if he starts to make sense."

Brand scowled at his chief. "I'm actually feeling better."

"Let me have a look at least, sir. It can't hurt." The sergeant pulled a small penlight from his pocket and flashed it across Brand's eyes. "How does your head feel? Any nausea?"

Brand nodded and winced, instinctively reaching up to grab the back of his head and neck. "Um, that would be an answer I think." Came the sarcastic shot from Prim.

Brand shook it off and looked to the Sergeant. "Head hurts around the neck where I hit the wall. But I know this pain. Bruising. And I'm already feeling better. What I want is a shower and shot of coffee."

"Sorry, sir. I'm supposed to take you to Arifjan for observation if I think you've got a concussion. And I think you do."

"Hey, sir. Look at the bright side. The hospital probably has nurses." Prim chuckled.

Brand laughed. "Gunner. I'm betting you're looking at him."

The sergeant grinned. "I've got a mean bed side manner, Chief. And we've heard about Navy patients. We don't let the females near your type. They might catch rabies or something just being in the room with you."

"Ah shit. This night just keeps getting better, doesn't it sir?"

Brand resigned himself to being taken to the hospital and leaned his head back. "It can't get any worse." He winced as pain tore through his shoulder and tendrils of fire wound down his bicep and across his chest. He felt a fever burning behind his eyes and the comment about rabies the sergeant just made suddenly seemed a great deal more serious.

Chapter 2

Hospital Visits

IT WAS JUST past midnight when they arrived at the hospital. The NCIS agents were rushed in through the emergency room doors followed by Brand and Prim on foot. Sergeant Wise stayed with them and led them into the emergency room, where a young female corporal directed them into two triage areas next to one another.

Sergeant Wise indicated they should wait in their triage area while he checked on the status of both Ross and Minos. As he departed, he pulled the privacy curtains closed, leaving the two alone. It was late and there were no other patients in triage. Brand sat upon the bed and lay back, closing his eyes and starting to swim into unconsciousness.

"Hey, Jackass! Wake up." Prim barked, grabbing his shoulder and pulling him to a sitting position.

A wave of liquid flame shot through his chest and down his arm from where his shoulder had been grabbed. "I'm up. Jesus!"

"No sleeping until the docs clear you from a concussion. Do you know how hard it is to train a good officer?"

"Alright. Alright. You're worse than my mother."

The curtain pulled back and a fit female sergeant stepped in, wearing battle dress pants and boots, and uniform green t-shirt, which fit tight. "Good evening, sailors. What have we here? Sergeant Wise warned me not to get too close, or I might get fleas." She grinned at Prim but upon noticing Brand she straightened up. "I'm sorry, sir. I didn't know there was an officer here."

Brand shrugged with his good shoulder and tried to smile. "Don't hold it against me. And don't worry about fleas, my chief wears a collar."

His joke lightened the mood and she stepped in, pulling the curtain behind to retain their privacy. "That's good. I like collars." She grinned. "I'm Sergeant First Class Reece Summers. Looks like you took a bath in ketchup. Whose blood is this, Commander?"

"Not all mine." He replied.

She reached for his wrist and looked at her watch as she took his pulse. "Reports sounded like you were hit by an IED. Vehicle was thrown upside down and your passengers seem to be pretty banged up. How does your head feel?"

Prim kicked back on the bed in his area. "Well, if you're asking . . ."

Sergeant Summers continued watching the time. "Wait your turn. You seem fine, Chief. Were you sitting in the baby seat?"

Brand caught himself laughing. "Your pulse is a little elevated, but considering what you've been through, it seems normal. How does your head feel?" She asked a second time.

He looked to her as she flashed a light in his eyes and checked the dilation of his pupils. "I am feeling better. I'll be honest; initially I was a bit unsteady. But I'd just been thrown into a wall. My shoulder feels hot and bruised. It hurts worse than my head. I'm kind of concerned because of all the blood that spilled on me."

She stopped and pulled back. "Wall? I was told your vehicle took an IED and flipped. Were you ejected before you hit the wall?"

Brand looked to Prim and back. "Who told you it was an explosive?"

"We heard your vehicle took an IED and there was a firefight. The Kuwaiti police arrived and secured the area. We just heard bits and pieces as they were bringing you in. To be honest, it's the first event we've had in Kuwait in years so we were all waiting on pins and needles, expecting more casualties."

"I don't remember an explosion. I remember we were rammed and flipped over. And we did have a firefight. Were there any casualties reported?"

"None. Just injuries. Initial reports indicated two NCIS agents pretty banged up, with the female being the worse of the two. Did she go through the windshield?"

"Hell no!" Prim protested. "I was driving. We flipped and we all had seatbelts on. She was in the back seat behind me."

"Then how did she receive all the cuts and lacerations? She's lost a lot of blood and her neck was severely torn."

The two men exchanged glances and Brand shook his head. "I don't know. It was dark and things just lost control. She was attacked by some sort of animal like a big dog."

The curtain pulled back and a small group stood before them. Two U.S. Army Colonels were front and center. The first was a portly man pushing the limits of the battle dress uniform he wore, with medical corps insignia on his shoulder and webbed nametag reading Pinson. The second Army Colonel stood tall and thick with a square jaw; dark, cold eyes and webbing that read Shaker on his broad chest.

Behind the two men stood a third in British combat fatigues, armed with a drop holster and sidearm as well as a large combat knife strapped to his right calf. His black hair was cut neat and short, while his uniform was devoid of any nametags or insignia.

The remaining individual to enter was a female who could have passed for government or military, with blond hair tied in a tight bun, and sharp features, attractive yet cool. She stood dressed in civilian attire, similar to the NCIS agents, with khaki pants and polo shirt.

"Thank you, Sergeant Summer. I'll take it from here, if you will." Colonel Pinson directed, motioning for her to depart.

She snapped to attention and immediately slipped past the entourage, disappearing elsewhere in the emergency room.

Prim watched her go and then turned his attention to the second Colonel. Brand had locked his eyes on the British officer the moment the curtains had parted and never let them stray.

"How are you feeling, Commander Brand? I'm Colonel Pinson, attending physician tonight. Looks like your team took quite a spill. British explosives ordinance teams are canvasing the neighborhood to pick up the pieces from the device that took your vehicle."

"I'm sorry, sir. The what?" Brand took his eyes off the British officer to look to Prim and then to the Colonel. "I don't recall any explosion." His eyes shifted back to the British officer.

"Excuse me, Commander." The second Army Colonel barked. "Come again! British EOD confirms explosives. What's your story on this event?" He cast a short, sidelong glance at the British soldier.

Brand stole his eyes from the British soldier for an instant to look at the Colonel. "We were attacked. It felt like an ambush. And . . . I think it was . . ." He was at a loss for words.

"Dogs, sir." Prim interjected. "They had big dogs. Attacking everywhere."

"What in Sam Hill? Are you saying your vehicle was overturned by a French Poodle?"

"No sir. It was big. And black. Bigger than any dog I've seen. And the Chief is right. They had dogs. One tore into Special Agent Chavez and dragged him from the vehicle.

His throat was ripped open! And one pulled Special Agent Minos down an alley."

"And they didn't fight like pussies, so they couldn't have been French." Prim added.

"Did you hit your fucking head?" The Colonel bristled, casting a sidelong look at the Chief before turning back on Brand. "We've got evidence of explosive devices being collected right now and we didn't get any word there were attack dogs around. I'm certain Colonel Khalil wouldn't have left that part of the story out."

The British officer stepped in, smiling and maintained his eyes locked on Brand's. "Colonel Shaker is correct. My boys are collecting the evidence from the underside of your vehicle as well as the neighborhood. There was light charring of the streets and your vehicle took quite a blast on the front under fender. If the charge had been set right, you would find yourself with Saint Peter at the gates right now. Consider yourself lucky." His English was refined and polished, denoting birth of gentry. "Of course, we didn't hear the reports of canines being involved, but we can expand our search to see if any evidence supports. Perhaps dog hair or prints in the dirt and sand."

"I'm sorry, but I didn't get your name. I'm Lieutenant Commander Brand." He stuck out his hand towards the British soldier.

A smile flashed upon gentleman's face. A moment passed before he accepted the grip for a quick shake and released. "Major Samuel Valko: British Royal Marine. Call me Sam. How did you fair tonight, Commander?"

"I'm alive; which is more than I can say for my charges. I was supposed to protect them, and I'm officially missing one. Did anyone find Special Agent Chavez?"

Colonel Pinson looked to both the Colonel and Major. Valko responded, "We have men on the scene tracking and Colonel Khalil has his men canvasing the neighborhood. We will find him. What was his condition when you last saw him?"

"Initially, I would say dead. What do you think Gunner?"

The Chief gave a curt nod of agreement. "Yes sir. I'm going to have to agree on dead. And taking a turn for the worse."

"That is a shame. And was he sitting on the side that took the blast?"

Brand's eyes tightened as they drilled into Valko's. "Well, considering I didn't remember a blast, I'm not certain. He was sitting on the passenger side, though. Behind me."

"The report definitely indicates an explosion, Commander. I am certain the blast shook you both up and you may not remember. That would explain things, I do believe. It would have resulted in the vehicle flipping."

"Get your head back in the game, Commander." The square-jawed Colonel barked. "We'll be back in a day or two once we've collected all the evidence and we'll need your statement. And for the record, I don't want to hear that Lassie and Rin-Tin-Tin had a hand in a terrorist attack unless you have proof." His stare bore down upon Brand who ignored him and kept his eyes locked on the British officer.

The triage area remained awkwardly silent until Major Valko spoke up, breaking the tension.

"Gentlemen. If you have no further questions for the two, I am certain they need to receive triage. I would like to stay and ask a few more questions before their nurse returns. Colonel Shaker, you will receive a copy of my troops' report within the week once we finish with the scene."

The square jawed Colonel clinched his teeth tighter and shook his head. "I'll look forward to it, and I'll forward you a copy of mine. I've got my men heading to the sight of the attack if they aren't already there by now. I'll be joining them shortly."

As if queued the two Colonels nodded and stepped away, leaving the others to the tense silence. Both Brand and Prim exchanged glances. The female shifted to the edge of the triage to ensure their privacy.

"Alright, now that we seem to be alone, are there any details you feel you should tell me? Were you injured excessively?" Valko locked eyes with Brand again.

Brand felt his pulse quicken and the burning in his blood seemed to calm. "Like what?" His breath was shallow and came in little gulps.

"What attacked you? Did you see?" His tone was almost hushed yet serious.

Brand caught himself. "Do you mean who? Or what?"

"Same thing? Did you get a glimpse of them? How many were there? Did you get a good look at them? Did either of you shoot them?" He felt as if Valko was boring into his mind.

Brand looked down to his body armor, breaking the tie between them. "I'm covered in blood, and it isn't mine. Not all at least. Nor is it anyone's from my vehicle. So I'm guessing we did hit one at least. Which reminds me: I'm missing my knife."

Valko seemed taken back. "Did you get into a tussle with one of the . . . did you say dogs? What happened? Be precise. How many did you see? And where were they? Were either of you excessively injured?"

Prim held his arms up in the air. "I was going to let the Sergeant check me out when you all showed up. But I wasn't injured. Not a scratch. Just really shaken up and confused."

Brand continued looking down at his shredded Kevlar and his mind began to race. Maybe the Colonel was right, he just had hit his head too hard, he thought as he started to doubt himself. And then he calmed himself and it sank in. There was no explosion, and a dog wouldn't have attacked him like he had been attacked nor could it have torn his Kevlar like this. No, he knew what he saw. "I did get into it with a dog that Colonel Shaker says didn't exist. And you can call me crazy, but it wasn't like any dog I've ever seen. I stabbed it as it was trying to get through my body armor."

Valko seemed intent upon the description, leaning in closer. Again Brand felt their eyes locking as if mesmerized. "How did it happen? Did its bodily fluid make contact with you? Any blood? How did you break free?"

"I followed Agent Minos. She was pulled from the car and dragged down an alley. I left Gunner with Ross and told him to call in for help. When I caught up to the … whatever … it had Minos in a courtyard waiting for me. I was jumped from behind and a second one tried to get me by the throat. Ambushed. My Kevlar kept me safe but I wasn't doing well. Whoever ambushed us sent in their dogs to finish the job. One of them pulled Chavez out of the vehicle. Tore his throat out and I'm certain he's dead."

"How did you manage to survive? Did you get any numbers? And how badly were you hurt?"

Brand shook his head. "I don't know how we survived. Something else showed up; a different creature. Or dog. Or whatever. It's pretty confusing."

"We shall call it a dog for now. Will that help?" Valko smiled a genuine smile.

Brand felt calm and nodded. "Yes, it will. So, this other dog chased the first two."

"You said one chased two. So there were three?"

"Four." Prim added. "I saw someone watching from the dark, but he left when I pulled my M4 from the back. I couldn't make him out, but maybe he was the handler. He was just watching from the shadows and then he disappeared."

"Ok. This is good." Valko commented. "So there were at least three dogs and one man. One dog chased the other two away. And then what happened?"

"Well . . . he didn't just chase them away. He tore them apart. Or it. Whatever. And that's when Chief opened up with his automatic weapon."

"Excuse me?" Valko interrupted again. "You shot him?"

Both Navy men looked to each other and considered their statement. After a moment of contemplation, Prim shook his head. "I thought I did, but I must have missed. He ran off."

"Negative, Chief. You hit him dead on. But that didn't stop him. Didn't even slow him down."

Valko seemed excited and snapped his fingers for the female to come forward. "Where did you leave the two dead dogs?"

"We didn't." Brand corrected, and Prim added. "The white creature took them." "I apologize." Valko hesitated. "Did you say the white creature took them?"

Prim nodded. "Yes, sir. Picked them up one in each hand and hauled them away."

"You described it as white, with hands? Now Chief, how hard did you hit your head?" The Major smiled again. "Do you recall where you saw the dogs last?"

"It was silver-white or maybe light gray. Shouldn't be too hard to find if you follow the trail of Special Agent Minos's blood down the alley. She lost a lot of it before we reached her but it was a straight trail to where we saw them last."

"Yes. Well now, regarding Special Agent Minos: Did she get any . . . dog blood on her? Rabies and other bacteria, you know." He stated as if a matter of fact.

Both Brand and Prim nodded. "I'll say. She was already bleeding. And the grey dog shredded both of the smaller black dogs before the Chief made it down the alley. They all bled over her. It was quite literally a blood bath, no pun intended."

Valko's face took on a concerned look and he turned to the female beside him. "Pass that word and make sure we have vaccines administered to her." The female nodded.

Valko looked Brand in the eyes again. "One more time, Commander. Did you receive any injuries perhaps we should be aware of?"

Brand felt a wave of fear roll through his stomach as his mind raced. All of Valko's question and his constant, intense gaze were not helping. It seemed like there was something more the British Major was trying to hint at without saying, as if he knew something more but refused to openly admit.

Finally, Brand swallowed his fear and responded directly. "If you're asking whether I was bitten by a werewolf or some other monster, the answer is no, not directly. My Kevlar did the job just fine. I'm bruised but that's about the extent of it. I did get a lot of blood on me, and my shoulder is kind of raw and burns." He thought a minute before adding, "Come to think of it, there was enough blood that seeped down my collar into my shoulder. I hadn't thought of it before, but now that you mention it, my shoulder does burn."

He closed his eyes and took a deep breath. "Ah crap. What kind of vaccine is it?"

Valko stepped back and the female stepped forward, pulling two syringes from her pocket. "If you would be so kind as to remove your shirt, Commander." Similar to the Major's, her accent was very formal English. "I'm afraid you will need a dose."

"Dose of what?" Prim asked before Brand could.

"The blood and saliva might be rabid. It would best we not take any chances. Two shots will boost your immune system. We should keep you under observation the next seven days."

Brand pulled off his uniform blouse and rolled up the sleeve of his t-shirt. The blood had seeped through and covered the collar and shoulders of his shirt. Beneath the skin around his collar was discolored and with tendrils creeping up the side of his neck from bruising. He kept his eyes on Valko while the shots were administered, both in quick succession.

"Perhaps tomorrow you can provide a description of the dogs to an artist. Dogs here in Kuwait should not be too hard to find." He chuckled and stared Brand straight in the eyes again. "And I would definitely leave off any jokes about werewolves. I doubt your Colonel is in a humorous mood."

"Thank you, Major. But why are you interested when Colonel Shaker so obviously isn't?"

"Call me Sam. And perhaps we tend to be a little more open to an eyewitness account. We have experienced trained animals assisting in terrorist acts before. It wouldn't be the first time a dog was used to lead to a man's demise."

"Thank you, Sam. You can call me Liam."

They shook hands again. "I hope they don't keep you here too late. Get some rest. I believe you shall be seeing a great deal of Colonel Shaker in the near future. And more than likely you'll have the opportunity to get sick of seeing me around as well."

"Before you go, is there anything I should be looking for: Side effects from the shots? Rabies?"

The female nodded. "Fever, chills, aches, pains. Blurred vision. Weakness."

"Sleeplessness as well." Valko added. "But my team will be keeping an eye on you."

"I'm sorry. Is that for the rabies or the shots?"

"As luck would have it, both." Valko smiled. "We are heading to visit your Special Agent Minos before we adjourn for the evening."

"More like morning." Prim muttered. "Enjoy."

"Thank you. Oh, and just to make this official, British Intelligence is working with you Americans on extremist cells operating in country who are utilizing trained canines. It is all extremely classified, so I appreciate your confidence in this matter. Until the proper authority reads you in, I recommend you maintain confidentiality on this matter. I estimate your safest bet is to minimize all discussion on this subject to . . . well, myself for now. Have a good rest."

Valko gave a friendly nod and he led the female agent from triage. Brand lay back upon the bed and kicked his feet up. As he watched them disappearing from the triage area, he whispered to Prim. "I don't understand why Valko is covering up."

"What do you mean, sir?"

"The Colonel indicated the Brits were claiming the attack was IED, but we both know we weren't hit by an explosive. And although we both saw what we saw, he's more willing to believe our story than either of us. He wants us to keep our story under wraps and go with the IED version. He knows something and he isn't sharing with the Colonel."

"Yeah, I caught that somewhat. What do you think, sir? We play along?"

Brand thought a brief moment before shrugging, which brought a wince of pain in his shoulder. "For now, yes. When we can, we talk with Ross and see what his take might be. I don't know what we've gotten into, but at least the Brits seem to be on our side. Keep your wits about you, though."

Both men waited patiently as the long night was just beginning.

Chapter 3

Um Ghar The Den of the Mother

The young Kuwaiti officer approached the sight of the ambush and saw U.S. and Kuwait military personnel scouring the area. The vehicle had been moved hours before as foreign investigations proceeded at a much faster rate than his countrymen would have. In Kuwait, it was common for a car that had been in an accident to sit on the side of the road for months until the trial and although his Colonel would have wanted results from an immediate investigation, he doubted any effort would have been wasted to look into this incident from his countrymen. He stopped to watch for a moment and waved with a smile when one of the Americans turned and saw him.

The gruff looking officer with square jaw glowered at him and he hurried on his way. He was off duty and had spent hours the previous night with his fellow soldiers patrolling the immediate neighborhoods. Although Colonel Khalil had assured the Americans his soldiers would canvas the entire area, he personally had noticed few of the soldiers moved beyond the immediate block. None dared leave the safety of the street lamps. They had all heard rumors and it filled them with fear.

As he moved past the foreign soldiers, skirting the scene, he noticed two of the largest men he had ever seen. The men, one black with shaven head and one white with short cropped red hair, were dressed in business suits and conversing at the spot where the vehicle had been. The two men knelt and examined the ground before heading off following an invisible trail towards an alley. They disappeared from sight before the Kuwaiti officer had cleared the scene.

He continued on, moving rapidly through neighborhoods very familiar to him. Within minutes he came upon a row of houses and approached the third one. Glancing up and down the block, he hesitantly stepped up to the door and reached to ring the doorbell.

The door swung in before his finger reached the button and a young Middle Eastern man stood before him. Lean with short cut black hair; the host greeted him in traditional formal fashion. "As-Salamu alaykum."

He replied, "Wa alaykum as-salam." Bowing to the host of the house.

"Welcome, Abdulla. I hope you've brought good news. You're the last to arrive."

"Thank you, Hassem. I appreciate your hospitality." He stepped inside and the door was shut and locked. The young officer followed the host of the house to an inner room, where five others waited. Four younger men were seated and one middle-aged balding man stood in the back smoking a clove cigarette.

Hassem offered Abdulla a seat and waited for the young officer to settle in. Finally he greeted the group, "Um Ghar is pleased with our actions to date; however, she's displeased with the results of last night." This caused the others to shift nervously.

"Our preparations were flawless and our cause just. Allah should have seen us to victory. Instead, we failed Allah because of our arrogance. What news from the house of Khalil?" He turned to the newest member in the room.

Abdulla bowed his head and stood. "Thank you, Hassem. My uncle had his staff and soldiers canvassing the neighborhood, but found nothing. I assisted in the search, and was able to divert some attention. The Americans were too confused and failed to actually see the attack. I didn't hear any description of the Sons mentioned. And further I've heard it's being referred to as an IED attack."

"That isn't what I saw." Hassem stated, shaking his head. "Is the Colonel telling you the truth? I watched the American officer. He saw Halil make the first kill. The American fired at him; yet praise to Allah, the bullets found no target. I was able to pull the body of the American agent from the scene when the American soldier followed his officer. I believe one of the soldiers may have seen me, but I doubt he saw me well enough to recognize me. I was deep in the shadows watching."

"How did this fail?" Questioned the balding man as he fingered his thin mustache before taking a drag from his cigarette. He blew smoke and continued. "How did our brothers fail? They had the strength of the Sons. And why did you take the body of the dead agent and leave the Senior Agent in the vehicle? The Senior Agent was the target."

Hassem shot an angry glare at the balding man. "Thank you, Kumar. I appreciate your support when you weren't there. I grabbed the agent our brother had pulled from the vehicle as I thought he was our target. More importantly to me, there was another about."

"Another what?" one of the younger members asked.

"Mustadhyib." Hassem responded. "Werewolf."

"Perhaps it was one of the Elder hunting." Kumar seemed to smirk, rather full of himself. "Are you sure you sensed another mustadhyib?"

The seated members seemed to turn, looking to one another nervously. Abdulla was the only member in the room who seemed unable to grasp the relevance.

"If an Elder was hunting it would explain why our brothers didn't report in. Perhaps they're hiding." Another of the seated members spoke up.

"The Elders are just tales of old women. They haven't been seen in recent memory, if they existed at all. And if they do exist, why would they be here and we not know?" The smallest member of the group stated, standing to be seen and heard by the others. He glared directly at Kumar and returned to his seat.

"And what do you consider Um Ghar to be, Raheem? I believe in the Elders, but other than Um Ghar, I don't believe any hunt here, so in that I do agree with you. I believe our brothers are casualties of our cause. My brother, Udei, sought them out last night and found their trail in the courtyard of their battle. He is certain they were slain, and their blood marks their last stand. He's certain there's another of us in this area, hunting: there may be a den. We may not have realized we entered their territory when we came here, but we'll have to make due."

"Where is your brother tonight?" Kumar asked, almost derisively.

Hassem turned his eyes on Kumar. "Udei is busy tonight. That's all Um Ghar feels you need to know."

Kumar smiled and directed his comments to the others. "Perhaps Um Ghar feels none of us need to know, and you aren't aware either."

The entire room hummed with tension as Hassem seemed to grow in stature. "Don't forget that I am one of the first of Um Ghar. I am well aware of where my brother is and what he does. And Um Ghar has directed I not tell you or the others yet. Do you question the will of Um Ghar?"

Kumar's smile seemed to fade and he attempted a shrug. The others noted his demeanor change and he seemed to back down. "No, Hassem. I would never question the will of Um Ghar. I live to serve Allah. And Um Ghar is a servant of Allah."

Satisfied, Hassem looked to Abdulla. "What else?"

The young officer shook his head. "The Americans are currently looking the entire neighborhood over. When we attempted to question the residents, they wouldn't open their houses. I am certain the Americans will have less luck. The legend of the Sons is growing and already we hold fear in the hearts of the Kuwaiti people."

"I did see two others though. They were in suits, and they were following, as if they saw the trail of blood from the car into the alley. I don't know who they are? They seemed different."

"I thought we cleaned all the blood." Kumar mumbled, shaking his head.

"Find out who they are, Abdulla. And your efforts will be rewarded." Hassem stated. "You've done well and I'll personally tell Um Ghar of your support."

The young officer brightened and could not hide his pride. "Thank you brother. I hope that my services find favor in Allah."

"I am certain they do, Abdulla." Hassem smiled. Looking to Kumar, he added, "The blood was cleaned, as best as possible, considering the area was crawling with the Colonel's men as well as the Americans. Once we know who they are, we'll know how they were following the trail. Now, let's have tea and make our next plans. What do you have for the group, Kumar?"

The bald-headed man crossed his arms. "I will continue with my plans towards the military base itself. I think we need to escalate our attacks and announce our presence. The Kuwaiti people need to know we are here. The infidels need to know we are here. And they all need to fear us!"

"I agree." Hassem stated, nodding and looking around the room. "Our intentions had been that this attack announced our presence to the coalition and the Americans in particular. I suspect they doubt the stories of their own soldiers, so we will have to make them believe. Our next attack must be larger, and leave no doubt as to our presence. They must know of the Sons of Anubis."

"Perhaps we should make a video to post to the Internet. They aren't intelligent enough to know our forms if we change. If you agree, we can prepare a statement in advance to send out immediately following our next attack. The great imam himself has established the method we should use."

"I like it, Raseem. We should. For now, we have a more pressing concern. What should we do with the NCIS agent's body?"

The room again buzzed as they each talked aloud, offering suggestions. Sitting quietly on the side, Abdulla raised his hand and sheepishly offered, "Perhaps we should leave him in the house of Khalil. It could serve as a warning to all Kuwaiti to chose the righteous side while furthering to announce our presence."

The room went silent and Hassem looked to him. "Go on."

"If my uncle does not immediately notify the Americans, I can notify them. We can be certain of the Americans finding out, and of the Colonel understanding our strength."

Hassem smiled and placed a hand on the young soldier's shoulder. "You are a gift. That is an exceptional idea. Now, how shall we move the body into the house of Khalil?"

"We continue to keep him chilled in the freezer until the time is right, and then I transport him in my Mercedes." Raseem offered. "The trunk is massive. Can Abdulla meet me and get me in?"

All eyes again fell on the young officer. He looked around, realizing he was the center of attention again. Smiling, he nodded. "Yes, Raseem. If we coordinate in advance, I can insure no others are around and we can bring the body in. I'll keep an eye and ear out, to see when we might have a window of opportunity that might work."

Even Kumar seemed pleased as the room boiled with excitement. Hassem scanned the room and smiled. "We need to look to the future and select another target to hunt. I want all of us to keep ears out and I want another prey. Someone of importance to send a bigger message."

Kumar lit a new cigarette and took a long drag before exhaling and smiling. "We still have the Senior Agent from NCIS. We never did complete that hunt. I say we finish."

"And what about security?" One of the others questioned.

Hassem looked to Kumar, catching the veiled slight Kumar implied by noting the failure of the original mission.

After a moment, Hassem nodded in agreement. "You are correct, Kumar. We need to finish what we started, and regain the approval of Um Ghar. We should target the Senior Agent."

Raseem spoke up. "I'll find where he is. And report back in the next day or so. Once we find him, we can determine how best to proceed."

Again one of the others questioned. "What about the security? He has been attacked once, won't they be watching?"

Kumar responded arrogantly, "And what of them? Fuck the Americans! We are the Sons of Anubis. Their weapons hold zero threat to us."

"I doubt they will have much security about him." Hassem stated. "They may watch the senior agent tonight, but I doubt for more than a few days. Find him and we'll find a way to him. Remember, we aren't trying to be silent and unseen. We want to be known. Plus, as Abdulla has indicated, the Americans suspect an explosive device on the road, not an attack against the senior agent. I doubt the focus will be on us or on him."

After a moment of thought, Hassem added, "And we need our next target, after the Senior Agent. Or before, depending upon how long the Senior Agent remains under guard. Someone important. Check for any incoming visitors, especially senators and politicians. Americans love to travel and love their fame. We should know in the news who is coming and when."

"How about recruits?" Kumar asked almost nonchalantly. "Shall we grow our numbers now?"

Hassem considered it a moment and slowly nodded. "We must be cautious. Not many yet. We have more preparations to do, but then we can grow our numbers. For now, we still must remain small enough to hide. We need to stir up fear among the people while causing fear in the Americans and breaking the trust between the people of Persia and the infidels. A larger show of force to soon will have a negative effect and bring the U.S. to our doorsteps before we are ready. For now, let's keep it to only the most fervent of believers."

Abdulla lifted a hand almost plaintively. "Would you consider granting me the gift of Um Ghar, Hassem?" He smiled sheepishly.

Looking from Kumar to Raseem and then across the room, Hassem smiled and nodded. "Yes, Adbulla. We can grant you the gift of Um Ghar. I will give it to you personally tonight. You've more than earned it."

....

The two British male agents in civilian attire followed the trail of blood from the spot where the Pathfinder had come to rest down and alley. It was past midnight and quiet. Both men were massive, with the chiseled muscles of body builders or strongmen. Once outside the immediate vicinity of the main road, they found the ground appeared to have been cleaned recently.

The first and larger of the two, the black male, knelt and rubbed his fingers along where the trail had been. He brought his fingers to his nostrils and sniffed deeply. "Do you smell it, Fergus? Bleach. Someone attempted to clean this, poorly." Unlike Valko and the British female, he bore a less refined British accent, educated yet not higher society.

"Would have been easier to burn it, don't you think Cedric?" The second observed, his accent strongly Scottish. He was younger, with bright red hair cut short. "Let's see where it leads. Thankfully those Yanks will lose sight and won't follow."

"Right. Stay on your toes."

It was a short walk to the courtyard, where the first of the two once again knelt in the center and felt around the ground with his hand. "The Yank was right. Cleaned it good, but there was blood here." He bent down to place his nose against the dirty courtyard. "I've got six or eight scents working here. I'd make out four or five shifters, distinct and one female's blood. One of the shifters, he's a strong one: real strong. An Alpha among alphas doesn't come close to this one. We'd best tell the Major, promptly. If what the yank said is true, I'm wagering he made short work of the other two."

"So the story seems to correspond. Can you get a gage on the strongest?"

"I'm afraid not. But I can sense in his blood that he's strong. More than anything I've ever sensed, he's Alpha.

I've never sensed anything so powerful. Whatever he is, he's unlike anyone I've encountered."

The second knelt and touched the ground, sniffing around. "You've a good snout. I can barely make it out, but you're keen on it. Now that you mention it, I can sense he's strong. His mark still resonates here." He took a deep breath and let it out.

Both men stood tall and looked around, sniffing at the air. The younger man scratched his short, red hair. "He's not here, but we'd best head back and make our report."

Cedric looked towards the corners of the buildings and shook his head. "I believe his trail goes cold once he took to the roof tops."

"How do you make that?"

"He scaled the wall at the corner of the building. You can see where he dug in, carrying the weight of the other two. It probably didn't slow him down, but he did have to draw his claws in deeper. He went straight up and over the roof."

Both men nodded and then turned back down the road they came, returning to the original scene of the ambush. Shortly thereafter, the two climbed into their transport, an armored HUMVEE, and sped back to meet up with their Major.

Chapter 4

Ancient Dreams, Living Nightmares

The hospital released Prim shortly after the British team departed, however they kept Brand through the night and into the morning until Colonel Pinson was satisfied his eyes were normal and he no longer presented symptoms of a concussion. Brand found the Chief waiting for him just outside the hospital, parked in a HUMVEE, and the two drove back to their base. The hospital was located inland at Camp Arifjan, whereas they were based on the coast at the Kuwait Navy Base.

The morning dawn was peaceful with a light breeze coming in from the Northern Arabian Gulf. The smell of the saltwater embraced them as they approached the Navy Base and passed through security, parking on the backside of the base. The heat of the desert was just beginning for the day as the sun began to rise.

After dropping off his weapons at the armory, Brand returned to his quarters and immediately stripped his body armor, throwing it aside on the tiled floor. He lived in a small room with one door and one small window in an old, battle-worn building on the edge of the Kuwait Naval Base. It had belonged to the Kuwaiti military, but when the Iraqi Army invaded, they had slain so many Kuwaiti soldiers within the building, they gave the structure to the U.S. forces when they arrived.

His room was one of a dozen on the second floor. All the rooms opened into the inner courtyard of the building, with two stories of like-sized rooms. His room had a metal-framed bunk bed, of which he slept on the lower bunk and threw his uniforms on the upper bunk when he didn't throw them in the corner for laundry. Sand was constantly blown in through the window or under the door, and his floor and belongings were covered under a fine layer of the soft grains. His chief maintained a similar room next to his, their doors facing one another.

A makeshift wooden desk and folding chair, a short bookcase and a pair of footlockers under the bed frame furnished his room, and a waist high wooden cross stood in the corner for his body armor and holsters to hang.

He started to remove his torn uniform but thought better of it. Instead, he gathered a towel and clean uniform, to include under attire, and headed out from his room to the showers.

Halfway across camp a group of trailers were set up with showers, toilets and sinks, recently replacing the portable potties that had dotted the base.

It was still early in the day and the camp had not quite come alive, even though there were always operations going on, twenty-four seven. He made it to the shower trailer and hung his towel and clean clothing before turning on the always-hot water. In the desert, cold water was a luxury.

His torn uniform was shed in a pile and he gingerly touched his swollen and bruised shoulder. It was hot to the touch, burning with fever. Blood caked around the bruises, and it appeared as if someone had taken a cheese grater to him. Before stepping into the shower, he threw the shredded blouse and t-shirt into the trash bin, opting to keep the trousers to wash. With his clean clothes neatly set aside near his combat boots, he stepped into the shower and felt the hot water course down his back.

Leaning against the wall, he let the water rush over him. Brand stood for a while, feeling his sore muscles relax. He gently ran a hand over his injured shoulder and grimaced in pain. The caked blood washed off slowly and streamed a river of red down his body and into the drain.

He felt a wave of nausea course through him and the shower stall darkened as his vision narrowed into a long, dark corridor. His knees buckled and he felt himself starting to sink. Grabbing the shower knobs he held himself up, fighting the urge to pass out.

Brand closed his eyes and felt himself sinking inside. He felt himself falling back through a tunnel that closed around him. He tightened his grip and slid to his knees. Releasing his grip he leaned back into a corner and took a deep breath as water washed the caked blood from him.

He felt himself falling deeper into an abyss and was unable to stop. It seemed to go on forever.

Brand found himself kneeling in the shower, the water coursing over his shoulders and down his back. Prim was calling his name and he tried to pull himself to his feet.

"In here Chief." He managed to turn off the water and reach out for a towel while leaning against the wall of the shower.

"Jesus, sir. You ok? You've been showering for half-an-hour. Hope everything is clean."

"What are you, the shower Nazi? I was getting the blood off of me."

"Yeah, right. I'll have to remember that one next time I'm in the shower taking care of business. I just know the medics told me to keep an eye on you. Can't have you fainting from the heat."

"Thanks. I can always count on you getting my back." He dried off and started to dress in a clean uniform.

"Not while you're in the shower. I draw the line there." He snickered. "Want to get some food when you're dressed, sir?"

Brand took a moment to consider. "Come to think of it, I am kind of hungry. Sure."

It took him a few minutes to throw on the clean set of camouflaged desert fatigues and then both men crossed the camp to return his dirty clothes and towel to his room. Feeling just a bit fresher, Brand walked with Prim from his room towards the large DFAC, the base dining facility.

As they entered, a soldier sitting on a stool clicked a counter in his hand and they grabbed trays, following a growing line to obtain food. The DFAC was serving breakfast, as it was early morning. Prim opted for the waffles and sausage patties, while Brand could not decide and went for scrambled eggs, bacon, sausage links and toast. They ate in silence, Prim watching Brand closely.

"After we finish eating, you should go get some rest, sir. I'll find out what our schedule is. I think we're off the next few days while Ross recovers. I'll come by and check on you later."

"Thanks, Chief. Good idea. And maybe get a number for someone at medical to keep tabs on both Ross and Minos."

The Chief smiled and nodded. "Good idea, sir. I think I know just the person."

Brand laughed under his breath and shook his head. "You never change, Gunner."

"Man's gotta eat, sir."

"I'm going to get some rest. I feel awful. Give me a few hours and then come by. We'll find out if they completed a SITREP and what information needs to be followed up." The situation report would be the official message the military submitted recording the incident.

Prim shrugged. "I'll find that out while you sleep. I can visit the comms shack and then I'll grab a few hours before I come get you. Officers need more beauty sleep then Chiefs. We're just naturally good looking."

They laughed and took their trays to stack. As they exited the DFAC, Brand stopped to glance around the base and ponder the situation. "We need to figure out who had knowledge we were going to be there. We were ambushed, regardless of by what."

Prim nodded and shrugged. "Just make sure we carry bigger guns wherever we go, next time. But I'm with you."

Brand took in a deep breath and agreed. "Find us some bigger guns then, Gunner. And wake me up in a few."

Prim started to turn and then stopped. "We're going after them, aren't we sir? Whatever they are."

Brand took a moment before shrugging. "I haven't figured it out yet. I don't think I'm that stupid . . . but I could be wrong."

"I think we are, sir." He grinned, and they split in different directions. Brand headed to his bunk to catch some sleep, and Prim crossed the camp towards the operations center.

Once he reached his room, he pulled off his uniform blouse and sat down on the edge of the bed. As he leaned forward to untie his boots, he felt his head roll through a wave of vertigo and he started to slip back into tunnel vision as everything faded to black. He felt a wave of heat roll through him and he tried to sit up. He only managed to fall back across the bed as he fell deeper and deeper down a dark hole.

In a sudden flash, his mind flooded with scenes and faces almost too fast to make out, yet with the scenes he also heard voices and smelled scents. Hazy and vague, it was as if a deluge of his memories rushed through him, yet they were not his memories. Faces and places flashed and were gone: a man here, an animal there, a building, a tower, a river. He saw the desert and then a jungle, and the pyramids, though new and incredible to behold. And then it stopped.

Deep within he saw bright sun shining from above as he stood in a courtyard. Palm trees stood about gently swaying in a warm breeze. As he moved, he saw guards placed around the corners of the courtyard, dressed in ancient Egyptian attire with long, sickle swords held in a double grip.

He passed by a pool of water and glanced down, catching his reflection. His face was different and foreign, though young, strong and handsome, with jet-black hair and piercing silver eyes. He wore an Egyptian Nemes, the striped gold and white head cloth of royalty in ancient Egypt.

He continued on, and his eyes lifted towards the entrance of a palace building ahead. The armed guards seemed to stand a little taller as he walked by.

The room he entered was large and plush, with divans around in a circle and a fountain in the center. Pillows were cast about and gossamer curtains separated corners of the room from view.

Standing across the room was a young woman of surpassing beauty, with exotic Persian features and long, raven hair. Her full lips, touched with deep red color, parted in a smile, accentuated by extraordinarily long canines.

As he approached, he felt her saying something in greeting to him, and he knelt before her, lowering his head ever so slightly.

....

Chief Prim crossed the base from the DFAC to the communications building. One of the few intact buildings on the base was a three-story structure in which communications had been established. A field of antennae and radar dish were arrayed on the roof and several offices on the first floor had been set up with the gear.

The heavy metal door to the communications room was always secured, with a small barred window in the center. As the chief approached, he reached up to press a small button and a buzzer sounded inside.

The small window swung inward and a black Navy chief looked out. "What's up, Gunner?"

"I'm looking for the status on a SITREP. Would have gone out late last night? Possible IED in the city." Prim responded cordially.

"Sure enough. We received a copy of it early this morning. Army sent it out. We wouldn't have seen it but we saw a reference on a FRAGO and one of the petty officers looked it up. It was hidden in the details."

"Great detective work. You'll get your Dick Tracey badge before you know it. Anything interesting in it?" Prim asked, pulling out a cigarette to light up.

"Those things will kill you, Gunner." The black Chief nodded towards the cigarette. "Why are you asking about the message?"

"Oh, I don't know; maybe because I was the driver of the vehicle involved. Anything interesting?"

The chief behind the window shrugged and held up one finger. "Give me a minute. Put out that cancer stick and I'll let you in. You can read it yourself. The weird thing is you'd think it would have made front-page news, so to speak; but not a peep. It's like it didn't happen, except they put out a short SITREP and followed with a FRAGO to limit all off base activity to groups of four or more."

Prim took two more extremely long puffs on his cigarette before snubbing it on the doorframe. As the chief inside opened the door, Prim stepped past and let his lung-full of smoke blow out, followed by a childish grin.

The chief shut the door behind him and shaking his head muttered, "Dick."

....

Brand opened his eyes to see his Chief standing over him. "Jeese, you sleep more than a woman. How's your head?"

Brand shook his head and rubbed his eyes, sitting up. He stretched and yawned. "How long have I been out? I'm starving again like I haven't eaten in a week."

Prim looked at his watch and seemed to be doing simple math. "Let's see, counting the last ten minutes I've been at your side . . . two days."

"What?" he exclaimed, bolting to his feet. "How's that possible?"

The chief shrugged. "We saw you shuffling out of your room like twice to hit the head to piss or whatever and then you'd disappear back in your dark cave. I popped in a few times and watched you. Did you feel creeped out?"

Brand shook his head. "No. Actually, I feel great. My head doesn't hurt at all and I'm not feeling like I'll pass out at any moment."

"Yeah, well those Brits were visiting you a good deal the last two days; especially the female. You know, if she didn't seem like a cold bitch, I'd say she was hot."

Brand shook his head again, this time smiling. "And the world is right again. Only you have the propensity to go from me sleeping through a two day coma to concepts involving you having sex with a British . . . what is she? Special agent?"

"Hey, sir. I keep trying to broaden your horizons. Maybe she can show you why she's special." He grinned.

Brand turned away, trying to hide his smile and shaking his head more. He reached a hand up and stroked the course stubble across his chin. "Anything else I should know while I was asleep?"

Chief shrugged. "That Army Colonel, Shaker, sent a first lieutenant over yesterday afternoon. Said the Colonel wanted a statement from you when you woke up. I told him we'd send it over later. I took the liberty of writing one up for you, but figured you'd want to look it over.

You know, to touch it up with those frilly metaphors you officers use."

Brand grabbed his blouse and cover. "Come on. Is the DFAC open?"

"Nope, sir. Just missed lunch. But the schwarma shop is open. I had lunch but I can always go for a schwarma or two. I'm buying."

The sun was high and bright and the air was warm and heating up. During their walk from the building, Brand looked his thin companion up and down. "Where do you put it all? You eat all the time."

"Smoking and coffee keeps me fit." Came the patent reply as they stepped into the courtyard and mid-morning sun. "Anyhow, you had a fever that seemed to break early this morning. You were sweating more than a politician passing a whorehouse with his wife in the car. After we eat, you might consider a shower."

When Brand stepped from the shade he winced at the sunlight. He fumbled around in the pockets of his blouse and was rewarded with a pair of Wiley-X sunglasses. He slipped them on and the two men continued across the base towards a small shopping area complete with local mercantile and local food.

The shopping area had been set up in a fairly poorly constructed set of one-story buildings. There was a small military exchange with US goods, a barber shop, a tailor and cleaner, as well as a few small shops which sold local Middle Eastern trinkets, and a food court.

As they approached the food court, Brand eyed the Kentucky Fried Chicken and Burger King while they made their way to the schwarma shop. Across the air, Brand smelled the soft fragrance of jasmine and lavender almost hidden under a stronger musky sent of sandalwood. He breathed it in, capturing the jasmine and lavender and could almost taste the soft skin it caressed.

A female stepped from the schwarma shop, covered by a black hajib with dark blue niqab covering most of her face. Crystal blue eyes peered up at the two men, locking securely on Brand. She froze and Brand could feel her breath stop in her chest. Even from a distance, he could smell and taste her. Something came across the warm wind that smelled of lavender mixed with other fragrances.

"Welcome Chief." Called the schwarma shop owner, a portly and friendly Middle Eastern man. His short hair was combed sharply down the right side and his thin mustache was tightly groomed. "Are you hungry?"

Brand shook his head and the covered female turned and disappeared back beyond the shop owner. Her fragrance lingered for mere seconds, the subtle mix of jasmine, lavender and her slowly overtaken by the musky sent of sandalwood and the shop owner.

"Hey Abdullah. My officer is starving. Fix us up a bunch."

The portly shop owner grinned and clapped his hands. "For my best customer, of course. Have a seat and I will send them out to you."

As he turned to rush back to his shop, Brand called to him. "Abdulla; what is that you're wearing? That smell."

"Ah, you like? It's sandalwood. I have it made by a friend for me. It hides the smell of lamb and schwarma so I go home to my wife and she let's me in." He laughed. "It's only made for me here in Kuwait. I can get you some, if you want. The ladies like it. I can't keep them off me, especially your American women." He grinned and nodded emphatically.

"No thanks!" Prim snapped, shaking his head. "I don't need to be stuck in our vehicle smelling that next to me all day, Abdulla. And certainly, I don't need any of the ladies fawning all over my officer. I have enough trouble keeping him out of trouble."

Abdulla went off laughing loud as the two men found their way to a small, plastic table. Brand was still walking in a haze as they sat and waited.

"What's with the smell, sir?" Prim lit another cigarette and put his feet up on an empty chair at their table.

"It's not his cologne. There was something else underneath. The girl was wearing it. More intoxicating."

Prim winked at him. "Sounds like you're getting better, sir. Luckily I'm here to run interference and make sure we keep a distance between you and international incidents."

"Thanks. I appreciate you watching out for me, mother."

The shop owner quickly sliced meat and crafted a number of the delicious, aromatic wraps. Within a few short minutes, Abdullah brought full plates of schwarma with cans of Pepsi to place before the two men.

Both men took their time eating, although the chief only ate two shawarma, an Arab sandwich-like wrap of shaved lamb, goat or other meat inside a pita bread with tabbouleh, fattoush, tomato and cucumber. Some of the shawarma were topped in tahini, a sesame paste, or hummus. Brand ate four, and felt as if he could eat four more.

As they sat, Prim reported to Brand regarding the situation report. "SITREP indicated an explosive device that flipped our vehicle. Two injured and one missing person. No mention had been made regarding the disposition of his body.

Upon finishing their meal, Brand felt someone watching and his pulse quickened. He turned to face the approaching Major Valko, with his female companion following at his side, both with Styrofoam cups from the shop.

"Liam. It's good to see you up and about? How are you feeling?"

He felt his pulse hammering in his ears and his breath came in short gulps. His eyes settled on the female. Suddenly he could feel her pulse and her breathing. Something about her pulled him to her and his vision settled across the curves of her body. He could smell her and felt heat beginning to rush through him.

"Liam?" Valko stepped into his sight, drawing his vision from the female and forcing their eyes to lock. "Is there something about Siovhan that intrigues you? Or are you still somewhat dreaming?"

"Siovhan?" Brand queried, coming out of his trance.

"My assistant, Special Agent Siovhan Watson, Captain in Intelligence Corps originally. You seem somewhat enthralled by her. Or perhaps, as the young chaps might say, a bit rat-arsed."

"Excuse me?" Prim asked.

"Drunk." Valko replied.

"I'm sorry. I didn't mean to stare. You just smelled . . . fresh."

The chief leaned in and chuckled. "Good one, sir. Another one I'll have to write down when I consider talking to women. As long as they're hookers, it should work."

For a brief moment, Watson smiled. "Thank you, Commander. Considering the company, I assume I have been complemented. And I am certain that line would work on women other than your chief's hookers if received from the right individual."

"Siovhan has visited you a few times while you slept. How do you feel?"

"Better." Liam replied. "I can't put my finger on it, but buzzing. And I had incredibly vivid dreams all night . . . or all two nights." He felt the approach of two more figures from behind and knew them to be the remaining members of Valko's team.

"Must have been the shots. They can do that. Siovhan gave you a few more while you slept. I do not think you have been properly introduced, though she may have taken the liberty to pull down your trousers to administer a few."

"I can assure you, I took no such indiscretions." Brand could barely make out a mischievous smirk beneath her forced indignity, with her extremely proper English.

"Liam and Chief Prim, allow me to introduce my team. Siovhan Watson, Cedric Churchill and Fergus Williams." The three stepped forward to shake hands, Cedric being the largest of the group, his muscles barely contained within the suit; and Fergus being the youngest with short red hair, Scottish accent and almost as large as Cedric.

As Brand shook hands with each member, he felt them almost as an extension of himself. With Cedric, the large man was sheer physical, brute power and a calm center. Fergus handshake was excited and young. When he touched Siovhan's hand he felt her pulse accelerate to match his own and he saw her eyes grow wide.

Fergus moved closer to Brand, his eyes wide with a friendly smile. "I've heard you practice martial arts. Your Chief said you were pretty good."

Brand looked up to the massive, young man who seemed truly intent upon befriending him. "I've been practicing and teaching a few decades now. I started when I was younger. Do you practice?"

Cedric laughed in his deep baritone voice, "He does, and when he heard you teach he had to meet you."

"What style do you practice?" the young Scott asked.

Before Brand could answer, Valko interrupted with a smile, "We can discuss close quarters combat at a future date, Fergus. For now, I believe Agent Watson might have more pressing questions to ask our friend, while it is as fresh as possible in his shaken brain."

The big soldier nodded and gave an embarrassed grin. "Right, sir. My mistake. Perhaps later."

The four sat down around the table from the two. "So what did you dream about?" Sam asked.

Liam looked down at his empty plate and shrugged. He thought long and hard, trying to recall his dreams as they floated in his mind like true memories. "It was unusual to say the least. I've never had a dream like it before. It was like a flash of pictures that went through thousands of years in a blink. At least that's what I felt it was. Like flipping back and forth through the encyclopedia and just spotting various times and places. And then I found I was in ancient Egypt. It felt so real, and I could smell the air."

Valko smiled with just a hint of anxiety. "I apologize, but did you say ancient Egypt? How ancient?"

Brand looked Valko squarely in the eyes. "Why do I always get the feeling you ask questions because you know a great deal more than you let on? It was very ancient. BC if I were to guess based upon watching the Discovery channel. It just felt like early Egypt."

"I'm fascinated by dreams, myself." Siovhan spoke, drawing his attention. "What did you see?"

Liam thought for another minute before recounting the first dream, which lead into a host of others, many blurring into the next. "I don't recall all the events, but it was like watching myself in a movie."

"I was in a courtyard with a fountain. And I saw my reflection, but it wasn't me. I was dressed in a white kilt with a gold and white striped headdress. The kind you see in Moses or Egyptian movies. But my face was different."

"Did you do anything?" Valko inquired, continuing to lean forward as if to pull the dreams out.

He shrugged. "I turned and found myself facing a woman. But for some reason I didn't feel she was Egyptian. She was royalty, I could tell, because guards surrounded her; and I felt that she was Cleopatra, but I can't be sure. The memories are fading."

"Memories? Or dreams?" Siohvan asked for clarification.

Liam thought about it a moment. To him, it felt more like memories and details of his life and less like a dream or fantasy. He nodded to confirm. "I guess dreams, but they feel like parts of my life."

"What else?" The Major urged.

"That was it for the first dream. After that, I felt myself going in and out of other dreams, all very similar: same time frame. In one I was leading a hunt on foot, while the Queen followed in a chariot. I don't know what we were hunting."

"You said queen? How do you know this?"

Liam realized Siovhan was taking notes on a small flip notepad while Sam continued what began to feel like an interrogation. "I just felt it. She was the queen, and I was her hunter. Ok, what gives? It was just a dream and I get the feeling I'm being psycho-analyzed."

"Oh, my apologies." Siovhan spoke, flipping the notepad closed. "I like to catalog the various dreams the vaccine imparts upon the recipients. Medical purposes, if you will. And considering you're in the middle of the desert, its no small wonder you're dreaming of Egypt and Cleopatra."

"Awesome. Just as long as you don't ask me to complete a Rorschach test I think we'll be fine."

She smiled politely. "I don't put any faith in inkblot tests, thank you."

The Chief stood up and collected their trash. "Hey, sir. I was thinking we might visit our two remaining agents in the hospital. When I visited yesterday, Agent Ross was awake. They still didn't let me see Minos. Maybe you can use those collar devices to get us past the back door." He nodded towards the rank insignia on his collar.

Sam offered. "We visited your special agent late yesterday. Although she had yet to come out of her coma, the doctors have her stabilized. They indicated she had lost a considerable amount of blood, but otherwise seemed to be on her way to making a full recovery. A few transfusions and stitches and she was resting. If you find her awake, let us know."

"Thanks, Sam. We appreciate that." Liam responded, standing. "We'll stop in on them both, as well."

"Right. Well I've an errand to run, but if I'm quick, I might meet you over in the vicinity of he hospital. Watson might want to check up on our patient Minos. And perhaps we can have tea later this afternoon. We shall be around this camp most of the evening, so feel free to look us up."

"First things first, sir. I'll get our weapons while you wash off two days of funk. I'll meet you at your hooch in thirty minutes."

Brand bent his nose to sniff at his own chest and screwed his nose. "Good idea, Chief. See you at the tent in thirty."

The British officer and his entourage watched the two Americans depart from the food court, heading back across the small base.

"Churchill. Williams. Follow them, but stay out of sight. Just make sure they are ok. And keep your eyes on Lieutenant Commander Brand. I have a worry about that one."

"Aye, sir. We're on it." Replied Williams, and the two stood to follow.

Churchill shook his head and looked to the Major. "Is he changing? And how old is his maker, sir?"

Major Valko shrugged. "Based upon what he has divulged to us, I'd say he is changing. As to how old his maker is, I cannot even begin to guess. I don't know exactly how it works, but I have heard visions and dreams are passed during the change. They are supposedly snapshots of the past from the maker's life. What he is describing is . . . ancient. We've administered the shots, so hopefully he'll accept the change as easily as possible."

Watson looked to Valko and shook her head. "Snapshots of the maker's? The dreams he described would have been from eons ago. How would he possibly see those visions? It wouldn't pass from one maker to another down through, would it?"

Valko shrugged. "I don't know. We have two possibilities. He was made from a line of makers: Each one passing along the thoughts, visions and dreams of the original. The second possibility is he encountered an Original. His maker might simply be that old."

Churchill took a breath as he paused a moment to think. "If his maker is that old, will the vaccinations be enough? The dreams might be right. From what I could smell, the Elder hunting here is considerably powerful, which might make him considerably old. I would never have guessed two-millennium or more. Is that even possible? It definitely was like nothing I've ever encountered, sir."

Their major shrugged his shoulder and lowered his eyes. "My grandfather spoke of the really old, but he had never met any of them. I have absolutely no idea if it is possible. This one might be a pureblood."

After a moment of silence, he looked up. "Then let's be about our business with our heads on straight. Look alive and stay alert. If we are in an Elder's territory, regardless of age, we definitely don't want to agitate it when it may not be against us. Mind you, from the Chief's reports, he took rounds from a weapon and didn't seem to flinch. And from Commander Brand's description, tore through the other two shifters like a hot knife through butter. This may be dangerous."

"When I get a moment, I'll contact London and see if there are any historical reports of lycans in the court of Cleopatra or Ancient Egypt; especially a silver lycan.

It might at least give us an idea of who or what we might be dealing with if we find ourselves in their presence.

With that said, the two large men nodded and turned to follow the Americans. As they watched them depart, Valko sipped his tea and turned to Watson. "We'll have to set up around the clock to watch him if he is changing. Make certain he is safe."

"And to make certain others are safe from him, especially the females." Siohvan commented. "Dear god, his heat is palpable. His attraction is . . ." She stopped and smiled. "Delicious."

Valko turned away as she giggled softly. He shook his head and stood up, sighing. "You will not be on first watch. As a matter of fact, perhaps we should just keep Churchill and Williams on the night watch."

She laughed for a brief moment before turning a serious eye on Major Valko. "Do you seriously believe there is a shifter in this vicinity that is two millennium?"

Valko shook his head. "I don't know. I've never encountered any, although my grandfather swore they still existed. It's not like they advertise. He always said lycans came from purebloods and the purebloods were immortal. I always thought it was a bedtime story."

"If he is here, why haven't we heard of him? How come we've never received a report of any activity here?"

The Major laughed and sipped his tea. As he sat the cup down he looked at Watson. "Who knows? No one I know is immortal, just long-lived; but there are always the old tales that the first generations were extremely long-lived. My grandfather said his grandfather met a Nordic shifter who claimed to be Fenrir. My grandfather swore he was, that his grandfather described Fenrir as old and strong but looked as young as I do today. When I asked him why we didn't all know about Fenrir, he said Fenrir chose to let his grandfather know, and only Fenrir knew why he kept his silence."

"Fenrir, as in the Norse wolf of mythology?"

"The one and same." He stated. "Most myths are based in some form of reality. Fenrir was the father of the Norse bezzerkers, the Bwazara. They were warriors in legend who clothed themselves as bears and came in savaging any living creature before them; men, women, cattle. None were safe. We know the Bwazara were and still are shape shifters. My grandfather said they came from Fenrir."

She nodded. "So if the bwazara are real then Fenrir was real. I can believe that. But any lycan living for two-millennium; that's a bit far fetched to believe."

"Two millennium on the low end; possibly considerably older. Let's just hope he's on our side." He finished his tea. "Cedric might be right. If the Maker is an Elder, will Commander Brand be able to accept the change? Even with the vaccines?"

Siohvan shook her head. "I have no earthly idea. I guess we'll all find out together."

Chapter 5

NCIS

Colonel Shaker sat in the office of his hard-shell building on Arifjan reviewing a PowerPoint on the number of IED attempts in the region when a younger sergeant knocked and entered, followed by two individuals in black suits and dark sunglasses. The first of the two was a tall, thin Chinese male with short-cropped black hair and almost pale skin who moved with a dancer's grace. He was followed by a female of mixed-Asian race, with long, black hair tied in a tight bun and a lean, athletic build.

The Sergeant cleared his throat and grunted, "Sir. Two new NCIS agents have requested a meeting."

The Colonel glowered at the intrusion and started to stand as the male moved towards him, extending a hand and a warming smile. "Greetings Colonel. Thank you for receiving us on short notice."

"Don't you mean no-notice?" The Colonel began to growl. As their eyes locked the Colonel seemed to deflate, his barrel chest relaxing. "Welcome. Come in."

The female spoke up from behind her male counterpart, not offering a hand. "I am Special Agent Wong. This is Special Agent in Charge Huang." She flipped open her credentials and badge and slapped it shut abruptly as if the mere action was a nuisance.

Special Agent in Charge Huang spoke again, drawing Colonel Shaker's attention back to himself. "We have just arrived from a long flight and as you can imagine, we are acclimating to the sun and heat. I have read your initial situation reports, but would like to review the scene of the attack first hand. The Navy appreciates your support in our investigation."

Colonel Shaker grimaced and then nodded. "Sergeant! Get a ride for the Senior Agent and have them taken to the site of the explosion."

"Also, may we have a list of all witnesses to the accident? And perhaps any of your first responders who were on scene?"

The Colonel looked at the Sergeant and nodded. "Give them what they want."

Huang broadened his smile, barely showing his white teeth and gave a short bow. "Thank you again. We shall return with any of our findings or thoughts."

The Sergeant called up a second Sergeant and a few Corporals to take the two agents to the site. A short ride later pulled an armored HUMVEE up to the intersection where the attack had taken place.

As they stepped out of the vehicle, the heat and sun beat down upon the black suits, but neither agent seemed to notice. The Sergeant who drove pointed across the short area. "When we arrived, the vehicle was overturned here. We saw blood here." He gestured towards the ground and immediate surrounding area. "Sir, we have plenty of water in the back of the HUMMER. You two have got to be burning up in your suits in this heat. It's almost 110."

"Thank you Sergeant." Huang responded, walking in the direction the Sergeant had indicated the blood was found. "I appreciate your concern. But I shall be fine. Please provide one to Agent Wong."

As Huang walked around the site, Wong pulled an MP-5 from inside her jacket and kept watch around the immediate area, eyes both high and low while gripping the small machinegun at the ready. She accepted the large bottle of water in her free left hand and drank from it, never letting her watch waver.

The Senior Agent sniffed at the air and seemed to follow a trail as if in a trance, kneeling to touch the ground and lift a few grains of sand blown in from the desert. As it sifted through his fingers, he turned towards the alley and stood tall, following the hidden trail.

Wong and the Army soldiers fell in line behind as he tracked across the ground. He entered the alley and stopped to sniff again, taking in a deep breath. Glancing over his shoulder, he whispered in Chinese back to Special Agent Wong, "Blood. Quite a bit."

They continued tracking the unseen trail until they ended in the courtyard between buildings. Huang knelt in the center and touched the stone and sand. "Someone attempted to clean this rather poorly. A great deal of blood here." He lifted a handful of dirt and sand to his nose and sniffed. He grimaced and again in Chinese muttered. "Láng rén." He shook his head as Wong nodded, understanding the term "Wolf man."

Huang stood, wiping his hands off as if offended. "They were here." Again he changed from English to Chinese. "Some died on this spot. And I sense something more. Much older." He shifted his eyes to the corners of the buildings and looked upwards, following to the edge of the roof.

Turning back to Wong and the soldiers, he stated. "Nothing more to see here. I have all I need. Please take us back to your base. I would like to visit the hospital and our Agents there."

"Yes, sir." The sergeant responded.

....

Prim pulled his HUMVEE up outside the hospital structure located on Camp Arifjan. The hospital was a hard-shell structure fairly large in size and oval in shape with a domed top. Hard shell structures were starting to pop up more and more across the military facilities in Iraq and Kuwait, to include being used as dining facilities as well as gymnasiums.

Both Brand and Prim stepped out of the vehicle and walked towards the entrance. They were dressed in their body armor and were armed with their weapons, which they downloaded at the door, using the clearing barrel to the side.

"See if you can talk to your sergeant friend once we get inside, Chief; if she's on watch. Find out where Minos is. I'll find Ross. I don't know why, but I have this feeling we weren't just targets of opportunity. We were targeted, or rather I believe the special agents were."

"How do you figure, sir?" They entered the lobby where a few soldiers sat in folding chairs to the side of the front desk, waiting to be triaged. Both officer and Chief removed their covers and folded them into their large side leg pockets.

"It's a gut feeling, but when we arrived and when we departed the Colonel's home, we were being watched. They were waiting for our arrival, and they were ready to attack when we departed. I don't think it was random. They knew we were going to visit Khalil."

"Roger, sir. I'll make contact with the Sergeant. I'll come looking for you when I'm done. I know where she hangs her hat when she's on watch. I think she should be on shift for another hour, so I might get lucky . . . I mean we should be in luck." He winked.

"Sounds good. I'll take luck." Brand headed for the front desk while Prim continued on past as if he belonged.

Behind the counter sat two army enlisted, one young Hispanic male and an older black female. The female looked up behind thick, wide glasses and spoke in a very stern yet professional tone. "May I help you, sir?"

"Good morning, Master Sergeant. How's business today? Slow I hope." He smiled.

She responded with a smile, warming to him. "Blessedly slow, yes sir. How may I help you?"

"Special Agent Ross. I've come to visit my charge."

"Visiting hours just started, so you're in luck, commander. Do you know where he's resting?"

"No, Master Sergeant. This is my first visit since the night of the incident. A few directions should send me on my way."

She nodded, pointing with a pen. "Head past triage and the emergency room. We've a number of private rooms down the hall on the right. He's in room 18-alpha. The door should be open and he was awake during breakfast."

Brand nodded and gave a short salute. "Much appreciated. Have a great Navy day."

Brand passed the triage area, where he saw Prim laughing with the female Sergeant from their first night. Other than Prim and the Sergeant, triage was empty save for a few other medical personnel on watch.

Just beyond triage, flaps opened into the emergency room area. The activity was low key, and there were no major injuries being treated. Only two military members were being treated at the time, probably having reported earlier during morning sick call.

Just beyond the flaps to the emergency room two corridors opened up, one marked A and the second marked B. Brand followed the first corridor to the right, checking the doors to either side as they read up in numbers, odds to the right and evens to the left.

He found 18A a short march up the hall and stopped to look in. Special Agent Ross sat up in his bed, watching a television against the far wall while holding the remote control in his had. A tray of empty plates sat on the nightstand next to his bed and light filtered in through a single, large window of opaque shatterproof glass.

Looking up from the news, Ross managed a weak smile. "Liam. It's good to see you. How are you?" He straightened himself up.

"Top notch, sir. How are you? You took it pretty hard during the attack."

"Doctors told me I had a concussion from the accident. They said we were hit by an IED and we lost Chavez. Can you fill in the blanks? I can't remember a thing after leaving Colonel Khalil's home."

Brand grabbed a folding chair from the corner and pulled it closer. "I don't know if I can, sir, but I'll try. Mind if I sit for a while?"

"Please do. I've only had a few visitors, and of them, only the Chief came to see how I was doing. Most of them either want to stick me with needles or take my pulse, or wanted to know what I recall from the events. Once they hear I was unconscious, they lose all interest and that's it. Like this morning."

"What happened this morning?" He pulled a small flip notepad and pen. "Mind if I take notes?"

"Not at all. Washington sent a few more NCIS agents to take over the investigation. Army CID was pretty pissed I heard. I can't see that really mattering to the agents that were sent. They were ice cold." He extended the remote control and the television turned off. "The SAC was just cool. He asked a few questions. Then his assistant asked some questions, and they left."

"What questions, if you don't mind my asking?"

Ross laughed. "I'll let you know if I mind. About the meetings I had with Khalil. They didn't seem too concerned with the accident. Of course, maybe they already guessed it would be a waste of time asking me, since they probably read the reports that I was knocked unconscious. Army seemed a bit slow in picking that piece up."

"What did you tell them about the meeting? What was it about?"

"Khalil was worrying about a number of attacks that have happened recently. Over the past few months, they've lost a few goats and dogs, and in recent weeks, three camels. The animals were found in the mornings, disemboweled and dismembered. There were no witnesses; however, the locals are afraid and the Colonel was hoping we could investigate. His own police force is too afraid to look into the issue and his soldiers refuse to address it."

"Why is that, sir? You'd think they would be interested in animal mutilations. Potential serial killer in the making."

Ross nodded. "Yes. And it's real investigative work. I asked Khalil, and he just indicated they had superstitions that his men refused to buck. His men were afraid. Khalil is well educated and thinks beyond local folklore, but he did say something strange. He said his police force had mentioned some religious sect from pre-biblical times. I don't recall the name, but something like sons of something."

"Khalil may be educated, but he's not an investigator. He's royalty and he's military. His own police force won't investigate and he's losing support to superstition. He seemed concerned that the superstition would turn the local Kuwait people away from supporting U.S. forces."

Brand continued to take notes and asked, "Why didn't Chavez want to investigate? He seemed like this was a waste of time?"

Ross shrugged and smiled. "Chavez is. . . .was upset at being in the Middle East to begin with. Everything was a nuisance to him. He saw this whole episode as some local teenagers playing with Satanic rituals."

Brand shook his head. "He didn't take the culture into consideration. But in his defense, I wouldn't have thought much of the incidents either if we hadn't been attacked." He paused for a brief moment. "How did Khalil contact you? And who else knew you were going?"

"Khalil sent an invitation over requesting we visit as soon as we were able. That was about two days before we went. I really don't know who else knew beyond his Major. Now it's your turn, Liam. What happened?"

Brand flipped the pad of paper closed and slid it back into his blouse pocket while he glanced over his shoulder to insure privacy. Looking back he leaned in and spoke cautiously, sighing deeply before beginning.

Prim continued to flirt with Reece, sitting on the edge of a gurney while she stood. She laughed and shook her head. "I appreciate the attention, Chief. But I doubt you came here just to talk to me. I do have the best bed side manner, but my shift is ending soon and I figure you're here for some other reason."

"Hey, can't I just improve Army-Navy relations? Why's it got to be like that? I'm hurt."

Again she laughed, lifting a hand to pat his chest. "I'm sure you don't have any pain in here, Chief. But maybe I can make it up to you later. In the meantime, what can I help you with?"

"As long as you're asking, how's our Special Agent Minos? My officer is meeting with her Senior Agent, but we haven't been able to see our other charge."

"The small female? There were a few other special agents who showed up today and took charge. If I heard correctly, they were transferring her back to the states immediately."

"Excuse me? Where is she now?" Prim bolted from the edge of the gurney to his feet.

Reece pointed back down the passageway. "End of Alpha corridor. I think 26 Alpha."

"Thanks, Sergeant. And for the record, you were my first reason for being here today. Everything else was secondary.

We should have some coffee at some time." He started heading towards the Alpha corridor.

Reece laughed. "Just coffee, Chief?"

Prim froze in his tracks for a brief moment before shaking his head. "Eh, duty calls. I'll be back." And continued on his way.

As he made his way down the A-corridor, he ran across Brand exiting Ross' room. "Come on, sir. Minos was in quarantine down the hall. 26 I think."

"Ok. Why the hurry?"

"Little birdie told me spooks from stateside are moving her out of here. Figured we'd want to at least check on her and see her ourselves before she's gone."

"Good thinking, Chief. You constantly remind me why I keep you around."

"I'm hurt, sir. And all this time, I thought it was on account of my good looks."

They found room 26-A and Prim pushed the door in. The four-bed room was empty with the exception of a single female in black suit and white shirt. She stood in the center of the hospital room watching the door as if waiting for their arrival.

"Good afternoon, Commander Brand. Chief Prim." The greeting was cold and formal. "I am Special Agent Wong, NCIS from Washington DC. Senior Agent Huang felt you would be visiting here and sent me to retrieve you."

Brand pegged her at five-five, with black hair tied back in a tight bun, tight athletic build and mixed Asian lineage.

Dark glasses covered her eyes and her black suit fit more in a movie setting or Washington DC than in the military hospital in Kuwait.

"A little over-dressed for the part, aren't you?" Prim asked. "Dark suits don't go well with the desert heat."

She didn't respond to his sarcasm. "If you have time, we would like to converse with you regarding the incident."

"Right away. Just, right after we get to visit with Special Agent Minos." Brand stated. "We haven't been in to check on her yet, and we were hoping to see her."

"Special Agent Minos has been moved from this hospital to receive better treatment. She'll be repatriated back to the US where she'll be treated at Walter Reid. She will receive the absolute best care possible."

"If it's all the same to you, we'd like to at least see her before she goes." He stated emphatically.

"Yeah, the commander is right. We've grown kind of fond of her, and it wouldn't seem right if we didn't get to see her off. So, be a good agent and point us in the right direction." Prim added.

Special Agent Wong looked from Brand to Prim and back to Brand. "Your current concerns are of little consequence. We have more urgent matters to attend to than satisfying your base needs. This investigation takes priority, so if you will come with me, we can speak with my Senior Agent in Charge and you can be about your business."

The NCIS agent nodded at the door and gestured for the two to lead the way. As they stepped from the room, she moved past to take the lead. They had only gone a few yards down the passageway when they heard the familiar British accent call from behind.

Turning back, the two men saw Major Valko hurrying to catch up. "I hope you don't mind, but thought perhaps your luck might be better than mine, if your Special Agent Minos is awake. Mind if I join the party? I've been informed she isn't accepting any visitors and they plan to move her.

Special Agent Wong shook her head but before she could refuse Brand had responded, "More the merrier, Sam. Come on. We're on our way to meet the new Senior NCIS Agent before we can visit Minos."

"Do tell. Well, I'm always in the mood to meet new members of the U.S. Navy. Lead the way."

Wong seemed a bit upset but shook her head silently and led the small group down the passage way. At the last door, she knocked.

Although they waited a few long seconds, they did not hear a response before Wong pushed the door in. They entered to a room that had been made into a makeshift office. A large, metal desk sat in the center, with a number of simple, metal chairs around the room. Various medical reports and military messages were strewn across the desk.

Sitting behind the desk was a tall, lean man of Chinese descent with short cut, black hair and porcelain skin. Like Wong, he wore a black suit with white shirt and black tie. He rose from behind the desk, his dark, cold eyes capturing first Brand, then Prim, and finally settling on Valko.

Valko seemed to bristle at the door and looked around nervously before stepping in. "Well that was fast." He stated quite simply. "Although not entirely unexpected."

"You are quite done here, little bulldog. Run away and fetch a stick." He spoke in near perfect English, an almost indistinguishable hint of Asian accent hidden in his words. Although outwardly he seemed to emit little emotion, Brand could feel a tension building between the two men.

"I think I'll stay, if Commander Brand doesn't mind."

Wong looked from the Senior Agent to Valko and back, shifting across the room to take up station at the corner of the desk. She opened the front of her suit, displaying the butt of her MP-5.

"This is a US investigation. We are quite confident we don't need you." The Senior Agent spoke emphatically.

"I don't believe you have any idea what you're up against, and perhaps I have more experience in these matters, all things considered." The British officer responded.

The verbal sparring match continued as the Senior Agent commented, "You are barking up the wrong tree."

"And you've bitten off more than you can chew. I claim this." The Major seemed agitated and grew taller in stature.

The Senior Agent seemed to grow colder and as he did, Special Agent Wong lifted a hand towards the grip of her sub-machine gun.

"Hold on!" Brand called out, stepping between the Major and the two agents. "What's up here?" Between the two men, Brand felt a veritable wave of energy. From Valko, it felt almost bestial, while from the Senior Agent it felt cold and dark.

Both the cold Senior Agent and the British officer looked to Brand, while Wong kept her eyes trained on Valko.

Turning to the Senior Agent, Brand spoke. "You wanted to see me. I'm here. Major Valko is with me. So ask your questions and let me be on my way. I want to see Minos before you ship her off to Walter Reid."

The Senior Agent took in the entire group with one glance before speaking in his monotonous tone. "Out of the question. Special Agent Minos is under quarantine until further notice. If you wish to assist her, you will provide me with a few answers." He pulled a wallet from the inside pocket of his suit jacket and flipped it out nonchalant, displaying his NCIS badge. "Senior Agent in Charge Huang. I've taken over this investigation from all parties. Please take a seat." He sat back in the chair behind the desk. "Special Agent Wong, please be seated."

Wong relaxed and let her jacket fall shut before sitting in a chair off to the side. Brand and Prim exchanged glances before pulling up two chairs to the desk. Valko remained standing.

The negative energy around Huang seemed to dissipate while the British officer still seemed on edge. Brand considered what he had just felt passing between the two.

Huang looked to Valko, but the British officer simply smiled. "I prefer to stand, considering the company. Don't want to get caught flat footed."

Seeming to ignore Valko, the Senior Agent looked to Brand. "I've heard some of the rumors from Colonel Shaker regarding the events of the other night. Please, lead me through them and do not spare any details. I am especially interested in the additional elements of your report."

"Additional elements?" Brand asked quizzically.

Valko leaned over his shoulder and audibly whispered. "He means regarding the canines involved in the attack. Unless I've judged these two incorrectly, he has his cold little heart set upon hearing about the beasties."

Huang gave a curt nod and commented. "You are exceptionally perceptive for one of your kind. I am most interested." Looking back to Brand, he stated again. "Lead me through the events of the other night and do not spare any details."

Glancing over his shoulder at Prim, he shrugged and began to recount the events leading up from their arrival to when he was knocked unconscious. Upon completion of his telling, Prim took up and added the remaining events up until Colonel Khalil and his troops secured the area.

When they had finished their report, the room sat in silence until Wong spoke up. "What type of rounds do you use in your weapons, Chief?"

Prim shrugged. "Standard military issue. And you?"

She shook her head. "And your accuracy? Are you an acceptable shot?"

"He's the best gunner I know." Brand commented. "He's an exceptional shot."

"So it's safe to assume you didn't miss your target?"

"Considering how many rounds I put down the alley, I'd say I hit my target about ten times before it moved, if that's what you're asking. All shots were solid, center mass. I saw them penetrate and I saw the blood."

Wong looked from Prim to Brand. "And you were covered in the blood? Was Special Agent Minos covered in blood? We've seen her injuries. How about yours?"

"Yes. I got some blood on my uniform. And to my knowledge, my injuries were superficial." Brand replied.

Wong continued. "Where are your uniforms? The uniforms with the blood."

"Back in my room at KNB. I was going to throw them out later."

"Negative, sir." Prim corrected. "You threw them out after your shower. They were in the trash bin in the shower trailer, unless the hajis already did a cleaning sweep."

Huang looked to Wong who shrugged. Brand noticed and elaborated. "Third-Country Nationals: camp support personnel. They normally clean mid-morning, so they may have already cleaned the showers before I got in there. Or they may be there now. They don't follow any set schedule I can tell."

Wong nodded to Huang and left the room.

"She will take care of having them retrieved." The Senior Agent stated. Leaning forward, his cold, dark eyes focused intently on Brand, locking him into place. "Is there anything else I should know? How do you . . . feel?"

Brand felt himself drawn towards the eyes as if he were being pulled from his own body. For a brief moment, he felt light and almost out-of-body, and then he felt Major Valko's hand placed solidly on his shoulder and he was pulled back.

"I believe the report sounds fairly complete, don't you, Huang?"

Again the Senior Agent glowered at the British officer. Looking back to the Naval officer and chief, he directed. "If you recall any additional information, you will let me know immediately. Further, you will maintain confidence on the particulars of this event. Do not divulge any of this information to anyone without first requesting permission from either myself or my assistant, Agent Wong."

"Ok. Now about Minos." Brand stated, standing. "I want to see her."

"No. Suffice it to say, she is being treated with the best care and under constant surveillance. We can keep you informed of her status should it change."

Brand stared at Huang to get any read from his body, yet the Asian man stood completely still. Finally, he shook his head and agreed. "I'd appreciate that, Senior Agent. Hopefully you will lift her quarantine before she leaves the country."

"You will be one of the first to know, Commander. Now, if you will. I must attend to other matters regarding this investigation. I will find you if I have additional questions."

Valko lead the way out and the three departed. As they made their way back through the hospital, Valko whispered to them. "Be careful of those two. They aren't all they appear. And I daresay you will not likely see Special Agent Minos again on this side of the pond."

Brand grunted. "I felt that. He's very dismissive. And he doesn't like you at all. Do you two know one another from a previous life?"

Valko shook his head. "You might say we have family disagreements, between his kind and mine. You know. Investigators versus operators." He smiled. "I shall be off now, gentlemen. I've a report to make. But I'll see you later."

They exited the hard-shell and Valko departed their company, heading towards his HUMVEE. Once he was beyond earshot, Brand turned to Prim.

"Our next stop should be Khalil. I doubt we can get to see him today, but we should try to schedule a visit with him tomorrow."

"What time sir? And where? Early morning in his office on base, or are you thinking later in the evening at his home?"

Brand pondered the question a moment before looking to the sky. "Evening. He met our agents at home for a reason. He didn't want to be overheard. Which begs the question, who doesn't he trust?"

"So how do you want to play this, sir? Random drive by his house or shall I call and make an appointment?"

"Good question; if it was just his office, I'd say random drive by. See if you can make discreet contact with his aid and set something up in the evening at his home if he'll see us."

"Roger, sir. I can make contact and set it up. Are we going in alone or should I bring a few bodies?"

"Who did you have in mind?"

Prim shrugged. "I've got a few weapons types I'd ask. I figure four for backup just in case. We don't have to brief them up; just let them know we're looking for additional bodies since the IED event. They'll come along just to break up the monotony."

"Ok. We'll leave them in the vehicle and make our visit short. Set it up. Discretion."

"Sir, I'm hurt. I am positively the poster child for discretion."

"Oh, yeah. You." Brand smirked, shaking his head. "Let's grab some dinner and you can make your contacts."

....

An hour later found Brand and Prim entering the DFAC as a Staff Sergeant clicked the counter in his hand twice. Each grabbed a tray and walked the line, pointing at the food they wanted while contracted workers spooned out portions. The workers were third-country nationals, brought in from various countries such as the Philippines, Malaysia, Pakistan and others, employed by the American company for cheap labor.

Brand loaded his plate with sliced roast beef and little else and filled up a large cup of iced Pepsi. As they sat at a table off to the side of the somewhat crowded DFAC, Prim looked at the plate and laughed.

"What?" Brand asked as he cut into the roast beef with his fork.

"Sir, I can't believe your choice in food tonight. What's come over you? I mean, I got the beef, but you never drink soda."

Brand looked down at his plate and then shrugged before gulping a large bite of beef. As he swallowed he lifted the Pepsi and sipped before responding. "I just felt like I could use the sugar. And I've got a HUGE craving for meat."

"I see. Are you going back for seconds, or just grabbing an ice cream float?" As Prim sipped some of his coffee, he noticed his officer suddenly staring off in a daze.

Prim watched for a moment before turning in his seat and looking over his shoulder. A young female Army corporal was following a group of male soldiers towards a table. As she continued past, she glanced back at Brand hesitantly, and when she reached her table, she placed her tray and sat down facing him.

Brand had sensed her as she had walked by passing within inches of him and almost brushing his shoulder. He could feel her pulse pounding; or was that his own, he wondered. Heat rose within him with an undeniable urge to move towards her.

"Um, sir." The Chief turned back. "What gives? I'm the horny one. You're the rock of Gibraltar." He stared and received no response from his officer.

Looking back over his shoulder, he noted the corporal still staring intently at Brand, and now her fellow male soldiers at her table were turning to look. Prim also noticed a few other female soldiers and Navy sailors were starting to turn towards their table.

He spun back to Brand and waved a hand directly in front of his eyes, but only earned a half-blink in return. Brand's breathing was growing deeper and deeper and he leaned forward in his seat, pushing his tray of food and starting to rise.

"Sir?" Again no response, so Chief Prim swore under his breath and picked up his cup of coffee. "Fucking waste."

He dashed the cup of hot coffee down across Brand's lap, which brought an immediate startled response from the officer. His eyes going wide, he swatted at the hot liquid and shuffled back. As he looked up from his lap to Prim, he mouthed the question, "What?"

"Sir, we've got to go!" Prim stated, grabbing the plate of beef and stacking it on his plate of food, taking the plates with them. "Come on."

Brand followed Prim towards the exit of the DFAC, leaving their trays on the table. The females behind watched Brand move across the room and out the door, and the table of males watched intently too.

Once outside the DFAC, Prim handed the plate of beef over and shook his head. "Seriously, sir. What the fuck? You acted like you didn't hear me."

"Totally surreal. I don't know what just happened. I just . . . smelled her. I could almost feel her pulse. I just had this intense . . . lust for her. And I could feel her drawn to me, like she could feel me."

"I'll say. And every other split tail in the place. I don't know what you're wearing, but we should bottle it up and sell it. That was insane."

They kept walking across the base, heading for one of the large Texas barriers: tall, heavy cement barriers that formed a protective wall around the living areas. They sat on the base of the barrier to continue their meal while Prim kept an eye on the exit from the DFAC.

"If any of those women decide to follow you out here, I'm taking you off base. I don't know what's going on, but I don't need my officer appearing on the cover of the Navy times. How's that going to look for me?"

"Thanks, Chief. I'm glad you're looking out for me."

"We finish eating and you go straight to your room, sir. I'll make my connections and work our team. I can swing by later once I've got us set up. I should be able to reach Colonel Khalil's aid now and I know where Timmons and his crew hang their hats, so I can reach them anytime. I'll be able to give you a download as to who is going and when tomorrow."

"Good. I'll stay put and away from any females. I'll try to think of questions we'll want to ask the Colonel."

"While you're at it, maybe you should stay away from everyone, sir. Not just females. Who knows how you officers swing?"

"Ha-ha." Brand replied dryly. "Finish your meal."

Chapter 6

Hunting

Prim found himself across from the Kuwait Naval Base, leaving the US zone and making his way towards the Kuwait military offices. Although it was past dinner, a few members of the Kuwait military kept watch through the evening, and the Chief knew Colonel Khalil's aid worked various odd hours.

He approached their watch center, taking the uneven stairs down to the basement room. In the heat of the summer, the basement rooms were cooler than the upstairs. He rang the buzzer on the double doors and waited. A large sign in both Arabic and English declared the area restricted.

Presently, one of the double doors opened to a younger, enlisted member. The Chief noted to himself with a wry smile that the door had not been locked.

"Is the Major in?" Prim asked.

The younger soldier seemed somewhat annoyed and nodded silently, turning without further response and leaving the door open as he returned to the watch room. The room had a number of workstations around the four walls, with dim lighting overhead. Against one wall was an array of state-of-the-art monitors with pictures of both the port area of the Kuwait Naval Base as well as the piers of Ash Shuyaiba depicting one or two ships moored with US Navy small boats guarding the water.

A few older computers were arrayed around most of the workstations, of which none were on. A large plasma screen television was broadcasting a Middle-Eastern version of music television, with a young Arabian blasting a very tech-centric song while surrounded by gyrating young, scantily clad European women. Two other enlisted and one young officer were engrossed in watching the television, while across the watch room in the corner sat one middle-aged officer reviewing documents.

Prim headed to the older officer, ignoring the sidelong looks from the remaining Kuwaiti soldiers. As he approached, the officer turned from his work and upon recognizing his guest, smiled warmly.

"Chief Gunners Mate Prim. To what do I owe this pleasure?" His English was impeccable with barely a note of accent.

"Major. I figured I'd find you here. How's it shaking?"

The Major stood and the two men shook hands. Major Mohammed offered a chair and they both sat, facing one another. "My sincerest condolences on the incident from the other evening. I am so sorry that should occur in my country and after visiting my Colonel's home. I've been checking daily and I'm pleased that Senior Agent Ross is recovering."

"Yeah, he's doing better; although we haven't seen Minos, yet. They've kept us at arms length from her. I was hoping you might be able to help me."

"I will try, Chief. But I don't believe your military medical staff would be dissuaded by me when they won't allow you or your officer to visit."

"Not with that; we'll sneak in to visit her on our own. Commander Brand was interested in visiting your Colonel. Can you set it up for tomorrow? Just us two."

The Major shrugged and replied, "That's simple. Just come by his office in Kuwait City tomorrow. He should be in early."

Prim shook his head. "Commander was thinking more of a private meeting. Either at his residence or somewhere else."

Mohammed looked somewhat concerned and sat quiet for a minute. Finally he nodded. "All things considered, I believe I can. He normally takes tea right after the last call to prayer. Tomorrow he has no visitors scheduled, so this should be acceptable. I will inform him this evening and plan on being at his house for your arrival."

"Thanks, Major. And keep this between us. I don't need any chit-chat around the water cooler to ruin a perfectly good, discrete meeting."

"Should I be concerned, Chief Prim? Do you have reason to believe there may be danger to the Colonel?"

"Always, sir. Always be concerned. It'll keep you alive. It keeps me alive." He winked. "Now, if you'll excuse me.

I'll sit down for tea with you another time. I've got a little more work to do and a cup of coffee calling my name."

The Major stood and again the two men shook hands. "It's a pleasure as always, Chief Prim. If you see the Special Agent or Senior Agent soon, give them my best."

"I will, Major. Take care. And I'll see you tomorrow evening."

From the Kuwaiti watch center, Prim headed across the Naval Base to the piers, where he found the water front boat operations center. A tent had been established within a small, protected compound and hardened with Texas barriers and sand bags. Heating, Ventilation and Air Conditioning was piped directly into the tent from units erected within the compound and powered by a large diesel generator.

Towers were erected in a similar fashion to the operations center with protective hardening around the base and sand bags around the gun mounts up top. Two crewmembers manned the two towers; one located overlooking the operations center tent and a second on the far side of the inner basin of the Naval Base. Prim could make out the beefy barrel of an M-2 .50 caliber machine gun peaking through the sand bags with a solid angle of fire across the waterfront and out past the protective wall of the basin.

Two heavily armed boats sat at the pier near the operations center and a third boat sat floating lazily across the basin, sailors onboard barely visible from the pier.

He approached the entry control point of the pier and waved at the two petty officers sitting aside their M-2 with their protective body armor hung on the fender of an armored HUMVEE. The HUMVEE had another M-2 mounted on the top.

"Good evening, Chief. Are you here to see our Chief?"

"You know it. That fucker owes me a coffee. Is he in or is he down on the beach like a bloated whale?"

The two petty officers laughed and pushed on the counterweight to lift the metal arm out of Prim's way. "He's in the tent watching Band of Brothers."

"Again? Jeese, you'd think he'd get tired of that show. I mean it was good, but really. Maybe I need to send him some good porn."

This brought more laughter as he passed the two and made his way through a sandbag maze to the operations center. Inside he found a small ready room complete with table and chairs, large screen television and DVD player, as well as several gaming consoles wired in. A coffee mess, refrigerator and microwave finished out the ready room, with a handful of enlisted hanging out watching a World War II series on the television.

"Timmons. Wake the fuck up and get me a cup of coffee!" Prim barked as he entered.

Most of the petty officers in the room shot up out of their folding chairs and turned to see the new chief entering the room. One particularly large, barrel chested member with crew cut dark hair sat closest to the television and barely registered the arrival.

"Get it your self. I'm not your mother."

"Good thing. At least I know who my mother is." Prim responded, heading straight to the coffee pot. "What the fuck are you brewing over here? This isn't that haji shit is it?"

Timmons stood up, pressing the controller to pause the DVD player and looked across the room. "Language, chief. Just because you can swear doesn't mean you have to abuse it. I'm trying to train my boys not to talk like you."

"Yeah, but if they're going to swear, who better to learn it from? Anyhow, I need a favor." He poured a cup and held it to his nose, inhaling deeply. He immediately screwed up his face and shook his head. "God. I've been ruined. My officer only brews Starbucks. They send him eight pounds a month from the Starbucks near his home; Komodo Dragon and Sumatra. Naturally I had to teach him how to brew it, but we don't drink this drivel."

"Bring me a pound next time you come and take care of a fellow chief. Now, what's this favor?"

"I need your three best on short barrels, so that would be you and any two you pick. We've a short excursion and Commander Brand and I don't trust anyone else."

Chief Timmons stopped and stared intently at Prim. "What are we talking about here, Dean?"

"Can we get some privacy? I'll give you the short version, but I need to keep this close to the vest."

"Everyone out. One minute." The barrel chested chief barked and the tent quickly emptied, leaving the two men alone.

Taking another sip of his black coffee, Prim stated, "We believe we were set up the other night and the Commander wants to interview Colonel Khalil. We don't know how dangerous it is, if anyone might be watching us, or the Colonel. So it makes sense we take along more fire power next time we visit."

"Do you think the Colonel set you up? He seems like the straightest shooter in country."

Prim shook his head. "Commander doesn't think so. But who knows? Best be safe than outgunned, right?"

"When do you need us?"

"Let's just say take yourself off the watch bill tomorrow and maybe the day after. Be ready to rock sometime in the afternoon or evening. We'll call and you can meet us."

"Negative. You meet us. We'll take my ride, Fat Bertha. I heard about your IED and I have zero desire to take one in the shorts driving the streets of Kuwait."

"Suit yourself. We'll come here when we're ready to roll. And pick good, aware members. I hope nothing happens, but if it does, it goes off quick."

"What does?" Timmons asked.

"Hopefully nothing. I'll tell you more once we load up tomorrow. Until then, not a word to anyone."

"Roger, Chief. Now finish your coffee and get the fuck out of here. I have my Band of Brothers to watch."

Prim soured and shook his head. "What ever happened to the no swearing?"

"I said not in front of my sailors. They aren't here, so get the fuck out. And have a nice night."

"You too, Chief. Talk to you tomorrow." He slugged back the coffee and put the cup on the table before heading out the door.

....

Major Mohammed finished a cup of tea and lit a cigarette. After glancing around the room and noting his staff engrossed in the music videos, he picked up his phone and dialed. A moment later a young male voice answered the phone in Arabic.

"Colonel Jassim Khalil Al Azzaan. Abdullah speaking."

"Abdullah. Major Mohammed. Is the Colonel available?"

"One moment, sir. He is taking tea. Can I inform him of why you are calling?"

"No. It's best between the Colonel and myself. I'll wait for him. Put him on when he is available."

"Yes, sir. One moment." There was a gap of dead air and then the voice of the Colonel came across the receiver. "Khalil speaking."

"As-Salamu alaykum, Jassim."

The Colonel replied, "Wa alaykum as-salam. What's going on this evening Major?"

"I had a visitor, sir. The chief who supports the NCIS. He was requesting an audience with you."

"And what did the chief desire to talk about?"

"I believe his officer wished to talk. They were asking to take tea with you tomorrow evening. I believe it might be in our interest, sir."

There was silence on the other end of the phone and then the Colonel responded. "I agree. I'm concerned about the events of the other night. I'll be awaiting them."

"Thank you, sir. I'll confirm with the chief and plan on being there as well."

"Thank you; and Major . . . be careful. I don't know what is going on, and I'm not superstitious, but something is scaring the people. Whatever it is it's dangerous."

"You too, sir. I'll see you tomorrow."

As he hung up the phone, Colonel Khalil turned to Abdullah. "Thank you, Abdullah. I am done with tea this evening."

They stood in a large, ornate office with leather furniture and a large, mahogany desk. The young officer bowed and went to clear the tray of tea from the corner of the desk. "Is there anything I can assist with, sir? You seem concerned by Major Mohammed's phone call."

Khalil shook his head. "No. I will be fine. But we will have visitors tomorrow evening. American soldiers."

The Colonel did not see the sidelong look cast by Abdullah in the moment. After a brief pause, he offered, "Shall I prepare tea for the event? How many guests shall there be? And who do you anticipate?"

Colonel Khalil shook his head. "I'm not certain: two at least. Make the preparations, thank you. That is all for now."

Abdullah gave yet another low nod and carried the tray of tea from the office. The moment he was out of eyesight, he quickly hurried to the kitchen to drop the tray and continued out beyond the mansion and the compound, and more importantly, out of earshot.

When he felt he was secure, he pulled out his cell phone and dialed. Waiting only a few seconds, he immediately spoke in hushed tones, glancing around nervously. "I have the perfect opportunity to deliver the dead agent back into the hands of the American forces. We must move tonight to get everything in place."

....

After dinner, Brand made his way back to his living quarters. He wasn't feeling tired enough to sleep so he changed into shorts, t-shirt and his black Vibram Five Finger running shoes before running across the camp to the massive, hard shell gymnasium.

For the thirty minutes, he rowed on a Concept-2 rowing machine, increasing the tension and pushing his limits. He stood up from the machine, sweating but barely breathing hard, and went to the weight room. He went through a circuit of weights, covering chest, triceps and biceps, followed by pushups and sit-ups.

As he finished his first workout, he found the all-purpose room off to the side was empty. Covered in sweat, he sat cross-legged in the far corner and began to meditate, palms across his lap, breathing deep and slow. After a few long minutes, he stood to practice his martial arts.

He started one form with an elaborate bow and then launched into the movements, gracefully shifting across the floor in a violent dance of kicks, strikes and other moves. Midway through the form, he felt the approach of another. As he finished the form, he stood and bowed once more, closing the dance out. He turned to see Fergus watching from the door.

"Impressive form. You move like water. What style is that?"

"Family art. From Tzu Jian. Taoist along the Silk Road of China." He squatted into a horse stance and held it low. "Art of war."

"How does it compare to Shaolin or other arts?" Fergus asked. "I've trained with a few other styles. I learned my Scottish family art of punching, which hails from the Vikings and the berserkers. Plus I trained in judo as well as Shaolin for about a bit and some Japanese arts."

"Martial arts can be like religion. When you find the right one, it seems all others are less." Brand laughed. "It might be easiest to describe as this. Japanese arts tend to be hard and linear. They come straight in and pound. Kung fu and Shaolin are soft and circular. They move around an attack. As they say, fight hard linear with soft and circular.

Fight soft and circular with hard linear. What I practice and teach is war. It's gung fu: hard and soft, linear and circular. From the basics it is hard, with long, low stances to increase leg strength. In the advanced, you learn the hardcore Chinese arts. Even the soft is hard and the hard is soft. Hard to grasp the concept."

Fergus nodded. "Watching you practice, I can see it. You have directed jing in your strikes and kicks."

"You understand the concept of jing: the snap at the end of the strike? Nice."

"Aye. I learned it first when my father taught me our art, except we didn't call it anything. It's just how we punched. One of the Shaolin teachers I practiced with worked on striking a good deal. He was pretty fluid in his movements. But not like you. You've got very solid stances, kicks and strikes. I see a fight when I see you. That is a war art."

"Thanks. That's what it should feel like when you practice."

"I'd enjoy working out with you. Would you mind teaching me some?" Fergus asked, his eyes wide with hope and excitement.

Brand smiled. "Sure. Let's see what you know and we'll start at the beginning."

They continued working out for another two hours, going through a few basic forms and concepts. As they finished, they sat back against the wall.

"Thank you, Liam. Mind if we practice more like this tomorrow?"

Brand nodded. "I could use a workout partner."

"Thank you. I look forward to learning more. So, tell me about yourself Liam. Where are you from? I'm from Scotland, outside Edinburoughshire. I'm from a small family of just my mum and pop and my sister. She's a tad older than me but just like me, a firebrand."

Brand lifted himself and crossed the room to an organized pile of large bottles of water. He took one and drank from it. "I'm from a slightly larger family: one brother, three sisters and our parents. I've already got a bunch of nieces and nephews running around. They send me care packages every week and I've got too many baked items to eat." They laughed and he threw a second bottle towards Fergus.

The large, young man caught the bottle and twisted the cap off to take a long swig of water. "How long have you been practicing martial arts?" Fergus asked.

"Give or take a few months here and there, about thirty years. I started very young, but really got into it while I was in college. Besides swimming, it was my sport of choice, and I slowly slid more into martial arts and less into swimming. Every once in a while, I'll jump in the pool, but I've been so passionate about the arts since I was young. I used to watch Black Belt Theater on Saturday mornings. I think the Five Fingers of Death was one of the first movies I recall having martial arts in it and I was smitten."

Fergus sat listening with fascination. "Wow. I don't think I know that movie; but aye, same with me. My father started me and my older sister off learning our art of bwazara: it's a Nordic punching art my father learned when he was a boy. But then as I grew up, I was really excited about all different arts. Same as my siùir. Dadaidh taught us both and we both enjoyed tussling. She was always the tougher of the two until I grew into my body. Then I was stronger, but she was still a better scrapper."

Brand laughed. "I know what you mean. My brother is younger but a much better soldier: A Marine, through and through. Better officer too."

"Maybe we can grab a bite later and talk more on this art you're teaching me, Liam. I would enjoy hearing more."

Brand nodded. "Certainly. Its history is rich. I'm the same way. I love all aspects of the arts. History as well as practicing."

Fergus pushed himself to his feet and reached out to shake hands. "It's been fun Liam. I look forward to more. I'd best be off or the Major will skin me for taking up your time."

....

Brand's return back across the base was relaxed and he pushed the door of his room open to find Prim sitting inside.

"Is this what you consider laying low, sir? I said come back here and stay here."

Brand laughed. "Thanks, mother. But I felt great, so I hit the gym and worked out hard. Best workout I've had since I arrived in country. And one of the British team joined me. The young one, Fergus."

"Great. As long as the workout didn't include a horizontal grinding action with an enlisted girl, I'm ok with it. Burn off that . . . whatever you have going on."

Brand grabbed his towel and a change of clothes, kicking off the Vibrams and slipping on flip-flops. "What's the word, Chief?"

"We're on. Teatime at the Colonel's tomorrow evening. And I've got Timmons onboard bringing solid shooters. And I do mean shooters. He'll also be driving Fat Bertha."

"The tricked out Hummer? That thing's a tank!"

"Absolutely, sir. When you go on a date with me, it's in style."

"Good job, Chief. Let's plan on having breakfast in the morning. I'm hitting the shower and then catching some sleep. I feel great, but I am starting to sundown and feel a bit light headed."

"Ok, sir. Make it a shorter shower than the last time. You've got to save some water for the rest of us."

"Ha-ha. Thanks. I'll carry a timer with me."

....

Following the shower, Brand returned to his bunk and kicked off his shower shoes, laying back. He started to reach for his copy of Homer's Illiad but thought better of it and lay back, folding an arm over his eyes. He felt a cool breeze blow across his chest and he sank into his dreams.

The dream came to him sporadically as if in a daze. He felt a warm breeze caressing his skin and he could tell he was under a starless sky. His bare feet dug into sand and the sounds of the desert night called to him.

Brand found himself on all fours, sniffing at the air and feeling in a daze. Something was running from him, scared, and he was following it. He could feel its pulse and smell it as it ran erratically ahead. He hunted, moving forward on hand and foot silently while closing on his prey.

Though still unable to see, he charged through the utter darkness, his senses leading him as some primal force drove him. He felt his body leap and he heard a scream as he pounced. His teeth sunk into flesh and he drank deeply the warm blood.

....

Somewhere in the distance, the first call to prayer roused the land, and Brand shook his head and opened his eyes. He felt dirty and encrusted with mud and sand as he pushed himself up. The chill from night was already giving way to the warmth from the early morning sun as it slowly crept into view.

He looked down to find himself covered in sticky blood and sand, caked across his chest and chin and through his fingers. Sheer panic welled within as he spun around and found a dead goat, its throat torn open and head nearly ripped from its neck. The ground was soaked in blood.

He fell back in shock, shaking his head and staring at the gruesome sight. It took him some time for the call to prayer to bring him back to his senses and he looked around. He was behind a sand dune but he could hear sounds of traffic not far off, so he cautiously crept up the dune and looked.

A myriad of thoughts raced through his mind. How had he woken outside the base? Did he kill the goat? Why did he kill the goat? And more importantly, what was happening to him?

He found himself on the outskirts of a housing district not far from the highway. He saw the signs on the highway and knew he was approximately halfway between the Kuwait Navy Base where he lived and Ash Shuyaiba. He also realized he was less than half-a-mile from the Northern Arabian Gulf.

Looking down, he realized he was completely naked. Taking grasp of his situation, he crept across the dune towards the housing district and hurried. It was still early but the call to prayer was going to wake the devout. His only hope was that they would be attending to prayer and wouldn't be paying attention to the naked, bloody man running for the water.

It was a short run from the dune to the housing district, where the houses were cloistered close together. He saw a goat pen torn open, still populated by a handful of goats who began bleating wildly as he snuck past. He continued on.

Two blocks beyond he saw clothing drying on clotheslines stretching between the second floor balconies of two adjoining homes. He veered in the direction of the homes and spied around. Ensuring he was alone and unobserved, Brand ran up and leaped to grab the ledge of the balcony, pulling him self up and climbing over the railing. The railing was loose and almost pulled free of the structure, but was strong enough to allow him to crawl over and take clothes from the lines.

He chose a black burka and a pair of wide-wasted men's slacks. He quickly pulled the pants on and jumped over the rail, landing lightly on his feet and continuing on towards the water. His trip was quick, taking less than a few minutes, and he followed the water south towards the Kuwait Navy Base.

When he was beyond eyesight of the housing district, he stripped down and slid into the water, washing the blood and sand off as best he could. In minutes, he was back out of the water and on land heading south again, wearing the slacks sticking to his wet legs and the burka to cover his identity.

It took him the better part of an hour to reach the outskirts of the base. Although fairly secure, he knew how to gain entry into the compound hopefully unnoticed. Throwing the burka aside, he waded out into the water and swam carefully.

As he neared the piers, he was able to close the distance enough to swim unseen beneath the wall until he entered the basin. A short swim took him to the far pier, on the opposite side of the inner basin from the manned operations center. Glancing around, he reached up to a metal rung and pulled him self up a rusty ladder to the pier edge.

Another glance around and he quickly pulled himself up and over the edge and hustled from the pier towards the base. Once beyond the pier, he scurried between structures and tents and made his way towards his room. It was already morning and the camp would be coming alive.

He was able to make it into his room and strip down without being seen, and quickly grabbed gear to shower with. Throwing a towel around his waist and slipping on his shower shoes, he headed back to the showers.

Brand had barely returned to his room when the door pushed in and Prim stood before him, a cigarette in hand. "Sorry. Forgot to put this out. I'll be outside."

"I'll just pull on my boots. Be right out."

Within a few short minutes, Brand pulled the door shut behind as he stepped out. Prim was smoking a new cigarette and looked around the courtyard. "Is there ever anyone else in this building? It's like you and I have both floors to ourselves."

"They're currently on liaison to the ships in the NAG. They won't be back for at least three weeks. So, no there isn't. Didn't anyone ever tell you there's a smoking gazebo across the compound?"

"Sure, they told me. But it's so far away it takes me like two cigarettes to get to it. I smoke less if I don't have to walk all the way over there. It's like I'm cutting down by not walking across the compound."

"You slay me, Chief. Let's go eat."

"Sounds good. We'll sit in the corner with your back to the crowd. Any idea what you plan to do today while we wait?"

"I'm feeling pretty good. I think a workout will help settle my mind. Are you going to visit the hospital?"

"I can. Do you want me to?"

"If it's not out of your way, check up on Ross. And find out if anyone has been able to see Minos or if they have word that she left the country. I don't know, but I don't get a warm and fuzzy with those two new special agents."

"I don't get a warm anything from those two ice bricks. I mean, I've gotten warmer receptions from my ex-wife."

"I know. I get the same read on them. If you see them or can get a gage on what they're up to, let me know. Other than that, we can meet up for an early dinner if you want before we go. I'll work out this morning. Make sure we're packing big guns on the drive today."

"Sir, I'm hurt. You know I only bring the best to a dance. I've picked up a few nice guns. We'll be fine."

"I have complete faith in you, Chief. As a matter of fact," he stopped walking and took a deep breath. "I trust you with my life. And I'm kind of more than just worried about the situation we're in."

Chief stopped and turned back to his officer. "What's up sir?"

"I don't know. I woke up outside the base this morning."

"Scuse me, sir? Where were you? And how'd you get there? Possible prank?"

Brand shook his head. "Negative on the prank, Prim. I was a few miles up the road, inland. I had to hustle back during Morning Prayer and swam the last bit in through the water. I have no recollection of when I got up or how I got out. I just know I woke up near some houses."

"That explains why I didn't see you in your room when I went for a smoke this morning early. I thought you might have hit a port-o-pottie or something. I should have checked on you. Anything else?"

Brand looked down, snubbing his toe in the sand before turning an awkward glance back at his chief. "I was somewhat naked and near a dead goat."

Prim pulled a cigarette from the pack in this chest pocket. As he lit it, he took a few puffs as they stood in silence before finally responding. "You do know at this rate I'm not going to quit smoking anytime soon, sir?"

Both men grinned and the chief continued. "I'll need to keep a closer eye on you. Should we tell the Brits?"

Brand shook his head, "I don't know. Should we?"

"Well, they did give you that vaccination. Maybe this is a side effect. They did say sleeplessness or sleepwalking, I think. Can't hurt if they have the answer."

After a moment of thought, Brand nodded. "Good idea. But let's focus on meeting with Khalil first. After we meet with him, we can look into what happened to me this morning. If I bump into Major Valko or Special

Agent Watson, I'll disclose to them, but only if it's a target of opportunity."

"Roger, sir. Now let's get our breakfast."

They continued on their way towards the DFAC for breakfast.

Chapter 7

Colonel Khalil

After breakfast, Brand dressed for the gym and went to workout. He felt his strength was fully returned and his stamina was through the roof.

As he arrived at the gym, he found Cedric and Fergus just finishing a workout. Cedric nodded to him as he approached, reaching out with his massive hand to shake. Fergus was beaming with excitement.

"Care to work out some, Liam?" the younger Scot asked. "I've just finished a bit of the weights with Cedric."

"Certainly. We can practice a bit before I hit the weights."

The two men continued back into the gym as the larger British soldier went his way. Once inside, they returned to the all purpose room to practice and train.

Brand and Fergus reviewed what they had previously worked on. After half-an-hour of review, Brand offered to teach Fergus a form.

"This is the first form: the first kata. Typically I wouldn't teach this until you'd learned more of the basic exercises, but you have enough martial training that you should be able to adapt to this. So we begin in the horse stand, Kiba Dachi. Are you ready?"

"Born and bred." Fergus smiled, standing at attention and following directions.

After an hour, they broke. Brand smiled. "You're doing great. You pick it up quick. That's about halfway through the form. Practice that some more and we can add the rest tomorrow. Let's practice some one-step drills."

They spent the next half-hour going through attack-defense movements. Brand worked with Fergus on moving from the direction of attack and working on angles.

Although Brand was fast, Fergus had a natural grace and speed that almost defied Brand's skill. He had to work to keep from getting hit by the larger man. The more they practiced, the more relaxed both men practiced and the faster they moved. On several occasions as Brand attacked Fergus, he struck or kicked past the larger man's guard. And likewise, when Fergus attacked, he struck Brand on several occasions, shaking the smaller man to the core with his huge fists.

When they finished, both men were sweating and bruised, but laughing. Brand looked at Fergus. "You did great. We can finish Kata Ichi tomorrow. And do some more one-step. Maybe even some waza and kumite."

"That would be awesome. I loved the lessons on shifting from the line. Makes perfect sense."

"I'll finish my workout and catch you later." Brand stated, grabbing a sweat towel from a stack near the door as well as a bottle of water. "Don't forget to hydrate."

"Great talking with you about the history of the art, and about your family. I could tell you had a bit of the Scot in you. Fascinating they came over the pond in the 1700s."

Brand nodded. "Yes, my mother's side left Scotland with her great-great-great-something grandfather. Our family name was Hogg until we came across. I look forward to meeting your family some day. They sound like fun. And your father might teach me something."

"Well, since you've a bit of the Scot inside you, my dadaidh would find you almost acceptable." He laughed. "He's a bit of a sod when it comes to non-Scots and talking fighting. But my siùir will absolutely adore you." He winked with a grin. "My sister."

"Then I'll definitely have to meet them. If she fights like you, I'll have my hands full."

Fergus' grin broadened. "You will at that."

As the young Scot departed, Brand continued working out another hour in the gymnasium structure before he returned to shower.

....

After his shower, Brand did not see Prim and decided against the DFAC for lunch, so he headed across the base to the schwarma shop, enjoying the warm, dry air. It took him only a few minutes to reach the shop and he sat at one of the empty tables. Although open all day long, the shop did most of its business in the evenings and in between meals when the DFAC was closed.

As Brand sat, he smelled jasmine and lavender and looked up. The young woman approached and bowed slightly, staying at arms length while she looked at him with her blazing, blue eyes.

"Two schwarma and a Pepsi, please. Can and cup of ice will do." His eyes closed into slits as he breathed in her aroma and felt a heady buzz overcome him. As he closed his eyes, he had a quick vision of running across the desert sands alongside her as she glanced at him with her wide, clear eyes.

As he opened his eyes, she had disappeared and he grinned. His pulse quickened and for a brief moment he almost pushed himself to his feet and went in search of her. And then it passed and he sat forward, gripping the edge of the table.

"Get yourself together!" He growled under his breath, pinching the table edge so hard that he heard the plastic crack.

"And who are you speaking to, Liam?" Came the familiar British voice.

He released the table and turned to look over his shoulder. Both Major Valko and Special Agent Watson were walking towards his table. As he watched their approach, he was conscious of their smell when they were still halfway across the dining area. Valko was clean and wore a musky scented aftershave while Watson wore a body lotion of sage and cream. Her natural scent intermingled with the lotion and Brand smiled, his eyes dancing along her.

"May we join you?" the British Major asked, grabbing the back of a chair yet waiting politely. He lifted his chin and sniffed ever so subtly at the air before smiling and looking back down to Brand.

Brand tore his eyes from Watson and looked to Valko. "Please do. I could use the company."

As they both pulled chairs to sit, Valko laughed, speaking quite comfortably. "Each time we meet, you are intent upon looking my special agent over from top to bottom. Is there something that intrigues you about her?"

Brand noticed Special Agent Watson turn a shade of red and look away. He looked back to Valko and shook his head. "I can't tell you why I'm doing this. I am never this rude, believe me." He looked back to Watson and apologized again, "I am so sorry. I just seem to be aware of so much lately. I just noticed how deep blue your eyes are and how intense smells are around here."

Valko laughed, waving over the shop owner as he approached with Brand's Pepsi and cup of ice. "Two more Pepsis, please. And make hers diet."

"Thank you." The hefty shop owner replied, always smiling. "And perhaps some schwarma?"

"No, thank you." Watson stated. "We just ate. The soda for him will be fine, but make mine a water please."

"Right away. And will my best customer be joining us for lunch?"

Brand shook his head. "Chief and I might make it for dinner. I didn't see him earlier."

"Ah, too bad. I like the Chief. I do hope to see you both tonight." And he bounced away.

"Any word on Minos?" Brand asked while he poured the Pepsi over the cup of ice.

Watson shook her head. "No. When we visited this morning, we were instructed that NCIS had tightened the quarantine. No visitors beyond immediate medical personnel and unfortunately, I don't qualify."

"Thanks for trying at least."

"Any plans for today?" Valko asked.

Brand nodded and sipped his Pepsi. "Might get another workout in this afternoon. I'm finding I'm full of energy today. Must have been the two nights of sleep I got. It's funny, but I thought you said the vaccination might give me sleeplessness."

Watson shook her head. "I believe you misunderstood. I should have elaborated. You might be prone to sleep walking or acting out in your sleep. You will definitely sleep, as evidenced by your two nights comatose."

"Ah." He looked down at the tabletop and pondered waking up outside the base. "Well, about that. Something funny did happen last night."

"Oh? Do tell?" She queried, reaching for her pad and pen from her front pocket.

"And the doctor is in." Valko laughed. "She'll be asking about your dreams next. You really should start writing them down for her, to save her the trouble."

"Yeah, about that. I woke up outside the camp this morning." He shrugged.

"Excuse me?" She glanced at Valko and returned her attention to Brand. "Where outside?"

"Don't know. A few miles up the road. I had to make my way back through town and swam back in. I didn't have my identification on me."

"How the blazes did you get out?" Valko asked, intent yet polite.

Brand considered the question before shaking his head. "Not certain. I know there's an area of fence line with a soft patch you can pull the chain link up from. I might have squirmed under it, but how I did that without waking up is beyond me. I just know I woke up out in the desert."

"Anything else unusual about the event?" Watson asked staring into his eyes.

He rolled his eyes looking to the ceiling and squinted his face. "I don't know. I was naked."

Valko laughed and Watson immediately turned a scowl upon him. "Sir, this isn't a laughing matter."

Brand shrugged and a grin crept over his face. "Actually, it kind of is. I don't sleep walk, but waking up in a foreign country naked in the desert is funny. Except of course that it happened to me."

Watson tried to hide her smile while both men laughed. Shaking her head, she redirected, "You have no recollection of how you got there? What was the dream of?"

Brand thought a moment before replying. "I was out hunting in the desert. It kind of seems hazy, like in a fog."

The heavy-set shop owner came back to the table with a small round tray. Smiling at the three, he promptly placed their drinks and the schwarmas on the table. "Let me know if you desire anything else." With a quick bow of his head, he spun and headed back to shop.

Brand took one of the schwarma and bit into it. Watson continued writing while Valko sipped his Pepsi.

"How are you feeling today? Did you receive enough rest?"

"I feel great." Brand commented between bites. "Although I'm hungrier than I recall, I feel well rested. And I'm working out like an Olympic athlete."

"How's your shoulder?"

Brand stopped eating long enough to glance at his shoulder and turned his eyes back on Watson. "I don't know. Come to think of it, it feels just fine. I haven't looked at it today, but it feels like the bruising and pain are all gone."

He finished the first schwarma and raised his arm overhead, flexing the shoulder and rotating his arm. He brought it back down and took up the second schwarma.

"Would you mind if I took a look at it later? Perhaps after your meal?" She asked.

"I'll be along to assist, for proprieties sake, if you're concerned about that sort of thing." Valko stated, glancing at Watson and then smiling to Brand.

Brand looked around the immediate vicinity and saw only a few other soldiers and sailors in the food court, space around the various tables in the open-air courtyard. Without another word, he quickly unbuttoned his uniform blouse and removed it, laying it across the chair next to him.

Next he pulled his t-shirt up over his shoulder, exposing half of his chest.

The abrasions were gone and most of the discoloration of his shoulder was centered in a one-inch slightly black-and-blue circle under his collar. Watson stood and leaned across the table, reaching forward to touch the area.

"Does it hurt?" She pushed around the bruise.

He shook his head. "Negative. Feels fine."

"Well, it has been several days." Valko commented. "Do you normally heal fast?"

"I don't generally bruise. But when I do, it's deep and stays with me. Thinking about this one, I would have expected to have some discoloration for at least two weeks. And probably some pain for at least one. That creature bit down hard and ground my body armor. Broke the front plate."

"It has been several days." Watson stated. "But this does seem a bit accelerated. You seem to have full mobility. Have you had any blood work done?"

"Not that I'm aware of. They didn't take any when I first came in after the attack. And I haven't given any since."

Watson glanced at Valko and back. She stated as a matter of fact, "I wouldn't be overly concerned about your healing. Considering you're getting more rest than normal, it might just be your body responding accordingly. I will keep an eye on you, if you don't mind. And perhaps I can examine the bruise again later. Tomorrow?"

Valko laughed. "For heaven's sake, Agent Watson. Take a photo. They last longer."

She turned bright crimson and swung an angry eye on the major before promptly taking her water and standing. "I will check in on you later, commander. Apparently, my major has succumbed to his courser nature and allowed his imagination to run away with itself. Have a pleasant afternoon."

The two men watched her as she stormed away without a second glance back at them. Brand pulled down his shirt and buttoned on his blouse as Valko sat back laughing.

"She seemed very angry at you, Sam. I'd sleep with one eye open if I were you."

The British officer laughed harder. "I don't think it was anger, my good friend. I would place that more in the embarrassment category. And I don't believe I'm the one who should sleep with their eyes open. You might have just placed yourself on her list of prey."

Brand took a bite of his schwarma and lifted his Pepsi, pausing for a moment. "List? Is it long?"

"Positively short. To my knowledge, you may be the only one." Valko stood; finishing his Pepsi and leaving the empty can on the table. "Look me up later and we can have dinner if you are available."

"Better make it mid-morning coffee. Chief and I have dinner plans. If anything comes of it, I'll keep you informed."

"Thank you. Oh, and did you ever pass your report to that Army Colonel? As I recall, last I heard, he was hot to receive yours."

"Crap. Totally forgot. Chief wrote my statement up, but I never submitted. I'll take care of that after lunch. Thanks."

Valko gave a polite bow of his head and walked away.

....

Prim swung by the building with weapons for both himself and Brand. He found his officer in his room, dressed and wearing body armor. Prim presented a Beretta 9mm for Brand as well as an M-4 with laser site and four magazines for each weapon.

"Beretta has standard 9mm rounds. I've loaded both our long guns with tracer rounds. The tips will burn when impacting, so I'm hoping that gives us added punch should we need it. Or burn. Whatever."

"That should work. Hopefully we don't have to worry about that tonight. How about our ride?"

"Waiting on us at their boathouse. They got the Hummer armed and ready. Timmons mounted an M-2 on the turret for the 50 millimeter crew served weapon. He'll drive. It'll be a tight ride, but a safe one."

"Let's hit it then. I want to arrive at the last prayer if we can. Does Timmons know what to expect?"

"No, sir. I felt that might be best coming from you. He might think you're crazy, but he won't second-guess your orders. If I told him, we might not have a ride tonight."

"Good point." The two started their short walk across the compound towards the waterside.

....

Once they loaded up the HUMVEE, Timmons drove the vehicle out through the gate, flashing his security brassard at the Army soldiers who manned the post. One of his petty officers manned the M-2 machine gun on the turret while the second sat shotgun in the front seat. Brand and Prim sat in the back seat to either side of the turret. Within minutes, they were on the highway speeding towards the housing district where Colonel Khalil lived.

As they entered the highway, Brand took a moment to catch them up on the initial attack. With minimal details, he briefed them on the potential for animals in the attack.

"What kind of animals?" Chief Timmons asked.

"Weren't you listening?" Prim responded. "Dogs. Big, black dogs."

"Sounds like a bad SciFi flick." Timmons laughed.

"Or a really good porno." The turret gunner added.

Brand looked up and shook his head. "I don't know what kind of porn you've been watching, but maybe we should switch up your venue to some Disney movies."

Prim looked over and grinned. "Boat crew are some sick fuckers, aren't they sir?"

"Cut the crap, Prim. My boys get all their porn from you." Timmons barked from the front, which brought more laughter from his sailors.

"Nice. Well, just keep your guard up for anything. If anything pops its head up, shoot it. Hard and fast." Brand spoke. "And if you see a big, black dog, aim for the head. They move fast, so you might only get one shot."

"Roger, sir. Head shots."

....

The rest of the ride was in silence and went fast. They entered the wealthy neighborhood and pulled up to the colonel's home. As they arrived, the front door opened and Major Mohammed came out to greet them.

Chief Timmons and his side gunner stepped out first; sweeping the immediate area with their eyes, M-4 machine guns at the ready as both Prim and Brand exited the vehicle from either side.

Mohammed approached brand first, offering his hand to shake. "As-Salamu alaykum, Commander Brand."

Brand replied, "Wa alaykum as-salam, Mohammed. Good to see you this evening and thank you for coordinating this on short notice."

Mohammed smiled, shaking his head. "I did nothing. It is good that you are meeting with Colonel. And he appreciates you taking time."

As Prim came around the HUMVEE, Mohammed turned to him and extended his hand. "Good to see you again, too, my friend."

"Thanks, Major: always a pleasure. Next time, I should bring some Crown Royal."

Mohammed looked over his shoulder to the house and back, grinning. "That would be greatly appreciated, just don't say a word before the Colonel. He doesn't appreciate whiskey."

"That's cause he's a good Muslim. And you're more like me." Prim winked. "Don't worry. That's our and Allah's secret."

Mohammed shook his head and ushered them towards the house. "Please come in. Colonel is waiting in the tea room."

As they moved towards the house, Brand looked back at Timmons. "Keep it tight, chief. We'll be in and out quick."

"Roger, sir. Maintain your situational awareness in there. We've got it out here."

....

Colonel Khalil was waiting for them in his small tearoom: a square room with approximately ten chairs lined on each wall with end tables between every other chair. In the center of the one wall was a larger backed chair. Brand and Prim followed Mohammed into the tearoom where they approached the Colonel and greeted him, shaking his hand in turn.

Beside the Colonel stood a young Kuwaiti officer in uniform with thin mustache. As they greeted the Colonel, he introduced the young man as his nephew, Abdulla.

"Thank you for coming to visit. I know these must be trying times, Commander. What can we do for you?" He sat and gestured to a young boy across the room near an open doorframe. The boy quickly disappeared.

Brand and Prim followed suit, sitting near the Colonel, with both Mohammed and Abdulla sitting on the opposite side of Khalil. As he sat, Brand smelled the air and caught a strong sent across the room of jasmine and lavender. He noted fresh plants placed in the corners of the room.

"The plants smell incredible, Colonel. Very … refreshing."

Khalil smiled and nodded. "Yes. My wife decorates the house with her plants. She has her assistants make a perfume from the jasmine and lavender. She sells them on her website and has become somewhat well known, although it is expensive. She gives it to the wives and daughters of our prominent friends as a gift. Would you like some? For your mother or other?"

"Thank you, Colonel. I appreciate that. But I'll be direct. Who knew about your meeting with NCIS the other day?"

Khalil looked to Mohammed and back. "Mohammed and I were the only ones who knew."

"And you didn't tell anyone else?" Brand asked, as he watched the young boy return to the room, carrying a tray full of cups of tea that he offered the men.

As each man accepted a small cup of hot tea, Mohammed shook his head, taking a quick sip, and responded. "Only we knew; and my assistant. It was his suggestion that we include NCIS."

"Include them in what?" Prim questioned as he finished his tea in one gulp, returning it to the tray and accepting a second glass.

"We are having an issue locally and we sought assistance. We needed an investigator." Khalil answered.

"For what?"

"We've had a rash of animal deaths and a few attacks on old women late at night over the past few weeks. We were concerned some animal was doing this, but now we are concerned we have a group terrorizing our people. Some of our own police are somewhat superstitious. Mohammed's assistant recommended we ask NCIS to conduct the investigation, so we set up a meeting to discuss."

Prim finished his second glass of tea and returned the empty to the tray. The young boy quickly took the tray of empty glasses out of the room.

Prim waited until the young man was gone and asked, "What superstition is causing the rub, Colonel?"

The older Kuwaiti officer shook his head and looked at his hands. "I don't know. Rumors really."

Before Colonel Khalil could continue, Abdulla blurted out excitedly "The Sons of Anubis, dark hunters in the night."

Colonel Khalil looked at his nephew with reproach and spoke. "Local whispers, nothing more. But with the sudden animal mutilations and the animal attacks at night, we are concerned. And our own police refuse to investigate."

The two Americans exchanged glances as Brand pulled out a small notepad and pen. "Who are the Sons of Anubis? And you mentioned possibly terrorizing the people? How so?"

Mohammed answered. "We don't know who the Sons are. There are only whispers from the street."

Abdulla interrupted, speaking in a rush. "A group of hunters and assassins for the Pharaohs. They came at night across the sands of Persia exacting justice and retribution. There were fleeting stories that the Sons were tied to Saladin during the conquest of the Crusaders."

Mohammed shrugged and shook his head. "If they were involved with Saladin, their impact was minimal if any in the histories. I'd never heard of them. At best they were a mythical group probably in the time of the Pharaohs."

Abdulla sat back somewhat nonplussed. "That or they were written out of the history to hide them."

Colonel Khalil shook his head at his nephew and took a brief moment to collect his self before continuing. "After the first few animal mutilations, there were rumors they were being sent as a sign to warn the people away from aiding the Americans. And then when older women were attacked, what they witnessed did not make sense. Great beasts walking on two legs and warning them to turn on the Americans."

Brand finished jotting down notes before asking his next set of questions. "So who else knew you contacted NCIS? And how did you invite them? Did you contact them yourself, or was it Major Mohammed? Who else knew besides you two? His assistant? Anyone else?"

"My nephew, Abdulla knew." Khalil motioned to the younger officer.

"And no-one was around when my assistant suggested it. But even he didn't know the time and place of our meeting." Mohammed stated.

The young boy entered the room again and collected the remaining dirty glasses. As he departed, Brand watched him go and turned to the Kuwaiti officers.

"Does your tea boy walk in and out of your meetings?"

The men looked to each other and back to the Americans. "Yes, but I would trust my tea boy. He has been with my house since he was young and we treat him well."

"But Uncle, he has been seen outside the house with strange men of late." Abdulla quietly offered.

Both Colonel and Major turned to the younger officer. "What? Are you certain?"

"I saw it myself. I thought it strange, but didn't address it and didn't think I should mention it."

Brand looked to Abdulla and back to Khalil. "How well do you trust him?"

The Colonel shook his head and sighed. "Up until now, implicitly. After this revelation, I am not so certain."

From outside the room there came a shrill scream and the clattering of metal and shattering of glass. Both Prim and Brand shifted, moving to cover Khalil and turning towards the door, drawing their weapons. With 9mm weapons drawn, Brand whispered back over his shoulder to the Kuwaiti officers.

"Where did that come from? And who was it?"

"It sounded like my tea boy from the kitchen. It's just down the hall." Khalil responded pointing towards the door.

Nodding to Prim, Brand gestured with his 9mm. The Chief took point and moved across the room towards the door the young boy had exited through. Brand was on his back, at the ready.

As they neared the door, they stacked one behind the other. Both listened. Brand took a moment and inhaled deeply through his nostrils, sniffing at the air. He whispered to Prim, "Blood. I can smell it. It's old. And death."

Prim nodded as his eyes focused on the entrance. Brand squeezed Prim's shoulder giving signal and the Chief burst through the door, followed closely by his officer. They quickly covered down the short hall and entered the kitchen, splitting in opposite directions and clearing the doorway as rapidly as possible. In a sweeping pattern with their weapons, they canvased the small kitchen from both sides to the center.

The tea boy was kneeling in the center of the room, covering his face and sobbing. Across the room lying atop the kitchen counter were the torn remains of Special Agent Chavez, his head severed and laying upon his chest.

Brand looked around the kitchen and immediately stopped in his tracks. "Prim, back out! Try to retrace your steps. Don't disturb anything."

"IED, sir?"

"No. Evidence. But that's not a bad idea either. Back out the way you came in. Step for step." Looking back over his shoulder, Brand saw the Major in the doorframe. "Major. Please call the boy and have him come out of the room. Take him back down the hall and keep him with you."

The Major called in and the boy looked out, tears still streaming down his cheeks. He took a moment and additional direction from the Major but finally stood up and hurried from the room. Both Brand and Prim backed out of the room, attempting to follow their own footsteps without disturbing any potential evidence.

At the entrance, Brand pulled the swinging door shut and motioned to Prim. They hurried back down the hall and found the Colonel and Major waiting for them, the Colonel's nephew comforting the tea boy across the chamber.

"Prim, call it in. We'll need EOD to sweep the room. Colonel Shaker will want to know. And send a text to Ross. He'll want to know we have Chavez."

Prim pulled his phone from the front pocket of his blouse. "What about the new NCIS agents? I don't have their contact information."

"Neither do I. They'll find out soon enough. And let our boys outside know."

"Aye-aye, sir. I'll be right back in. Shall I bring them in?"

"Yes. I'll keep eyes on here with Colonel Khalil. Bring them back in and let's stick together until Shaker and EOD arrive."

Prim hit the dial button and threw out one last question. "Anyone else?"

"By anyone, are you referring to our British friends? Since this happened outside U.S. control, I'm assuming it will be ok to at least let him know we've found Chavez. I'll text him. We may need to sit down with NCIS and the Brits to determine where we are in the contact of classified information and sharing. At this point, I'm willing to be a little liberal. Lord knows this is way outside any classification authority I'm aware of."

"Yeah. I'd love to know who has Original Classification Authority on this one. Bela Legosi?"

"Funny, Chief. But I think you meant Lon Chaney. Legosi was Dracula."

"Hey, sir. I figure you'd at least know the reference points." And he immediately fixed his attention on his phone as it was answered and he spoke. "Chief Prim. I'm looking to talk with one of Colonel Shaker's staff." As he waited for someone on the other end of the phone, he spoke again to Brand. "I feel we can strike the tea boy off our list of suspects. He was honestly shaken up."

Brand agreed, his eyes on the poor boy that stood near the Colonel, shaking and crying. "He's legitimately disturbed by this. I can feel it in him. Yeah, he's not on the list."

After making the call and texts, they rejoined the Colonel and the others. As they approached, Abdulla declared, "This is a warning, Uncle. The Sons of Anubis are warning us to separate from the U.S."

The Colonel shook his head and stared directly at his nephew. "We will not be subdued by cowards and villains. The U.S. is not our enemy. Those who would invoke the name of Allah for their own personal gain . . . they are the enemies of Kuwait. Those who would slaughter innocents through terrorist and cowardly acts: they are the enemies of Kuwait."

....

By the time Navy explosive ordinance arrived, Chief Timmons and his team had secured access to the kitchen. The two Petty Officers had been sent around to cover the back entrance while Timmons and Prim stood cover at the hall entrance. The Navy EOD technicians from the Kuwait Naval Base were first to arrive, followed shortly by Colonel Shaker and his staff. The explosive ordinance team cautiously went down the hall and swept the room, clearing it within minutes and reporting back.

As the chief from EOD team was reporting his findings to Prim and Timmons, Colonel Shaker stormed in with his staff in tow. He honed in on Brand as he stood with Colonel Khalil and Major Mohammed.

"You are fast getting on my shit list, Commander. How come every time something ruins my day, you're at the center of it?"

Brand shook his head and looked to both Khalil and Mohammed before replying. "Bad luck on my part, sir. Thank you for coming."

"No doubt you couldn't have found this in the morning." Shaker stated, looking to both Khalil and Mohammed before turning an angry gaze towards the chiefs across the room. "What's the situation?"

"EOD just cleared the room. We initially entered and saw Special Agent Chavez in the kitchen. We immediately pulled out and notified your staff. We've kept the perimeter secure."

"And why were you here, Commander?" The Colonel turned his eyes on Brand, locking stares.

Brand did not turn away. He felt a general anger within the Colonel, not just focused on him but inherent in his personality. Instead of shying away from the intensity, he chose to meet it head on. "Following up on why we were attacked, sir. We had a few questions for Colonel and his staff?"

"Army has this investigation, Commander. Or did you miss that discussion?"

"No offense, sir, but apparently I did. And my SAC is aware of my intentions to meet with Colonel Khalil."

"I assure you I was not aware of your intentions, Commander." The men turned to see Senior Agent Huang enter the room, Special Agent Wong in tow. "Luckily, we did receive notification of the incident and finding of our Special Agent Chavez."

"This is an Army investigation. Why are you here?" Shaker growled, settling his hands on his hips and puffing out his chest.

"Colonel Shaker: Naval members have been attacked and an NCIS agent killed. I've replaced Ross as Senior Agent in Charge for the duration of this investigation. As I am certain you will appreciate, with the attack on our agents and loss of our life, NCIS is extremely interested in this investigation. And we will work closely with Army CID." He flipped out his badge holding it for Colonel Shaker's inspection. "I assure you, although I have authority over this investigation, I want to work with you and your team."

Shaker turned from Huang to Brand. "Well?"

"I was still reporting to Senior Agent Ross when we made arrangements to meet with the Colonel. I failed to back brief our new Senior Agent. It slipped my mind."

Huang smiled as he turned to Brand. Beneath his eyes he could see something else, both cool and inviting yet deep and possibly dangerous. "Not to worry, Commander. We'll look past this. What is important is the location of Special Agent Chavez." He could not quite place whether Huang held disdain for him or simply no emotion.

Looking from Huang to Wong, Brand could see the younger female was not adept at hiding her emotion. Her eyes flashed and he noted she kept grip of her MP5 as if she intended to draw down on him.

The three chiefs approached and Colonel Shaker used their arrival to interrupt the tension. "What's the status?"

The Chiefs acknowledged him but turned to Brand as the Navy EOD Chief responded. "Clear. No sign of explosives. The body is clean and we checked the kitchen. It's safe to enter, sir. We tried not to disturb anything beyond sweeping the room."

"Thank you, Chief. Appreciated." Brand spoke.

"Sir, if we're done, I'd like to pull my team and head back to KNB. It's late and we have an early morning pier sweep to complete."

Glancing from Shaker to Huang and back, Brand nodded. "Roger. Take off, Chief. Travel safe and get some rest."

Colonel Shaker gave a quick salute to the Chief who almost attempted to respond and instead nodded before heading from the room.

Huang spoke quickly, stepping between Shaker and the hall towards the kitchen. "Colonel, if you will indulge. I would prefer to quickly view the room and the remains. I've considerable experience here and will be only a brief moment. Then I would appreciate your team performing your forensics on the scene."

Shaker locked eyes with Huang for a moment as if to disagree and stood silent. Brand felt as if an unseen battle of wills was taking place in the brief silence between them. The U.S. Colonel gave a curt nod and gestured towards the hall. "Let us know when my men can come in."

Huang glanced at Wong and gestured for her to follow. The two headed for the door.

Brand watched as the remaining individuals moved about. Colonel Shaker directed his team to set up security within the room, having already secured the exterior of the home with half his team when they arrived. He noticed Major Mohammed follow Prim and Timmons to the corner of the tearoom for a smoke, the three men standing silently.

The two Petty Officers found their way back into the house once the Army arrived and Chief Timmons sent them to their HUMVEE to wait out the events. Brand stood near Khalil and Shaker a moment more in awkward silence before nodding to Khalil and joining the Major and his chiefs. As he approached them, he slid into the corner, watching the rest of the room.

Khalil attempted to engage Shaker in polite chatter while the Army Colonel waited impatiently for the NCIS agents to finish their work. After a few minutes, the elder Kuwaiti Officer smiled and nodded and moved to join Brand and the others in the corner.

Brand felt them before he heard or saw them, so he was not surprised when the door swung in and Major Valko entered, followed by his team. Colonel Shaker noticed their arrival shortly after Brand, and immediately cast a glower upon the Naval Officer before crossing the room towards the British.

"Who called you?" the square-jawed Colonel blasted.

"I did." Prim called, waving a hand with cigarette between his forefingers, leisurely adding after a moment. "Sir."

Shaker shook his head. "We've got this one pretty much wrapped up, Major."

"Well, considering we're involved, I believe first hand inspection should assist us in assisting you. Wouldn't you agree, Colonel?" Valko offered. "You won't mind if we take a look after your team is done, would you."

"I don't believe I see the value added." A voice called from further across the room, and both Valko and Shaker turned to see Huang returning from the kitchen, followed by Wong. "We have what we need, Colonel. The room is yours. We were careful not to disrupt any evidence or the scene."

Valko's attitude shifted in an instant, going from friendly to hot. "Well, none the less, I intend to investigate the scene. Should I put in a phone call to your chain of command? Who would that be again, Special Agent?"

Huang outwardly seemed amused as his eyes locked with Valko's, yet Brand felt a wave of energy exchange between the two men like before. Even Shaker seemed a bit unnerved by the sudden intense friction between the two men.

"This isn't the crime scene." Brand called from the corner, breaking the tension and calling all attention to him. "It's where Chavez was dropped, but there isn't any blood. He's been dead a few days. This was just where they staged him. And they did it for our benefit."

"Whose benefit?" Huang asked; his curiosity piqued. "And how do you know?"

"Ours. US military. We arranged a meet with Colonel Khalil tonight as a follow-up to the meeting from the other night. It was after the first meeting that we were attacked. Tonight, we were trying to find out who may have had reasons to set us up. It makes sense they were intending to leave Chavez as a message to us and an example to Colonel Khalil."

"And what is the message?" Valko questioned, moving towards Brand.

"There's a new player in the game: a hunter; and we're the prey."

Shaker shook his head. "What game, Commander? And what hunter?"

Brand looked back to Mohammed before continuing. "A new group, maybe using the name of an older organization. Probably considering themselves defenders for local causes. I'm guessing they are siding with the insurgents in Iraq and Afghanistan. And they tend to hunt at night."

"So, terrorists?" The Army Colonel asked.

"If you say so, sir; but not in the traditional sense. More like . . . hunters and assassins."

Huang moved closer, keeping opposite Valko and Shaker as they all closed on the corner. "What do you know of them?"

"Major Mohammed and the Colonel were just telling us about them when we heard the tea boy's screams. That's when we found the body in the kitchen. They can tell you more."

"Not much more." Major Mohammed clarified. "That is about it. We've heard rumors on the street recently. When we show up at the scene of a dead goat or animal, we hear the whispers of the Sons of Anubis. We know little more. They were a mythical group that has appeared over the centuries from time to time. Most of it is old tales, generally righting wrongs or bringing justice. Occasionally it's darker. But other than tales, there is very little actually written about them."

Huang looked to Valko and Shaker before turning his eyes back on Brand. "Do we know anything more about this group?"

"We just found out they exist tonight, sir. We'll have to look into it more."

"No, you won't." Shaker snapped. "You're security for NCIS and your charge is in the hospital. This isn't your investigation, so consider yourself off of it. We'll do the investigating. Do I make myself clear?"

Brand felt an urge to rage as a hot flash swept through him. The thought of sweeping out and tearing his fingers through the Colonel's throat, spraying blood across the room rolled instantly through his mind.

A steady hand reached out to grip his wrist and he looked to see Prim taking a drag from his cigarette and giving him a wink. "Come on, sir. We can use the break. Let these cool investigators do their thing."

When he turned back to Shaker, he found Valko standing between them, smiling. "Are you ok, Liam?"

"I'm good, thanks." Glancing over the British Officer's shoulder to the Army Colonel, Brand shook his head. "You're crystal clear, sir. And I'll continue to follow the orders of my chain of command, with all due respect."

"Which by the way, means as little as possible." Prim added, laughing, as the Army Colonel seemed to boil, his face turning bright crimson.

"What did you fucking say, Chief?"

Stepping between them all, Huang placed a hand on Shaker's chest and stared straight in to his eyes. "I'll take care of my personnel, Colonel. I advise you to take your team into the kitchen and perform your forensics. I'll be here when you return. My men will not, as I will send them back to base. Do you require any additional information from Lieutenant Commander Brand or his Chief?"

Shaker seemed to be struggling with his response and finally shook his head. "No, not now." His anger deflated and he led his team towards the kitchen.

As the army team of investigators disappeared down the hall, Huang turned to Brand and the others. "I recommend you depart back for the base. I have no need for you here. But I also recommend you coordinate with me before you take any further action. I feel we may have gotten off on the wrong foot earlier, and I believe we can correct this."

The Naval Officer looked over the Senior Agent's shoulder to see Wong staring at him; her passion or anger subsided as she followed Huang's lead. Looking back up into Huang's eyes, he felt almost mesmerized. "Good idea. I think we will."

He motioned for Prim to follow and they lead the way as Timmons followed. Valko gave Huang a quick, hot nod and rushed after Brand. His team followed.

They reached the parking area outside the residence and Valko pulled Brand aside. "What did you see? I have no doubt when I get inside, the Army will have disturbed or negated any evidence I could gather."

Brand took in a deep breath and tried to recall all details. "Not much blood. He was on the counter. Torn to pieces and thrown in a pile. His head was just sitting on his chest."

"How was he torn apart? Did it look neat and clean like a surgeon, or pulled apart? Or could you see . . . anything?"

Brand stood deep in thought, trying to recall exactly what he had seen. After a moment, he looked back up, his eyes locked tightly on Valko's. "Torn, like something bit through the neck and arms. Although I didn't get close enough, I'd say teeth marks and deep scratches. If I were to describe it the way I saw."

The British officer nodded. "Thank you, Liam. That's what I needed to hear. Get back to your base and get some rest. We'll come visit you tomorrow for tea. And coffee of course."

The Navy crew loaded into the HUMVEE and they made a quick turn to head back to the Naval base. Shifting in his seat, Brand looked to his Chief.

"Prim, let's find this assistant of Major Mohammed. I want to talk with him as soon as we can. Trail leads to him. Do we know where he might live?"

Prim shrugged, pulling a cigarette from a pack in his breast pocket. As he lit the cigarette, he exhaled a puff of smoke and replied. "Many of the enlisted live on the base in those buildings near their offices. If he isn't married, we'll find him there. Otherwise, he'll be out on the economy. But should be easy to pick him up. I'm guessing we can just find him at the office in the morning."

"Good idea. After a quick breakfast, we'll head there."

Timmons let out a forced cough and shook his head. "Sir, doesn't it bother you in the least that your Chief is attempting to kill us all with his cancer sticks?"

Brand turned back to the front and smiled. "Yes, it does Chief. But I've learned which battles are worth fighting and which ones are just painful from the start."

"Besides, Chief." Prim added, taking a deep drag from his cigarette before exhaling towards Timmons. "What doesn't kill you makes you stronger. And I'm trying to toughen you up."

"While slowly killing me." The massive Chief grumbled, shaking his head.

....

Upon arriving back at their home base, Timmons rolled the HUMVEE to the weapons tent and they all crawled out.

Taking Brand's M-4 and 9MM, Prim gestured with a nod of his head and remarked, "It's been a long day, sir. I've got one more smoke left in me so I'll handle our weapons turn in. You go get some rest and we can meet for breakfast."

Brand nodded in agreement and said his thanks, heading towards his building while the Chiefs and enlisted took their weapons into the tent.

Brand made it to his room and felt a wave of exhaustion overcoming him as he attempted to strip. He threw his gear into the corner and unlaced his boots before sitting down heavily in a chair. Following the boots, his blouse came off, followed by his t-shirt, all on the floor. He had barely slipped the trousers off when he crawled onto his bunk face first and darkness enveloped his thoughts.

Somewhere out across the dark sands he felt a howl lifting in his dreams. It was a summons and an invitation and a welcome all in one.

The deep sleep pulled him into an ancient dream as he felt the warm sun waking him. He found himself back in Egypt, yet there were plush forests outside the windows of his palace room. For some reason, he knew he was in Lycopolis, the city of wolves, and he lived in his palace. He thought he must be dreaming, but it was so vivid and real. He could smell and taste the desert and feel the warmth of the air.

Looking in the tall, golden-framed mirror, he found himself face to face with a different man, powerful with long black hair and silver eyes. Although deep within, he felt he was in a dream, in his heart he felt this was his true self, preparing to lead the way.

Turning, he left his large chamber and headed through the halls, his passing but a blur of memory before he stepped out into the waiting evening light. The warm sun was already beginning to set, with warm, desert winds racing through the city.

Waiting outside the palace he found several chariots and mounted men. The men arrayed in a semi-circle with weapons; spears, bows and scimitars and he knew them to be the royal guard. The first chariot drew his attention, as it was resplendent with golden leafing along the rails and frame. Standing beside the chariot even more radiant was his queen, Cleopatra, and her daughter at her side, smiling up at their huntsman.

Although he saw the Queen was smiling, the small child was beaming with joy and anticipation at his arrival, almost jumping anxiously. The child rushed forward to grab his leg and squeeze him. The Queen greeted him as he approached almost informally, with a slight nod.

He noticed standing behind her a tall, black warrior, a scowl of disdain on his stern face. His adornments placed him above the other royal guards but below the title of the Queen.

Brand could not help but smirk at the warrior. Standing before the Queen he knelt and knew keenly it was because he desired to kneel not because he was forced to. As he stood, the Queen leaned in to grace his cheek with a soft kiss. Her sharp canines delicately glanced across his skin without drawing blood and he saw her smile.

Without a word, he fell to all fours and went bounding from the courtyard and out of the palace walls, heading through the city as nighttime fell. He knew his queen and the princess would mount the chariot behind and he could already hear the pursuit as they followed him.

Following the wind, he set out for the outskirts of the city, heading for the main gate. As he moved through the city, the few citizens of Lycopolis still roaming about saw his approach and pulled back from the street, bowing low. He knew they would remain averting their eyes until the chariots passed. In short time, he was through the gates of the city, the guards snapping to attention and remaining so until the chariots followed.

Brand glanced back, looking at his exotic queen and the young princess riding in their chariot behind him. Their look was of excitement and thrill as he raced ahead, following prey he could feel on the wind.

Looking down, he saw he was hirsute with a fine layer of silver fur and his digits were extended with long, sharp claws. He raced faster than he should have been allowed as his body extended and raced on all fours, similar to the racing stride of large cats.

He was the Opener of the Way and the Master of the Hunt. And he was taking his Queen and princess on an adventure.

Chapter 8

First Attack

Silver eyes looked across the sands from the desert. It was evening and the sun was already setting. The eyes closed and a massive chest took in a deep, slow breath. All the different scents were in the air. A hunt was on and the silver eyes could almost see the new, young lycan that was growing. Others were around, their musk lingering in the wind. He would call to his new lycan and see what had been made. Only then would he decide whether to let it live.

Prim took his time walking across the compound from the weapons tent towards the buildings. He had spent the last hour cleaning his weapons as well as Brand's and insuring their ammunition was loaded and ready. As he approached, he noticed Brand leaving their building in just a pair of shorts and heading towards the fence, his movements somewhat different and his appearance almost entranced. He increased his pace as his officer disappeared around the corner.

As he reached the corner of the building, he saw Brand disappearing under the fence, scurrying under on his back. Before he could shout out, Brand's bare feet disappeared.

He hurried towards the fence line and as he did, saw an approaching Army soldier on perimeter watch. Turning to the enlisted soldier, he shook his head and pointed to the gap under the fence, "Did you just see someone, I don't know, crawling out under the fence?"

The soldier shook his head smiling, "No, chief. I didn't. And I didn't see him crawling out yesterday either. Don't worry. Most of us like your commander. He doesn't have a stick up his ass."

Prim shook his head, looking down to compose himself before raising his eyes. "Did it occur to you that perhaps my officer is acting a bit strange? Did he appear to be sleepwalking? I mean, how many officers do you know crawl out on their belly in shorts and no shoes?"

The soldier looked rather dumbfounded, glancing from the Chief to the gap under the fence and back. "Sorry chief. I didn't think about it. I just assumed . . . "

"Don't assume. Fuck! Just do your job. If you see MY officer sneaking out in the middle of the night in nothing but shorts, call me. Or throw hot coffee on him."

"Hot coffee?" the soldier scratched his head.

"Don't ask. And just call. But don't ignore him." And he spun to head back into the camp.

"What about your officer?" the soldier called after him.

"I'm a Chief, I don't run. I can't follow him on foot. I'm getting a car. He won't get far . . . I hope." Prim pulled a cigarette to light it and picked up his pace just a bit.

....

Brand ran through the desert, feeling the cool, night air across his face and chest. He closed his eyes and took in a deep breath, smelling and listening. After a short mile he came to the top of a sand dune and knelt on all fours, closing his eyes again and paying attention to the night.

Somewhere off in the desert he kept hearing a calling. He wasn't certain who or what it was, but he knew it was for him. Some echo of the past and call to the future humming in his thoughts. Quiet yet almost insistent.

Lifting his nostrils and inhaling, he turned and started off, crawling and then moving into a run. He ran somewhat upright, leaning forward and occasionally, reaching forward with one or both hands to gallop on all fours.

He smelled his prey ahead of him, a lamb separated from its flock and wandering in the sands. The beast was taking over and he had one intention: to hunt.

In moments, Brand knelt over the torn body of a young lamb. In the back of his thoughts, he still felt a faint call, yet the fresh kill preoccupied his attention as his fingers and mouth ran with blood and tufts of fur. He buried his teeth in the soft, warm flesh and tried to tear a piece of meat when suddenly he felt another close by.

He came up, staying on all fours to cover his kill, but lifting his head to look around. At the top of a dune rose a dark figure with a wide, gaping grin. Behind it raised a second and a third.

The beast in Brand let out a guttural growl and his muscles tensed. His eyes tightened on the first of the three and he bared his teeth.

The three lycans barked in response and the first among them launched forward, clearing the distance between them in one leap. As he landed, he swiped at Brand, who shifted back, lifting his left arm to deflect and instead receiving deep lacerations on his forearm.

As the lycan came down on all fours, it snapped its jaws forward, attempting to lock onto Brand, but the man shifted to the side instead and delivered a roundhouse kick to the creature's chest followed with a punch to its jaw. The creature rolled with the blows, sweeping out with a hind leg as it did and raking up Brand's abdomen as it went.

He fell back, clutching at his torn stomach and landing hard on the ground. He rolled and came back up on all fours, as he was aware of the two remaining lycans rushing down the dune to engage. He dropped under the first of the two, catching the creature under the chin with his foot and throwing him over, while the second slid to the side and came in snarling.

Brand howled as the lycan snapped its jaws on his right forearm and tugged. Before he could defend himself, he heard the loud retort of a rifle and the lycan's side erupted in blood.

The lycan whined and let go, falling to the side and rolling, both clawed hands gripping the side of its chest. A second crack followed and then a burst of rounds slapped into the creature and the surrounding ground.

The first lycan to attack was back on its feet and it shifted its gaze from Brand towards the new menace. Prim stood on a dune overlooking them, his M-16 with M-204 grenade launcher trained on the attacking beasts.

Before the first lycan could initiate an attack in either direction, Prim swung the barrel and fired a burst. The three rounds hit dead center and threw the beast back. As it attempted to gain its feet, Prim fingered the M-204.

"Heads!" He shouted.

Brand rolled to the side, covering his head as the grenade launched and landed on the opposite side of the first lycan a good distance from him. The explosion lifted the lycan and threw it over Brand's prone body.

He lifted his head as sand continued to descend upon him. The first lycan took more rounds from Prim's deadly barrage and was attempting to limp back over the dune. The other two lycans were nowhere to be seen.

Prim came down the dune, dropping an empty magazine to replace with a full one. He slapped the slide back into place and kept the butt of the machine gun pocketed in his shoulder with the barrel pointed towards the disappearing creatures.

"On your feet, sir. They might be back and I don't think I've done much more than slow them down and scare them off."

Brand shook his head and looked around, trying to take in the scene.

"How the hell did I get here?"

"Strange story. I'll tell you on the drive back. To coin a phrase, let's get the flock out of here, sir. My Hummer is just over the dune. I parked it there when I saw you take down the lamb. I didn't even see those three."

"Don't you mean to borrow a phrase?" Brand asked, pushing himself to his knees. "Coining a phrase means it original. That's from Lethal Weapon."

"Really, sir? Now you pick the time for an English language lesson?" He kept his eyes peeled and finger extended past the trigger.

Brand followed the chief back over the dune to the HUMVEE and they climbed in. As they started to drive, Prim stated, "Keep an eye out sir. I don't know how fast they run. Once we're on the highway, I'll open her up and get us back to the base. When we reach the highway, see if we have a towel or some shit to wipe you down. You've got . . . uh, your midnight snack all over you."

Brand pulled the side mirror around and looked at the mess of blood on his chin and chest. Looking down, he saw the gouges on his forearms and across his abdomen. Although initially deep, the wounds were starting to close up and heal while the bleeding has almost stopped.

"When we get back to KNB, I need a shower and to speak with Major Valko."

"Figured as much, sir. But might I suggest it wait until morning. I'll hunt him down when the sun comes up, but they don't live on base and I don't think either a – we want to go look for them, or b – they are awake right now. I'll keep an eye on you the rest of tonight, so let's figure once you're cleaned up, I'll get comfy in a chair in front of your door so you can't sneak out and you climb in bed to sleep."

"Thanks, Chief. Good points across the board."

"One last question, sir. We're in the middle of a horror film now, and it's looking a lot like Underworld. I don't even believe the shit I've seen tonight, except of course the part about you killing that lamb. I always knew you officers were sick fuckers. But seriously, should we let anyone else know about the werewolves? I mean we saw them. We saw them the first night and we just saw them again tonight. We already know Colonel Shaker doesn't believe us and I have no desire to explain to him why you were outside the fence line; but what about Huang? I figure we'll include the Brits, but Huang?"

Brand took a moment to respond, again thinking things through. "I'll talk to Valko first."

"I'm thinking the DFAC is still off limits for you, especially after last night. Once we wake, I'll go find the Brits and we can have breakfast in the usual spot."

Brand agreed with a nod. "Yeah . . . you think? I'll see you at the tables. Might be too early for schwarma, but we can grab some coffee."

....

As they arrived at the base and slowed on their approach to the gate, Prim flashed his shoulder brassard indicating he was attached to NCIS. The guard nodded and then cast a quizzical look at Brand. The Chief shook his head and muttered, "Don't ask."

Once they pulled onto the base, Prim drove to their usual spot not far from their cluster of buildings. As they exited the vehicle, Brand went to his room to gather shower gear. Prim took his weapons to the armory to clean them and restock ammunition.

Within the hour, both men had returned to Brand's room. As Brand climbed into his bed, Prim set up a plastic chair, wrapping in a blanket and leaning his head against a pillow, propped against the door. He placed his feet on a small wooden crate he brought in with himself, effectively making his self an obstacle against the door.

"I dare you to try to escape now, Sir." Prim snickered. "You're worse than my daughter when she was 16."

Both men laughed and Prim hit the overhead light switch. As the room fell into darkness with just soft moonlight spilling through the small window, Prim hesitated and finally asked. "Sir, what took you outside the fence line? I saw you slipping out. You looked like a man on a mission."

They lay in the darkness and silence a moment before Brand answered. "I don't know. I heard something. Someone. Out in the desert. And once I got outside, I just found myself hunting. It's all like a haze and a dream."

"Roger, sir." And with that the two men let silence take over.

....

Brand woke up, stretching as he rolled over to see Prim already standing with coffee in hand. Looking down upon his officer, the Chief grinned. "About time. I keep telling you, Chief's need less beauty sleep. I've already been up and enjoyed my first two smokes of the day. I also called the Brits and got ahold of the Major. He and his crew should be on their way. You get ready and I'll head on out. I'll meet you there."

"What time is it?" Brand asked.

Prim sipped his coffee and responded. "Time for my third smoke of the day. At this rate you're going to kill me - but late morning. Hurry up."

"What've you been doing while I was sleeping besides smoking?"

Prim nodded towards a laptop computer sitting on the floor.

"Watched Team America."

Brand grinned and finished the title of the movie, "World Police. Nice. Are you dedicated?"

"And loyal, sir." Smirked Prim, adding, "But I won't suck your dick."

Both men laughed at the inside joke from the movie and Brand pushed himself out of the bed as his Chief disappeared through the door. He threw on running shorts, shoes and a t-shirt and set out from his room, jogging across the base towards his meeting.

Brand found Prim was waiting with Major Valko and Special Agent Watson at a table. Prim had a coffee for himself and a fresh cup waiting for Brand, while Valko and Watson had Styrofoam cups of hot tea.

As Brand sat, Valko blew across the piping hot cup of tea and smiled. "It's a shame the quality of life we have to put up with while deployed. I mean, Lipton tea: really? I guess it will have to do."

"Good morning, Sam." Brand sat, lifting his coffee and taking a sip.

"Good morning, Liam. How did you sleep?" The British Officer smiled.

There was a chuckle from Prim who immediately glanced away and responded almost under his breath. "Not enough coffee in the day to cover this one."

"I feel fine, but I wound up outside the fence line. And I had another run in with the werewolves."

There was silence at the table for a few moments before Valko finally spoke. "Not the normal response one would have expected. We'll have to get your Chief more coffee. But how did you wind up outside the fence?"

Brand looked from Valko to Watson and then Prim. His chief cast a quizzical stare at the Major. "Interesting, if you don't mind me saying, sir: The fact that my Commander mentions being attacked by werewolves as if he just ordered another schwarma and you don't bat an eye, but you key in on how he wound up outside the fence line like that's the odd thing. Am I missing something?"

Valko looked to both the Chief and Officer and continued to smile his warm, inviting smile. "We've already established some abnormalities in our enemy. Suffice it to say we're beyond labeling who or what we are facing, so whether you call it a werewolf or a lycan or a Beast of Bray road, I am certain it doesn't change the fact that I already believe you. What I am interested in is how your officer may or may not have simply appeared outside the fence line and do we need to be concerned with that. Do we?"

Prim considered the statement a quick minute before turning to Brand. "He's got a point, sir. And you have changed your appetite to more meat, and rare at that."

"As we indicated earlier," Watson offered, "some of these changes might be a result of the inoculations we provided. They do have the potential for a heavy impact."

"And the change in appetite?" Prim asked.

Watson looked to Brand. "I get the feeling you've always liked your meat tending towards rare. So instead of how you've been eating it, let's go with you're just ingesting more protein and fewer vegetables. Another result of the inoculation."

All were silent until Prim shook his head and took another gulp of his coffee. "Ok. So we don't have to worry about my officer turning into a stark raving wolf man?” It was as much a statement as a question.

Valko laughed. “Now I didn’t say that. But right now I wouldn’t worry. Just continue to keep an eye on him and keep us informed of his . . . where-abouts. Now, back to how you found yourself outside the fence and about the attack. Can you describe what happened?”

“Not really certain.” Brand began. “I felt like I was in a haze or dream state. I had returned from Colonel Khalil’s home and was about to shower. I had barely unlaced my boots when I just decided to pass out instead. And my mind slipped into somewhere else, some-when else.”

Watson produced her flip pad and pen, and started scribing notes. “Can you estimate where and when?”

“Same as before. Egypt I’d guess, and B.C. I vaguely recall leading a hunt.”

“I’m sorry, but did you say leading? Were there others? Who?” Watson was intrigued, leaning closer.

Brand thought deeply, attempting to recall details. “A queen and her daughter. I’m certain it was Cleopatra. And she had guards around her. They were in chariots and I was on foot.”

“I lead them out of the city and then I found myself in the desert kneeling over a dead lamb and facing three black . . . creatures.” He paused on the last few words, unable to articulate.

“Three?” Valko gasped incredulously. “How on earth did you survive? I mean, what were you armed with?”

Prim chimed in, filling in details. "I tracked him. Wasn't hard. I saw him scurrying out under the fence in a pair of shorts. Didn't get to him in time, so I had to grab a vehicle. I don't run." The last few words were very matter of fact and brought smiles from the two British officers.

"Once I was on four wheels, I pulled out of the gate and saw him in the distance under the starlight. I hurried to keep up, but he lit out across the dunes so plowing through the sand took some time. Lucky I have four wheel drive."

"When I caught up to him, he took down a lamb. Bit it on the throat and shook it like a dog with a chew toy."

"Thanks for the description, Chief." Brand interrupted.

Prim laughed. "Don't mention it. To be honest, I'm glad that's all you did with it. Sometimes I'm not certain how you officers swing. The moment he finished the lamb off, the three werewolves showed up and came down the dune on him. I had my M-16 so I fired into them. All three turned tail and ran, so we did the same thing. After I opened fire, he seemed to come out of his trance and was the same old mindless officer I'm used to."

Both Valko and Watson stifled laughs at the Chief's nonchalant description of both the event and his officer.

"He took some bites and scrapes from the first one before I was able to open up on them. But his scrapes and bruises seem to already be healing. Whatever you're giving him, you can give me too! He's got Wolverine like healing factor."

Watson gave an inquisitive glance from Prim to Valko, who shook his head. "I assure you, there are no comic book like factors going on here. The inoculation does have a natural beneficial effect on health and healing, but nothing super special."

"And it is limited in its effects." Watson commented. "Your officer already has a naturally impressive immune system. This simply enhances the effects to stave off any maladies presented by close contact with the . . . creatures you've mentioned."

The Chief cast his officer a sidelong look and shook his head. "Too bad. If I keep hanging around with this guy, I'm thinking I'll need a Wolverine healing factor before too long."

"You might be correct, Chief. As for Special Agent Watson and myself, we must be off. Perhaps we can join up for lunch or dinner later this day."

Brand nodded. "We should be available for either. We're continuing our non-investigation, just trying to get a few facts in order. Anything we learn, we'll pass on to you."

"Thank you, Liam. We'll dial you up on the cellular."

Prim took a drink from his coffee and set the cup down, glancing his officer over. "Does he need another shot or something? After last night?"

Valko shook his head. "No. At this point, we just have to let it run its course."

As they rose, Watson looked to Brand and smiled. "If you don't mind, we'll have a look at your injuries to see how they're progressing later. And I may have additional questions for you regarding your dreams."

Valko laughed. "I'd recommend you keep your Chief close by in the event she wants you to take your shirt off."

Watson turned red and drew in an angry breath. "You males never cease to amaze me. I assure you, Commander Brand is perfectly safe under my care." She stomped away and Valko cast a grin back at the two Americans before hurrying after her.

As he caught up to Watson, he whispered, "Dial back to London. What do we know of Cleopatra and did she have a guardian?"

"I had already considered researching her, Major. Although I will be giving you a very cold and silent treatment for the rest of your day." She pushed ahead, leaving him behind.

Brand sipped his coffee and sat back. "Once I finish this cup, let's go find the Major's boy. I want to know where the idea came from and who set us up."

"Think he'll talk, sir." Prim lit a cigarette and took a long drag.

Brand considered the question and stared off intently at nothing. "All things considered, yes. I think he will. Whether he tells the truth is another story. Just keep an eye on him."

"That's what I'm thinking. By the way, do we want to inform Huang?"

Again, Brand took a moment to consider the question. "After we talk to Major Mohammed's assistant. I'd rather get a few more answers before I talk to the Special Agent in Charge. And maybe visit Ross again. See how he's doing."

"Roger, sir." Prim was silent for a moment before looking across the table somberly. "Sir, I know we figured the first night they were waiting at the Colonel's house for us, so that's how they caught us driving. I'm figuring someone in the Colonel or Major's house knew we were coming, so they planted the body for us to see. But how did they find you last night? I mean no one knew you were heading out, right?"

Brand took in a deep breath and sighed, looking down into his black coffee contemplating. "Well, certainly I didn't tell anyone. Did you? Did anyone else see me leave?"

The Chief sucked in air and whistled. "Yes. A private had the watch and mentioned he and others saw you sneaking out before. It might have been him or one of the others on the watch if he spread the word."

Brand considered the words and shook his head. "In which case we have an insider threat. And probably an American soldier."

"Great. As if this wasn't bad enough already." He shook his head. "Roger, sir. We tighten our circle of trust."

"Agreed. Timmons and his boat crew are good as long as they don't talk. But who else do we know?"

Chief shrugged. "The Brits seem to be on our side. I don't know how I feel about the new NCIS agents.

They seem pretty uptight, but mission oriented which probably means we can trust them."

"Agreed Chief. We should enlist Timmons and his crew into asking around the base. See if anyone is acting hanky or if there are any rumors."

Prim nodded. "Roger, sir. I'll visit the docks again and enlist them. That's a lot of geography to cover. Shall I recommend he look into the MPs on watch here?"

Brand nodded. "That makes sense. Start there and work our way out."

They sat in silence until Brand finished the coffee and then stood up to set out across the base.

....

The walk across the base was short and direct, leading to the waterfront and piers where the Kuwaitis maintained their offices above the port. Nearby stood a few two and three story buildings with double occupancy rooms for the enlisted Kuwaiti soldiers.

Prim looked to Brand and offered, "I can enter the offices and see if he's on duty today. If he's not, I'll see if he's on for tomorrow. Considering last night, if the Major is here, I'm certain he'll be compliant in pointing the way."

"Good idea. I'll be out here. If he is in, bring him out and I'll wait. That way we can talk to him privately without a crowd."

Prim departed and Brand leaned against a short, marble wall along the edge of the steps leading into the building.

As he waited he lifted his nostrils and sensed something in the wind. Turning, he saw the young, female corporal from the DFAC, dressed in just her battle dress pants and boots, with a tight, army green t-shirt watching him from a short distance away. Her strawberry hair was tied in a bun as she stood the short distance away, eyes locked on him. Just beyond her, a group of Army soldiers were stacking crates and organizing a large CONEX box.

He smiled and her eyes went wide. A slight, almost drunk grin crossed her lips and she turned almost beet red. Hesitantly, she started to take a step towards him when Brand heard Prim returning. She saw the Chief behind him and quickly turned away, moving back towards her unit.

"Sir, Major wasn't in, but the sergeant on staff . . . whoa. Good morning." Prim moved around in front of his officer and broke his eye contact. "I'll have none of that, sir! I have standards for my officer."

Brand grinned almost mischievously and shrugged. "I don't know what's gotten hold of me. But I was fine. Just . . . taking in scenery."

"Right! Note to self. Don't leave my officer alone. Even for a moment." He shook his head and lit a cigarette. "Anyhow, sergeant inside indicated the Major's aide didn't come in this morning and wasn't on yesterday. They were light on work anyhow, so nobody cared. He's in one of the rooms on the second floor. Shares it with one of the other enlisted. Shall we go knock?"

Brand nodded. "It would be the polite thing to do."

"Sir, this whole ordeal begs the question. Are these creatures thinking? I mean is this some clever plot? And if so, what? Or are they mindless beasts … like in the movies?"

"What do you mean Chief?"

"Well, the more we talk about it, the more I agree they were waiting for us, or at least you this last time. Maybe you're just really bad luck."

"Wow, thanks Chief. At least I know where I stand with you."

The thin man grinned and winked. "You know it sir. But I'll still stick with you."

"Great question, Chief. When we find out we'll both know." He looked ahead, turmoil churning in his stomach for what he might become. "And what about me?"

Both men stood silent, pondering the stated question but failing to find an answer.

"Whatever it is, Sir, I'm still your Chief. We'll figure it out. Just might take a bit more coffee and a lot more Whiskey."

….

The two men crossed the short stretch of the base to where the junior Kuwaiti soldiers shared rooms. Brand looked to Prim and glanced at the stairwell leading to the second floor. He scrunched his nose and shook his head, taking the steps a few at a time.

"Did you get a room number? God something reeks like … death."

"Yeah. Two-twelve. Second floor just to the left." He followed Brand up.

As they cleared the stairs and started towards the room, Brand followed the scent in the air and reached back to halt the Chief. "They're in there." He gestured to the room ahead.

The door of the room stood cracked open. "I smell blood."

Brand nudged the door open further and saw two men lying across the floor inside. Pools of blood were already congealing around them, their throats and bodies shredded and torn.

"This is starting to get old, real fast." Prim stated, looking over Brand's shoulder.

"This happened last night or yesterday. The flies are all over the scene and the blood is congealed and drying." Brand stated, looking across the room.

Prim shook his head. "I don't know about the blood, but flies are everywhere all the time. This is Kuwait. How do you figure when it happened?"

"This is different. I'd say these two have been dead a good number of hours. The smell of decomp and the number of flies."

"Shall I call NCIS and CID?" Prim pulled his cellphone and flipped it open.

Brand looked around the room, leaning across the threshold while avoiding stepping in. "In a minute. Let me take this in first." He closed his eyes and let his senses take over, drawing in a long draught through his nose.

His senses were initially overcome by sickeningly sweet rust and dry sand. Just below the smell of drying blood he touched on a faint, sweet piney floral with a mix of pepper and clover as well as earthy, spicy undertones. Some of the scents almost disappeared beneath the overriding scent of carnage.

Opening his eyes, he looked intently at both bodies. "Which one is the Major's boy?"

Prim knelt at the door and peered in. "The closer one. He was always the one serving tea."

"He's got a phone in his hand. Think we might want to check it out?"

"You mean before anyone else cleans the evidence? Now you're thinking. I'm glad I brought you along. Can you grab it without disturbing anything else?"

Looking across the room Brand eyed the floor, which was splattered with blood, and then he eyed the furniture. The Major's assistant lay closest to one of the two beds, which appeared to have the least amount of blood spray.

"I think so." He shifted inside the doorframe and knelt down, coiling into his legs before springing.

Prim stepped back to watch. "What are we looking for?"

"Who did he call recently? And what number did he call most? Does he have any texts?"

He launched across the room, landing softly on the metal bedframe in a crouched position, perched on the balls of his feet. Prim gaped in open astonishment and shook his head.

"Sir, you've been holding back. We need to get you a job in Cirque De Soleil."

Brand leaned down, grabbing the cellphone with two fingers and pulling it free. It slid free easily. "They've already passed through rigor mortis. Fingers are no longer stiff." Glancing around at the rest of the scene, he leaned closer and took another deep breath, inhaling as he filled his lungs through his nostrils. He looked intently upon the lacerated throat, and the shredded forearms.

"They attempted to defend themselves. It was quick." He eyed both corpses, shifting his eyes back and forth between the two. "Whoever it was, they let them in. They trusted them. Or at least didn't think they were a threat. The assistant died last. Defensive wounds on his arms and face indicate at least he attempted to defend himself. His roommate died from one quick slash across the throat. Four raking marks."

"Four. Like four long fingers with claws?"

Brand looked back to his Chief. "From what I can see, that's what I'm thinking. Looking at the spray, the roommate spun as he went down, I'm guessing putting his arms up in defense and then clutching his throat and spraying blood across the room. The Major's boy tried to fend off the attack and took a few across the forearms before he had his throat torn out. Looks like he went straight down."

"Good eyes, Sir, or a good imagination. And looking at the wall to the right, their assailant was standing about here." He pointed. "Some of the wall was shielded from spray. Now jump back out and let's call this in. And may I recommend we call NCIS first? Maybe let them call the Army. That Colonel positively hates you."

"So I've noticed. Good idea. Dial it in." He opened the cellphone and tried to look at numbers. "Password protected. Do you know anyone who can crack this locally?"

Prim nodded. "Sure. I've got the team in the communications shack. They could probably have the phone done in a few hours."

He leaped back across the room effortlessly, landing beside Prim without a sound. "Take this to them and leave before anyone else gets here. I'll hang out until they arrive." The two men started moving from the building out into the common grounds.

"You sure, Sir?" Prim listened as his phone began to ring.

"Positive. We can pass the information from the cellphone once we know what's on it. No need in both of us being here until lord knows when."

"Sir, that's positively selfless of you, taking one for the team." He heard Special Agent Wong answer the phone and he changed his tone to respond. "Hey, it's Chief Prim. You and your Senior Agent might want to meet the Commander over at the Kuwaiti enlisted quarters. We found a body and it might be important."

"What happened? Where are the Quarters?" He heard her ask.

"Head to the Kuwaiti port operations building near the waterfront. Just beside it are a few two-story buildings.

You'll see the Commander and he can take you to where the bodies are." He replied.

"Bodies? I thought you said a body."

"Ok, so they're multiplying. There are two in the room. He'll see you when you get here." Prim hung up the phone and looked to Brand. "Yeah . . . about me hanging out . . . glad I'm not. Enjoy her company."

"Who's that?"

Prim lit a cigarette and started walking. "Special Agent Wong. She's a special kind of angry I think. And she's on her way here."

Brand shook his head and just had to smile. "She does seem to always be in a mood. Straight business. Oh well. Have them put a rush on breaking the passwords and bring it back. Stay with them until they're done."

"Aye-aye, Sir. Have fun. Maybe you just need to take another one for the team and offer to break the ice with her. You know . . . it might remove the stick up her ass. And since she ain't military, I don't have to worry about you . . . well, not that much."

"Thanks, Chief. But I'm going to have to draw the line on that one. I appreciate you looking out for us." He leaned back against the wall as his Chief started moving away.

As an after thought, Brand called out. "I smelled something in the room. Something else. Something I've sensed before."

Prim looked back. "What are you talking about, sir? What'd you smell?"

"Under the blood, sweat and body smells. Something else. I can't place it yet, but I think I recall it somewhere else recently."

Prim shook his head and then nodded. "Roger, sir. Put some thought into it and we'll see where it leads. Was it coming from the room?"

Brand shook his head. "Negative, Chief. It's around the room but not from it. And it's dissipating fast."

"Aye, sir. Put some thought into it before Wong shows up. And then maybe stop thinking about it and it'll come to you."

"Thanks. Good idea."

And Prim was gone.

....

Brand was waiting patiently when he saw Special Agent Wong approaching. He greeted her with a smile as she approached and he received cold indifference in return.

"Good morning . . . or afternoon. Is Huang coming?"

"Senior Agent Huang is preoccupied at the moment. He directed I come interview you. I'll follow you. Lead on."

Brand gave a quick salute, "Aye-aye, sir." Followed by a friendly smile. "Follow me, Special Agent." Her reception was cool as she gestured for him to lead.

"We haven't contacted the Army, yet. Prim and I felt it best to contact you and Special Agent Huang before anyone else." He glanced back at her as he led the way.

She nodded and responded. "Thank you. That's wise. Did you also contact your British friends?'

"Actually, not yet: although we may since we seem to all be getting along better now. I thought we'd give you right of first review. If you don't mind my asking, what's the issue between Huang and Valko? Do they have a past?

Wong followed in silence for a moment until Brand slowed down and looked at her. "If I'm going to be working with you, I'd like to know what's going on with my team. I won't endanger my Chief if you two groups are sniping at each other."

She looked at him and for a brief moment her cool exterior seemed to relax, as she seemed to re-evaluate him. "Have you asked your British friend?"

"Yes, but he didn't seem forthcoming with information and he was a bit vague, so I thought I'd ask you. We are on the same team here."

Wong turned her eyes away and focused on their current task. "It's not my place to say what's going on between Special Agent in Charge Huang and the British. I will say the Special Agent in Charge did not know them prior to our arrival in this country. Their issues exist beyond us."

"Fair enough. Thanks. The room is just up ahead."

When they arrived, Brand quickly detailed what he had observed. Wong looked around, kneeling at the doorsill and turning a keen eye on the scene. After a few moments, she looked up to Brand with a renewed respect.

"Your observations are good." She stood, turning to look him in the eye. After a moment, she broke eye contact and looked back into the room. "Did you sense anything else? Did you smell anything?"

Brand considered the question and the source, glancing at her from behind and then turning to the scene. He took in another deep breath, inhaling through his nose intent upon what he could sense.

He held the air in his lungs and focused on the sensations in his nostrils. After a long minute, he released it, letting the airflow through his nose once more.

"Iron. Blood. Schwarma. Sandalwood. And a faint smell of jasmine." He looked at her. "Do you smell it too?"

Without looking at him she shook her head. "No. Just the blood." She eyed the floor and stepped inside, careful where she placed her feet. From a pocket she pulled a pair of latex gloves. "How far in to the room did you step? Did you disturb the scene?"

She did not see his smile as she continued to tiptoe through the blood spray. "I made it to the bed. And no, I didn't disturb the scene."

She knelt and delicately lifted the closest hand by the wrist. "What's missing here?"

"Good eye. It was his cell phone. I passed it to my Chief who's getting it run through one of our IT's. A quick forensic will tell us who he was texting and calling. That might tell us who else he might have spoken with regarding the meeting we had with Colonel Khalil. Once we have the information, we'll pass the phone back through you and Senior Agent Huang. We felt it best to get it done in-house before the Army took it."

She looked up to him and nodded. "Good thinking, Commander." She continued to glance around from within the room for another few minutes before stepping back out.

"I will report to Senior Agent in Charge. Then we can contact the Army." She dialed her cell. Before she pushed the call button, she looked at him for a short moment. "Call your friends. We are, after all, starting to get along better as you say." For a moment, it appeared as if Wong attempted to smile, and then in that moment she turned her eyes away and called.

Brand pulled his cellphone and dialed. A moment later, he heard Valko's voice and he spoke. "We found the Major's aide in his room, dead. Looks just like we saw at the Colonel's. It's a bloody mess. Care to join us?"

The proper British voice at the end of the call responded promptly. "Wouldn't miss it for the world."

"We're across the Kuwaiti Navy Base in the Junior Officer's building, second floor. Hard to miss us." He hung up his phone and turned to Wong.

She hung up after a quick conversation with Senior Agent Huang. "I'll take a few photos with my phone and report back to Senior Agent. Thank you for calling. And . . . I'm sorry for earlier. When we first met. I was following my instincts and they were off."

Brand smiled and shrugged. "No worries. The deserts hot and it can make us all edgy. Glad we're working together now." He held out his hand.

She gripped it firmly. "Senior Agent said to give you his thanks as well. I'll report back to him immediately. He recommends you call Colonel Shaker after the British investigators finish investigating the scene. He also recommends you contact the Kuwaiti Major since these are their soldiers. I'll try to return before the army arrives. I've seen how the Colonel may not appreciate you as we do, and although I don't have the same personality as my Senior Agent, perhaps I can distract him."

"Thanks, Wong. I appreciate the gesture. And . . . I hope you make it back in time. He definitely has it hard for me." He laughed.

She bowed her head and said. "Bai. You may call me Bai."

"Bai Wong?" He repeated.

She shook her head. "My family still follows the older Chinese method, even though we're several generations in the U.S. So, yes Bai Wong. But in family, I'd be Wong Bai."

"I'll remember that. And please feel free to call me Liam."

She smiled and turned to report back to Senior Agent Huang.

····

Prim moved across the base faster than he normally would have, cigarette held tightly in his lips with cellphone clasped tightly in hand. Rushing as he went, the cigarette burned faster although he took shallow breaths.

He reached the communications shack and leaned against the doorframe, breathing hard. Knocking, he stood and took one last drag on the cigarette before dropping the butt and snubbing it out with his boot. The door opened and an older, black female Chief answered the door. The nametag on her uniform read Colter.

"Can I help you, Chief?" she asked.

He nodded, pushing into the communications shack. "Absolutely. I need a huge favor, Chief to Chief. Can you do it?" He pushed the door shut behind.

Within the communications shack were two other sailors, both enlisted, to include a First Class Information Systems Technician and a Third Class. Prim took a seat at a counter covered with electronics gear, computers and radio parts.

"Where's Chief Jefferson? He's normally my go to guy."

The female chief looked at him and placed her hands on her hips. "Whatever he can do, I can do better."

Prim eyed her top to bottom and winked. "I bet you can. But I need to get right to business."

She shook her head dismissively as he offered the cell phone. "I need this hacked. We're supporting NCIS in an investigation and we need to know who this guy has been texting and calling the past few weeks."

She accepted the cellphone and glanced it over. "Wouldn't it be easier to just ask him for his password?"

"You'd think. Except we just found him expired, so unless you can talk with the dead, I'll need your super technical hacking skills. Think you can do it?"

She glanced over the phone; flipping the case and pulling the back cover open. She shrugged and looked across the room to the First Class. "We can probably have it done in an hour or so. It isn't complex and I doubt it's encrypted. Whom did it belong to?"

Prim responded as he sat back to wait. "Kuwaiti aide to the Major. Thanks Chief. And until we hear back from NCIS, let's keep this under wraps."

She nodded and passed the phone to the two petty officers.

....

The British team showed up directly at the room shortly after Wong departed. As they approached, Watson noted. "Did I sense a Special Agent departing?"

Brand nodded. "She was closer when I called and made it here first. She took some photos and is heading back to her Senior Agent. She might return shortly. They advised not calling the Army until we're done reviewing the scene to give you more time."

Valko smiled and bent his head to the side. "The gesture is appreciated."

"Give us a tour, Commander." Churchill spoke in his deep baritone. "What did you see when you found the room?"

Brand knelt at the door and pointed across the room. He gave a short synopsis of the scene they found as well as how they found the phone.

"Chief is taking the phone to have forensics done immediately. Hopefully we'll get information soon."

Valko looked across the room taking in the scene as if all his senses were extending and he was absorbing every scent and sight. After a moment, he looked to the largest member of his team. "Cedric. What do you make of it?"

The huge man stepped across the threshold with the grace of a dancer. Each step was calculated while he moved into the room, his eyes taking in every corner.

"One perpetrator, sir. Two victims. As the Commander pointed out, blood-spatter points to where the perpetrator stood." He stopped and closed his eyes. Opening them, he looked back. "Older. And female. Powerful."

Brand cocked his head and looked from Churchill to Valko and back. "Was it the smell? Under the blood?"

Churchill nodded. "Faint. Very faint. I'm surprised you caught it, sir. I'm impressed."

Valko leaned in and shook his head. "I'm not getting it, Cedric. What am I missing?"

Fergus moved in closer with Watson. The three paid close attention.

"Hard to taste the perfume as its disappearing fast, but whoever was visiting was small framed. You can barely see how the spray pattern gives just an outline from the first victim. The Commander was right. First victim spun and blood sprayed. I'd say our perpetrator was shorter than either victim, which judging by the size of them I'd place at about five or five-foot-one."

"How'd you get older?" Brand asked, intent upon Churchill.

Fergus laughed. "Cedric has a knack for those things. If he says older and woman, I'd go with it."

Cedric moved in through the room, taking photos with his phone. He knelt over the bodies one at a time, closing in on the wounds and taking numerous photos. When he had made the entire room, stopping to take photos around every inch, he stepped out of the room.

"I've got what I need, sir." Churchill stated to Valko. "Anything else?"

"No. I think we have what we need." Looking to Brand he spoke. "Thank you again, Liam. Please give the Army my regards.

....

Brand wound up hitting the gym with Fergus for a few hours before showering. As he came out of the shower, he met up with Prim.

"Seriously, sir. Every time I see you, you're either coming from or heading to the shower. Are you a neat freak or just horny?"

"You're just lucky I guess." Brand responded. "What's the word?"

"Chief Colter in the comms shack was able to hack the password on the phone. They had a bunch of texts which were in squiggly writing or whatever their Sanskrit is over here. And a bunch of numbers that might take us forever to figure out who they are. I should be able to get a list from the shack after we eat."

"Good. Keep it low profile. Once we have the list, I think both the Brits and NCIS will be able to play a role in figuring it out. Hopefully it leads us somewhere. And I'm guessing they can use google-translate or something to decipher his texts."

"You think? So how about a quick bite? I'm guessing you and Fergus had a workout and you're probably hungry."

"He's a good kid. I worked out with both Fergus and Cedric, the big one. We did a quick weight workout, and then I taught Fergus some more martial arts. He's got the same fascination and drive towards learning that I do. And it's great working with a huge uke to throw around."

"Jeese. That big guy: how much does he lift?"

"Couldn't tell you. He wasn't even trying and seemed to press the bar with maxed weights. I stopped counting when we slapped on five-hundred. But Fergus was putting up some impressive iron, too. Personally I'd have to say I wasn't unhappy with the plates I was lifting myself."

"Remind me to avoid any close angry encounters with that big guy, though. I'm certain I'd need to put a number of rounds center mass just to get his attention." The Chief quipped.

Brand shrugged. "He's the most peaceful of the bunch."

"Yeah, but it's always the quiet ones who go high and right when they explode. Kind of like yourself." Both men laughed.

As they approached their building, Brand stated, "I could use some dinner. Let me change and I'll meet you at your room. DFAC should still be open."

"Negative, sir. I've got a better idea. I'll swing by the DFAC and grab you a plate of whatever they are serving, heavy on the meat. We can eat in the food court area near the schwarma shop. I'm still not trusting any of the females around you."

Brand shook his head and acquiesced. "As you say, mother."

"Hey, sir. Let's call both NCIS and your Major. I'm guessing they can meet here, while we eat. If I take my time bringing the food back, I might be able to swing by the communications shack and the IT's might have their work done. Worst case scenario I wait a minute and your food gets cold."

"Good idea, Prim. I'll make the call while you're hustling for chow. What do you think? Forty minutes?"

"Make it an hour. Gives me time to get the food back, gives the comms shack a few more minutes, plus we can actually eat some before they all show up."

"Nice. I'll ask them to show up in an hour."

As Prim started towards the DFAC, he glanced over his shoulder and smirked. "Oh, I meant to ask you. How was your date with Wong?"

Brand tried to hide his smile and shrugged. "I think she's actually warming up to us. She didn't threaten to shoot me this time. Although now that I think of it, you weren't there, so maybe it's really you she has a thing for."

Prim shook his head, laughing. "Nuh-huh, sir. She's all yours. She scares me." And he was gone.

Thirty minutes later, Prim returned with two Styrofoam containers of food as well as a small canvas bag and a beverage holder with two large coffees. He found Brand sitting with Special Agent Wong in the inner courtyard of their building. He slowed as he approached, smiling as he looked to see whether she was armed.

"Hey Special Agent. You're here early." He glanced at his officer.

Brand shrugged as she replied. "I came as soon as your officer called. Special Agent in Charge Huang will be joining us shortly. He had some more phone calls to make. Did you retrieve the phone?"

As he neared the two, he extended the small canvas bag to Brand. "Two thumb drives and one cell phone. Did the commander indicate what we were hoping for?"

"Yes, that we could use our resources to decipher the texts as well as pull forensics on the phone. I will wait for Senior Agent in Charge."

Prim passed one of two coffees to Brand. "Tonight was meatloaf and mashed potatoes. Sorry. No rare meat." He grinned.

Brand sighed and shrugged. "It's a shame. I had my mind set on a rare steak."

"Sorry, sir. The closest we get here is the London broil. How about you, Wong? Does NCIS ever get to eat out on the economy?"

She glanced between Prim and Brand. "We haven't so far. Our days have been pretty busy, so we've kept to your food hall."

Brand laughed as he accepted his container of food. "That is a crying shame. You have the luxury of being able to eat fine Kuwaiti food and you're stuck here eating from our DFAC. You should at least try to venture out into Kuwait city and eat at one of the restaurants. It's not that far of a drive."

"I'd avoid the Sharq Souq, though." Prim added. "Nothing but American fast food, like McDonalds and KFC. And I think an Applebees."

She glanced from Prim to Brand and back. "Souq?"

"A market or mall." Brand responded. "The gold souq has great shopping for jewelry if you're into jewelry. The Sharq Souq is a mall, similar to any mall across the U.S. If you want to try some authentic, high-end local food, try Jamawar. It's Indian cuisine. Our previous Senior Agent ate there once when he visited with Colonel Khalil. He gave it great reviews."

She caught his eye and held, nodding. "I'll take that into consideration. Perhaps when we are done with the investigation, Senior Agent Huang will allow an evening out."

Prim winked with a smile. "Don't forget your security team. We'll make certain you get home safe."

"Is this a private dinner or can anyone attend?" Valko's proper British accent called from across the atrium.

All three turned to view the arrival of the British in force. Fergus nodded and smiled at Brand and shifted towards him while Cedric took a seat near Prim.

Siovhan looked around the courtyard to where Prim and Brand sat to either side of Wong in collapsible camping chairs and reiterated the question. "Yes, can anyone attend this dinner?" She moved to take a seat between Brand and Wong, pulling up one of the several other collapsible chairs leaning against the wall as she glared at Wong. Wong noticed the movement and gave a slight grimace before turning towards Valko, who watched all with great amusement.

As he moved to join the group, he nodded to Wong. "Good evening, Special Agent. Shall your Senior Agent be joining us?"

She nodded. As if on queue, he floated through the entrance with disarming grace. He smiled at the Major as he passed him. "Good evening, Major Valko. A pleasure to see you again."

"Positively charmed, I'm certain." The Major responded, smiling with a polite tilt of the head.

As he passed through the group, he stopped to consider Brand and his eyes focused in on him. For a moment, his eyes tightened and then softened back into a smile. He nodded and greeted the American officer. "Commander."

Brand nodded back and then looked around as he held up the canvas bag. "Let's get straight to business. Chief Prim and I were the first on scene. I believe we've already shared the information we found while on scene. We all seem to be in agreement that whoever or whatever lacerated the two soldiers did so with extreme efficiency. That being the case, it would stand to reason the Major's aide was probably targeted once we visited the Colonel. He was on our short list as to who knew and would have set up our meeting for attack."

Valko smiled and looked from Brand to Huang and back. "That would make the most sense."

"The texts are all in middle-eastern. We would like one or both of your teams to decipher the texts and see where they might lead. Further, can either of you run forensics on the listed numbers he called in the past month or more, specifically the days leading up to our initial attack and the meeting we had with the Colonel."

Cedric Williams spoke first. "I'm certain I can translate most of the texts once I download them from the phone."

Huang looked to Wong who shrugged. He returned his gaze to Brand and gave a tilt of his head. "I am somewhat fluent in many of the written and spoken languages of this geography. I will offer my services in reading through the texts."

Valko laughed beneath his breath and shook his head. "Why am I not at all surprised?"

Brand reached into the canvas bag and pulled forth the two thumb drives. "Chief Prim had copies of the texts made for each of you. We figured in the new spirit of teamwork, we all get a copy. Just share with us once you have an idea, please."

Valko took the first thumb drive and handed it directly to Williams, who pocketed the device. Huang gestured to Wong, who accepted the second thumb drive.

"That's the team!" Prim quipped, smiling as he pulled a cigarette and lighter from his pocket.

"Now, who can pull the LUDS from the phones?" Brand held up the phone. "We saw the numbers, but we don't have any access to connect with local cellphones. Can either of you tap into an international data base?"

Huang looked to Valko and his team. "We don't have access to local urban directories here. We might if we sent them back to Quantico, but that will take time. Would the British have better success?"

Valko extended his hand towards Brand. "I'm certain our connections might provide a quicker access to the local numbers." He took the phone and passed it to Williams as well.

Prim offered quickly. "I took some of the numbers from the phone and visited the Kuwaiti office. I asked some of the others in the office if they recognized a few of the first few numbers. One in particular: Abdulla, nephew of the Colonel. But that could be anything, as the Major and Colonel often coordinate. Still, bears notice. The others in the office said that often Abdulla would visit and spend time with the Major's boy."

Brand sat back down and picked up his coffee. "I also think it bears mentioning: I believe we have at least one if not more infiltrating the base. Chances are they are third country nationals, posing as one of dozens of hired cleaners, trash men, etcetera. Like the Major's aide, they would fly beneath the radar. No one looks twice at the tea boy here, so I doubt anyone, including our military, are looking at these third country nationals as anything other than they are. We need to keep an eye and ear out, because I doubt they've met their agenda."

"And what do you presume their agenda to be?" Huang inquired, staring intently into his eyes.

Again Brand felt an unnerving invasion and shook it off, dropping his eyes and turning to the others. "My guess, to make a scene. Since the attack didn't raise a big fuss and it was effectively glossed over by Major Valko and his team, I believe they will try something larger next time. Terrorist acts only inculcate fear if they are seen and heard as something to fear. Passing this attack off as a standard roadside IED effectively defeated their initial purpose, but planting our Agent's body in the Colonel's house was a message directed at us."

"What message do you believe they are sending, Liam?" Valko took a turn at asking.

"That they are here."

"And who might they be?" Siovhan followed the line of questioning.

Prim took in a deep breath and exhaled a cloud of smoke that lingered over his head. "Werewolves of course;

or some genetic creature from a government lab. I don't know which Sci Fi movie we're in. But both you guys," He waved his cigarette towards Huang and Wong, "as well as you guys," He completed with waving the cigarette towards Valko and his team, "have skirted the actual topic of what attacked us, twice, and whatever it is, is starting to leave a wake of bodies torn to shreds. Now we're not saying what it is. Or at least I'm not; I can't speak for the Commander. But with a lack of any hard evidence, I'm leaving the door open to anything at this point." He took another long drag and blew smoke. "For all we know, they could be using great Bollywood special effects and trying to convince us of some terrifying movie monster. Regardless, the body count is rising and they have specifically targeted my boss."

The group sat in silence as everyone looked around until finally Brand shrugged. "Well, there it is. And the silence is deafening. Let's just continue with the investigation and hopefully we can follow the trail to our culprits. Ok?"

Huang nodded and gestured to Wong. "We shall promptly do our best and get back to you as soon as possible. Good evening all."

Valko agreed, motioning to his team. "Same here, Liam. We'll put a rush on the information. Shouldn't be an issue."

"Thanks, Sam. We'll stand by."

"Care to join us for a late dinner?" Siovhan asked as she stood.

Prim held up his empty Styrofoam container. "Thank, Agent. We just finished eating and I need to keep an eye on the good Commander. We'll just have to take a rain check."

She smiled and followed the others, leaving Brand and Prim.

"Ok, sir. What's your plan?"

Brand ran a hand over his head as he took a sip of his coffee. "I need a haircut, so I'm going to run and see if the barber is open."

Prim scrutinized him with a grimace. "Um, since the barber shop is closed I'm assuming you're going to see if the boat unit's Petty Officer Ship Serviceman can cut your hair."

Brand shrugged. "I was going to, yes. She gives a good cut."

The Chief shook his head. "Looks like I'll be going with you. As I recall, she is a she; and kind of a freak by the looks. Thin, very short blond hair, glasses and a few hidden tats. No way you're going alone."

Brand laughed and then slugged back the last of his coffee. "Thanks. After that, I'm up for crashing early while watching a movie on my laptop."

"Good to know. I'll walk you back to your room and then check on you every hour or so. I need to set up some alarm system on your room so I can sleep through the night."

....

An hour later, they returned to their building. Brand ran a hand over his head, shorn down to just stubble.

He smiled and sighed. "Much better. I was starting to feel like a hippy."

"Yeah. Positively out of control. I almost considered putting a bow in it. Ok, sir. Lock it up tonight. I'll secure your windows. Bolt the door. I may put a line on your doorknob with a bell."

"Have at it, Chief. I have absolutely no desire to find myself out in the sand."

Brand adjourned to his room, followed by the Chief who checked the windows and locked them before heading out through the door, pulling it shut. Brand slid the bolt and kicked off his shoes to prep for bed. He pulled off his shirt and crawled into bed wearing his running shorts. Outside his door, he heard a short commotion, which sounded like glass bottles being tied to his door.

As he fell into slumber, he felt the warm breeze coming in across the desert. A moment later, he opened his eyes and stared into a golden-rimmed mirror as he dressed himself in bronze arm greaves, set with the symbol of a hybrid Wolf Jackal Man. He wore a cloth shendyt, the simple kilt often worn by the military, both soldiers and officers of rank, and sometimes peasants. To one side of the mirror on a rough metal mannequin sat his khepresh, his official blue headdress with cobra as well as golden sash and khopesh, a long curving sickle sword. To the other side of the mirror was a stand with a long, heavy bow and quiver of long arrows. His silver eyes appraised his form as he turned to the four men waiting for him, dressed in similar fashion.

The four followed him as he set through his magnificent dwelling, passing a long hall from his bedchambers towards the outer atrium of his dwelling. The house was magnificent with more than thirty rooms.

As the five men exited his home, he came upon a scene inspiring great awe. From the steps of his home he overlooked his city, Lycopolis, and the Northern Nile. An Army was arrayed along the banks of several thousand Egyptian soldiers, ready for battle.

The five hastened, moving with great speed through the streets to the edge of the city and passed through the gate towards the river. As he raced through, he heard the guards call out and the great gates were swung and secured behind them.

When he reached the army, he strode straight to the head where several chariots stood apart from the rest. Of the chariots, he saw his queen mounted in one. Beside her stood the tall, black warrior from an earlier memory he vaguely recalled. Again, he recognized the scowl of disdain upon his approach, and also noted the golden Cobra wrapping around his thick right bicep.

Just behind the small ring of royal chariot and guard stood one hundred men dressed similar to the four at his heals. Each of the men wore the shendyt kilts and only the bronze greaves on their arms, set with the symbol of the Egyptian wolf hybrid similar to the ones he wore.

Queen Cleopatra smiled at him, as he felt she always did when in his presence, and he heard her strong voice speaking in ancient Greek, although he understood every word. "Are you ready my faithful Guardian? Open the way and lead the army to victory over these Nubian invaders."

The four men in his entourage all knelt as he stood before her. He nodded with a wolfish grin and felt himself begin to change. The change was natural as his digits extended into long, sharp claws and a fine layer of white fur covered his body. His jaw extended out and formed the sharp jackals maw and his ears pricked up.

Lifting his lips he let our a sharp bark and immediately his four followers and the one-hundred men lined behind the chariots began to change, taking the forms of black, brown, red and grey lycanthropes. All were lean of bodies, with distinct sharp, long jackal-like snouts and thin fur. Even in hybrid form, they remained silent and reserved, waiting for their master's orders.

Turning he looked across the field and down the river, where he saw a massive army of Ethiopian soldiers arrayed, chariots at the forefront but directly behind them at least one-hundred elephants saddled with soldiers and archers. Behind the elephants stood row upon row of dark soldiers, armed with spear, shield and short sword.

He started off with a gentle stride that began to elongate as he sped into a run. He felt the others fall in behind him and before long the entire pack of lycans were racing across the field. Behind them he heard a roar ripple through the

Egyptian army shortly before Queen Cleopatra gave the order to charge. He knew that other then her royal guard, the remaining retinue would follow and several thousand Egyptian soldiers, both chariots and footmen, would be hurtling across the field of battle.

He was thrilled as he drove forward, launching into a full-body run on all fours similar to the great cats, stretching forward. Across the field, he saw the Ethiopian king raise a scepter and drop it, signaling the charge of his own army. A quick estimate put the Ethiopian army at almost twice the size of the Egyptian army, with the additional elephants adding to their might.

The armies clashed just past the center of the field and he felt himself drawn towards one of the mightiest of the elephants and riders. His agile frame eluded the arrows that rained down from above and he slipped beneath the massive tusks of the pachyderm. As he slid past, his long talons raked the sides and back of the front leg, just above the knee joint, and he was delighted to hear the scream of the beast as it tried to pull back and turn to follow him.

He rolled beneath and as he did, he kicked with his foot, using the talons on his toes to slice open the beast's huge, exposed belly and groin. He continued past the savaged elephant towards the next beast, knowing full well the fight had been taken from the first as it turned from battle, wounded, and ignoring the directions of his riders, began rumbling back towards its own army.

As he approached the second beast, a rain of arrows descended upon him and he rolled to the side. Two scored hits, one in his calf and the second grazing his shoulder, and he caught himself leaning just off before gaining his stride again as he reached down to tear the arrow from his leg.

The momentary pause was enough for the charging elephant to sweep its massive trunks across and catch him as he gained speed again. The heavy ivory tusks slammed against his ribs and he felt his body lifted and flipped into the air. Ignoring the pain in his side, he caught himself as he spun end over end and came down on all fours, turning back towards the elephant and rider.

Again, he came in underneath, slashing out in both directions with his long, sharp nails as he passed. He felt thick hide and muscle rend and the elephant trumpeted in agony. He dove into a forward roll and kicked up his hind paws, raking the sharp talons across the pachyderm's belly. As he continued his roll out from under, he felt the beast toppling behind him.

Chaos ensued as the throng of lycans tore into the elephants. Arrows wounded a few of his retinue, but that only served to slow them down. They would heal. Of those, one or two were caught by the elephants, and either trampled or gored by the massive ivory.

To his right, he saw a younger grey lycan caught through the abdomen by a tusk tipped with sharp silver. The gored youth was lifted and driven back down into the ground as the angry pachyderm tore into him, savaging him and crushing down with its heavy forehead. From the saddle, two archers launched long arrows into the trapped lycan, drilling through his head and chest. Soldiers swarmed up around the beast and started hacking at the dying lycan.

He veered off and drove into the soldiers, swiping them with his razor-like talons and spinning through them. He launched himself to alight the back of the head of the elephant and growled as he slashed at the rider, spraying blood when he opened his throat. Before the body toppled from the saddle, he had already slipped past to the archers and then to the elephant master himself, catching the man by the wrist of his sword arm and then disemboweling him with his free hand.

As entrails spilled out across his feet, he spun to drive his long fingers into the neck of the elephant, tearing through thick hide like it was papyrus. The beast squealed and lifted its long trunk to reach for him. He slid down to the side, coming up beneath its jaw and raking his long talons across its exposed throat. Blood showered down upon him and he launched past the dying beast back into the battle, leaving his downed lycan behind to be retrieved later.

In short order, he was beyond the elephants and racing towards the advancing line of chariots. He snarled in sheer joy as he launched into the Nubian army. To his right he saw one of his lycans catapult over the advancing horses to land within the chariot and make short work of the archer and driver.

The pack of wolves would drive the Nubians back and send them running home to Ethiopia. Brand felt the thrill of battle coursing through him.

Chapter 9

Dog Soldier

Liam rolled over and felt sand shift beneath his naked body. His eyes opened to the dawn and he sat up, a warm breeze bringing the smell of blood to his nostrils. A goat lay torn and dead on the ground at his feet, and he felt sticky, drying blood across his lips and chin. He fell back and rubbed his eyes shut, moaning. He could taste the blood and felt a small piece of the flesh stuck between his teeth.

"I've got to stop doing this." He muttered beneath his breath.

"I suppose you won't need breakfast, but can I spot you a cup of coffee?" he heard the familiar British accent.

Brand opened his eyes and rolled over to all fours and found Sam kneeling nearby. They were in the desert, not far from the edge of the highway and within sight of a cluster of homes. It was still early and even the animals were asleep.

"I've been watching you, although I missed you the first night you slipped out. I wasn't certain you'd go out so soon. I watched you last night after you returned. You are a natural hunter. Very efficient kill." Valko assessed, glancing at the dead goat. He held out a box of baby wipes. "Still a bit messy eater. Clean yourself up." He laughed.

Liam accepted the box and pulled out a double sheet. As he started to wipe himself off, he looked to the British officer and asked, "What's happening to me, Sam? What happened last night?" He paused. "What am I becoming?"

"You are not becoming anything. You already are." Sam corrected. "You seem to be a natural."

"What am I?" He realized he felt unnaturally calm in the moment.

Valko tossed a knapsack on the ground near Brand as he continued cleaning himself. He sighed deeply before speaking. "Now please do not get excited, but you are . . . one of us. You are," he paused again, offering a warm and welcoming smile, "a Lycanthrope, my friend. You've heard various names in movies and literature; werewolf or shapeshifter. Lycan if you prefer. That would be my preference. A young one, but one nonetheless."

Brand stopped cleaning and looked at Valko for clarification. "One of us, Sam? What are you talking about?"

"Lycanthropy, although generally passed down through birth, has also been found in a few rare cases to be passed through one other means: massive blood transferal, generally consensually from a lycan to a non-lycan. There are other mythical methods mentioned in literature, of course. But I've only ever heard of this being passed through blood."

The American shook his head considering the revelation. "This isn't possible. I wasn't bitten. Not really. They didn't get through my body armor." He stopped and considered his words. "What am I saying? Werewolves don't exist. Am I having some psychotic episode, probably brought on by PTSD? Or . . ."

Valko placed a hand gently on his shoulder. "I thought we were beyond this discussion point. You have personally met and fought several. This wasn't in casual passing; you saw them up close and personal. Plus, I did say it was through blood transfer, not through bite or scratch like in some movies."

Brand continued to remain calm, going through the events in his mind. His eyes lifted and he queried, "The shot you gave me?"

"To be precise, Special Agent Watson administered the shot, and I assure you, it wasn't the shot. In most cases, the shot staves off the worst effects."

"Do I change? Did you see me? Am I dangerous? And what effects does the shot fix? Why didn't it work? Why didn't it stop me from this?" His comments although one after the other came in a calm, even tone.

Valko pointed to the knapsack. "I brought you a set of your clothes and your identification, too. I had my men run by your living quarters after you left and I followed you. I stayed a distance back downwind to let you run. You are quite agile. My men brought me your clothing and are waiting up the highway. We felt it best you and I chat. Less imposing just one on one."

Brand began to open his mouth and Valko held up a hand. "I'll answer your questions, Liam, just hear me out please. We have a bit to cover and I shall try to be thorough. Unlike you, I was born into this. I, too, am a Lycan. My family is many generations, going back to early Roman invasions into Britannia. My father was a Lycan and my grandfather too. So for me, it was natural and accepted within my family."

Liam continued to listen calmly while he cleaned himself up and pulled clothing from the knapsack. The British officer continued. "It was impossible to tell when we first met. You had yet to begin to change. It affects one on the cellular level. As it advanced within you, I could start to sense it about you."

"Do I get all furry?" He slipped a shirt on. "Those creatures that attacked us: Lycans? Did I look like them? And . . . am I a danger?"

"I watched you when you left your building last night. You haven't changed yet; at least not fully. You looked like you, only with an edge. You haven't matured enough to shift fully. And yes, those creatures that attacked you are lycans. It is possible you will take on their appearance if they are the ones who made you. You mentioned the other: the silver lycan. It's also possible you'll take on an appearance similar to him, but in the end you will look like you . . . or rather, you will be distinct in your appearance, if that makes sense."

"As to whether you are dangerous, yes and no. In time, you will develop control over this gift. But until then, we need to keep an eye on you. The trouble with not being born to it, your body is changing abruptly and it can have both physical and psychological challenges."

"Why do I lose control at night? And how do I get control over this?" Brand interrupted.

Sam smiled. "You go to sleep and the primal side of you takes over. Your inner instincts want to hunt. Lord knows they want to do much more, but you are just getting into this and you have to adjust. Once you master yourself, you'll be able to change at whim and you will not be running about at night unless you desire. There really is something to a late night hunt, though."

"As for how do you get control over this? I do not know for you."

"But you said you are one?" Brand protested. "How did you get control?"

"I was born to it." He shrugged. "When I turned of age, which for me was when I was around fourteen, I started feeling the urges and my father took me in hand; my grandfather and great grandfather too. All three gentlemen took me to the woods and explained it. They explained my desire to hunt, and all the other urges that a young pup goes through. And by the end of the summer, I had it under control."

"Ok. What about the vaccine? Can you give me another shot? Double it?"

"I'm sorry, Liam. The vaccine isn't a cure and certainly not after you've begun the change." Again he sighed. "It counters the intense internal affects as the body becomes accustomed to lycanthropic blood. It also helps take the edge off the . . . mental stress of this. If you hadn't been . . . predisposed for want of a better term, the vaccine would have simply reduced the overall pain the body initially suffers as it becomes accustomed. Without the vaccine, there are two options: lycanthropy or painful death. Most will change but there are a few who are allergic to our genes and it's not what you could call pretty. For them, the change is much more painful and tends to leave them with a severe case of post-traumatic stress to put it in terms you might understand. This is also sometimes the case when a more powerful or possibly elder lycan passes their blood. It's sometimes too much for a body to accept."

"How often are people infected?" Brand asked.

"There are effectively two accepted thoughts on the subject. In most cases, an individual willingly elects to become a lycan. A man or woman develops a relationship with one of us and readily accepts our gift to join a pack. In those cases, the individual will accept a transfusion from an Alpha, who becomes their maker. This is a fairly rare occasion, as the pack is involved in the decision and it isn't taken lightly."

"Even more rare would be an unwilling recipient of our blood, or someone who steals our blood to gain the transformation. As you can imagine, we are kind of possessive of our blood." He smiled. "Even more unfathomable, one who receives a massive amount of blood in combat from a wounded lycan, like you apparently did. That is, to be rather brutally honest, unheard of. You are exceptionally unique." He nodded as if in approval.

"There are very few instances of lycans combating non-lycans as a means for the blood transfer. It obviously has happened, hence the old wives' tales, but the battle is always one-sided in our favor. Of those attacks, there are even fewer instances where the non-lycan survives. As a people, we are rather superb at combat. We are considerably stronger, much faster and our constitution is rather impressive. Any lycans out of their teens are by nature quite proficient. Of the recorded events between lycans and non-lycans, non-lycan survivors hardly ever do any real damage to lycans and hence little blood transfer. I would imagine though, if there were a significant enough transfer of blood, they would become lycan. I've never encountered any individual who became lycan as you did. Nor has Watson, who has found you to be extremely interesting as a test subject."

"The vaccine staves off most of the impact and pain of the initial body accepting. Being born into this, our bodies accept this life gradually from birth and it's as natural as you growing through puberty to adulthood, which can still be somewhat painful physically and emotionally. But for someone like you, your body is accepting the transformation over a short, rapid and painful period. Like going through puberty in a matter of days as opposed to a year or two. In a few rare cases, where such a small amount of blood transferred, the vaccine has been known to reverse the effects and beyond an increased sexual drive and desire to eat more red meat, they never fully become lycan, but there is speculation the recipient was not going to accept the transformation regardless of the serum."

"My body armor kept that creature's teeth and blood off of me." Brand argued.

Valko shook his head. "It doesn't work like that, Liam. I've told you, it's not in the saliva or by a claw like in the movies. It's in our blood, and it has to be a substantial amount. A drop or two more than likely won't have any effect other than to cause a localized infection or fever. But you and Special Agent Minos were covered in their blood. It saturated your body armor and seeped into your skins. And you . . . well, from all we can determine, your Maker is considerably older and more powerful than any lycan we've ever encountered. Even if there were an actual vaccine that could reverse the effects, it's possible his blood was too powerful. The vaccine may have saved your life. Or, you may just be predisposed to lycanthropy."

"I'm sorry, but what does that mean, Sam?"

The British officer sighed, taking his time to consider his words. "This is just supposition on my part, but your family line may have lycan blood in it from generations ago. Married into or out of a family of lycans, and you might have a recessive genetic trait waiting to awaken. Like I said, most lycans are born to this life. Very few members are made, so in this area I am not the most knowledgeable. Our reproduction is rather limited, but our lifespan is impressively long, so it balances out. My great grandfather, Caderyn Valko for example, appears to be a man in his late fifties with the same jet black hair common in the Valko lineage."

"My great grandfather married a lycan. Likewise, my grandfather and father both married lycans. In my bloodline for the past four or five generations, each generation has had only one child, with the exception of my grandfather, who had two sons. I've heard of lycans marrying outside the bloodlines, and from those unions there is a chance the children will be blessed one way or the other. For us it is far from a curse."

"The vaccine was developed in the United Kingdom and only works to assist in preventing much of the pain of the initial acceptance if administered shortly after the transfer of blood. As you have felt first hand, the transformation starts almost immediately. I've never heard of the vaccine being used on anyone accepting our gift from an elder lycan, but typically elders don't offer their blood. I've heard rumors from my great grandfather of ancient lycans that still appear from time to time, but most of us believed them to be old wives' tales. Again, being honest, if an ancient did pass you this gift, I have no earthly idea the total effects. Further, although I've never met an actual ancient, I would have assumed that the blood of an ancient would be too much for anyone to survive, with or without the vaccine. So you, my friend, are anomaly."

"How many?" Brand asked, looking up. "How many are there and how come no one knows about you? Or . . . us?"

Valko laughed. "Obviously the myths are based somewhat in reality, so we have been seen and heard. But over the centuries we've kept to ourselves. We minimize the public's knowledge of us. We live in cloisters and enjoy life. Or packs may be a better term. I work for the Queen and country. And I couldn't tell you how many, but from time to time we've had events that reduce our numbers, like any predatory creatures. At certain levels of the government, they are aware of our existence. And obviously there are others who know about us, but overall, we exist as old wives tales and science has made the belief in lycanthropy silly."

"How many are like me? Made?"

"There's no way to know exactly, but today the numbers would be drastically low, at least in Europe. I would say most of those made are welcomed into the family of their own choice. That would be why we made the vaccine, to assist those coming into the pack to reduce the initial pains of transformation and to offset any allergic reaction. Today, very few if any normal persons perish from the transformation."

"So people chose this? Why?"

"I don't know. The same reason any man or woman joins another family or changes religion. Love would be the initial response. My uncle fell in love with a normal woman of England and revealed himself to her before they were married. She accepted him and loved him and ultimately joined the pack. Her body accepted the gift and she became one of us. He was an Alpha and became her maker. Of course, joining through his blood bound them closer than you can imagine. She would tell us when I was younger how she could see how much my uncle loved her in her dreams. I don't have that bond as I was born to it, but I've heard you have the visions of your Maker when you are given the gift through transferal."

"You, however, are a true rarity. You mention your dreams and it sounds as if you are remembering times from your Maker. If those truly are his dreams from his life, then he is considerably older than any lycan I have met. To imagine an ancient has existed beyond a few hundred years is hard to believe, but one who is well over a few thousand is impossible."

Brand took in a deep breath and sighed. "This is a lot to take in. How dangerous am I?"

"For now, let us just set up watch. You can be dangerous and I have no idea how long you may be in this stage."

"What stage is that?"

Sam chuckled. "Adolescence shifting to puberty. You are almost the equivalent of a teenager, and I do not envy you for what you are about to experience. My god that was a painful spot in my life."

"What do you mean you don't know how long this stage will be? How long does it normally last?"

Again, Valko shrugged nonchalantly. "For me, it lasted through my teenage years, but my father was there to mentor me and I grew up in a lycan community. I am most certain you could say the same about your teenage years.

But considering you are not a teenager, I have no idea how you will react to this situation. The best I could guess, the sooner you get yourself under control, the better. Otherwise, you might find yourself chasing more than goats at night. You may find yourself howling after a few skirts, and we cannot have that, can we? As for my teen years, I at least had the fortune of living around other lycans, to include females my own age, so it made some transitions easier."

"I find this all hard to believe, Sam." He shook his head. "I mean, I saw those creatures who attacked me. I wasn't making them up; but this is . . .a lot. How do you expect me to believe?"

Valko sat back and pointed to the dead goat. "I would say your night time behavior is an indicator, my friend. But if you require additional proof . . ." He sighed and started to unbutton his uniform blouse. "Just do not run. I shall make this quick, but do not run. I would hate to have to chase you for fear some local would see us."

As he lay the uniform aside neatly, he slipped off his t-shirt and seemed to tense. His eyes took on a look of anguish and he let out a deep breath. He leaned forward and planted his palms in the sand and his shoulders broadened ever so slightly.

Suddenly and quite rapidly, his face began to change. His nose and chin began to elongate and form into the muzzle of a creature as he began to sprout hair along his chin line flowing up his cheeks. His brow and forehead began to pull back and his ears began to extend. Within seconds his face had taken the form of a wolf, with dark black fur to match his hair color and large, white canines. A light grey streak ran down his chin and throat. Fur sprang from his skin all over, with a darker streak down the back of his neck disappearing between his shoulder and down his back. His fingers extended and his nails thickened and sharpened, digging into the sand.

Brand sat transfixed, unable to move as he faced the hybrid half-man half-wolf before him. He felt his heart rate skyrocket and the blood pounding in his ears. And underneath it, he felt his senses reaching out and he could feel Valko's pulse and smelled the Major's musky sent across the short distance.

As suddenly as the transformation had happened, it reversed. In seconds, Major Samuel Valko sat before Liam again; his face human and smooth. Liam found he had fallen back from the scene, yet had been fascinated by the incredible alteration.

When he found he could talk again, he sat forward. "Ok, I guess I'm somewhat convinced . . . or totally insane. Now what?"

Sam extended his hand. "Welcome to the family, Liam. You are in for quite a ride."

Brand accepted the grip and could not quite grasp the emotions coursing through him. He had so many questions.

"What will this be like?"

Valko shrugged and then grinned with a wink. "You won't be some slavering Lon Chaney from the movies.

You'll be you, but much more. It can be a gift if you embrace it and you don't let it overcome who you are. We all need a guide up the path and through the change. Your maker would normally be the one. If you hear a calling from him, you might consider answering. Otherwise, we can try to assist you. Initially, you'll find you are two distinct creatures. As you evolve, you'll become just one."

"As for what you'll look like. Normally you take on the appearance of your parents. In your case, I'm guessing you'll take on the appearance of your maker. Do you recall what he looked like?"

"Lean. Silver or white. Not quite like a wolf. More like a jackal if that makes sense. But . . . I don't know. Elegant. Regal."

Valko considered the description for a moment and murmured. "Hmm."

"What about Minos? How did she fare?"

Sam shook his head as he leaned down to pick up his t-shirt and blouse. "We don't know. Your NCIS agents took her away shortly after the third day. We were able to administer the vaccine to her, and Agent Watson gave her a double booster the second day. But when we returned on day three, your agents Huang and Wong refused to let us near her. Even your Colonel Pinson was in dismay. I would bank on those other agents knowing her current where about though. I have had Watson keeping tabs on all outgoing flights, and unless they snuck her out, Minos is still in Kuwait. Although I wouldn't place her being here long."

"Then seeing as she's still my charge until further ordered, I guess I'll need to interview those agents. Care to join me?"

"Wouldn't miss it for the world, Liam. I rather look forward to our next meeting with them." Sam smiled and Brand continued dressing. "But I will warn you: those two aren't NCIS and they aren't normal."

"Are they lycans?"

"No, Liam. They are a completely different sort of monster." He sighed. "But one we may have to ally with, so we must tread carefully."

He stopped midway as he pulled on his t-shirt. "What about the moon? Will I be affected by the moon?"

Valko shook his head, chuckling yet again. "Old gypsy tale. Truth is, once you master control, you can change whenever you desire. Night or day; morning or midnight; regardless of the moon. As it were, many young lycans would run around at night, and when there was a full moon, they were seen. I guess we lycans are a romantic lot, and cannot help but feel the same pull of the moon as the normal men. Obviously, it is much easier to see someone with a full moon overhead then when it is pitch black. And I'm guessing most were young pups, not too cautious."

The Major pulled a cell phone from his pocket and hit one button. Shortly he spoke into the receiver. "Pull the Hummer up. We shall be taking a short drive."

As Liam tied up his boots, he followed Valko with his eyes as he stood. "Where does lycanthropy come from?"

Sam looked down and shrugged. "Great mystery of life, my friend. I do not know. Neither did my father or great grandfather. Perhaps you can ask your Maker." He smiled and the HUMVEE arrived with Williams driving and Fergus sitting passenger in the front.

"Where to, sir?" He asked leaning through the open window.

Looking to Brand, Valko grinned. "To chat with Senior Agent Huang. Any idea where he is?"

"Certainly, sir. We've kept track of his movements, as ordered. He has an office on Arifjan. Do you care about his assistant?"

"Not at the moment. Drive on." Both Brand and Valko climbed in the back seat.

Looking in the rearview mirror at Brand, Williams grinned. "Watson is going to be quite gutted that she wasn't here when you told the Seppo he was one of us. I would not want to be you when she finds out Major."

Valko snickered and shook his head. "Yes, well, she'll be a bit engrossed in chatting up our good pup and what he's going through, so I've faith her anger towards me will be short lived and quite rapidly replaced with a different, more intense focus."

Williams laughed. "Poor Yank. I wouldn't want to be on the end of her microscope when she goes research on you."

"Are all four of you . . . werewolves?" Brand asked, looking from Williams to Churchill to Valko.

Young Williams grinned and the Major nodded. "Yes. The Crown sent us out when we heard word of potential supernatural events occurring. We operate as a small, select Special Operation for Her Majesty."

"Wow." The American muttered, pausing to consider. Looking back up, he spoke. "You mentioned events that reduce your numbers. What events?"

"Although we consider ourselves at the top of our food chain, from time to time, we have found ourselves at odds with others. We've kept to ourselves and hidden from society the past few centuries due to normal men often purging our numbers out of fear. From time to time, we suffered pack wars, but that hasn't occurred in a generation at least. At least not in Europe." Glancing to Williams, he nodded.

Churchill looked over his shoulder at Brand and grunted "Buckle up."

Fergus turned and his grin widened. "Welcome to the pack."

The doors shut and the HUMVEE spit up sand and rocks as it kicked into gear, cutting across the desert towards the roads that would take them towards the American military base.

The HUMVEE pulled up to Arifjan and they passed through the gate. By the time they had arrived, Brand had his armband on indicating he was security and was properly dressed in uniform.

Churchill drove the HUMVEE through the base towards tents centrally located, just beyond the hard-shell gymnasium. He pulled up near a black Toyota Pathfinder and parked.

"Shall I accompany, sir?"

"No, thank you Cedric. I think it best that Liam and I handle this. Hopefully we will have some privacy and his assistant won't be in. Although I do not favor Huang, his assistant is a cold yet hot one and quick to draw her weapons."

"I've noticed. You're going to have to explain to me what kind of monster she is?" Brand commented.

Valko laughed as they exited the armored vehicle. "One monster a day, Liam. You've already had your world shaken a bit once today."

"True, but it might be tactically expedient to know what I'm walking into."

They entered the tent, a medium sized DRASH with two office desks towards the front, with two areas sectioned off towards the rear for two cots and living areas, although only one appeared to have been used.

Sitting at the second desk was Special Agent Huang, his eyes upon the entrance flaps as if he had anticipated their arrival.

"Please do come in, by all means, Major." He spoke, almost pleasantly as if the earlier exchanges had not occurred. "And Commander, a pleasure to see you again."

"Thank you, Special Agent." Valko replied very cordially. "It is special agent, correct? NCIS?"

Huang waved his hand towards two folding chairs near his desk as if to offer both men a seat. "Please join me."

"Will do, sir. But forgive me if I jump right into our business. Where is Special Agent Minos?"

Huang waited for both men to sit and then locked his eyes on Brand's eyes. He held them transfixed for a few silent moments, smiling pleasantly. And then his lips parted and Brand barely made out the slightly elongated canines. As he did, he felt his mind slowing, as if caught in cobwebs.

"You seem different, Commander Brand." Huang stated as a matter of fact. "Almost . . . lupine if I were to qualify it."

Valko started to move as if to stand and Huang held up his palm, swinging his eyes on the British officer. "Please. We are being polite right now. I wanted to know what I was facing and I believe I know. Does he know is the question?"

"As of this morning, yes. We weren't quite certain."

Huang shook his head as if enjoying a great joke. "Yes you were. You just weren't in a mind to share. So he's transforming."

Brand shook his head to clear his mind and looked to Valko before returning his eyes to Huang. "Whatever you are, stay out of my mind!"

"No offense meant, Commander. Just trying to assess your threat. Now, you had asked a question. Minos is fine. We've shipped her home, back to the states."

"What's her status?" Brand asked.

"Probably the same as yours. I am not certain, nor was that my primary concern. Our current threat is a pack of lycanthropes hunting in Kuwait. I am quite impressed that you survived your initial encounter with them."

"Thank you. No offense, but my concern is Minos. Where is she going and how is she being helped?"

"Excellent question." Valko piped in. "As you can see, I may be in a better position to support any questions she is bound to have."

"She'll be taken care of once she arrives in DC. As you can imagine, you British do not hold a monopoly on . . . well, the underworld." He smiled politely.

Valko growled under his breath, "I would concur regarding a monopoly on the underworld. That is entirely your kingdom."

Huang laughed and shook his head as if scolding a child. "No need to be rude. We are getting along quite famously now and making progress."

Brand felt more at ease and sat back. "So you aren't really NCIS, correct?"

Huang shook his head. "Suffice it to say I do represent the government, but just at a different level. No I am not NCIS. I'm in an organization that reports outside normal chains. Rumors surfaced of . . . super-natural incidents . . . if that description captures the situation properly. We were already traveling when the report came through of your attack. I wasn't expecting Major Valko and his team when we first met, so when I sensed his presence, I initially thought he may have been my target. But I quickly dismissed him as our adversary. He did have a bit of animosity towards us, though and that was a bit disconcerting."

"My apologies, Senior Agent." Valko responded, nodding acquiescently. "I was as much taken back by your arrival as you were by mine. And you'll understand if we perhaps are apprehensive of each other. I'm not even remotely used to friendly terms between . . . well, our kinds."

Huang gave a polite nod. "So I have heard. And I've experienced in the past. Needless to say, we are working together and recommend we comport ourselves professionally. At least until this event is fully realized and dealt with."

Valko nodded and stood to extend his hand. "I concur, Senior Agent Huang. It will be a unique experience and hopefully pleasure to work with you."

"Likewise, Major Valko. And as a show of faith, I'll make every attempt to discover Special Agent's condition and report back to you when I can."

....

Prim had already enjoyed his morning coffee and smoke as he made his way to the armory. He pulled both his and Brand's weapons from the armory and took them outside to benches set up for cleaning, to include two M-9 semi-automatic handguns and two M-4 machine guns. The armory also had a metal dunk tank for soaking larger weapons and cleaning parts near the wooden benches located outside the structure.

Prim set up on the first bench and had disassembled one M-4, cleaned it and reassembled it when Chief Timmons approached. "Mind if I join you, Dean? I've got to clean my long guns." He dropped his M-16 with 204 on the underbelly.

"Please. The more the merrier."

"So how's the Commander?" He slung a knapsack onto the wooden bench and started to strip the weapon.

Prim pushed cleaning supplies across the tabletop, offering to share. "Doing better. He's got me worried."

"How so?" Timmons asked, starting to wipe sand and grime from the parts.

The thinner Chief shrugged. "Too many things have happened in a short amount of time. It's a long story but kind of hard to take in without at least a pot of coffee or a bottle of Jack."

"I hear your Commander enjoys Crown Royal." It was as much a question as a statement as he gestured towards the knapsack.

Prim placed the barrel of his M-4 down and opened the knapsack. He smiled, "To what does he owe this? And I'll offer now that he appreciates it."

"Give him my thanks. We appreciated being invited to the adventure. That's from me specifically, but my team feels appreciated already."

Prim cinched the knapsack closed and nodded. "I'll pass on your regards. And I'll probably help him empty it. Lord knows he's causing me to drink." He winked.

"Ok, Dean. What's next?"

"Canvas the neighborhood. And I do mean on base. We've probably got a rat onboard of the two-legged variety.

Have your boys hit the three main bases and ask around: Anyone out of the ordinary or peculiar. Any Third Country National who just looks out of place. And just because I don't trust no-one, see if there are any of our troops who fall outside the norm."

"We can do that. I'll send my boys out first thing. I'll have them look for any of the hajis that appear suspect. We can probably scout out today and get a preliminary report tonight. I've got some of my boys running to the other bases to get supplies."

"Have them eyeball everyone. U.S. forces too. Especially the MPs on this installation." Prim stated.

"MPs? What makes you think it's one of them? Have you hit your head? I mean again? Those guys seem to be on our side. Always pretty decent to us considering they're Army."

Prim laughed and shook his head. "Never trust the friendly hooker. You never know what she wants. Always go for the angry one. You know she's just there for the money, and the sooner you have your happy ending, the sooner she gets paid."

"Eloquent words from the sage. We'll keep an eye on friendlies too. But just remember: maybe the hooker just likes sex."

"That's never been my experience. Normally, she wants more money."

Both men laughed and Timmons quickly went through the components of the machine gun he had disassembled. The weapon was fairly clean as he wiped it with a small cloth and CLP oil. "I'll check in for a daily update." He began to reassemble the weapon. "If I hear anything, I'll let you know. Dzigeleski and Parker will be on their way to the other bases shortly, hitting Ash Shuyeba and Arifjan. I'll have them scout out and get a tally on TCN activity. We've got a few trusted Army and Navy security forces at both bases who we can ask to give us the straight skivvy. I'll let you know what we hear, but it might take them a few days. Oh, and don't forget to give your commander his Crown."

"Thanks." Prim responded and gave a mock look of pain. "I'm hurt, Chief. Don't you know me by now?" He patted the knapsack.

Timmons shook his head. "Yeah, I do. Which is why I'm considering taking the Crown back and giving it to him myself. I'll talk to you later."

Timmons set the cleaned and assembled weapon down on the bench and turned to depart. As he did, Prim's cell phone rang. He flipped the phone and barked, "Yellow! What's up sir?"

Brand's voice echoed across the line. "We need to talk. Where are you?"

"Cleaning weapons at the armory. Timmons just left and his boys will keep a look out for us. What's up?"

"I'll see you at the building. My life just got a whole lot more interesting and complicated."

"On my way in about fifteen minutes, sir. Let me finish and reassemble your M-4, although I don't know why I clean it. You can't shoot worth a shit. Hold tight."

He heard Brand laugh and then respond. "Great. That gives me time enough to shower."

Prim couldn't help but laugh out loud himself. "Seriously, sir? Your showers last longer than a porn movie. I can finish cleaning all the weapons in the armory and still have time to smoke one."

"Ha-ha. I'll make it quick."

The Chief snapped his cellphone shut as he chuckled and continued cleaning the weapons.

Prim met Brand in the courtyard of their building, returning from the showers in his shower shoes, shorts and t-shirt with towel hung over his shoulder. Prim followed him to his room and shut the door behind them as they entered.

Prim held out the knapsack. "Gift from Chief Timmons. Said thanks for bringing his team along. Most fun they've had since they arrived."

Brand unzipped the bag and glanced inside. Nodding, he zipped it shut. "We can drink it later. Send him my best, if you haven't already. And give him something in return. Lord knows I think we'll be using him again."

"I've got Scotch, sir. I'll take that today."

"Thanks. Now down to business. I woke up outside the fence line again. Valko was squatting nearby."

Prim shook his head. "Sir . . . we've discussed this. I thought I trained you better than that. Major Valko?"

"No." He shook his head ignoring his Chief's humor. "But all these changes overcoming me . . . the large white creature that saved us the first night: they are connected. His blood washed into my body armor and into my skin. It managed to get into my wounds and there was enough of it that I'm . . . affected. Apparently he is my maker."

"Affected or infected? And what is your maker? And what the fuck? Seriously! I mean, we both knew something was going on. But I thought maybe you had a case of the rabies. Do you turn all shaggy and shit?" He sat in a chair in the corner of the room.

Brand shook his head as he hung his towel from a rack on the end of his top bunk. "I don't know. I haven't been awake, or aware, when it happens. But I think yes, something like that will happen. I had another intense dream and I need your help. In my dream I was leading an army defending Lycopolis against an Army of elephants. I had with me at least one hundred werewolves and an army of Egyptians. I think this really happened."

Prim looked squarely in his Officer's eyes. "Ok. We've been having some strange shit happen lately, so I'm in. You said Lycopolis? Got it. Is that a city?"

Brand nodded. "Lycopolis was an ancient city along the Egyptian borders, if my geography is correct. It was the city of wolves, according to legend. But that's about all I recall. If you can, check online. I'll see what I can find as well, but when you're not surfing porn, you're actually quite good at finding information for me."

"Just think how good I'd be if I didn't have porn to distract me, sir?" Prim winked. "Now, back to your maker. Seriously, what the fuck is that?"

Brand shrugged and sank down to sit on the edge of his lower bunk, looking at his hands. "He would be the one whose blood infected me. The creature we saw that first night. The one you shot."

The Chief took this information into consideration for a moment before nodding. "Ok. I've seen the movies. Do we have to hunt him down and kill him or something to break the curse? We're going to need bigger fire power than we have."

It was Brand's turn to smile as he shook his head. "Sorry, Chief. I think there's no going back. Valko told me it's a cellular level. And I doubt he meant for this to happen to me. Although Valko and the others don't see this as a curse."

"I've been sleep-walking at night as this is overcoming me, and the Brits are all werewolves, too." He watched Prim for his reaction.

The Chief simply smirked. "Well, I always knew you were a bit of a horndog hidden underneath all that officer's trappings, so it doesn't surprise me about you that much; but the Brits? I can see the young Scot maybe, but what would the female be like I wonder?" The Chief tried to hide a sarcastic smirk.

Brand watched him for a moment as the Chief sat back. "That's it? You're ok? I mean, the revelation wasn't too much? I'm still in fucking shock."

Prim leaned back and laced his fingers behind his head. "I figure from what I've seen of you lately and your antics, if this explains it, then they being werewolves isn't that far fetched. And I figured something was up after the attack. Those weren't dogs, and I wrapped my head around something weird pretty early."

He took in a deep breath and sighed. "And it makes sense them being dog soldiers." He grinned. "So, how would you do it with the girl? Is that like doggy style?"

Brand took in a deep breath and exhaled loudly. "Leave it to you to normalize everything around sex."

Prim pulled a pack of cigarettes from his front pocket and chuckled. "We all have our strengths, sir. I'm just glad I'm not in this alone. Otherwise I'd think I was crazy."

Standing, the Chief pulled a single cigarette from the pack. "I'll head back to my hooch and check online regarding that wolf city. Egypt right?"

Brand nodded. "After I change, I'll look it up as well. Shall we meet up for lunch? I think I'm not up for schwarma today, so how about the DFAC?"

Prim nodded. "I'll keep my coffee in hand, just in case."

Brand smiled. "I've got it under control. These late night runs have helped."

"Hey, I'm not judging. But I also see how you're starting to affect the ladies. Coffee might not just be for you." He winked and was out the door.

As lunch arrived, Brand found his way to the DFAC and flashed his ID card as he entered. A young Army female enlisted lifted a hand counter and clicked it as he entered. She smiled at him.

He moved to the line, taking a tray and plate. He offered the plate to the worker behind the counter and pointed to the vegetables. The Middle Eastern worker smiled and spooned the vegetables on the plate.

"Yes, sir. Next item?"

Brand glanced down the counter and thought a moment. "I'll take pasta with meat sauce, and can you throw on a few Italian sausages and onions?"

Again the worker smiled and piled the pasta and food on his plate. "Garlic bread?"

"Not today. Thanks." He took the plate and made his way to the tables.

Glancing around, he found Prim in the far corner sitting with Chief Timmons. He made his way to them and slid next to them. "Greetings gentlemen."

"Sir." Timmons acknowledged. "How's your day been?"

"Don't ask." Prim responded for him. "Sir, you are going to be amazed at what I found out."

Brand poured a mass of grated cheese on his pasta. "I already am. Tell me what you found. It'll probably confirm what I think I know."

His Chief sat back. "Sometime BC, there was in fact a Nubian army encroaching upon the city of Lycopolis. I think the numbers had them outweighing the Egyptians. Legend has it that dogs saved the day and were the cause of the Egyptian victory but that's a modern rendition of what may have happened. History has a burial site dedicated to dogs or Egyptian wolves near Lycopolis, putting them in a place of honor similar to Pharaohs. Your city was the city of Wepwawet or something like that. He was an Egyptian god of war."

Timmons sipped a cup of coffee and looked between the two. "What's the homework? What's this history lesson have to do with us?"

Brand looked up with a mouthful of pasta and swallowed. "We're looking into the terrorist group we're dealing with. All facets. The Sons of Anubis may be inspired by the Egyptian gods, so we're looking at others. Anubis is a wolf god."

Prim nodded. "Nice." He winked at Brand. "Anyhow, seems to support what you were asking about. There is some veracity to your . . . images."

"Thanks." Brand responded. "I don't know if that's comforting or concerning. And when did you start using big words?"

A cell phone chimed and all three reached for their pockets before Prim could answer. Brand pulled his phone out and his eyes went wide with amusement. Looking to Prim, he held it up for both Chief's to read. "Major Valko sent me a warning. Apparently Special Agent Watson is on her way to find me."

Prim looked to Timmons and shook his head. Timmons laughed as he stood, picking up his tray. "That's cryptic. And my cue to run. I'll catch you later, sir."

Prim chuckled. "I'll go along with my Commander to our hardshell and I'll stop by later to chat, Chief." Looking to Brand he continued. "But once Watson gets there, you're on your own." He winked.

Chapter 10

Running the Blood

Brand smelled her before he came around the corner of the building as he approached his room. He could taste Siohvan in the air as she sat in a folding beach chair in his way. He slowed, lowering the body armor he had carried slung over his shoulder, heat rising and his breathing coming sharp. She wore tight running shorts and a British Marine t-shirt with crimson Vibram running shoes.

"Greetings, Captain." Brand called as she came into sight.

She stalked across the courtyard straight to the two men, eyes narrowing upon Brand. "Hello, Commander. I've been briefed about your . . . " She glanced at Prim for a moment before turning back to Brand and finishing her statement, "situation."

"Hey, Captain." Prim waved as if seeing her for the first time. He winked. "I'm on the inner circle. My Commander trusts me so you don't have to talk in code. I'm aware of his condition, so I'm here for him."

Glancing between the two, Watson acknowledged with a curt nod. "Then you'll understand that I may wish to speak with him about his condition with a little privacy."

Prim chuckled. "Love the way you Brits says stuff like "privacy" and make it sound so formal, yet at the same time naughty."

Watson blushed with a gasp and turned away. "I assure you, Chief, my request for privacy is completely in consideration of Commander Brand's feelings."

"No worries, Captain. I'm off to watch some Team America. That's a great comedy. Have you seen it?"

She shook her head.

Prim pulled a cigarette and spoke to Brand. "You'll let me know if she's dedicated, sir?"

"I am absolutely dedicated, Chief." She retorted to the question, failing to catch their inside joke.

Brand shook his head, looking from the Chief back to Siovhan. "Not in the way he is asking." He tried to cast a disapproving glare at Prim but barely hid his mirth. "I'll let her watch my copy of the movie so she can catch up."

"Great." Prim mocked exasperation, looking up and shaking his head. "Just give me a head start when she's halfway through the movie so I can turn myself over to a terrorist cell. At least I know they'll only torture me before they behead me."

Agent Watson glanced back and forth between the two men before glaring at the Chief. "Why do I fail to sense I will be amused by your humor, Chief?"

"Good instincts, I'm guessing, Ma'am." He winked at her and took a long gulp of his coffee.

She attempted to hide her own grin but failed as she turned a blushing face down away from the two men.

As she heard Prim departing, Siovhan leaned closer to Brand and whispered, "Ok, I'm dying to know. What does dedication have to do with me?"

Brand smiled and whispered back. "I'll let you borrow the movie. It's a comedy, but during a specific scene, the hero must prove his dedication to rejoin the team."

"Oh? And this is funny somehow?"

Brand shrugged. "Well, considering to prove his dedication he has to provide services, sort of like the ultimate show of dedication to the team."

"Well, that doesn't seem so bad. What kind of services?"

Brand leaned in just a bit closer and whispered under his breath, "He must provide another male a blow job. The ultimate sacrifice."

Her mouth gaped open with a startled look, her eyes opening wide and then narrowing to a glare. Her continence softened as she giggled. "He is a little miscreant, isn't he? I think I will borrow that film, thank you. And you can warn him in advance, I may put him on my short list of prey."

They both laughed.

"Now, Captain. To what do I owe this pleasure?" He smiled, narrowing his eyes as he acted beyond his own control.

"Well, Commander, I did not feel it was exactly fair, you having to suffer this without the support of a community. Most of us have several dens to watch over us, and normally at least a few pups our own age to run with when we go through this."

He smiled and felt the heat roll through his head making him quite light-headed. "I appreciate your concern, Agent Watson. Feel free to call me Liam."

"On one condition, Commander." She stepped closer to him and he could feel her pulse quickening to keep pace with his own as he saw the pupils of her eyes dilate. He had a deep and sudden urge to reach out for her.

"What . . ." His voice was lost in a hoarse whisper and he quickly corrected himself. "What is that?"

"Call me Siohvan; at least when we're in private. In public, we should respect the rules of propriety."

He took in a deep breath and attempted to calm himself, clearing his head, but it only managed to shift through some of the dizziness. His breath was short as he replied, "I can do that."

"Good." She smiled genuinely. "Then I propose we go for a run. Care to throw on your jogging gear?"

"Certainly. Just give me a few minutes. How far are we running?"

"That depends, Liam. How fast do you believe you can catch me?" There was a husky tone in her voice, almost cutting with an animal's growl. "Your Chief wasn't entirely off about my request for privacy. I just don't wish to give him credit."

Brand gulped audibly and could barely hide his smile. He was in and out of his room in minutes, wearing running shorts, desert brown under armor t-shirt and his black Vibrams.

"By the way, I like your choice in shoes." He smiled, pointing to her feet.

She lifted her right foot to show off the five-finger running shoes in blazing red. With a wolfish grin, she snarled. "I wear these, or nothing at all."

They stood so close that the energy popped between them, drawing them closer. She stepped even closer; sniffing at him and eyeing his neck and chin.

"So, here's the plan, Liam. We are going for a run, as long and as hard as possible. The plan is to run you into the ground so you sleep peacefully tonight. We need to boil off your blood." She leaned in closer, her lips near his ear breathing hot. "And the prize: You catch me, you get me."

His eyes turned down to meet hers and they locked. "Do you get a head start or can I just grab you now?" He felt himself falling towards her.

She pulled back, pushing his chest and moving towards the break in the wall. "I would not need a head start. Plus, who's to say I am not intrigued by what you would do once you caught me. But you will have to earn this." She gave her hips a defiant shake.

He stopped in his tracks speechless as she continued on. He heard her giggle as she knelt near the break in the wall. "Fergus wanted to come run with you tonight, but I pulled rank. He is absolutely on to you. Thinks you are quite his hero."

Brand broke his silence by awkwardly responding. "Yeah. He's a good kid."

Once outside the wall, Siohvan looked back at him and smiled. "Just so you know, there has yet to be a wolf who can catch me. And tonight, you won't be the first."

Brand started out after her, setting his pace to warm up and take the first mile in stride. After the first mile, he picked up his speed, reaching to catch her. He gained ground, and immediately she picked up her pace, glancing back with a grin.

This went on for miles, each time he started to gain ground she would pick up her speed to stay just a few strides ahead, sometimes opening the gap enough to push him on faster. They ran for hours across the desert, she occasionally taunting him, speeding up and bursting ahead only to stop and shake her hips at him before starting up again.

Their run continued on as the evening sun began to set and they kept the gap close enough to talk about each other, asking questions and giving answers. Brand found it kept his head clear and mind on target. He talked about his life, growing up in his family with brothers and sisters. He talked about attending college and practicing martial arts, and he talked about past relationships, while at the same time Siohvan spoke about herself and even about the rest of her team. After a while, he wound up telling her more about his recent dreams to include the battle at Lycoplis and the Nubian army.

By the end of the fourth hour, Brand started to lag behind, panting and sweating. Halfway through the fifth hour, he stumbled and fell in the sand. As he knelt on hands and knees, Siohvan came back and squatted just outside his reach, grinning her wolfish grin.

"Looks like tonight you won't be claiming my prize. A shame. I thought you might be able to put that rough tongue to use on my camel's toe."

He lifted his head and growled, launching forward and snatching out towards her. His elongated fingers stretched incredibly fast, yet somehow Siohvan eluded his grasp and laughed.

"Better luck next time. Come on, Liam. We can run back to the base and you can catch some sleep."

"You run like a gazelle." He grunted, breathing hard and falling over onto his back. "You weren't even trying, were you?"

"No, not really." She crawled over next to him and lay down on her side, looking at him. "You haven't been at it long enough. Once you come in tune with yourself, you will run faster. But I warn you, I am the fastest." She reached a finger out and ran it down his chest and his abdomen.

He closed his eyes and licked his lips. "I can taste you from here. I can feel your pulse."

"It's an intoxicating rush, wouldn't you say? To tell the truth, I haven't felt this from anyone since I was a young pup and I began my change. You are quite . . . delicious."

"Thank you, I think. You aren't going to eat me, are you?" He laughed.

"Not literally, not yet." She laughed back.

Liam rolled onto his back and laced his fingers behind his head, staring up at the sky. His breathing was slowly returning to normal and he felt his pulse calming. Siohvan inched closer, placing her head on his bicep and rubbing her hip up against his. The warmth of her body was like a match that ignited a small fire, which quickly set to racing through him. Before his breathing could accelerate, she rolled onto her side and placed a hand on his chest softly and she took in a deep breath.

"You do smell good." She spoke softly. "We'll just rest here a minute before we head back."

He felt everything relax and his mind was clear. "Sounds good to me." He replied, and closed his eyes. "You have this incredibly poised exterior; but I see you slip in this extremely . . . sexually charged you."

He felt her purr deep in her chest before she playfully giggled. "I have many facets, all meant for the right time . . . and very specifically for the right person. I can be professional and prim and proper while having my hidden wanton desires. It's up to me as to who I share them with."

"I feel very honored." He grinned as he watched the sun setting.

"You should be." She poked him in his ribs lightly. "We'll rest here another bit and then head back to have dinner. Care to join me in the DFAC?"

"My pleasure." And he opened his eyes to watch the sun disappear.

....

As Prim finished his dinner, he exited the DFAC and lit a cigarette. Looking up, he watched as the sun was setting. He glanced across the base towards the waterfront and started walking towards the docks.

From the exit of the DFAC, a lone soldier followed at a distance. He was tall, lean and dark skinned and kept his eyes trained intently on Prim.

Prim swung by Timmons office on the waterfront and knocked as he entered through the wooden framed canvas door.

"What's up chief?" He called, swinging a knapsack off his shoulder and onto the table.

Timmons was in the middle of watching a war series on the large television, from which he paused with a controller and turned. "Band of Brothers. How're things?"

"My commander offers his appreciation in return." He motioned to the knapsack.

Timmons stood and crossed the tent space to the table. He opened the knapsack and a grin crossed his face. "Scotch. And the good stuff. You can tell him thanks yet again. Every time I think I square with him, he ups the ante."

Timmons pulled the bottle from the knapsack and placed it on his desk. Crossing his space, he went to a row of lockers and spun the tumbler on one. Opening the locker he pulled two glasses.

Returning to the table, he opened the new bottle of Scotch and poured two glasses. Offering one to Prim, he took a sip from his and moaned as it burned going down. "That is smooth. I'm guessing you picked it up for him. He doesn't seem like the type to know how to acquire this in country."

"You'd be right on that, Chief. But they are his sentiments."

"Thanks, Dean. Other than enjoying this bottle with you, what else can I do for you and your Commander?"

"Any word on canvasing the neighborhood? The more I think of it, the more I'm certain we've got a rat onboard of the two-legged variety. Did your boys have any luck yet? Anyone out of the ordinary or peculiar? Any Third Country National who just appears too interested or any U.S. who looks out of place?"

"I sent my boys out when I returned from lunch. They're looking for any of the hajis that appear suspect. And I had a few of the smarter ones eyeballing our own forces. What defines out of place?"

Prim sipped the scotch and breathed out. "Good stuff. I'm glad we gave this to you." He took another mouthful and swallowed, savoring the moment. "Right now I'd say anyone stepping out of their swim-lane. Especially anyone who might also be keeping an eye on my Commander or our building."

Timmons swallowed a mouthful of the scotch and murmured something unintelligible in agreement. "I'll refine their search parameters. Why would they be concerned with your Commander?"

The thin chief shook his head and took a gulp of Scotch. "Gut instinct tells me someone set us up, several times now. They would have to have inside information. We're looking into our host national friends for their leak, but it just makes more sense it came from here. Specifically, information U.S. forces might be in a better position to overhear or observe."

The larger chief nodded and stood a moment in silence. After taking another swig of scotch, he finally spoke again. "Yep. Painfully makes sense. I'll let you know if we hear anything."

Prim threw back the rest of his scotch and placed the glass on the table before turning to leave the soft-shell structure. As he swung open the wooden door, he glanced back and called. "I'll check in for a daily update. Thanks."

"You're welcome. On your way out, send in Dzigeleski and Parker. I'll pull them off the boats tonight and send them to scout around Ash Shuyeba and Arifjan. Maybe get a tally on TCN activity. We've got a few trusted Army and Navy security forces at both bases I feel safe asking to give us the straight skivvy. I'll let you know what we hear, but it might take them a few days. Oh, and did you actually give your commander his Crown?"

Looking back, Prim gave a mock look of pain. "I'm hurt, Chief. Don't you know me by now?"

Timmons shook his head. "Yeah, I do. Which is why I'm considering calling him to verify. I'll talk to you later."

As he exited, he didn't notice the young black enlisted Army soldier scurrying out of sight around the edge of the soft-shell structure.

Within the city of Kuwait, Hassem hung up his cell phone and walked into the living room of the house. Others waited, sitting around and watching television. Raseem looked up when he entered while Kumar sat back, smoking a cigarette and smiling.

"Udei's agent just informed him. The Americans are searching the base for informants. They are enlisting the aid of the waterfront crewmembers."

Raseem looked around the room at the others and back to Hassem. "Do they have any idea where to begin looking?"

The elder Son shrugged. "Does it matter? I think not. But they have become our target."

"Are you suggesting we attack them?" Kumar questioned.

Hassem thought a moment and slowly began to smile while he nodded. "Yes. As a matter of fact, tonight. And Raseem had the perfect idea of videotaping. But we'll make it easier on the Americans. We'll let them capture the event on their own equipment. They won't be able to deny us any longer."

"How so?" Kumar inquired.

Hassem poured himself a whiskey from an open bottle of Jack Daniels. "The Americans maintain video surveillance on the waterfront and on their boats. Even at night. And they capture everything on video day or night. With night vision. They'll capture it themselves. All we have to do is attack."

"How shall we attack?" Kumar asked. "Just run up to the front gate and smile?"

Raseem grinned wolfishly, looking from Kumar to Hassem. "We go in by water. I can get us a boat to take us just off the port entry. We can swim in below the lights. They won't see us until we are on them."

Hassem smiled at the younger man. "You are just full of great ideas. Call your friends and get the boat ready. I want to attack when the sun goes down."

Chapter 11

Agents of the Night

Night had fallen quickly and dark as it was the rainy season in the desert and the skies were clouded. Chief Timmons boat squad had the watch and sat in their two 32 foot patrol boats as they had on dozens of night watches. Although Timmons tried to keep his crew attentive, both boats drifted lazily in the waters protecting the Kuwait Navy Base. There was one asset to protect, a small, British transport that had recently finished loading redeploying military gear ready to head back to England.

Water lapped against the underside of the bow, further lulling the sailors into a state of lethargy and the chief lit a cigarette. "Ok, boys. Let's make a round through the harbor."

"Come on, Chief." One of the petty offices groaned. "We got nothing to watch. There aren't any high value assets to guard and no one cares about that tramp." He gestured over his shoulder towards the British ship.

"Zip it Jones. Just crank it up a notch and bring us around the harbor. You got somewhere else to be?"

The three crewmembers in the first boat laughed while the vocal petty officer took the helm of the second boat. Chief Timmons stepped up behind him, lifting a backhand as if to strike. "The grief I put up with. Burns, get up front and man the fifty."

"Aye, Chief." The third man of his crew piped, hustling up to the front of the 32-foot boat and gripping the M2 machine gun mounted on the bow. Two more fifties armed the sides of the boats, with one MK-19 40mm grenade launcher mounted on the fantail.

His boat started forward but was quickly overtaken by the first boat as the chief scanned the fairly calm harbor. Timmons felt the calm across the harbor and let out a long drag of smoke. It was a quiet night.

Chief Timmons almost smiled when it suddenly hit him and stole the color from his face: a gnawing feeling in the pit of his stomach lit his nerves on fire. Every watch he had stood had been quiet, even the night watches with poor weather and sand storms; but this night was different. The air wasn't just quiet; it was virtually silent, as if the very harbor was holding its breath.

"Shit!" He grumbled, moving to the starboard gun. "Look alive!" He barked loud.

The sailors in the first boat did not hear the chief as their 32-foot patrol boat cut across the harbor and their engines drowned out his voice. The chief reached up and keyed the microphone in his black, tactical helmet, "Heads up fuck sticks! Shark One, mind your quarter. Something isn't right."

Petty Officer Jones pulled back on the throttle and turned an eye back over his right shoulder towards the chief. In that instant water erupted around the first boat as four dark figures launched from the water over the gunnels from all sides.

The boat crewmembers were armed with M9 handguns and M4 machine guns, but their primary mission utilized the M2 crew served weapons. Most of the time, the M4 were stowed below in the small cabin, while the M9 might be holstered securely to the sailors black vests. The unprepared sailors screamed as the creatures of sopping black fur tore into them.

The front gunner triggered his M2 heavy machine gun, launching .50 caliber rounds across the harbor into the hull of the British transport ship while trying to target the black figure that arced over his weapon and landed on his torso. He attempted to follow the arc by pulling back on the weapon in the flowerpot it was mounted in, but the elusive creature slipped over the muzzle of the weapon and landed heavily into his chest with sharp talons. Long canines and fierce teeth latched onto the sailor's throat and a spray of crimson showered the deck as his hands slid from the grips of the .50 and he sunk under the attack. The black lycan shook its maw violently and tore the throat free, splashing blood across the bow.

Two more lycans descended upon the helmsman, one snapping its vicious maw on his shoulder while the second, larger lycan bit down on the back of his neck, grinding long canines into vertebrae. They played a gruesome game of tug of war before tearing the sailor in two.

The fourth lycan followed the third member of the crew from the fantail into the cabin, where he attempted to grab his M4. In mid thought, he pulled at the M9 from his chest but did not quite get the semi-automatic weapons free before he turned into horrid jaws closing on his throat. The M9 blasted a hole through the lycans chest and two more holes through the side window of the cabin. The lycan shuddered under the impact of the M9 but renewed his attack and bore the sailor to the deck, tearing into the exposed throat with long fangs while shredding the sailor's arms and chest with piercing claws.

Chief Timmons was horrified at the unfolding scene. His hesitation lasted only a moment, but in that moment all members of the crew had been taken out. The soldier in him took over and he barked orders, crossing from starboard to port to man the M2 facing Shark One.

"Open up on those fuckers!" He racked the bolt back on the portside M2. "Jones, call it in! Now, damn it!"

The front gunner had been frozen in place until he heard the roar of the M2 and then he joined in, fingering the trigger of his heavy machine gun. The big M2s spit flame and heavy rounds tore across the harbor.

Jones picked up the microphone for the radio and started to call in the report to their operations center on the pier. The roar of the M2 deafened him as he screamed with incoherent words.

Across the short expanse of water, the rounds tore through the 32-foot fast boat. One of the two black creatures savaging the remains of the helmsman was riddled across the back and it's chest exploded. The other lycans on the bow and at the helm shifted low and dodged the blur of projectiles.

One of the black creatures rolled across the fast boat and disappeared over the far side into the dark waters. The creature on the bow sunk lower before launching itself impossibly high through the air towards the second boat. The bow gunner tried to elevate his M2 fast enough but fell beneath the fangs and fury of the lycan, dropping back and lifting his arms for protection.

He screamed as he fought the slavering creature off, feeling sharp talons tear through his black vest while fangs snapped towards his face and throat.

From further back on the boat, Chief Timmons heard the cries for help from his petty officer on the bow and he shouted at Jones. "Back us up and get us the hell out of here!"

He felt the boat suddenly kick into reverse and all combatants on the boat rolled. Timmons stumbled forward into the cabin, already catching his sea legs, and snatched up his M4, racking the bolt as he continued towards the bow. The fast boat drove backwards a few yards before it lurched in a tight circle and then Jones threw it into high gear forward.

Timmons felt inertia kick and he almost lost his footing. Years of serving on small boats gave him waterborne stability to handle most situations, including the sudden aggressive turns he stood against. Experience did not prepare his for what happened next.

The sudden change in direction caught the lycan and Petty Officer Burns off guard and the two tumbled through the open hatch into the cabin. Still entangled, the two rolled into Timmons, and the three fell back through the cabin and onto the fantail.

As the fast boat kicked into action and the bow lifted from the torque of the propeller, all three continued rolling across the desk past Jones. The petty officer watched them roll by but kept to his task of getting them moving fast. The roaring confusion hid the black talons that clung to the gunnel beside the helm.

The three combatants seemed to stand as one and then the black creature shifted weight, slipping over the stern and taking both Chief and Petty Officer with him. In the blink of an eye, Jones was alone on the boat.

He glanced forward and back, noticing the absence of his crew. For a few seconds, he continued to drive forward before it registered and he slammed the throttle into neutral. The boat continued to drift forward as the petty officer turned to search for his crew. He picked up the M4 that lay on the deck and stood at the stern, scanning the water while shouldering the machine gun.

Jones was breathing so hard and fast and his heart was pounding so loud in his ears that he did not hear the radio crackling with the warning from the harbor watch tower.

He was still scanning the water for his chief when powerful jaws snapped on his neck and twisted, shattering his upper spine. After a few violent shakes, the black lycan dropped the dead sailor and looked to the watchtower across the harbor. The creature gave a wolfish grin and waved to the guards he knew were watching before slipping over the gunnel into the dark waters.

Hassem changed while he floated and swam as a man. He approached where he had seen the sailors enter the water and the head of a black lycan popped up. A second head appeared, balding and in human form. Kumar smiled.

"Where is Raheem?" Hassem inquired, looking towards the torn first patrol boat.

"In his haste to enjoy his kill, he was shot by the machine guns. They split his chest in two. He looks dead." Kumar seemed almost happy to report the casualty.

"Pull him from the boat and let's go. The Americans will arrive soon in force, and we will be long gone. The watch tower saw us, so they will report this. They now know definitively, and their fear will grow."

As the third lycan started to paddle back towards the first patrol boat, Kumar shrugged. "Let's leave Raheem. Let them see us in our true form. If he is dead, he won't shift for hours."

Hassem looked to Kumar with disdain. "We bury our brothers, we do not leave them behind. And without a body, they can fear their weapons have no effect on us. It'll strengthen our impact."

The third swam back, pulling the body of Raheem. His entire chest cavity had been blown out and his head lolled to the side, his long tongue hanging out. The body floated lifeless on the water.

"We should hurry. Water will start to weigh him down." Hassem noted, shifting as he did into lycan form and kicking off through the water. The others followed and they disappeared back into the night.

....

Brand was just returning from a run with Siovhan when he smelled the cigarette smoke ahead beyond the fence. As they crawled beneath the opening, he looked up to see Prim.

"What's up, Gunner?"

"It's bad, sir: an attack on the waterfront. Chief Timmons boat crew got hit."

"What?" he felt as if he'd been struck in the chest. "How?"

"I just heard. I was at the Comms shack when word came over the PRC-119. Sounds like the same black things that got us. I don't know how badly, but I know the whole waterfront is in an uproar. I came to get you immediately. I've been waiting here about forty minutes."

"Crap. When did it happen?"

Almost simultaneously, Siovhan asked, "Was Major Valko notified?"

"Sorry, ma'am. I don't know. I've been waiting here for my commander and I didn't think to call him."

She turned to Brand and placed a hand on his arm, brushing softly. "I've got to go contact Major Valko, although I'd be surprised if he didn't beat your men to the scene. I have my pack just over near my jeep, so I can be back in a moment if you'll wait." Her eyes sparked and out of unconscious reflex she leaned towards Brand and pressed her forehead against his arm.

"Go. We'll see you at my room in one minute." As she turned and raced away, Brand noticed Prim shaking his head as he watched her running, his eyes focusing down. "You can stare later, Chief. We've got to run."

"Oh, my bad, sir. I forget, you've probably been watching her tail run all night." He took a quick drag from his cigarette and blew smoke before throwing the butt off into the sand.

Trying not to laugh, Brand added, "Call the NCIS agents. I think we're going to need the Senior Agent if the Army Colonel shows up."

"Roger, sir. I'll dial now." Prim pulled his phone from his chest pocket and dialed.

They ran through Brand's courtyard and he continued into his room, where he quickly changed into battle dress uniform. As he came out of the room, he found Siovhan approaching in her uniform, hastily buttoning the blouse and then the three headed for the waterfront.

From the shadows at the far edge of the courtyard a figure stalked, watching from a distance. The figure kept its eyes on Siovhan, watching as they disappeared from the courtyard. The three pressed on towards the waterfront as the figure melted away into the dark.

The figure shifted from the shadows through a bright fence line light. He was a young black Army enlisted in desert fatigues with the name Wilson across the webbing sewn into his blouse.

....

At the waterfront the piers were alive with lights and security. Both Navy and Army units had converged on the waterfront, to include additional boat units. Colonel Shaker stood at the center of the mayhem, surrounded by dozens of armed military police. A Navy Commodore, full equivalent to the Colonel, stalked along the pier followed by his staff.

Major Valko, Cedric and Fergus drove up as the three approached.

"Evening Liam. Watson. Chief. Thank you for the telephone."

Prim blew a cloud of smoke and dispensed with his normal witty greeting. "Sounded bad and felt we could use your perspective, Major."

"Sam, you'll forgive me but I believe it best if Chief and I stay a distance from the Colonel. He'll see we're here soon enough, but I don't need to agitate him."

Valko looked to the Colonel blustering about and turned back. Nodding he agreed. "I'll take point. We'll give him a bit. Any way you or Chief can skirt the edges and get a picture."

Prim dropped his cigarette butt and snubbed it out. "I'm on it. You officers wait for the work to be done." He shifted away towards the tower. "My guess is the TIS/VIS has the best view and they'll have pictures in the tower. If I hurry I can beat the Christmas rush."

As he moved smartly along the pier towards the tower, Valko looked to Liam quizzically. Brand replied to his silent question. "Thermal Imaging Sensor and Visual Imaging Sensor. TIS/VIS. It is electronic surveillance equipment that we maintain visibility and situational awareness across the water. The thermal images would see in the dark. Night camera. If it happened on the water, I'm betting the equipment picked it up. They have incredible zoom capability."

Valko looked to Cedric and the larger man nodded. "That won't do, now will it Mr. Churchill."

"I'm on it, sir. We'll see what the video captures and I'll adjust as necessary."

"Very well. Take Williams with you and insure there are no complications."

"Roger, sir." He touched Fergus and the two moved away, following in the path of Prim.

"Complications?" Brand asked while maintaining an eye on Shaker.

"No offense, Liam, but we don't need the world suddenly finding a video of a lycanthrope savaging a number of . . . people. It wouldn't do for relations. It's part of our reason for being here."

"Understood. I'm still adjusting and it's surreal. But what about actual witnesses?"

Valko smiled. "How is that working out for you?"

The American shook his head as he understood. "Ok. Without the video, you just have a few wild stories and no corroboration."

As the remaining three waited, Valko and Siovhan both turned and looked up the pier. Brand followed their attention and saw the approach of Huang and Wong.

As he neared, Huang bowed his head politely towards Brand. "Thank you for the call, Commander. I appreciate the prompt notification."

"I'm glad you were able to arrive so fast. We just arrived ourselves. Chief Prim is making his way to the tower to see what was captured on the surveillance."

Huang seemed mildly annoyed at the thought of surveillance and looked to Valko. "Good evening, Major. Are we aware of anything else?"

"No. I received the report from Ms. Watson and came directly. Like you, we just arrived. I've sent my men to follow Chief Prim to assist with any … shall we say cleanup of surveillance if we are able?"

Huang nodded and looked to Wong. "Stay with Commander Brand. I'll make my way to the Colonel to see what they are aware of."

As he seemed to float away across the pier, Brand noted the tense truce between Valko and Huang held in place. He watched Huang move and realized he was unnaturally graceful. Whereas Valko and his team seemed to move smooth and natural, Huang's movements had an almost ethereal grace to them.

Looking to Wong, Brand nodded. "Good to be working with you, Special Agent."

She looked at him and then to Siovhan who returned her glance with a glower. For a brief moment, it seemed the truce would explode between the two females. Brand shifted between the two to separate them as he addressed Valko.

"Sam. What are we up against?" His tone was hushed even considering the commotion across the water and along the pier.

The British major looked to the rest of the group and shook his head. "I'm not certain. We had heard through channels there was a potential supernatural contemplating actions against allied forces in the Middle East. Intelligence put the actor in Kuwait. We had no idea what or where beyond that."

"What do you mean by supernatural? Do you mean …" Brand hesitated a moment, glancing at Wong.

"I mean supernatural. I am assuming Special Agent Wong and her Senior Agent aren't here because of an IED against NCIS. I am assuming they are here for the same reason I am. Supernatural – something that isn't quite natural in accordance with the thoughts of "modern" man – and I say that in quotes."

Wong moved closer to the other three. "What type of supernatural did your report indicate?"

"Lycanthrope. But you knew that. I'm guessing you and Senior Agent Huang were placed on a jet the moment the initial report hit the airwaves."

The agent remained silent.

Brand leaned closer and whispered. "No offense, Agent Wong. But we are on the same side. Let's put whatever differences you and Huang have with Valko and his team aside. One fight – one team."

She locked eyes with Brand for a hot second and he felt Siovhan bristle and move forward. He also felt Valko intercept her.

Wong's eyes shifted to Siovhan and glared but the flash disappeared as she returned her gaze to Brand. "Ok. We received word of a possible incident. We were dispatched to respond if necessary."

"Who dispatched you? You aren't NCIS." Valko questioned.

Wong shook her head. "And you aren't whoever you say you are. So we are back to square one."

"Jesus Christ. Can we all just whip 'em out and throw them on the table already." Brand snapped, anger ripping through his voice. "Enough grandstanding. We can figure out which spy organizations you are both from later. Right now we're on the same side and we're working together. Do we understand?"

Valko was taken aback and blinked, smiling and nodding. "Yes, Liam. I understand."

He turned to Wong who took in a deep breath and nodded silently, eyes wide at his sheer primal fury. And when he turned to Siovhan, she bowed her head in acquiescence, docile as she almost shifted within his shadow.

"Good. When Prim returns we'll collaborate with Senior Agent Huang and decide what our next course of action is . . ." He stopped and lifted his chin, sniffing at the air and listening across the water.

His eyes tightened and honed in. Across the dark inner harbor, he barely made out a dark figure in the water floating in the choppy waves. Taking two bounds towards the water he launched himself, clearing the edge of the pier and a good fifteen feet before landing in the water and kicking forward. Even with combat boots and fully clothed he sped across the water with strong strokes and kicks.

He approached a figure that was barely floating, waving an arm and gasping between waves. Wrapping an arm around Chief Timmons massive chest, he turned him on his back and started to scissor kick back towards the pier. The Chief grunted and almost struggled before going limp.

As he approached the pier, he heard Major Valko barking orders and boats approaching across the water. Arms reached down to grab the Chief and pull him from the water and Brand felt a separate hand reach down for him.

Pulling himself from the water, he sat down next to Chief Timmons as the boat turned and sped the short distance to a floating dock. From the floating dock a ramp lead up to the main pier. He could already see emergency vehicles rolling up the pier towards the ramp and medics were heading towards the boat.

He climbed over the gunnel to the floating dock where Siovhan greeted him. Wong was immediately at her side and someone placed a towel over his shoulders.

"There are more in the water." He stated. "I saw one of the enlisted. He didn't make it. He's just below the waterline." He pointed generally towards where he had found Chief Timmons.

The boat turned back out and headed towards the location he had indicated. Valko moved in close and gestured towards the ramp.

"Shaker will be on you shortly, Liam. Look alive."

Colonel Shaker stormed down the ramp followed by Huang and an entourage of Navy and Army officers. "I should have known!"

"Good evening, sir." Brand threw the towel over his shoulder and unbuttoned his blouse, removing the dripping wet shirt.

Huang slid between Brand and Shaker and intervened. "Commander. What happened?"

"I noticed Chief Timmons floating in the water and dove in."

Shaker looked out across the dark inner harbor. Even with the spotlights scanning the water, it was nearly impossible to view more than a few dozen yards from the pier. "Bullshit! How on earth did you see him that far out? The boats didn't even see him."

Turning on the Colonel, Senior Agent Huang gave a sharp stare. "Colonel. This is a Navy matter and I'm on scene. I appreciate you consider yourself and any possible accusations you may have. Commander Brand was fortunate to have observed the Chief at all. Another second may have been too late. So he has exceptional eyesight. Do you have any other observations you feel are relevant for this evening?"

The entire entourage went silent as all eyes fell on Shaker. He was caught off guard and stepped back, unable to respond. Within the gathering group and both shadows and light, Huang seemed to grow in stature as the Colonel fell away.

"Thank you. Continue to support and secure the pier further. We will need the remaining bodies pulled from the harbor and I'll want reports from any witnesses. I have faith you and your team can provide?" The last sentence was more question than statement.

Shaker nodded absently and took a step backwards before turning and moving away, motioning for his team to follow. He gave curt orders for them to take statements.

"Thank you. I appreciate the support." Brand spoke.

Turning back on him, Huang focused his eyes and seemed to ponder something. "It is remarkable you saw him from such a great distance in such poor lighting; something to be considered. The medics have him."

"I'll go with the medics to the hospital and when he's available, I'll get a statement from him." Brand stated.

Huang again took a moment to consider and nodded. "Take Agent Wong with you. She will assist."

He felt Siovhan bristle in their direction while he felt Wong shift, looking to Huang for guidance. Valko reached out to take Watson by the elbow and she pulled her arm free. Brand glanced back to see her spin and move up the pier.

"Care to ride in the ambulance, Special Agent?"

She looked up at him and for the first time didn't seem to glare at him with daggers. Silently she nodded and followed as he moved towards the ambulance that waited.

Valko called after them. "I'll send Fergus to pick you up. We can all reconvene back in your building."

Brand glanced back for a moment to see the slight smile on the Major's face as he turned back towards the scene in the water and watched Watson fume.

....

Prim skirted the group around Colonel Shaker, keeping to the shadows and moving towards the short tower at the end of the pier. He climbed the short stairwell inside where the few enlisted on watch still sat their post with a young Navy Ensign standing as office of the watch.

"Hey, guys. Chief Prim. I'm with NCIS." He acted as if he was reaching into his pocket for credentials and at the same moment gestured around the room. "What did you guys see?"

The Ensign stepped forward and looked at him in disbelief. "Chief. I've seen you at the boathouse with our sailors. Are you certain you're with NCIS?"

Prim pulled a box of cigarettes from the front pocket of his blouse and tapped the box twice before pulling a cigarette out and lighting it. "Yes, I'm certain. Look down on the pier and you'll see a cold looking Asian in a black suit. That's my Senior Agent. Do I need him up here to chew a little ass, Ensign?"

"Um, no Chief. I mean, I just see you on the piers from time to time lately."

"Yep, conducting surveillance. Now about my question: What did you guys see?"

The Ensign turned to the petty officers seated at the monitors. "I wasn't up here when it happened. The two petty officers were manning the equipment. They called the Watch Center and I was sent up here by our commander."

"Very well." He noticed the arrival of both Cedric and Fergus, who collectively blocked the door and the stairwell down. "Ah, good. My associates have arrived. Now, you were saying . . . "

"And as you're saying it, we'll need you to secure all copies of the surveillance tapes as evidence in the ensuing investigation." Cedric stated, pulling his credentials from his pocket and flashing them around the room. "This is a joint operation between NCIS and our agency. Special Agent Williams, please be so kind as to obtain names, ranks and contact information of all members within this room." Looking to the Ensign, he pointedly asked, "Have you seen any of the surveillance video?"

The Ensign shook his head. "No. We haven't played any back."

"Good to know. You may give your name to Williams and then please depart down the stairwell while we conduct interviews. Be so kind as to secure the stairwell and keep all others out until we are done. It won't be but a moment."

"Further, we'll be initiating non-disclosure agreements with each of you through your government. This entire event is a highly classified incident: Top Secret on a need-to-know basis only. You are strictly forbidden to discuss this outside of our agency and the local NCIS agents. Isn't that correct Chief Prim?" The huge man glanced over to the thin Chief.

"Affirmative. We'll have those DD form something or other around sometime tomorrow for each of you to sign." The Chief stated, looking back at Cedric and shrugging.

Cedric corrected, "Chief means the standard form 312 non disclosure agreements. This restricts you from discussing this incident with other members of your command. If you need to discuss the issues, please coordinate with Chief Prim. We will take statements from each of you, and we will need all copies of the electronic storage for this evening. Please assist us as this is a National Security event, endangering both Great Britain and American lives. Thank you for your Patriotism."

The Petty Officers in the control center went to work downloading the video feed. Cedric stood behind them watching as Fergus took each member aside to privately interview them and write down their statements. Chief wound up moving to glance around Cedric's massive shoulders as the video feed played back and they watched the attack. They could make out the heat signatures as the bodies swam through the water and then swarmed the first boat. When the night vision hit the creatures, their eyes glowed and the creatures stood out in green. In the end, when the one lycanthrope waved from the boat before disappearing over the side, there could be no doubt as to what they all saw.

Prim shook his head as Cedric reached over and took the thumb drive from the Petty Officer operating the equipment. "Thank you, Petty Officer. I'll need you to erase the moments leading up to the attack through the attack."

"Sir, that's an official log of events. We aren't allowed to do that." The Petty Officer stated, looking up over his shoulder from where he sat.

"Sorry, junior. It's now part of an official investigation. We will maintain the evidence during the course of this, but it's best if you didn't have it. Support national security and all that." Prim commented. "Do as you're told. If anyone asks, just let them know NCIS has it."

Looking around from Prim to Cedric and finally to Fergus, the young Petty Officer turned back to the equipment and started procedures to erase the block of time. Cedric watched, ensuring it was done, and then nodded to Fergus.

"Thank you. Job well done. We will take the rest of your statements and you can expect we will have the forms around tomorrow. For now, once we depart, maintain silence. Understood, gentlemen?"

The remaining watch members replied and Fergus continued taking statements independently.

....

At the hospital, Chief Timmons was taken to triage first where Sergeant Summers was on watch. She led a team of Corporals as they shifted him to a waiting bed started to remove his torn soaked uniform. Both Brand and Wong followed until they reached the emergency room, and then they held back to wait. Colonel Pinson ran by to join the triage.

Looking to Wong, Brand offered, "Coffee? We might be here a short while."

She looked at him, sizing him up, before her demeanor softened and she nodded. "Thank you."

He smiled in return and nodded down the hall. "I've been here before. They have a coffee mess around the corner. While we're here, we can see if Ross is awake."

"I don't believe we should inform Special Agent Ross of the events of this past night." She stated, following. "The fewer who know the easier it is to contain."

Brand thought a moment as they walked before asking, "How many events do you contain? Is it that often?"

Wong looked to him, still uncertain of whether to trust him. "No it isn't that often. It is currently in the best interest of all parties though. This would be a first in a long time for something on this level."

"What level is that?"

Her response was very matter of fact. "You pointed it out earlier: they want to make themselves known: Active aggression towards the populace on a terrorist level. They want to kill people to cause a scene."

"Ah. Yes, I guess I can see that would possibly be an issue." They arrived at the coffee mess. A standard long folding table stood with three tall urns of coffee, a few towers of Styrofoam cups, and numerous shakers of sugar and powdered creamer. "Sorry, it's just your standard Folgers. Probably been here for hours and might be burnt and bitter. But it's hot." He poured a Styrofoam cup of coffee and handed it to her. "Sugar and creamer are on the table here if you need to cut it." He poured himself a cup as well.

"Thank you." She sniffed the coffee before joining him at the table to pour both sugar and creamer in her coffee, as he was already doing.

They returned to the Emergency Room and found folding chairs to wait until Chief Timmons was available. They sat and drank their coffee in relative silence, watching a flat screen television on the wall as local news from back in the United States played.

A short while later, Sergeant Summers found them and reported on Timmons condition. Although in shock and suffering a number of scratches and bruises, he was none the worse for the wear.

Brand thanked Sergeant Summers and led Wong to the triage where they found Timmons sitting upright in a bed. As they approached, the Chief straightened some.

"Sir."

"How are you Chief?" Brand asked.

The big Chief shook his head. "I'm in disbelief, sir. I didn't know what you were into, but I saw it first hand tonight. The Sergeant told me you're the one who pulled me out. I have you to thank."

Brand shrugged and shook his head. "Could have been any one of us. I was just the first to see you."

Wong leaned in. "Don't believe him Chief. He is the only one who saw you, and he acted without hesitation. You are absolutely only here because of him."

Brand looked at her and she gave a sheepish smile. "Regardless, Chief. The important thing is you're going to be ok."

"Am I, sir? I just lost my whole boat crew to a bunch of werewolves. Fuck the surreal situation, I lost my men."

Brand took in a deep breath and let out a short sigh, lowering his voice to just above a whisper. "You're right, Chief. And I'm sorry. But at least you made it. I'm sorry about your men. You had no idea what you were up against. Hell, no one could have guessed that would happen. It's insane."

"Is it, sir? What happened at the Kuwaiti Colonel's house? What are you chasing? Were we attacked by werewolves? Were you and Prim attacked by werewolves? I mean, what the fuck?"

Both Brand and Wong were startled by the abrupt question. Brand leaned in and Wong shifted closer for privacy. "Ok. The Colonel's house was involved. We were attacked the first night we visited and yes, by werewolves. And they have made other attempts, but none on the base. We're trying to figure this out, but we have to keep this need to know. Prim and I trusted you but we didn't tell you because . . . well to be frank, we didn't think you'd be in danger nor did we think you'd believe us. Now let's change the direction. What happened?"

Timmons looked from Brand to Wong. "Can I trust her, sir?"

Brand looked to Wong and caught her eyes. Looking back he nodded. "Implicitly. She's with me."

"We were on watch, I was on the second boat when we saw at least two of them attacking the first boat. We went to guns and were going to support when we came under attack. Everything went to hell in a hand basket before I could get my bearings. I know at least one of them was cut in half by our fifty. But then I went into the water in a pileup with one of my sailors and one of them. I don't recall what happened next. I just know I woke up here."

"Was there any indication? Did you see or hear anything leading up to the attack?" Brand inquired.

The big chief shook his head. "Negative, sir. Not a sound except the water lapping at the gunnels of the boats.

And then my boys were screaming and under attack." His eyes sunk and he shook his head. "Those bastards."

"Get some rest, Chief. And again, I'm sorry for your loss. They were good men." Brand offered, placing a hand on the Chief's shoulder.

He looked to Wong, who shook her head. She stared up at the Chief and quietly offered her condolences as well before turning towards the door and offering Brand the lead.

They walked out of the room and stopped just down the hallway out of earshot. Looking down to her, Brand took in a deep breath. "What're your thoughts?"

She stared up at him silently for a moment before nodding. "We return to Special Agent in Charge Huang. I had hoped he might have had more to offer, but I was afraid of this."

"No worries. I'll text Fergus and see how far out he is from us. Care for another cup of coffee while we wait?"

Again she stared at him silently before commenting. "You drink a lot of coffee, I've noticed."

He shrugged. "Eh. I like it."

She broke a smile and nodded. "I'll join you."

As they walked, Brand dialed Fergus and spoke briefly. As he hung up, he moved faster. "He'll be here in about ten minutes. Just enough time to grab a second cup."

....

Fergus parked the HUMVEE near the back gate and the three walked the short expanse to the building. The others were already waiting. Wong immediately moved to take up her position at Huang's right arm while Fergus stayed at Brand's side. Siovhan move to join the two and bumped up against Brand's elbow.

Valko glanced to the sky and looked around. "That was a long night. It's almost sunrise."

Huang nodded. "Almost. We should finish up and get rest. I foresee the next few days as potentially long. What were we able to discern? Anything from the tower?" He turned towards Williams and Prim.

The larger man shook his head. "It isn't good. The cameras obtained excellent footage with night vision. It was a concerted attack with the aggressors in the water. The tower crew was not able to see them until they breached the surface of the water."

"From the moment of the attack, they were in lycan form, so facial recognition software won't work through most of the electronic capture. One of the aggressors was shot directly through the chest by 50 millimeter rounds and they tore the cavity of his chest and heart out. At least one of the aggressors was killed; however, the others managed to secure his remains and swam the body out. Although the deceased remained in hybrid form, two of the remaining shifted into human form and we have a clear shot of one of their faces."

Prim presented a few grainy printouts centered on one black furred lycan and two men floating in a circle. Of the two men, the bald-headed man faced the camera and gave a clear shot.

"We're trying for facial recognition now. I think we might also ask both the Colonel and the Major if they have ever seen this one before, either in ranks or skulking around."

Brand took the photo and then passed it on. Looking to Cedric, he asked, "What's hybrid?"

The large man pointed to one of the photos circling in the group and responded. "Lycans shift in three phases. Man as you see the hairless one and the other with his back to the camera; hybrid, as the one swimming beside him, part man part wolf; and full on canine."

"Oh. Interesting."

Williams continued, almost clinically. "Although always maintaining their strength, the full wolf form allows for faster maneuvering and running, though not so much in the water. Hybrid form is better for combat as you can imagine. And man is just . . . well, it fits in."

Huang seemed amused with the discussion as he interjected. "That is rather fascinating, I must say. But back to what is at hand. Did we gain any additional information from the surveillance?"

"No, sir. I'm afraid not." Williams answered. "Although the fact that they took out the boat in broad sight of the tower without first taking out surveillance indicates they intended on letting us see them."

This brought a moment of silence. Huang nodded. "As Commander Brand indicated earlier, I believe this is the agenda that you thwarted. They are attempting to make a statement, only this time they were hoping to capture it on surveillance so that it could not be hidden away nor denied."

Major Valko held the photo of the attackers, analyzing the face as best he could. "What's our plan? We still need to keep this bloody thing under wraps."

Huang nodded in agreement. "Yes. We must. You have secured all the evidence and received statements from witnesses?"

Fergus spoke up. "The only witnesses were in the tower. Although they saw it in real time, it was in night vision mode so they weren't too certain what they saw. And we have the only copies, so I'm certain by the end of the week, they'll convince themselves they saw frogmen not wolfmen." He grinned.

Prim added. "We also had them sign non-disclosure agreements on the DSF 312. I swore them to secrecy based upon an NCIS investigation. I may have given them the impression we are . . . well agents."

"That is perfect. You did well." The Senior Agent commended them. "But perhaps you can provide me a list of names and we shall keep an eye on them."

Valko nodded and Williams pulled out a flip notepad. After a moment of glancing through, he took a pen and scribbled down a few names to pass to Wong. She slid it into her pocket.

"Anything more?" Huang continued his inquiry.

Brand shook his head. "You probably know more from the video surveillance than Chief Timmons could provide.

But he definitely knows they were werewolves. He fought them up close and personal. He's lucky to be alive."

"Quite." Valko commented. "And you would know."

"From a review of the surveillance feed, Chief Timmons was just knocked off the boat in the melee." Williams stated. "The others weren't so lucky. They all died on the boat. If the Chief had remained on the boat, he wouldn't have survived."

"I don't know." Prim quipped. "If a scrawny officer can survive an attack, a big, burly Chief ought to be able to make it."

Both of the big Brits chuckled before Huang interceded. "I believe we have a majority of the events. I recommend we adjourn until later. Rest and recover. We will also send the photographs back to determine if our recognition software pulls a name. Thank you all."

Huang led Wong and they quickly departed. Prim yawned and stretched, looking around the remaining group. "I'm beat. I'll see you later." Turning to Brand, he asked, "What're your plans, sir?"

"Kind of wound up. I think I'll grab another workout and maybe breakfast. I might catch a nap later."

Fergus nodded. "I'll join you in the gym. I could use a workout as well. And maybe practice some." He gave a silent nod towards Valko.

Cedric yawned and shook his head. "I'll submit the photos back to England and see what they can make of them. And then I'm off for bed. Good morning all."

Valko glanced around and agreed. "The rest of us should be off to slumber, too. We can perhaps have dinner later today. Come along Agent Watson."

Siovhan leaned her head forward and gave Brand's shoulder a slight head bump. Looking up at him, she sighed and turned to follow Valko.

....

Brand and Fergus changed and met up at the gym a few minutes later. Smiling to the American officer, the larger man offered his hand. "Major Valko believes you can use a different partner for you runs and workouts, so you get variation. I volunteered. If you wind up wanting to go for a run this evening, I'm your man. I don't have the speed as Special Agent Watson, but I've got the stamina to run all night. And this will give you the chance to hear a male's perspective of the life." He followed Brand as he entered the gym and headed towards the Fitness Room.

"Thanks, Fergus. I appreciate it. I might be up for a run. I seem to have an increasing level of energy all the time."

"Yeah. You better get used to that. You may need less sleep more and more."

The fitness room was a large all purpose room with mirrors across one wall, used for group exercises, stretching and other calisthenics. Noting it was empty save for the two of them, Brand spoke up, "So, Sam mentioned he grew up in a family of . . . werewolves? And lived in a pack. Is that how you grew up?" He started to stretch out.

Fergus nodded. "Aye. I was born into the pack. Both my parents were born into the pack. As far back as we can remember. And my siùir, Bridget. We grew up together with other Scot Wulvur. That's what we Scots refer to ourselves. Have you ever heard of the kindhearted Scottish Wulvur? It's the epic telling of many tales of the good deeds of our kind. We Scottish Wulvur have a much better reputation than the rest of the rampaging lot, I'll tell you."

Both men laughed as they continued to stretch.

"Aye, my siùir was eldest and taught me when I was coming of age until my Dadaidh took over. I was just about in my teens. And the other boys in my pack ran with me. I wish my siùir was here to run with you. I'm certain you'd get on great with Bridget. And I'm sure she'd love you." He winked with a smile.

Brand smiled in return and turned the subject back to questions. "So is your team a pack, or is it something else? I see Sam is in charge."

"No." Fergus shook his head. "We aren't a pack. At least not in a traditional sense. We are assigned through the program to this team and we sort of made a family." He grinned. "Major Valko is in charge due to his rank and his family connections to the program. Cedric is the strongest of us, and it's a toss up as to who is smartest between him and Watson. They are both pretty sharp depending upon the subject. I doubt Major would be our Alpha if we hadn't been assigned to our rolls, but we all work well together."

"What program are you referring to? What connections?"

"Ah, now you're touching on areas that it's probably best you ask the Major about. Or Cedric. We work for the Crown."

Brand nodded and shrugged. "Can't blame me for asking. But I understand. Shall we hit the weights for a bit before moving on to martial arts?"

"That would be great!" Fergus replied, following as they headed to the weight room.

They lifted weights for the better part of an hour, rapidly working through most of the body muscle groups. They continued, shifting to martial arts, which they practiced for another few hours before finally ending.

As their workout ended, Brand wrapped a towel around his neck and glanced at the clock on the wall. "I'm going to shower and grab lunch. Then I'll crash for a few hours. Want to grab some food in a few."

"Absolutely, sir. I'll meet you in a bit. Where?"

"Probably schwarmas. If I go to the DFAC without Prim, he might scold me." The two men laughed and headed out.

Brand made his way back to his room in the late morning sun, the warmth beating down up him. As he approached his door he lifted his chin and sniffed the air. He opened his door and smiled at Siovhan, who lay within his sheets. She looked up at him and smiled lazily, half asleep.

Pulling back the sheet, she lay in just one of his tee shirts from what he could see. "I hope you don't mind, but I wanted to curl up next to you. I figured after your workout with Fergus, you'd enjoy softer company."

"Completely unexpected but absolutely welcome. I did however let him know I'd be joining him for lunch after a shower."

She shrugged. "I like the way you smell right now. You can have dinner with him later." She offered a pleading face and batted her eyes up to him. "Just pull your shirt off and crawl in with me for a few."

Brand pulled his phone and tapped out a quick text as he kicked off his shoes. As he hit send, he placed the phone on his desk and pulled off his shirt, sliding in next to her as she wrapped him in the sheet and nestled her head into his shoulder.

She smiled and murmured. "Thank you, Liam." And he felt her peacefully drifting into slumber.

As sore and tired from the night and the workout as he felt, he also felt alive and full of energy. He felt her heart racing and then calming as she wrapped around him and he felt himself calming too.

He smiled down upon her and closed his eyes to nap.

Chapter 12

Mentor in the Night

Silver eyes stared out across the sand. Raising his chin, he let out a long howl, sending his thoughts across the desert. The ancient lycan called.

The team was playing a waiting game now. Churchill had sent the photos back to England as did Wong to the U.S. hoping international intelligence channels might identify the bald man. It would take a few days for the data to be mined if it were available.

The next few days and nights followed quietly. Although Brand met with Prim daily for meals and to catch up, he typically would work out with Fergus following lunch for a few hours, often with Cedric joining them for weights, and then run later in the evening when the sun was beginning to set. After his runs, he would sleep for a few short hours in the mornings, finding he needed less sleep daily. Each day he ran with a different member.

The first night it was Fergus, who ran and talked the entire time. Again they shared stories of families and martial arts and movies they enjoyed. Brand felt he was faster than the younger Wulvur but the younger man had great stamina and kept up through the hours. He liked Fergus and knew he would like his family.

The second night Cedric was waiting for him. The two set out at a fairly quick pace, though nowhere near as fast as Siovhan's. As they ran, they spoke and again Brand learned of the life of the lycans. Cedric was quiet and contemplative, but when he started talking, he spoke volumes. Huge Cedric offered his perspective on all the beauty his budding senses would someday afford him. Though the largest of the group, Cedric ran with incredible agility for one so massive.

The next night he expected the British Major, yet was surprised when Siovhan showed up at his room early. She met him with a wicked smile and rushed him from his room to sneak out under the fenceline.

As they started their run, she rubbed shoulders with him and whispered, "I couldn't wait another night to run. I'm sorry. Our poor Major will probably wonder what's become of you. But he wouldn't have given you much of a challenge. He isn't that fast."

"Does he know you're with me tonight?" Brand asked, quickening his pace as she led the way.

She laughed over her shoulder. "No. Tonight is ours."

"What's the plan?" He called forward, lengthening his stride.

There was a moment of silence before he heard her laugh. "Same as before. You catch me . . ." Her words trailed off as she took off running.

As before, there were several times Brand came close to her. But again, Siovhan stayed just out of reach. As their run came to an end, he could feel her breathing was labored and her muscles were pushing to their limits.

She called back to him, "We're done for tonight." And slowed her pace.

As she leaned forward to catch her breath he tackled her and they rolled in the sand. He came up on top of her, face to face, both breathing hard and intertwining their hands as he stared down upon her.

Her eyes were wide and for a brief second flashed hot. In that moment, a smile slid across her face and she wrapped her legs around him, pulling him into her while letting him hold her hands above her head.

They both felt the heat and he felt her starting to give way to let him in, all the while tightening her legs so that he couldn't escape.

And then she whispered, "You didn't quite catch me . . . but still . . . "

It was his turn to smile as he leaned in ever so closer and whispered in return. "Rules are rules. Next time." He gave her a quick, soft kiss on the cheek and rolled to the side, lying in the sand.

She rolled over next to him, nestling her head into his shoulder. "You're faster. And stronger. You'll change soon. I can taste it in your sweat."

He closed his eyes and rested. "I see myself in my dreams at night. Not like before. Not ancient; something different. And now." He breathed a deep sigh.

She leaned in closer and kissed him softly on the lips. "You are something special, Liam." And then she pushed herself to her knees and stood. "I'm both looking forward to and fearing if you ever catch me."

"Thanks for running with me." He opened his eyes and looked up to her. "I think I know exactly what you mean."

She offered him a hand. "We'd better be heading back. The sun will be rising soon."

As he stood he looked to the very early morning stars. "What time is it?"

She leaned in close and rubbed her head against his shoulder. "Still early enough that we can crawl in bed for a moment if that's ok." Her voice was almost pleading. "Before we shower."

"I'd like that."

They set their pace and ran lazily back to the base. After sneaking in, they crawled into his rack and she curled up around him, both of them breathing easily and relaxed although he could still feel the heat rolling from her everywhere they touched.

As morning dawned, he heard Chief Prim moving about and calling to him. Siovhan looked up at him and quietly giggled, crawling out of bed to pull on her shorts and Vibram shoes.

The door opened and Prim stood there with two coffees. The British agent smiled at him and walked silently to the door. As she passed, she leaned in close and whispered. "Yes, I am very dedicated." And she was gone.

Prim stood there dumbfounded and simply shook his head. Taking in a deep breath, he let out a sigh and held up one coffee.

"Come on, sir. I've got to light one just thinking about this."

"What? I assure you nothing happened." Brand protested. "I haven't caught her yet."

His Chief gave him a quizzical look and again shook his head. "Seriously, sir. I have no idea what you just said. But, if we were to go on evidence, I'm saying . . . guilty!"

Brand accepted the coffee, climbing out of his rack wearing his running shorts. "Thanks for the joe. I had a long, long night . . . running that is."

"Yeah, I'll bet." Prim snickered. "Whatever you say sir. Your secret is safe with me. But she did tell me how dedicated she was. And quite proud of it, too."

Both men took a moment of silence to sip their coffee as Prim pulled a cigarette from his pocket and Brand was quite frankly speechless. Prim broke the silence with a smirk. "I haven't heard anything from Churchill or NCIS regarding photo identification. The guy might not be in any intelligence data bases."

Brand set his coffee aside to pull on a shirt. "I was with a Joint Task force a few years ago focusing on terrorists. They had a database something like six degrees of separation from Kevin Bacon, only based on terrorist links. I can't recall if they shared this tidbit with anyone, especially intelligence. Might be worth a shot. I know an Agent still attached to them."

Prim chuckled and shook his head yet again. "Seriously, sir? Way to hold out. Do you want to pass the contact information on or do you want me to make your excuses?"

"I'll take this one. Thanks, Chief. You're always covering down on me. I thought their intel sources would at least yield some fruit and it didn't dawn on me until just now. I'll pass the contact information on. I also think I still have an Army Major JAG on their staff I used to run with."

"Run, sir? We're not talking gangs, 'cause you're white as snow and I don't see you having any street cred." Prim quipped.

"Ha-ha. I've got serious street creds. Just ask me. In my neighborhood." He winked. "But no, I mean running as in Hash Hounding: Drinkers with a running problem. We ran in the DC Hash Hound Harriers. The last I recall he was still attached as legal to the task force, too. I'll pass both numbers to Churchill and Wong, letting Valko and Huang know."

"Ok, sir. What are your plans for the rest of the day?"

"Probably see if Fergus wants to grab a workout and then I'll shower. Lunch with you and see where we are. I just get the feeling the rest of today is going to be a quiet one, so other than working out, I might catch up on my reading. I wanted to start on the Illiad again."

"Might try watching Troy. Great movie and it covers the same things without the hundreds of pages of exposition." Prim suggested, leading the way out into the courtyard where he promptly lit his cigarette. "Oh, and you forgot something, sir. Details. You know I'd tell you."

"Ugh. Nothing . . . I repeat nothing happened. She came in and curled up."

"Oh, sir." Prim took one long drag and hung his head as he exhaled out. "You have severely disappointed me."

"And with that, I'll see you at lunch." And he was heading off towards the gym.

....

Brand woke and it was late. The night seemed silent and yet he felt something in the air. Something stirred inside his chest. It was the same calling he had heard the past few nights, only stronger with more direction.

He crawled out of his rack and slid on his running shorts and a fresh workout shirt before slipping on his Vibrams. He grabbed the armband identification holder from the corner of his desk and quietly walked across the room. Once outside, he began working his way across the camp, heading towards another of the sections of the perimeter wall that he knew was unmanned and easy to slip through but heading into a different direction of the desert than he normally took.

As he approached the gap in the wall, he felt a presence in the shadows ahead and he slowed, pulling further into the darkness himself. A flash of yellow eyes caught his attention and he held his breath.

"No need to hide, Commander. We saw you coming." He heard the familiar British officer's voice. "We were waiting for you."

Brand stepped into the lights. Though the moon and stars were hidden, camp lights still provided some illumination.

Valko moved from the shadows as well, followed by his team. "Although we've taken turns watching you, tonight seemed like a good night for all of us. I missed you last night." He glanced over towards Watson and shook his head. "Regardless, we've all felt something in the air today."

Brand looked to each of the three behind Valko. Siovhan hid a wolfish smile, an unusual trait for her normal stern visage. Brand attempted to hide his smile in return and shifted his gaze to the Major. "I felt something too. I wasn't sure what it was but it's been out there on the wind the past few nights. Tonight I can't seem to shut it out."

"That would be your Maker if I were to guess. And he wants to meet you. He is exceptionally strong. Blazes, even we can feel him. He isn't making it a secret that he's calling you. I hazard to guess, but I would mark any lycans within twenty miles can feel his call. And if they are wise, they'll ignore it. It is a very specific summoning."

"Why are you here then?"

"We wish to tag along until we're no longer welcome. To make sure you stay safe. Like I said, any lycans within twenty miles can probably feel his call, and some might not be wise enough to ignore it."

"As far as I'm concerned, you can follow me all night. I welcome it."

Sam laughed. "Sorry, but it's not you who needs to welcome us. Your Maker wants you, and we are not invited; however, we can run along a pretty good stretch. He waits out in the sand somewhere, leading you."

"Thanks. I appreciate it." He took in a deep breath and looked up to the sky. After a moment of consideration he looked to the other perplexed. "How is he doing this? Summoning? How can I feel this from so far away? It's not words just a thought and direction."

Siovhan smiled and looked to Valko. He nodded and she explained. "Mind of the pack. When you're . . . for want of a better term . . . accepted by a pack, you share common thoughts during specific times, such as a hunt. It's how we can coordinate our actions in a group. An inherent trait, such as common speech patterns in family units and neighborhood slang. Only this goes beyond words."

"Like a whale song . . . only silent?" Brand offered.

Siovhan thought a brief moment and shrugged. "Close enough. He's letting every one of us know he is searching for you. He's also letting every one of us know he is here. And he is very strong."

Without another word, the British officer stepped aside and gestured for the American to move past him, heading towards the wall. One by one, each member crawled under the cement wall where the foundation had been shattered by explosives years before. The gap was large enough for a man to scrape through.

Once they were all outside the perimeter, Brand stood and lifted his face, sensing the air. It took him only a minute, and then he set off at a steady pace, followed by the four.

They ran for the better part of an hour, straight into the desert. They crossed the highway once, and kept going. As they neared a set of hills, the four behind him slowed down and he heard Valko call out.

"Keep going, Liam. We're at the limit and not welcome beyond here. You can introduce us later if your Maker allows it. I can feel him from here. He is letting us know. This is definitely his territory."

Cedric nodded. "I've smelled him everywhere for the last mile or so. I agree we've come quite far enough."

Brand turned and looked to the four. Each nodded and they sat down, patiently waiting.

Facing about, he continued on, leaving the four behind. Within minutes, he felt the connection. Sheer animal instinct led him to the spot. As he came over a short hill and climbed the ridge, he found himself face to face with the silver-grey lycan, squatting on all fours and looking at him through silver eyes.

Brand froze, his eyes locked on the massive creature. The lycan seemed larger than he remembered, muscles tight and rippling beneath its short fur. Without fully understanding, Brand squatted as well, coming down to all fours and looking up towards the great creature.

The creature stood in one very smooth and non-aggressive motion. Moving within arms reach of Brand, the lycan squatted again, close enough that the American could feel the rise and fall of its chest.

As they squatted transfixed with each other, Brand felt his breathing coming into rhythm with the lycan's. While he watched, the great lycan slowly changed, shifting in form. Limbs shortened and the jackal-like snout pulled in as black hair emerged from his scalp and within a few seconds, a man faced Brand, his eyes still silver. It was the face Brand had seen in his dreams.

The man appeared to be Brand's age, with handsome features. He was naked yet did not seem to care. After a moment of silence, he stood again, still as fluid as before.

"Greetings. It is my great pleasure to meet you." He smiled, nodding his head ever so slightly without taking his silver eyes off Brand.

The American nodded in return, his breath short and his heart beating rapidly. "Thank you. Pleasure's all mine."

"You have questions." It was a statement. His voice was smooth and ageless, and his English was impeccable with an understated accent.

"I'm Liam. Brand. What do I call you?" Questions flooded his thoughts, as he suddenly felt comfortable. "Who are you?"

The man before him grinned and Brand saw the jackal in his smile. "While in the sands I have been known forever as Amun-Ulric. But Ulric was always my first name."

Brand felt warm and safe, and he smiled in return. "Sorry, but you don't look like a . . . Amun-Ulric."

Ulric laughed. "So whom do I look like?"

Brand shrugged and thought a minute. "I don't know. Alexander? Baldur or Thor? Nordic or somewhere western Med."

Ulric laughed. "Alexander? Of Macedon? You must mean from the movies. He looked considerably different in life. Thank you but I am not he. He was a weasel. Why do you say that I do not look like who I am?"

"I don't now. You don't look Egyptian? Or even African?"

Ulric nodded. "I am neither. I traveled to the river Nile. Although over the millennia I have been known by many names, I was always Amun-Ulric here, and I liked Ulric. Long ago when I first came to these lands, those of the Nile called me Wepwawet. I was their guardian of the gate and the hunter for the Pharaohs. It was . . . a favorite time in my life."

"Pharaohs? How old are you? You look as young as . . . me."

"I'm very old. Yet always as young as I feel." His silver eyes sparkled, yet behind the light, Brand could see age and wisdom, the depths of which he could hardly begin to fathom. "Have you had dreams since we first met? What have you seen?"

Brand shook his head and looked down. Looking back up, he replied, "Egyptian. A female. Looks like a queen. That was the first, although it's fuzzy and hard to recall now."

Ulric took in a slow, deep breath and smiled. "Ah. Interesting. That makes sense I guess." He exhaled. "That was always a fond memory. I enjoyed those years the most and I often think about them." He seemed held in his own nostalgia. "It was not long after I first came to the lands of the Nile when I met her."

"Where do you come from?" Brand asked, correcting his train of questions. "How is this possible?"

The elder lycan grinned broadly. "I am me. You're you, and how do you exist? A few of the others as old as I am made up what they wanted people to believe and after a while, it became history. I always liked the story we were descendants of the Bene Elohim. Others liked being called children of the gods, angels or devils. We can discuss that much later. We have other, more current issues to cover I believe."

"But, what is lycanthropy? Where does this come from? How did I get it?"

Ulric smiled and looked to the sky. "Mysteries of life. I was born to this, although my mother was not. As far as I know, I am one of the eldest. My mother was like you were. She said my father came to her and used to run like a wolf at night. My brother is like me, from the same father although his mother was a Nubian. He was known as Anubis."

"Anubis? The Egyptian god?" Brand considered the revelation and tried to make sense of it. "So, you and your brother are the fore-fathers of all lycans?"

"Certainly not." He laughed, bringing his silver eyes back down from the skies. "That is hilarious! No, I have very few offspring, although Anubis himself had a few more. There are others of us, to be certain. Fenrir in the Norse lands. I do not know who is older between he and I or Anubis. But back to your question as to what this is: I consider it who I am. And I can feel it in you now."

"How?" the younger American asked.

"Don't take this the wrong way, but my blood obviously takes to you. It fits, so you can accept the change. If it didn't fit, your body would try to reject it."

"And what does that mean for me?"

Ulric smiled as a father to his son. "Many wonderful things. I've never been anything but this; however, I gave this gift to one other and she described how she felt." He sat back, his memories caught up in the past and a peaceful look overcame him as his eyes shut. When they opened, he nodded as if approval of his memory. "As was described, eyes see much clearer, ears hear sharper and smells have more meaning. Stronger and faster, the body becomes amazing. And other things. With all the affects, life is just so much more enjoyable."

"What do you mean smells have more meaning?"

Ulric took a deep breath and exhaled, using the moment to consider his answer. "I'll make it easy to understand at the most base level. Have you smelled any females near you? Have you seen their response to you?"

It was Brand's turn to take a moment to consider his answer. "Definitely. Although I don't seem to be myself, I sort of fall into a trans, I can almost feel them. Their pulse intensifies and they smell . . . welcoming. Almost like we have this intangible connection. And I get the sense they feel the same from me."

Ulric's eyes sparkled to match his smile. "Good. You are responding well. Let your body accept it, but know it for what it is. Your senses are becoming heightened. No other creature I know has our senses. You'll see farther, in dark and light. You'll hear more acutely. And you'll grow stronger. You will adapt to being you."

"You can sense and smell others. When they are emotional, they put out a different scent, whether it's fear or lust or anger. It is unique and you can tell. Likewise, you also put out the same scents, only stronger and more attracting. Hence others will pick it up and some will be attracted to you. In doing so you pick up their attraction. It can be intoxicating. But as a point . . . regardless of how you may feel, you are you. What you feel is simply the primal part of you."

"Wow." Brand sat silent, turning his eyes down to the sand. After a moment, he looked back up. "You were shot.

Numerous times. Prim is an expert gunner. How did you make it out alive?"

The ancient lycan smiled, his canines showing beneath his lips. "Those little things. My body heals rather remarkably; as yours will in time. You may have noticed already. You'll grow tougher. I mean to be certain, I felt them, but they were more an annoyance. And I was already somewhat annoyed at the moment, so your friend was in a very precarious position. But his intention was to save you and the girl, and I could sense that."

"Perhaps there is too much to consider for you to think of a question for yourself." Ulric suggested shifting the topic. "Maybe if we talked of you, we could bring questions to mind. Who are you?"

"Um. . .I am Liam Brand, Lieutenant Commander in the United States Navy. On IA orders. . . individual augment orders acting as force protection for the NCIS agents in Kuwait. I'm 38. I'm actually a Navy reserve officer."

"So you are military? Good. Then you have discipline?"

"Between military and sports, yes. I also swim and practice martial arts, which has always tightened my discipline. But I've been losing control . . . ever since that night."

Ulric smiled. "Yes, that tends to happen. I have seen it before in valps . . . as you would say, young pups. Although you were not born to his, you still must go through the same process."

"How many others have you seen like me? That weren't born to this?" Brand asked.

The elder lycan shook his head. "Just the one. I know of a few others personally, but I met them well after they had become who they are."

Ulric saw concern in Brand's face and his smile softened, "Little Hvelpr. I can help in a great many ways. I can feel where you are, and I can feel my blood coursing through your veins. I can help you understand this new life you've been given and how to master yourself. I can teach you a great many things. Because my blood courses through you, I can probably help you understand this better than I could my own pups." He leaned in close, almost nose to nose. "Will you accept?"

Brand bowed his head and replied, "I'm sorry, sir. I am just really . . . "

Ulric sat back and reached out a hand to place it on his shoulder. "I can imagine how this has probably shattered your concept of life as you knew it. We shall get beyond that. Now, let's first open your mind to understanding who and what you are, and how to grow. We'll have many, many days and nights ahead of us. I have made room for you in my house in the desert. When we are done this night, you may go back with your friends and gather what belongings you might need. You can return to me tomorrow here and we'll begin in earnest."

"How many days shall we be away? I'll need to inform my Chief and make excuses for my absence."

Ulric shrugged. "That depends upon you. How quick are you at learning? We can plan on at least a week initially.

If need be, you can return to your base for a short respite and then come back out to me for more time."

"Yes, sir."

"Now, before we continue, I wish you to tell me more about you. What you told me so far is what you do here. Who are you? And what are you like?"

Brand felt relaxed and sat back. He thought a minute before looking up and responding, telling Ulric what he thought of himself; his religion, his likes and dislikes, his confidence and his training. He had been born to a large family with several siblings and a Roman Catholic upbringing. They had all played sports and done fairly well in school, even allowing for Brand to attend a military school for college. His family was close. He enjoyed martial arts and outdoor sports, and had only a few longterm girlfriends, although his last had ended poorly. Ulric sat silent for most of the time, nodding or saying a word in response, while listening intently and paying as much attention to what was said as to how it was said.

When Liam had talked for the better part of an hour, he stopped. "There is more, but I've been talking a bit."

"Yes, and that is good. Now I know a little bit more of you. It is a good start. You are smart and thoughtful, yet thoughtless and reckless at times. You are compassionate and passionate, and sometimes let your concern for others impair your abilities. You are physical by nature, and a hunter at heart. Am I correct?"

Brand smiled in return. "Spot on."

"Good. Now tell me more about your family and who you came from. And then tell me about your dreams. Or should I say my dreams?"

....

Hours later as the morning began to dawn, Ulric looked to the sky and stood, stretching tall. "Thank you for coming to meet me, Hvelpr. It took you a while to answer me, but I am glad you finally came. Now go back to your friends. They worry. I will wait your return tomorrow."

"They'd like to meet you." Brand stated.

Ulric shook his head. "Not today. I am quite famished and need to go eat. In time."

"Yes, sir. I'll let them know." He seemed to feel it fitting to give a short bow. "I'll return this evening and I'll bring my gear. Do I need to bring my weapons?"

Ulric laughed. "I don't see that you'll need them. I would just bring the bare essentials. I will look forward to your return tonight. Now hurry along." With that, the great silver lycan transformed as he turned to run. Before he disappeared behind the dunes, Brand saw him change into a lycan form running on two legs, and then shift completely into a large silver canine, sleek and long with tight muscles under thin fur and a long, thin tail.

Brand still felt a bit surreal as he stood and made his way back from where he came. As he came upon Major Valko and the others, Siohvan was the first to notice and called to the team. They all stood and gathered around as he approached.

"Well, mate. What's the word?" Valko asked, standing with his hands on his hips.

Brand simply shook his head. "I don't know. It's a bit much to take in." After taking a moment to consider, he lifted a smile to Valko and the others, settling on Siohvan. "Very exciting, to say the least."

"Who is he?" Cedric asked, intent upon the American.

"Wepwawet, if I heard correctly. Guardian and hunter for the Pharaohs?" He stated, part in question. "And so much more. He goes by Amun-Ulric, or just Ulric, which sounds Scandinavian or Nordic. I have no idea how old he might be. To tell the truth, I doubt he knows himself. But . . . just wow! He's told me to return tomorrow evening and that I should be staying with him for a week. He has offered to bring me into this life."

"I asked if he would mind meeting you. He said yes, just not today. He said he was hungry and wanted to hunt."

Fergus grinned and nudged Cedric. "To be certain, I won't want to meet him on an empty stomach. He might just eat us all."

Siovhan looked to the younger man and winked. "I hope he goes for you two first. He might be too full to finish off the Major and I."

They all laughed and the Major motioned for them to start the run back to the base. Still laughing they set off on an easy pace as a pack of young wolves welcoming home one of their own.

Chapter 13

New Life

Liam slept in until almost noon. As he crawled out of his bed, he looked at his cellphone and noted text messages from Prim. He stretched tall first and then sent a text to his Chief to meet him for lunch.

As he started to dress, he received a text back with one word: Schwarma. He laughed as he sat down to put on his boots.

He approached the schwarma shop, taking in a deep breath of air as he saw Prim sitting at one of the plastic tables smoking. He caught the faint waft of jasmine and lavender across the air and glanced towards the shop. He barely caught the motion of the young girl turning back into the shop as the shop owner came hurrying out with a plate of schwarma and a coffee for the Chief.

"Sir! You must be famished. I took the liberty of ordering already, but all of this is for me." He chuckled as Abdullah placed the paper plate with food in front of him. "Hey Abdullah! Please bring my officer the same. One chicken, one beef and one lamb."

"Right away, Chief." He responded, laughing.

"What's up, sir? Another late night running?"

Brand sat and nodded. "Yes. And I had the most bizarre meeting. I woke up and I couldn't help myself."

"Seriously, sir? Did you make a film? And please tell me they were twins?"

Brand shook his head and continued to smile. "Sorry, more bizarre than that, and definitely more twisted. For lack of any acceptable and reasonable term, I met my maker."

Prim's face turned serious as the cigarette hung from his fingers inches from his mouth yet frozen in air. "Scuse me, sir? Did you say you met God last night?"

"No." He shook his head. "I did meet the one: the white werewolf."

"Who is he?"

Brand shook his head. "I don't know. He said his name was Amun-Ulric, or just Ulric. I know he's old. I mean really old, like millennia, but he looks as young as I do. When I met him last night, he was exactly as he was that first night, all silver fur and silver eyes. But then he shifted into a man about my age. I wouldn't believe it if I hadn't seen it."

Prim chuckled, "Did he have a bunch of holes in him?" And he took a bite of his schwarma.

This brought a slight grin to Brand's face. "No. Apparently those might be mere annoyances to him, but nothing more. He was fine. And after he changed, or shifted, into a human, he was the same man that has been in my dreams."

Prim stopped chewing with a mouthful of food and sat gaping at his officer. Finally, he commented. "Seriously, sir. While I'm eating you're going to go all Freud and tell me you've been dreaming of a man. I'm going to have to go back through all your training."

"Ha-ha. Funny. But seriously, when I've seen myself in the dreams, it was his face in the mirror. Now I know why. Those were his memories. I was reliving his life as this change has been overcoming me."

"So, what? Are you becoming him? And what does that mean?"

Brand smelled jasmine and lavender on soft skin in the air and looked past Prim to the shop. The smell was immediately overpowered by the smell of sandalwood and Abdullah as he appeared with a plate of schwarma and a can of Pepsi. The stout shop owner set the paper plate down in front of Brand as Prim pulled out several dollars to pay.

"Keep the change, Abdullah."

"Thank you, my friend." Abdullah responded, giving a short bow and heading back to his shop.

"No, I'm not becoming him. I'm becoming me, but I don't know what that fully means. I'm heading back tonight to spend the next week with him. I think he has the answers to what's happening to me. And when I said I couldn't help myself, I meant that. I woke up and could feel him . . . sense him calling me. So I ran out to meet him. Hopefully he can make heads or tails of this. Cover for me while I'm gone. If you need to get a hold of me, I'll have my phone, but I may not be able to respond immediately, so text."

"Roger, sir. Anything else you need to tell me?"

"Valko and his team ran out with me last night, but they kept their distance when we closed in on Ulric. They waited for me and we ran back together."

Brand took another bite of his schwarma and followed it with a drink. "I'm heading back out tonight. I'll be with him for a week or more. I'll take my cell with me but probably won't have it all the time, so if you need anything, leave a text and I'll try to get back with you."

The Chief blew out a long breath of smoke and nodded. "Will do, sir. You already covered that. While you're gone, I'll check on Ross."

"Be careful. I don't know what the endgame of this group, the Sons of Anubis, is. We don't know who they are targeting or for what reason. Maybe get with Major Valko and work it out what they believe their angle is. And find out what we're up against. Snoop around but be careful."

Prim smiled and flicked the cigarette butt across the food court towards a metal trashcan full of sand and cigarette butts. It missed, sending a small shower of burning embers into the sand. Prim shrugged and his grin widened. "Sir, I'll be the picture of subtlety."

Brand heaved a long sigh and bit into his second schwarma. They finished the rest of the meal in silence, enjoying a moment of peace while feeling the coming of the storm.

"While I'm gone be careful. Keep an eye out and see what you can figure out? We've had each other's backs since we got here."

Prim chuckled. "Aw, sir. You care."

Brand nodded. "You know I do. Now, after I finish my meal, I'm going to go grab a nap and pack a few things. I'll head out before dinner."

"Roger, sir. I've got to swing by the armory and clean weapons. Do you want to take a few with you? At least a nine?"

Brand shook his head before taking a bite of the schwarma. "Something tells me I won't need any. But thanks."

"Ok, sir. I'll be around before you cut out. Find me before you leave. Enjoy the meal." He grabbed his cover and departed.

Brand took his time enjoying the remaining schwarma and soda before wiping his lips and clearing the table. He tossed the trash in a can and returned towards his building.

As he crossed the base, he was so caught up in his thoughts that he missed a female figure catching sight of him and following him with her eyes. The strawberry haired corporal motioned to one of her fellow female soldiers and pointed to the officer.

After a quick word, both women took off to follow him across the based, mindful to keep a distance. As they entered his building, they took note that it was quiet and seemingly deserted. The strawberry haired corporal took the lead, moving towards Brand's door.

From nowhere, Siohvan stepped, intercepting the two Army women and glaring at them. "I'm certain you do not have any business with the Navy Commander. Do you?" She uttered a low growl and cast her sharp eyes from one to the next.

The two women glanced at one another and stammered, shifting nervously and turning away from the British agent to hustle from the building awkwardly. Siohvan watched them leaving, hands on her hips defiantly.

With a satisfied smirk, Siohvan turned and found herself face to face with Prim, who stood between her and Brand's doorway, arms crossed across his chest. "Thanks, I think. Are you protecting my boss or are you fighting off the competition?"

The British agent turned bright red and found herself speechless. Prim gave a wry smile and winked. "I've got the watch from here."

Siohvan turned, taking in a deep breath, and followed the exit of the two girls, leaving Prim chuckling behind.

....

Brand swung by Prim's room as he prepared to leave. He wore his desert boots, black cap, green t-shirt and blue jeans with a small knapsack slung over his shoulder.

"I've got a few changes of clothing and my running shoes. I don't know how long I'll be out, but I'm guessing at least five days if not longer. My phone should work . . . but to be completely honest, I have no idea where I'll wind up."

"Hey, sir. Are you going to be in . . . like a hole in the ground or a cave or something? I mean, where do werewolves hang out?"

Brand thought a second and shrugged. "I guess I'll find out. Valko and the others stay in rooms, so . . . hey, I'm flexible."

"Good luck, sir. Text me when you get there, if you can. Let me know you're safe. If something happens I'll get word to you as fast as I can."

"You be safe too. And keep your eyes open." Brand ordered.

As Brand turned to depart, Chief Timmons approached, nodding towards him. "Afternoon, sir. I'm here to coordinate with your Chief."

"You're up and about already, Chief? Shouldn't you still be recovering?"

"Negative, sir. I was fine shortly after you pulled me out of the water. Plus, although DFAC food sucks, it's one-thousand percent better than hospital grub. They discharged me this morning after 24 hours. I've got a follow-up appointment tomorrow. I'll be ok."

"Sounds good. Well, Prim's all yours, Chief. Enjoy. I'll be back." The Officer offered. "Take care of him for me. I'll be out for a few days. It's taken me a while to train him up and I'd hate to have to start over."

"Hey, now. Who trained who?" Prim protested.

Brand winked and smiled. "I always let you think it was you. I'll be back."

Timmons laughed as the officer disappeared from the courtyard.

"What's the plan, Prim?" Timmons asked, entering his room and pulling up a chair.

Prim thought for a moment. "First, I've got to get you caught up on the strange life I've been leading. I think we're going to need a drink first. Come in and shut the door." He knelt down and flipped open a locker at the foot of his bed to retrieve a bottle of Scotch.

....

Brand walked to the carpool and picked up a vehicle, taking keys for a new dark green Pathfinder. He soon found him outside the fence line and driving into the desert.

An hour later, following an internal calling across the sands, he came upon a turnoff from the highway where a tall figure stood. Brand not only recognized him but also felt him, as he pulled closer and slowed. Ulric stood there casually as if waiting on the corner of intersecting streets in a major city, wearing white linen pants and shirt, and matching khaki shoes.

The window rolled down and he leaned across the seat. "Greetings and salutations. Offer you a lift?"

The lone man turned his silver eyes on him and smiled. "I'm glad you came, little Hvelpr. Yes, thanks." He opened the door and slid in. "Follow this road." He bent his head past the turnoff and further up the highway. "I haven't had dinner. We can grab a bite to eat at the Sharq Souq and enjoy some conversation. Are you hungry?"

"Certainly. I haven't eaten yet, either. What's our schedule this week?" He shifted the Pathfinder into gear and the vehicle lurched forward.

Ulric glanced across the desert and up towards the setting sun. "Introduce you to yourself. And then teach you."

"When do we begin?"

Ulric turned his seeming eternal smile from the road upon Liam as his eyes sparkled. "We began when you first bathed in my blood. I've been tracking you since you were . . ." He considered his words carefully. "Reborn."

Brand sat silent for the next mile as they continued the drive and finally broke his silence. "How have you been tracking me? And how can I hear you from miles away? I did hear you, didn't I?"

The elder stared straight ahead along the road, watching while other cars zipped past. Though the speed limit was listed as 70 kilometers per hour, very few vehicles travelled at less than 100, including Brand.

"Yes, you did hear me when I called. You'll learn as we proceed. I am now a part of you. Initially, as a young pup grows, parents can sense and this helps raising the pups. Although you were not born to me, I am in you. For lack of a better word, I am also your sire: Your alpha. The beginning. I can sense you as your grow. As we get closer,

I can sense your emotions. Anger; fear; joy; sorrow. And as I can sense what you feel, I can sense what you sense. I'll be able to help you understand. As you grow and become who you will be, that will fade some, but we will always have a connection."

"As for how you can hear me, well you can sense me too. It works both ways, although obviously I'm older, stronger and have greater sense and senses." The elder chuckled at the last thought. "I would be able to feel you around the world if you were in extreme, such as extreme pain or elation. But that probably has as much to do with my age and strength as our connection. Likewise, when I call to you, you can sense or feel it. And if you call to me, I will sense it."

Brand nodded, taking it in. "Can you read my mind?"

Ulric chuckled as a father to his son. "No, Hvelpr. But some raw emotions leave not doubt as to what you may be thinking or feeling. It will be the same with others around you. You'll learn to open your senses to feel; especially if you are in a pack. And if you submit to someone or someone submits to you, you will have a tighter bond."

"What do you mean when you say a pack?" And submit?"

Ulric watched a herd of camels along the side of the highway. "Our social units. It's based upon family, but extends to all those who form the pack. For millennia the survival of the younger velps has depended upon pack mentality and grouping. And within a pack, members form bonds that allow communication. When a pack accepts a new member, one of the immediate benefits is acceptance into their feelings. It works both internally and externally."

"What does that mean? Internally?"

"If a member of the pack intends to harm the pack, the others will feel it. Lying isn't an option. When you were growing up, you might have told a few little lies to your parents and gotten away with it. Now assume you're a pup and you try that with your sire, yet I can feel your motives and emotions. You would give yourself away."

Brand laughed. "Hell of a parenting skill to have."

Ulric laughed with him. "Yes, it is. As for submitting, we always have a hierarchy. There are alpha and beta. And even within the alpha and beta, there is always a hierarchy. When you meet others like us, you will sort it out. And when relationships form, one is always the alpha and the other is always the beta. There is a tighter relationship and tighter communication. It can come between two friends, or siblings, or lovers."

"What about an equal relationship?"

Ulric's laugh was loud and full. "Seriously? And even in your short life, when has there ever been a truly equal relationship? Certainly, each individual should receive what they need, but in all things there is always one who leads and one who follows. At times it may switch as the need arises, but there is always one who will be lead."

"What am I?" Brand glanced over at Ulric.

The elder continued to smile and shrugged. "That depends upon who you're talking to or about. With me, you are my little Hvelpr, my pup. And I'm absolutely certain you can feel where you fall between the two of us. This is your beginning. But I not only feel me inside you, I can also feel you. You are strong and confident in yourself and were that way well before me. With others you will find yourself the dominant. It is just the cycle of life. You will find as others may submit to you, you will be able to feel them. It's . . . how the pack works."

"Not to change subjects, but I have to ask. What do you know about the Sons of Anubis?"

The smile disappeared from Ulric and he shook his head. "Those you speak of currently are just misguided children. The original Sons of Anubis were defenders and guardians centuries ago. They were the offspring of my brother or rather the offspring of his offspring. Is this what the group calls itself? I haven't been paying much attention of late, until I felt them."

"I believe so. Do you know them?"

"No. I have sensed them in my area although I could not discern their motives. I just thought they were passing through. But I felt them the night we first met. Or rather, when we first ran into each other. I could feel a tension in the air and their intention concerned me. Although I didn't know what they ultimately intended, I could feel they were hunting. When a pack hunts, they communicate through . . . well for ease of understanding, pack talk. Within a certain distance, a pack can feel itself. And if you are close enough to the pack, you can feel them. Like listening to whispers, but not necessarily hearing the words. As we have dinner I will talk as a pack occasionally so you can feel and understand."

"I followed them that other night. I was out hunting the week before and enjoying the quiet night air when I first felt them. Initially it didn't concern me, but one night I felt something else, so I followed them and I saw you. And you know the rest. I haven't felt them hunting since."

"Did you feel them when they attacked our base the other night?"

Ulric shook his head. "No. They know I'm here now, so it serves their interest to be cautious."

"Are these the original sons of Anubis?"

Again Ulric shook his head. "No." Again he laughed softly. "The sons were much stronger and I would know them if they were within my territory. Most of them have long since gone. These new lycans are just . . . young. They are not the sons of Anubis and they have probably just appropriated the name for their own use."

The two continued to drive and talk. A few miles later brought them to the Sharq Souq where Brand parked. They entered the mall with Ulric leading.

"Is Applebees ok?" the elder asked. "They have acceptable steak."

At the entrance, a Malaysian waitress greeted them with a smile. Taking them for Europeans or American, she spoke in passable English. "Table for two?" Her eyes fell squarely upon Ulric a moment before shifting down, her smile lingering.

Ulric nodded and responded. "In the center of the room please."

She took up two menus and turned to lead them, glancing back over her shoulder at the elder and giggling.

"Does that happen often?" Brand whispered.

The elder nodded. "Yes, when I let it. Have you been paying attention to others when you are on your base?"

The young American shook his head. "No, sir. I've been pretty much flaking out whenever I get around females, so I'm not paying any attention to how they act."

"Yes, well while you're with me I've got your attention so you won't flake out . . . much." Both men laughed. "But pay attention. All creatures are sensitive to some degree, and we tend to emote a level of . . . confidence just doesn't cover it. Just say we emote and others pick up on a very primal level."

Upon seating the two, the waitress lingered, glancing from man to man before catching herself and rushing away. Brand looked around the room and realized they were fast becoming the center of attention. Two men so obviously not Middle Eastern in Kuwaiti stood out.

As Ulric glanced along the menu, he casually spoke. "Note those around us; the man and woman sitting behind me; the three gentlemen in the booth to my right; the family with children at the big table. Focus on them first and tell me what you think."

Brand set his menu down and glanced. "Young couple. Middle Eastern. Well dressed. Early twenties.

He's somewhat ambivalent towards her and she's interested in her Smart phone. Three men in business attire, having a quiet discussion; one seems to be talking to the other two. Business dinner I guess. Family. Husband, wife, three kids."

The waitress returned, her eyes fawning upon the elder. "What . . . drinks . . . "

He looked up to her with his silver eyes and smiled warmly to her. "Iced tea, please. Sweetened. And my companion?"

Liam glanced down the menu. "Iced raspberry tea please. Thanks."

"And we will both have your largest steak, rare please. Just warm it up."

She jotted the notes down. "Your sides?"

He shook his head. "Nothing, thank you. And no need for a salad."

She finished the order and moved away towards the kitchen, her eyes continuing to spy back at the table, occasionally flickering on Brand but locking on Ulric. After she was out of sight, Ulric chuckled.

"You'll need to get control of that. We tend to be physical and even on a bad day are somewhat magnetic. I let my guard down simply to let you see. I'll be teaching you how to control it. Without control it can get a tad messy."

"What is it, exactly?"

"Animal magnetism. At one time, called mesmerism. Imagine an animal marking its territory. We tend to do that: Either warning off threats or attracting potential Betas, or

Alphas. But it's important not to be so blatant. So you'll want to control what you emanate."

"Now as to the three sets I mentioned, what else do you sense about them? You described what you saw. What do you feel?"

Brand looked around and shook his head. "I'm not sure I know what you mean."

Ulric placed his hands on the table and closed his eyes. "You've practiced breathing before in your martial arts. And sensing. Try to follow my breathing. Slow yours down and match mine." Brand watched and listened and slowly matched his breathing with Ulric. As he did, he felt an unfamiliar surge course through him and a connection between himself and the elder lycan almost pushing itself in against his will. As their breathing came into sync, he closed his eyes and continued sensing into the elder, trying to relax and allow the bond. Slowly, he felt the senses extending out, as if riding on the sight of Ulric. Through closed eyes, he almost felt like he was viewing the space in all directions, spreading out and noting each and every person further and further in the room.

Their senses began focusing in from the entire room towards individuals and Brand felt their combined vision wrapping his senses around the couple directly behind the elder. He felt them; their pulse; their smells; their heat. He could tell the man was interested, but not necessarily in the woman across the table from him. As one of the waitresses moved around the room, Brand could feel his attentions following her, and he could sense the man's motives towards the young woman. In contrast, the woman sitting opposite the man had two contrasting emotions battling within her. The first seemed to be abject loathing towards the man across the table from her and a seething anger; while the second was a new attraction, deeply sexual, and Brand almost blushed when he realized it was towards both Ulric and himself.

He shifted his thoughts towards the three men and realized there was an angry contest going on between the three, although they seemed to be covering it well. He could sense one of the three was veiling his anger but his focus was directed towards the second of the three.

Further rotating through the room, he closed his own eyes and surrounded the family, drawing in emotions and senses. He could feel tension in the father and mother as they focused on the children, while the children were excited; their excitement driven by being in the restaurant. Of the three children, one drew more anxiety from both parents; their eldest son, who was rambunctious and full of energy.

Ulric opened his eyes and Brand lost his connection. He opened his eyes and stared at Ulric. "How did you do that? Or how did I do that?"

The elder shrugged nonchalantly. "When you use just your eyes, you are limiting your total senses. You can smell, hear, and feel others around you. You can feel pulses. You can feel heat. Someone who is angry grows warmer.

Someone who is attracted grows warmer in a different way. You'll learn to sense where in the body the heat manifests, whether its in the head and shoulders or whether its in the abdomen, or whether its in the entire body. As a pack, we can align ourselves for a common vision. It helps in the hunt or in battle."

"When you practice martial arts, did you practice any blind training?" He waited for Brand's nodding acknowledgement. "You can sense the Qi of those around you. You can feel their movement, whether punch or kick. You do this by extending your Qi to extend your senses. But to truly feel, you have to use all your senses simultaneously."

"I brought you here for your first lesson. Using all of your senses at the same time. Most men tend to use sight or sound or smell individually. Combine them all and go deeper. Have you ever caught a scent and vividly pictured something from the past? From your youth or years before?"

Brand nodded and Ulric continued. "It is that but much more. It's combining all senses to form a fairly accurate picture. Now let's enjoy the rest of our meal. We will continue to practice through this meal and every other time we are in public. You'll pick it up fast. It's like opening your eyes for the first time and taking in all the sights and colors."

"When we return to my home, we'll start your physical training. And combat."

The steaks arrived and again the waitress lingered, her hand almost touching Ulric's shoulder as she stood by the table.

He looked up to her and smiled. "Thank you. That will be all for now."

As she walked away, Ulric cut into his steak. As he forked a piece of rare meat up towards his mouth, he spoke one last time before eating. "As we eat, I'll communicate with you, sending you my intentions and where I want you to focus. Try to follow. Right now, whisper to me who you feel me following." He bit into the steak and began to chew.

Brand hesitated and then sliced into his steak, watching as the warm, red juices spilled onto the plate. As he lifted a bite to his lips, he took a slight breath and felt towards Ulric. Right before he bit into the meat, he smiled. "The waitress."

Ulric nodded. "Good. Now let's enjoy our meal."

They ate the rest of their meal in relative silence. Ulric occasionally spoke as a pack, guiding Liam towards one individual or another. By the end of his meal, Brand had sought out every individual in the restaurant.

Ulric paid and lead the way from the restaurant. "We shall take our time as we return to your vehicle. The mall is an excellent place to learn to sense: So many people, so many emotions, smells and sounds. We will grab a Turkish coffee up ahead and then when we finish we will head back to my home. We still have time, so we can begin to train."

The Turkish coffee stall had a few tables in the mall corridor as well as seats inside. Ulric selected a table in the corridor and a small Turkish man rushed out to take their orders.

As before in the restaurant, they watched and Brand attempted to use all of his senses while enjoying a dark, Turkish coffee. The cups were small, but hot water was poured directly over thick coffee grounds. After a few sips, he took in a few grounds and crunched them between his teeth.

"About the sons or Anubis, or whatever this group is? Why are you hunting them?" Liam asked after a few minutes of silence.

Ulric took another sip of coffee and set his cup down on its saucer. "They are up to no good. In all things, we chose sides. I didn't like what they intended, so I intervened. They are in my grounds so it is my right and responsibility."

"What if they were elsewhere? What if they were in New York or Florida?"

"Not my land, not my concern. Still wouldn't support their intentions, but I wouldn't necessarily go out of my way to intervene. Now, whatever pack runs those grounds may have something to say about it."

The younger man sat astonished. "Are their werewolves in America?"

Ulric laughed loud bringing attention from others. He leaned forward and placed a hand on Liam's shoulder. "We are everywhere. It has been my experience most major cities have some pack. America is no different. The last time I was there, I recall visiting Louisiana. I forget when . . .

early 1800s I believe. New Orleans had a very social pack, thriving. I enjoyed the visit."

"Oh, wow. I mean, I've met the British officer and his friends, so I assumed they were in Europe. But I guess I didn't think beyond that."

"Liam, it's to be expected. I'm assuming the first you actually knew of our existence was after you had a run-in with the others. I was born into this life eons ago, but I can guess how it must feel. Changes your entire concept."

"Yes, well I'm having to reconsider a few things lately."

Ulric finished his coffee and looked around. "I believe we have done well so far. Let's head back to my home and we will start other training. We have years of lessons to cover in one week, but I'm certain we will get done what I need to start you on."

"Thank you, Ulric. I appreciate the lessons." He stood up to follow.

"Now certainly what sort of sire would I be if I left you to your own devices, young Hvelpr?"

They found Brand's car and started back. Ulric gave directions as they drove, lowering the windows and feeling the warm, desert air.

"You have plenty of training in combat and you move very well . . . for a non-lycan." He gave a slight smile. "In the same sense you learn to use your entire body when you fight, I will teach you how I fight. Some who are born to this only use their front claws and maybe their teeth. But in combat and in hunting, you have four paws, mighty jaws, plus countless other body parts such as knees and elbows. In the same way I am aiding you to use all of your senses combined, we will teach you to fluidly use your entire body as a weapon."

Brand nodded, paying attention to the road while listening intently. "Do all lycans learn combat like this?"

Ulric shook his head. "No. Like most predators, lycans don't typically need to use more than their teeth and jaws; or one or both paws to take down a prey. Most lycans will use one paw or two and don't ever really fight, much like most humans. Most will bite to finish off their prey. But only the ancients know how to truly fight. Anubis and I travelled for years, learning combat and practicing with each other. It was our mission in life for centuries to become warriors and then we became guardians and defenders."

The younger man took a moment to glance over in awe. He sat speechless and turned back to the road.

"You've already learned a great deal more than most people. It won't be hard to teach your mind: And your body will follow. I'll start you this week and you can practice more on your own. After we've trained a few hours, we will run at midnight. I want to take you on a hunt. Have you hunted yet?"

Liam turned red from embarrassment. "I've woken up outside the wire on a goat, but I don't recall hunting."

Ulric nodded. "It's your inner beast calling. We will let it out tonight. A great part of us is the hunter. But tonight and every night this week, you will run and hunt aware of who you are. And hopefully we can cause your shift. Running as you are isn't bad, but running as you will be . . . as lycan . . . is something else entirely."

They continued the drive following Ulric's directions back to the intersection where he had been waiting, where they turned. They soon found themselves approaching a large home surrounded by lush green plants and trees. A few cars sat in the driveway, to include two Mercedes and a Chevy pickup.

"Park near the Chevy. We'll head inside and change. I have clothing you can use to train in. Then, we shall begin in the courtyard."

For the evening, Ulric had them both dress in dark shendyt kilts and linen shirts without shoes. For the next five hours, they trained. Initially, Ulric simply had Brand move and defend himself. Then he transitioned to forcing Brand to attack. The elder moved with a grace and speed Brand could barely grasp, while he felt his own attacks were slow and predictable.

They transitioned to fighting drills in preset maneuvers, both attacking and defending. In each case, Ulric wanted Brand to use two or three limbs to defend and counter simultaneously. This continued for another hour, before Ulric called for a short break.

"I know you've learned forms and such in your martial arts. The rest of our time, I'll teach you a lycan war form. Anubis and I created it several thousand years ago, to train our children. It will assist you in a great many things, not the least of which is fighting."

Brand nodded. "I'm pretty adept at picking up forms and dances, but something tells me this is going to be something altogether different."

"We shall see, won't we young Hvelpr."And they began.

When midnight rolled around, Ulric had finished teaching Brand the last move. He watched him practice a few times through, the dance being fluid yet strong. Finally, the elder nodded and then shrugged. "Eh, it will do for now.You need to practice."

Brand laughed. "Thanks. I'll take that as a compliment for now."

"Good. Now, let's go hunt. I can feel you haven't shifted yet. Not into your true form." He removed the linen shirt he had been wearing. "Your mind fights against it and you aren't at ease."

He sat on a stone bench on the side of the courtyard and placed the shirt neatly beside himself. He took a moment to look to the sky and then stood.

"As before, extend your senses and feelings towards me." He removed his shendyt and placed it across the stone bench, standing naked in the warm night air. He took in a deep breath.

Brand thought he should have felt awkward, but instead felt like a child standing with his parent. He lengthened his breathing to match Ulric's and knelt down, leaning forward on his palms while watching the elder man.

And then he felt the change as Ulric shifted, soft white fur sprouting across his entire body. Ulric's jaw elongated and his ears extended up into sharp points and in seconds before Brand stood the great silver lycan. He had felt the energy coursing through the great lycan as he shifted from man to beast and even now felt the almost palpable charge in the air. He felt his own breathing deepened and his pulse grew rapid. He felt his body striving to follow suit, but he did not.

And then he felt the pack whisper in the back of his mind. "Hunt."

The elder lycan launched out from the courtyard and Liam followed on bare feet. They ran out into the night to hunt.

....

The two ran across the sand, Ulric taking lead while Brand struggled to keep up. The ancient lycan was incredibly fast, much faster than Brand, and even Siovhan for that matter.

They caught sent of many creatures as they ran. Goats, horses, camels, dogs and cats swam across the wind. As they ran, those creatures that caught their scent first or saw them approaching ran and hid. They even came upon a small pack of desert wolves, hunting. The pack gave way to the lycan and his pup.

Occasionally, Ulric would send a thought or intention and Brand would take lead. He would send him towards a specific beast somewhere ahead, and Brand would find it,

Finally, Ulric caught sent of a goat and Brand knew it was time. The two came in from opposite angles, both downwind. Brand could feel where Ulric intended to stalk from and he took up a vantage point opposite his mentor.

They both moved at the same time, launching towards the goat from its blind sides. The smaller animal sensed Brand, lifting its head to see his approach and turned to run, instead finding it facing the massive silver lycan.

Ulric stopped short of the goat, allowing Brand to tackle it. He caught the creature by its throat and jaw and snapped its neck, giving it a quick and painless death. The goat went limp in his hands and he looked up to Ulric.

The elder nodded and shifted back into his human form. "Well done tonight, young Hvelpr. Let us take this goat home and we can prepare it. Sometimes I like to flavor my meat before I feast. And we can rest some tonight, for tomorrow will be a much longer day."

....

Brand woke when he heard the first call to prayer, the Salat al-fajr, before the sun began to rise. The weather was beginning to change as the harsher summer days were ending. It no longer reached the mid-120s and was closer to upper 90s with a dry heat. In the early morning while the sun wasn't high, it was enjoyable with a soft breeze across the desert.

The following days were the same as the first. They rose early and when they did, Brand found an older British gentleman in butler attire preparing breakfast and tea.

He welcomed Brand graciously. "Good morning, sir. I am Jeremy. I am Master Ulric's personal butler. I trust the Master's accommodations were satisfactory. This morning we shall be serving breakfast with tea in the small dining room."

Besides the butler, there was a middle-aged middle-eastern grounds keeper as well as a younger, Philippine female maid.

Following breakfast, Ulric took Brand to the courtyard daily, working on combat and fighting for hours, followed by a quick jaunt to the Shark Souq to simply watch people. They would return for hours more training and then as night fell would head out to hunt. Following each hunt, they would return while talking and getting to know one another while Brand also learned more of Ulric's history and long life.

Brand stripped down to shorts nightly, running barefoot, while each night Ulric would shift into lycan form most of the time. On a few occasions he chose to shift fully into wolf. When he did, he appeared as a cross between a larger, more muscular wolf with the sharp, defined features of a jackal. In true wolf form, he moved faster than Brand could follow, darting ahead and returning.

The week drew to an end. On their last night, they hunted only for sport, tracking numerous creatures across the dunes. As midnight approached, they came to the top of a high dune and looked out across the desert.

Ulric shifted back into human form and looked to the sky. "This has been a good week, young Hvelpr. I am proud of how far you've come in such a short time."

"Thank you, Ulric. If I hadn't felt it through you, I would still be blind. I feel there is so much more to learn." He squatted on all fours.

Ulric tussled his short hair like a father to his son and laughed. "I have several thousand years ahead of you, so yes; there is more to learn. But you're doing well and most of it will come with time. You're already allowing your true strength to rise through and you are faster then when you arrived. You're hearing when I whisper and you use your senses as one born to it. All you need now is to let go and allow yourself to be . . . you."

The elder felt concern within his young student and he waited, watching. Finally he asked. "What's bothering you, young Hvelpr?"

After a moment of hesitation, Brand asked, "Why can't I change? Since the first time we met, when I was first infected, I was never scared. I don't know why. This should have been terrifying, but not once was I truly concerned. As I learned more, I realized I wanted this." He noticed the elder smiling at him. He continued, "I feel you shift. I feel you change. And I feel your blood in me. But why can't I shift?"

Ulric watched the younger man a moment and continued smiling warmly. "You may feel my essence in you, but rest assured it is all your blood. My blood touching yours was only a catalyst. As you grow, you become more of whom you will be. Right now, only you are holding yourself back."

"What do you mean?" Brand asked, looking up for answers.

"Although you believe you accept this, there is still some part of you that does not. It will come and probably when you least expect it. You have a lifetime of not believing to overcome. Give it time. And practice what I've taught you."

They remained in silence, watching the peaceful night. Finally, Ulric looked back over his shoulder. "We shall head back now. Return to your camp tomorrow after lunch. Enjoy the morning breakfast and news. No doubt your friends miss you. I've a short trip to take but I'll return. When I do, I will call you back to me. We have much more time ahead of us."

"May I bring the others next time?"

Ulric thought a moment before responding. "We shall see."

Brand stood and nodded as the elder lycan shifted. They started the run back to his mansion.

....

Across the desert, Hassem stood in the back courtyard of his home under the dark sky. Kumar stood at his side. He stared silent as stars gave faint light overhead. Finally he looked to Kumar.

"Everything we have done . . . for naught. We lost Raheem for nothing." His voice was angry. "They visited the Colonel's house. Abdulla heard them talking about the Sons of Anubis. They know we exist and yet still they say nothing."

Kumar lit a cigarette and stood silently, his smile hidden by the night. After letting Hassem suffer in his internal anguish, the bald man spoke. "We killed many more of them than our one. And we have been growing in ranks. The new Sons will be able to change soon and with them we shall have the numbers we need."

Hassem nodded. "Thank you, Kumar. But Um Ghar isn't happy with us or with me. My brother called me today. Um Ghar has decided we should take out the others immediately. She has devised a way. We will hunt as a pack and attack together."

"We need to pull them apart. Separate their strength and take them down individually. We can start with the weakest first. Their Major is too calculating to be caught alone, so he can wait for later. But we must take out his soldiers."

"What about the Chief? The one with the guns?" Kumar asked, lighting a cigarette. "He's caused us enough pain and suffering."

Hassem nodded. "Yes, I believe you owe him a debt of blood. He is yours. When we act, he is your responsibility."

The short man grinned and took a long drag from his cigarette. He blew it out in a large cloud.

"We need to select one of the others and pull them away. This new one is not our biggest threat. The British are. They are more experienced and dangerous. Um Ghar believes we must take them out and then their officer will be ripe for the killing, and this American will be a babe lead to the slaughter."

Kumar shook his head. "Um Ghar said to take them out. Let's take them all out. Even the American child."

Hassem looked at the shorter man and considered him for a moment. "They've managed to counter us every time to keep our presence quiet. A few whispers and other than that, they have successfully hidden our presence here at each turn. Even when I know they saw us and captured it on video, they were able to hide what we did. They are now silently hunting for our agents on the bases. We shouldn't underestimate them."

Kumar blew smoke and nodded. "True. But our soldier on the inside will be their undoing. We know the boat crew was looking for us. We know they were probably working for the American officer and his Chief. The two chiefs were often seen together. And now we have directly sent them a message that we knew by striking their boats. I agree with Um Ghar: It's time that we attack more decisively. We need to separate them. We need to strike directly at those who oppose us."

Hassem listened and waited for Kumar to continue. "We know the one U.S. officer sneaks out and often. He almost always has someone with him now; one of the British. We kill two birds with one stone. We need to hunt them when they sneak out but we need to send stronger numbers so they cannot escape. And, as you direct, I will take out the Chief. That bastard is hell with his guns."

"What're your plans then, Kumar? You have my attention and if this works, I'll give all the credit to you when we tell Um Ghar."

Kumar took in another long drag and blew smoke. "We wait. Send four to wait outside the fence line and when the officer is far enough from the base, slaughter him and whoever is with him. He runs and hunts like he wants to be like us, but he doesn't change, so now is our time. And if one of the British goes with him, slaughter them too. When they run with him, he leaves his Chief at home. I will take care of the Chief myself. I can get on base. Our Army soldier can get me in through the gate. When I know the officer is gone, I'll simply finish the Chief and be done."

Hassem took the plan in and mulled over it a moment. Finally, he began to nod and smile. "I agree but that is not enough, Kumar. It's a great start. As long as we're hitting them, we hit them harder. Who normally runs with the officer?"

The bald man replied, "The female or one of the two big males; but never all at once. And the American officer hasn't been seen at all this week. I heard he left the base in his vehicle and hasn't returned."

Hassem considered the new information. "We don't want to spoil the element of surprise, but should we target his Chief now? And maybe one of the British?"

Kumar shook his head. "No. You're correct. We don't want to ruin the surprise. In the words of Clausewitz, hit their center of gravity. We hit them hard at once and before they recover, we slaughter them all. If we can target one or two of the others, perhaps the large British soldiers, we can pull them away as well. If we leave three different scenes of slaughter, it will be impossible for them to hide us any longer."

Hassem nodded. "Good. I'll call Udei and have him keep an eye on the base. You call our Army soldier. When we know the American officer has returned, we'll send watchers to wait outside the fence line. When he decides to leave the base again, we'll be waiting for him and you can personally take care of the Chief."

"That honor is all mine; and my distinct pleasure. I still feel the prickling of his bullets that night he kept us from finishing the officer out in the desert. The next time, we won't be caught off guard."

"Good." Hassem said again and seemed to relax a bit as a smile started to form on his face. "We must grow more. I want our numbers to be more than one hundred. When we finally attack, I want it to be final."

Kumar shrugged. "We are already close. Of those who we recruited, we've only lost one to the change. All the others are either able to shift by now or close to it. Another dozen and we'll have more than your hundred. But we are only choosing the most devout and trusted. And that process with today's generation is long. They just don't care as much. Not with their smart phones and the internet."

It was Hassem's turn to shrug. "No matter. It's always been that way. Each generation grows less and less faithful."

Chapter 14

Return to the Pack

Brand returned to his room and dropped his gear in the corner, sitting down to remove his boots. From the door came a knock and he heard a male voice call out as a young Army soldier popped his head in.

"You had a visitor, sir. British chick. Pretty hot to look at but nothing but business."

Brand stood up and glanced around his room, calling back. "Did she say anything?" He lifted his chin and sniffed at the air, sensing around the room.

"Nope. I saw her just waltzed in without knocking and then I saw her leave. I think I recall her from a few weeks ago when you racked out for a few days. She came in with your chief a few times."

Lifting the pillow and blanket on his bed, he found a small, folded note hidden under the folds of the sheets. He let the sheet and blanket fall back in place and unfolded the piece of paper.

Before he read the note, he lifted the page to sniff deeply and he caught the scent of Siohvan. A short note written in delicate cursive stated simply:

Liam,

I've missed our runs. Looking forward to tonight. Try to keep up. See you at the fence at dusk.

Siovhan

He folded the note back and slid it back under the pillow, sitting on the edge of his bed to remove his boots. He quickly changed into running shorts and shirts, strapping his badge holder on his arm and slipped on his five-finger shoes.

He exited the building and headed across the camp towards the armory. As he arrived, he stepped in through the wooden door and nodded at the petty officer behind the counter.

"Sir." Came the greeting. "Can I help you?"

"Looking for my Chief. Gunner in here?"

"Back here, sir. Welcome home." He heard Prim call out from beyond the wall. "Just schooling these newbies on Xbox Burnout."

"Did you eat yet?"

"Sir, you know I wait for you. I'm not one way."

"You must be starving, then. Care for a schwarma? I'm buying." Brand offered.

"Hell, yeah. How often do you hear an officer offer that? Just give me a minute to log out and I'm there."

The petty officer at the counter grinned and lifted the counter top. "Care to come in, sir?"

"I'm good. I get back there and I'm likely to disassemble a few weapons for fun. Just love the smell of CLP in the morning. Or afternoon as it were."

"Roger that, sir. I put it on my Wheaties at breakfast." The Petty Officer quipped.

"Bullshit, Cobb." Prim stated, stepping past the petty officer. "You know you put fat free milk on your cereal: Special K at that. You ready, sir?"

"Let's go." And the two stepped out, heading for the schwarma shop.

They walked in silence until they arrived at the shop. As they arrived, Abdullah came out to welcome them, wiping a plastic tabletop and offering a chair.

"Hello, my friends. What shall we have tonight? The usual?"

"Does a hooker charge you twice in Amsterdam? Absolutely, Abdullah." Came the Chief's response. This brought a bigger grin from Abdullah who nodded emphatically and turned back to his stand.

As the two men sat down, Brand leaned in closer. "Update. Where do we stand?"

"What? No love? Just right to work? Sir, I'm hurt. You've been gone for a week and you don't care to hear about my day?"

Brand smiled, shaking his head, and asked, "How was your day, Chief?"

"It was great, sir. Thank you for asking. I had a date with the Sergeant while you were gone."

"You can fill me in on your exploits with the Army nurse later. Put your Dick Tracey hat on and tell me what you've found."

"I've been poking around and asking questions. Just nosing here and there. And I keep coming back to the base. We told Chief Timmons to keep an eye out for anyone or anything out of the ordinary. I'm sure he was asking around and then his boat unit gets attacked. And we both know what attacked him."

"Prior to that, one of Khalid's men comes up with the brilliant idea to invite NCIS in for a pow-wow. We've guessed that the real target was NCIS. We were duped into coming outside the wire and they were waiting for us. So who's been watching us? Who's our invisible stalker? Is it the Colonel's man here on base? It was his idea."

"I don't read him like that." Brand stated. "He's squirrelly but not against us. He's just shifty. Someone else is coordinating this. Someone who we can't see but who can see us."

He smelled jasmine and lavender and looked up as the young woman approached, burning blue eyes staring out from behind her niqab. She placed the two paper plates of schwarma on the table in front of the two men, never taking her eyes off of Brand. She froze, as if caught in a daze and Brand stared back intently.

"Um, sir." He heard Prim cough, and the young woman hesitantly bowed and turned away, hurrying back to the stand and out of sight.

"Jeeze. I need whatever you're on. It's like frickin' catnip for the ladies. Anyway, where were we?"

"I was just wondering who might be our invisible stalker."

"It's got to be an inside source. Someone nobody suspects."

Brand picked up his schwarma to take a bite and stopped. "Or nobody sees. Like a servant."

Prim glanced up, not fully comprehending. Brand added, "Think about it: third-country nationals are overlooked by everyone. They clean our port-o-potties and serve tea and no one even blinks when they're about. I'm guessing the Colonel has full-on meetings with his staff while his tea boy stands at his side."

"So we're back to the Colonel's man on base. Who gave him the idea?"

"Exactly."

"I say we visit the Major and ask to have a chat."

Brand took a drink from his can and took up his second schwarma. "Did we get anything back from the cellphones? Or on the facial recognition from the contact I gave. Have you heard from Cedric?"

Prim had a mouthful of food, which he chewed and swallowed before shaking his head. "Good point. They should have results by now, at least the LUDS. I haven't spoken to them yesterday or today. But your contact on facial recognition bore fruit. The bald guy is Kumar something. He's been attached to a few different groups, but all trails lead back to ISIS or al qaeda before that. He's wanted in a few different bombings across the Middle East, mainly in Iraq."

"Nice. Ok, let's find the Brits first. Then we'll check with Major Mohammed." The officer thought a moment before looking up and asking, "How is Ross? Is he out of the hospital yet?"

Prim nodded. "He took a flight home yesterday. We're back down to just our two new agents now."

"Good to know. Remind me to email him later when we know he's back CONUS to see how he's recovering."

The Chief nodded again, finishing the last bite of his schwarma in one large mouthful. He gave a muffled affirmation.

....

Following their meal, Prim texted the entire British team as well as the two NCIS agents. They all managed to meet in the courtyard of their building at about the same time, Brand and Prim arriving shortly before the British.

As the British team arrived, Siovhan attempted to hide her smile although Brand could feel the excitement rolling off her in waves. He could also feel a different level of excitement rolling from young Fergus as he pushed ahead of the others to shake his hand, grinning. Prim shifted back out of the way to give them room as they approached.

"Aye, welcome back, Liam. I mean Commander. How was your . . . visit?"

Brand thought a moment before shrugging and smiling to the group. "Exhilarating and eye opening. My life can never be the same."

Fergus continued to grin and stated, "I've been practicing the forms daily while you were gone. I'm looking forward to training some more."

Siovhan pushed past the larger Scot and leaned her head into Brand's shoulder, nuzzling against him before massive Cedric clapped a hand on his back. "You seemed a changed man in less than a week. I can see it in you." The large man was truly happy for him and welcoming.

Valko approached last, nodding and smiling warmly. "Churchill is correct. You are . . . much more than before."

"Even I can see you are more than meets the eye on this new day." They all heard Huang as the two Navy agents entered the courtyard. "Your absence has seen a . . . growth in you." He hesitated as he assessed the officer. "Welcome back."

"Thank you." Brand responded, looking around at the gathering. "We're all here. What did I miss and where are we? Who was the Major's boy in contact with?"

Cedric reached into his shirt pocket and pulled a small notepad, flipping it open. "A few of the numbers were 1–800 sex numbers, which isn't shocking. But there were two numbers he called often: both on the day of his demise.

One some hour before, followed by the same numbers minutes before." Flipping the pad shut, he looked up. "Abdulla, nephew to the Colonel."

Brand took in a deep breath and let it out slowly, turning to Prim. The Chief nodded.

"Well, that makes some sense. He's in the perfect position to play the Major's boy ten ways to Sunday. And he would know who is coming and going in the Colonel's house. What about the other number?"

Cedric opened the pad again and glanced. Closing the pad he shrugged. "It's assigned to the Army. It's a watch phone."

Prim turned his head and furrowed his brow deep in thought. Huang noted the movement and waited a moment before calling out. "What is your thought, Chief?"

Prim looked up and smiled. "Thanks, sir. I was just wondering. We know there's a snake in the grass . . . or sand as it were. I doubt it was the boy. He was just the patsy. We can see its possible the Colonel's nephew is involved. But someone else on this base has been watching us and providing information. I doubt it was the boy. He just doesn't know that much and he isn't in a position to find out. Or should I say he wasn't?"

Wong moved closer, staying at Huang's elbow. "Who would be? Not the foreign workers. They don't have access to much of the base or at least not without an escort."

Brand shook his head. "No. Regrettably I'm afraid it's not. Our problem is internal. That's what got the boat crew attacked. They were asking around for us. And someone overheard them and it made them a target."

Huang nodded. "So someone on this base then?" It was more question then statement.

Brand nodded his head up and down slowly. "I'm almost certain of it."

Cedric thought a moment and snapped his fingers. "I can run an app against Abdulla's phone and see who he was also chatting with. It might take me a moment, but I'm certain I can find something."

Huang nodded to the largest man and then turned his eyes on Brand. "Might I recommend we follow up on the second number as well? Our insider might be with the Army." He turned back to the larger man in a fluid motion. "Mr. Churchill, if you would be so kind as to see how many calls were shared between the second number and young Abdulla. If they do share a common communication, we might be able to narrow our search down."

Cedric looked back to Valko and then to Brand before nodding at Huang. "Yes, sir. I'll work on the connections immediately."

"Excellent." Brand spoke. "We'll be visiting the Major. At least we can confirm a few things regarding the initial meeting. I doubt we'll learn anything new, but we can confirm what we do know."

"And what's that?" Valko asked.

"That his assistant recommended they invite NCIS to talk. I'll also confirm what else he knew, which I'm guessing will be nothing."

Huang agreed. "Best practice to answer all questions. Leave nothing to chance. We will be available once you know more. Let me know if you require any assistance."

"And I believe I trust Major Mohammed enough to warn him about Abdulla." Brand added. "He's Colonel Khalil's nephew, so that might not go over too well with the Colonel right now. But the Major should be in a position to keep an eye on him."

"Another intelligent idea, Commander." Huang commented. "We will be in our office." He turned and led Wong from the courtyard.

The others started to turn away and Siovhan moved closer. Leaning in, she whispered, "Are we on for tonight?"

Liam leaned down to touch his fore head to hers and whispered back. "Absolutely."

She turned and ran after the others, leaving Brand and Prim in the courtyard alone. The two men looked to each other and then started across the base to find the Major. As they did, the young black enlisted Army soldier watched from a vantage point not far and lifted his phone, dialing. The nametag on the private's uniform read Wilson.

A moment later, across Kuwait City, Kumar hung up his phone and looked to Hassem and the others in the room. He took up a small glass of tea and sipped it before smiling smugly. "Our target has returned. We will move into position tonight and wait for our opportunity to strike a decisive blow."

Hassem nodded. "Al-ḥamdu li-llḥh." Praise be to the lord.

....

Major Mohammed was in his office when they arrived. Chief Prim led the way through their office, greeting the enlisted staff as they crossed the room. When they entered his office, he greeted them cordially and Brand closed the door behind them.

Mohammed had a concerned look as crossed the room to greet them with a handshake, "You seem solemn today, my friends. What concerns you?"

Brand moved closer and kept his voice down. "Mohammed, we trust you. Since we've been here, you've shown us respect and friendship and I haven't felt anything other: the same with your Colonel. There are easier ways of making a statement than calling us out and setting us up. But someone in your inner circle is playing us all and I'm wondering if you might know who."

The Major returned to his desk and sat silently, looking down across the tidy paperwork. Finally he looked up and shook his head and winced. "I was afraid of this. When my aid was slaughtered in his room I knew it was more than just violence. When your special agent was found in the Colonel's home, it could not have been coincidence that you were there. My Colonel and I spoke on this many times in the past week and we suspected someone in his home, but he refuses to say who that might be."

Brand spoke the thought out loud, "His nephew, Abdulla: we checked his LUDs and he was in contact with your aid right up until he was murdered. I know the Colonel trusts him, but how do you feel about him?"

Major Mohammed mood changed and he furrowed his brow. "How did you obtain his LUDs? We didn't find his phone."

Prim shrugged with an embarrassed look. "Well, you know we were the first on the scene. We were going to visit him and ask him a few questions. We took the phone."

Mohammed initially looked as if he were upset and then softened and his head bowed. "It makes sense. You would get the information faster than I would. I'm not upset. But why didn't you come to me sooner?" His eyes popped back up to Brand.

Brand responded in earnest. "We're coming to you now. We didn't know before. When we found the bodies and took the phone, it took a few days to get the forensic information. We just now received the report, so we're telling you immediately. How would you feel if we brought you accusations without some sort of evidence? We still don't know how Abdulla is connected other than he was the last person in contact with your aid before he and his roommate were murdered."

Prim piped up again. "Plus, every time we've been anywhere that something hanky went on, he was somehow one degree separated but close enough. He knew we were visiting the Colonel when we were first attacked. He knew we were visiting when Chavez's body was found. And he was in a position to put the bug in your aid's ear to invite NCIS to the party. When we questioned the Colonel, he was the first to shift the attention to others."

Mohammed shook his head. "I often wondered how my aid came up with the suggestion to call your NCIS. As your saying goes, he's never been the sharpest tool in our shed. And he just suggested it one day. I really started suspecting something when he volunteered that Colonel Khalil's tea boy might be involved. I've never seen that boy so much as sneeze in the Colonel's direction. He admires him beyond belief. That just didn't make sense." He took in another deep breath and let it out. "What am I to do? I have nothing to present to the Colonel and Abdulla is his family."

Brand thought a moment before speaking. "Just keep an eye on him for now. Fore warned is fore armed. But we may be able to use him to our advantage. And you can keep the Colonel safe. He's a good man."

Mohammed agreed. "Yes he is. I'll do what I can." After a moment of consideration, he took a deep breath and let it out slowly. "I should tell the Colonel. With this additional information, he might be more open to listening. He's actually a very practical man."

"If you think so. But be careful, Major." Prim said. "We seem to be a lightning rod for those around us. Keep an eye on Abdulla and don't let your guard down. And if you do tell the Colonel, be prepared for him to confront his nephew outright, which means you get a target on you, I'm pretty certain of it."

"Regarding the nephew: have you seen him around the base often? And if so, have you seen him with any American soldiers?" Brand shifted the focus of the conversation.

Mohammed nodded to the American officer. "Yes. There is a young, black Army soldier that he often meets with. I've seen then together around base and a few times in the Mosque. I never thought of Abdulla as a religious man, so it did seem odd. But he told me the Army soldier was converting."

Both Brand and Prim exchanged glances. "Yeah, I'll say he's converting." The Chief quipped. "Do you remember his name or rank?"

"Wilson. He's enlisted. Private if I recall." Major Mohammed answered.

"Thank you, Mohammed." Brand spoke, offering his hand. "Be safe and keep your head down. We still don't know what we're fully up against."

As he shook hands, the Kuwaiti Major replied, "You too, my friend. It's gotten a bit more dangerous lately."

"We'll see you again soon, Major." Prim added as they two departed the office.

....

Once outside the building, Prim looked back over his shoulder. "What do you think the Colonel will say?"

Brand led the way across the base, eyes straight ahead. "Not sure. I'm hoping he keeps an open mind and doesn't tell Abdulla until we're ready. As for us, we need to keep attentive. It's been quiet since the last attack and I can feel something in the air. Some tension."

"Did the others feel it?"

"I don't know. If they do, they didn't say anything. I'm going running with Watson shortly. I'll ask her."

Prim stopped short and watched his officer continue to pace away. "Really, sir? It's like that. You've been gone a week and I don't even get a reach around. It's all about you."

He heard his officer chuckle ahead of him. "It's not like that, Prim. I need to run and she offered for tonight. Besides, I haven't caught her . . . yet."

"Yeah. I'm sure she did, but I still don't know what that means, sir." Prim laughed, hurrying to catch up. "Ok. I'll see how Timmons is doing and maybe we'll watch a video. Just be careful."

"You know I will, mother. Hey, if you think about it, see if you can find out where this Private Wilson hangs out and who he's with."

"Roger, sir. If Timmons is up to it, we'll go talk to our contacts with the Army."

They continued on their way towards their building.

....

Brand stepped out of his room to find Prim waiting in the courtyard smoking. "Hey, sir. Don't forget to use protection."

"From what?" They heard Siovhan call and both men looked up. Her eyes honed in on the Chief.

"Oh, you know. Sun burn?" Prim snickered. "He's got such delicate skin."

She moved closer, leaning in as she neared him to whisper. "I'll protect him."

"Hmmph. And who'll protect him from you?" The Chief responded.

She grinned and stood straight. Looking to Brand, she smirked. "He'll just have to run faster." Turning, she strutted away, glancing back. "Are you coming, Commander? You may be slower and softer from being gone this past week."

Brand unconsciously growled under his breath and followed her while Prim continued to chuckle. From outside the courtyard, an enlisted soldier sat cleaning his M-16 and watching. As the two strode towards the fence line, the young, black soldier picked up his phone and sent a short text. Once he had sent the text, he clipped his weapon back together and moved away from the building.

As the two neared the fence line, Siohvan smiled up at Brand. "Thanks for running with me, Liam. I have missed you painfully so."

Brand laughed lightly. "Yes, well I've grown rather attached to our runs but a bit more attached to you."

She nudged her shoulder into his side playfully. "Fergus is positively beside himself. He wanted to come along, too. But thankfully Cedric intervened and took him to the gym. He really admires you."

He felt a bit awkward as he replied, "Well, he's a good kid. I like him."

She shook her head. "No, Liam. He's focused on you. You don't quite understand . . ." she hesitated. "He's sort of made you his alpha. At least while we're here. Even within the team with Major Valko, Cedric and myself here, he looks to you for his leadership."

"Oh?" Was all he could muster in response. "I'm still new to this whole thing."

She smiled up at him. "You can't help what you are. Neither can he." She slid under the fence and waited for him. As he crawled out, she quickly whispered, "Neither can I. You've become that for me too." Without another word she turned and sprinted away, her light laughter following behind as Brand pushed himself to his feet.

He waited a moment, watching her start to race away. He felt his desire rising to both run and to catch her but waited, holding the fire as it simmered inside.

He gave her a moment to gain a lead and when she looked back over her shoulder at him, he nodded and started out. Even from the distance, she could feel him approaching and she launched into a full run, a moment of panic gripping her.

She ran hard, breathing hard and fully sprinting. Without looking back she could feel him gaining on her.

He watched her, stretching out his stride as he pushed himself. She was fast; but he had been running with Ulric.

He let the race go on for a mile, heading out into the desert and away from the lights of the base.

As she topped a dune, she felt his arm close around her waist as he wrapped her up and they went tumbling down the sands on the far side. They rolled and tumbled, wrestling down the hill and came sliding to a stop, with Brand on top, gripping her wrists and holding her in place while she wrapped her legs around his waist, squeezing him and pulling him in.

She struggled yet smiled, lifting her head to snap at his chest with her teeth. He felt her laughter as she squirmed and felt her heat as she tightened her legs around him, pulling his hips into hers.

Tightening his grip around her wrists, he leaned in closer, just out of reach of her bite. He grinned and whispered, "Caught you."

He suddenly felt her relax and a look of pleading overcame her. "Yes." She whispered. She released her grip with her legs and squirmed underneath, rolling over onto his stomach. "I'm yours."

As she did, he released her hands and she used them to pull off her shirt and sports bra in one movement, throwing them aside. Watching her, Liam lifted himself to his knees and removed his shirt.

She looked over her shoulder, her eyes wanting him while imploring him, "Shift with me. This first time, please." And slowly she began to change.

He reached down to cup her left breast and felt soft white and blond fur sprouting to cover her skin as her internal energy shifted. Her energy continued on into him and he felt an urge deeper than just taking her. He wanted to join her.

Under a starry sky, he felt himself shifting as soft short silver fur began to cover his body. He felt his fingers tighten and extend as his nails hardened and lengthened. His face and bones shifted and although initially he felt pain, he also felt incredible pleasure as a vast amount of energy flowed throughout his body.

Watson watched him as he shifted for the first time, his face extending into a long, refined snout with high pointed ears similar to those of Wepwawet, yet distinctive to Brand. His body remained lean like his human form, yet his legs shifted into the hind legs of a hybrid, with his feet extending into the long, clawed paws of a lycan.

He felt an internal convulsion as the energy completed his shift to hybrid form and he looked down upon Siovhan, now also in hybrid form of a white and blond wolf with longer fur and more wolf-like features than Brand. She lifted her hips for him as she sunk her head and shoulders.

Brand lifted his chin to the stars and let out a long, powerful howl. Their night had just begun.

Chapter 15

Divide and Conquer

The Imam in the nearby mosque began the Salat al-fajr as Brand and Watson snuck back onto the base, the sun just barely making its appearance. She followed him to his room and as he entered she wrapped her arms around him and squeezed.

Brand turned and wrapped her up, lifting her and kissing her long and deep. As he let her down she continued to press against him, smiling and sighing.

"Get some rest. I expect my Chief will be waking soon to check on me."

She laughed. "I'll be surprised if Fergus isn't here shortly after to ask to train. He loves when you teach him."

Brand yawned and stretched. "I'll need some rest first. You wore me out, Siovhan, in a very good way."

She laughed into his chest and looked up. "Yes, well I'm sore in all the right places. And I've got sand in all the wrong places. I think I'll shower first. It's a shame you can't join me, but I believe that would be a bit too obvious."

He bowed and lightly tapped his forehead to hers before she turned to saunter away, glancing back over her shoulder to see if he was watching. She smiled again and blew him a kiss before disappearing from sight.

Brand continued to smile as he stepped inside his room and shut the door.

Siovhan followed the walkway towards the stairs as she looked down into the courtyard below. A mischievous smile crossed her lips as she stopped at Chief Prim's door.

She knocked and waited. Within she heard grumbling and the sounds of Prim moving out of bed and rumbling through his room.

"This had better be good. I was just in the middle of a great dream." She heard him say as she heard his bare footsteps approach from inside the room.

The door opened and he stood before her in boxers. "Scuse me, Ma'am. Do you have the wrong room?"

She leaned in closer and whispered, "In case your Commander fails to inform you, I've come to report I have definitely proven my dedication. Several times. For him . . . I'm extremely dedicated."

Prim choked up and stood speechless as she smiled coyly at him and turned away. "Perhaps I should go show him my dedication again." She departed, quite proud of herself.

As she disappeared from sight, the Chief shook his head and returned to his room to get dressed. "Looks like he's got some explaining to do." He chuckled.

....

The door swung inward and Prim stood watching Brand laying in his bed. The officer looked up to the Chief and covered his eyes with his arm. "Can you give me a few hours, mom? I had a late night."

"Or an early morning. Care to explain yourself young man? And I do mean give me all the juicy details. That British chick was simply beside herself quoting lines from Team America."

Brand sighed and rolled over, his back to the door. "I'll tell you everything. I swear. Give me two hours to sleep."

His Chief shook his head and grimaced. "Four hours. I'm going back to bed, too. And you're buying the coffee."

Mid-morning, Brand's phone rang as it received a text. He rolled over to pick it up and glance. The phone has received a short text from Fergus inquiring about working out and lunch.

He smiled and typed out a response with one hand. Ten-thirty.

He rolled over and tried to sleep more but found he was already wide-awake. Crawling out of bed, he grabbed his shower gear and headed across the base.

After a shower and shave, he threw on shorts, t-shirt and running shoes and waited. By ten, Prim was at his door.

"Ok, sir. Time for a coffee and smoke."

Brand acquiesced and followed the Chief across the base towards the DFAC. They entered, both showing the brassard strapped to their shoulders, and headed for the large coffee urns. By mid-morning, the dining hall was fairly empty: a few individuals or small groups were seen around the edges of the hall sitting at the long tables.

Each man grabbed a Styrofoam cup and filled it with the burned, black coffee. Brand put copious amounts of creamer and sugar in his coffee to cut the bitter taste.

He lead the way as the two men found a table away from prying eyes and ears.

He took a sip of the hot, acidic coffee and savored the flavor. His taste buds were different, as were all his senses. He could see more, hear more and smell more. Even his senses beyond those seemed honed to a higher level.

"Spill, sir. I've been limited to only my fantasies and what I've been doing with the army Sergeant these past few weeks. And although epic, it's about time I lived vicariously through you."

Glancing at his Chief, Brand contemplated the previous night's events and took another sip of coffee.

"First, it was phenomenal. The whole night."

"Now we're talking, sir. See? I have been a great influence."

The officer laughed. "Yes, but beyond just that."

"Oh!" Prim gasped. "Wow. I was joking. But, just wow. You did score. Sweet mother of God. My officer has busted his cherry. I'm proud of you, sir!"

Brand shook his head still laughing. "So . . . up until now, I haven't been able to shift. That's what they call it when you . . ."

"I'm following sir. That's when you go all fur and stuff; like the movies. How does that feel?"

Brand took in another deep breath just filling his lungs. He let it out, his eyes bright. "Incredible. Last night was the first night I was able to actually shift. And its like my eyes are open wide for the first time. I can see so much more. I can hear and feel so much more."

"When I shifted, there was pain. Major Valko had told me there would be pain the first time. It may be painful the first few times. He likened it to puberty and he was right. It was like every fiber in my body wanted to change. But it was great at the same time. There was so much energy. I feel so much stronger and faster. I cannot even begin to do it justice."

"Uh huh." Prim muttered, watching him as he drank his coffee. "And?"

Brand's smile widened and he turned his eyes down upon his coffee. "Ok. Just between you and me, and since apparently Major Watson saw fit to inform you . . . yes I did catch her."

"I am alive with questions, sir. What does that even mean?"

Following a sip, which he attempted to savor the bitter flavor, he replied, "When we first started running, she knew what I was going through. And just like puberty, everything has been active and chaotic, including my sex drive. And not just your normal deployment, I've been away from women sex drive. I'm on overdrive."

"Yeah, I've noticed, sir. And it seems to be both ways. Tails have been eyeing you like a holiday goose."

Brand chuckled boyishly. "That is a by-product of this change. And I've got to learn to turn it off. But Watson knew I'd be going through this, so she used it. She offered that if I could catch her . . . " He looked up knowingly to his Chief.

"Ah. If you catch her, you keep her. So I'm guessing she's fast?"

The answer came with a nod. "Definitively. She's faster than any of the others. Until I met Ulric, I've never seen anyone run so fast."

"Ulric?" Prim queried.

"My maker. The lycan whose blood made me."

"Oh." He nodded. "Go on."

"Ulric moves faster than anything I've seen. He's insanely fast. But among these others, Watson was the fastest."

"Was, sir? I'm taking it she isn't any more."

He shrugged. "The week I was with Ulric, I felt myself changing. I'm faster and stronger. And last night I caught her and I shifted. And it was awesome!"

Prim sat in silence, sipping his coffee while Brand seemed caught up in thoughts of the previous night. Finally, the Chief grinned and spoke. "Did you do it like doggie style?"

Both men laughed. As Brand finished his coffee he glanced at his phone. "I'm meeting Fergus in the gym in a few."

"He's a good kid. Tell him I say hi. Sir, what's our next move?"

Brand stood up and thought a second. "Did you find out where Private Wilson hangs out?"

Prim nodded. "He's one of the enlisted who is on the watch schedule. He apparently has been asking to patrol our sector of the camp and requested nights. His senior enlisted just thought he was a loner and thought it was a win-win."

"Nice. See if you can get a picture of him and we can share it with the others. If he's patrolling our sector then he's probably keeping an eye on us. That might be how Timmons boat crew was marked. If he passed word we were talking to the boat crew, that might have been the trigger."

"Which means we might be the next target, sir. Be careful when I'm not around you."

"You be careful, too, Chief."

"Come on, sir. I'm a Chief. It comes with the territory."

They laughed and Brand continued. "Between Wilson and Abdulla, we have at least two targets. We need to figure out how best to use them to our advantage. We need to smoke out the Sons of Anubis."

"We'll figure something out. You go burn a workout. We can grab dinner later. Are you running again tonight?"

"Hell, yeah! I love her dedication."

....

At the gym, both Churchill and Williams stood waiting in the weight room.

The giant man greeted him with his warm smile while the younger man grinned. "Watson reported that you shifted. Congratulations! I thought we might see how your strength is today."

"And maybe we can practice. I've been putting in hours a day on the forms you taught me." Fergus offered.

"Sounds great. And my maker taught me a form you'll find fascinating."

The three men entered the weight room and started with dumbbells. They worked their arms and core strength for an hour before shifting to deadlifts.

Cedric began arranging plates on the bar and looked to Fergus. "Are you feeling up to the big weights today, Williams?"

The youth nodded. "Load it up."

"We'll start at two-hundred and go up from there. Everyone in. We'll do ten deadlifts to warm up. Then we go up and lift five reps each increase."

The big man lifted the bar from ground to standing straight and back ten times like he was lifting an empty bar. Fergus followed and finally Brand. Each man did the reps easily, exploding to bring the weights up and down.

And then they added more weight.

They continued increasing by degrees of twenty-five pounds at first and then changed the twenty-five pound plates for the larger forty-five pound plates. Each increase they snapped out five reps and went higher.

At nine hundred fifty-five pounds, Churchill was still lifting the bar as if he was simply standing, although the bar sagged with nine plates on either side. Fergus bent and grunted as he lifted the bar, hissing on each lift as he brought the sagging bar up to his thighs and dropped it again.

When it came to Brand, he rubbed chalk on his palms and stood over the bar. Gripping the iron bar, he squatted and lifted. Exploding to a standing position, he brought the bar up to his thighs and back down in one even move. He ran through the five reps and dropped the bar on his fifth, feeling the burn in his thighs and breathing hard on the last lift.

Churchill shook his head. "You are definitely a beast. Even young Williams is breathing harder on that last lift. Too many others in the gym for us to continue increasing, but overall a great lift today. I'm off to clean up, gentlemen. Williams: Are we on for dinner in the DFAC later?"

"Aye, Cedric. I'll call you later."

As the largest man left the gym, the two remaining headed towards the multi-purpose room. Once inside, they found a corner and began stretching.

"Sir, you're positively a beast today. Cedric was right."

"Thanks, Fergus. It's been a great workout. And this whole event has been eye opening."

"Well, you probably have a great deal more to learn, so I requested a leave of absence from the service once this mission is over. If you don't mind, I'd like to return to the states with you. You'll need a pack, and I can help you with that. I can be your first. If that's ok?"

Brand looked at the young man and saw the pride in his eyes. Smiling, he replied, "I'd be honored to have you show me the way, Fergus. Thank you."

The young Scot was positively beaming. "I'll email my siùir. I've told Bridget about you some. Maybe she can come visit us in DC."

"I look forward to meeting her."

"Ha. She meets you and she'll probably want to be a member of your pack, too." Fergus grinned and winked. "You'll be stronger with a pack."

"How so?"

Fergus shrugged. "I don't know if I explain it quite so good as Watson or Cedric, but you've played sports. You know how team mates always amp each other up. Even the crowd cheering causes the athletes to perform better. Well, now imagine your pack all in communion and with one goal. You all cheer each other on and just grow stronger."

Brand nodded, considering the statement. "Ok. Makes sense . . . I guess."

They continued stretching and talking a bit more before Brand told Fergus about the forms and training Ulric had put him through. He discussed the ancient fighting style and even the techniques the elder had taught him. Young Fergus sat listening attentively.

When they stood, Brand stepped back and directed. "Do the form I taught you. Let's see how it looks and we can make corrections. Then I'll start you on the next form. We still have a great deal more to teach you."

They continued working out another hour before ending for the day. They hurried to catch the tail end of lunch at the DFAC and then separated.

As they went their separate ways, Fergus called back to Brand. "I'll email Bridget first thing. Major Valko already has my request for a leave of absence. When we wind down this mission, I'll just remain where you are if that's ok and I can follow you back to the states."

"I'll let Prim know we'll have a third with us." He nodded with a smile and waved as he continued on back to his building.

....

Kumar sat in the food court enjoying a Kentucky Fried Chicken meal. Across the table sat both Private Wilson and Abdulla.

The young Kuwaiti looked around nervously, apprehensive of any American soldier who walked by. "We shouldn't be seen together, Kumar. Why are we meeting here?"

Private Wilson snickered at him. "No one knows you here. And no one knows brother Kumar. You're safe."

"Major Mohammed knows me, and I don't trust him. He's like my uncle."

Kumar licked his fingers and smiled, smacking his lips. "One thing these infidels have is tasty food." He wiped his hands on a napkin. "You have seen our targets on base today, Private?" He turned his eyes on Wilson.

The enlisted man nodded. "Yes. I'll give them to you. But when do I get the gift?"

"Soon." The bald-headed man spoke. "Very soon. We will need your strength to join ours. Right now, we have men outside the fence line waiting for them if they should go out tonight. And I will be onboard. That Chief is mine. We will also target at least one more. Preferably the female if we can get her alone. If not tonight, then tomorrow night or the next."

"Why am I here then?" Abdulla asked.

Kumar looked at him and shook his head. "Stop being such a bitch, Abdulla. You are one of us. You are a full Son of Anubis now and if Um Ghar were to hear you whining she would strip the spine right out of you."

This cowered the Kuwaiti officer and he shrunk in his seat. "I worry that my Uncle will learn and we will lose my position inside his house. Right now, I know everything that goes on within the house of Khalil as well as on this base."

The bald-headed man shrugged. "And soon we won't need that anymore. Our numbers are finally high enough. Once we destroy these infidels we can focus on taking our lands back. Hassem believes we should let the whole world know we exist. Very soon we will."

Wilson grinned. "And I'll be one of you."

"Yes, you will. Now go keep an eye out for our targets. Let us know where they are. Abdulla, go swing by and visit the Major. Find out if there is anything new with the

American investigation and then go home. You'll hear from us if anything happens."

"Thank you, brother." Abdulla spoke, pushing from the table and hurrying from the food court.

....

Brand showered again and took an afternoon nap. When he woke, he found Prim waiting with dinner.

"They were having a special on schwarmas. Buy as many as you want and pay for them, regular price." He chuckled.

"How'd you do today?"

The Chief laughed. "I'm a Chief. Of course I was successful. One of his Gunnery Sergeants had a picture already on his phone from when he first arrived in country: the Gunny texted me the picture. I can forward the picture out to all members on the team."

"Do that, Chief. And thanks for dinner."

"Any plans this evening? I mean before you go running?" He laughed.

"Yeah. Thought I'd watch a movie before heading out for a run. Would have watched Team America: World Police but I lent my copy to Watson." Brand stated.

"Nice. Love that movie. Has me in stitches every time." Prim commented. "Should I bring my copy over?"

Brand nodded. "That'll work. I'll pull out my computer."

....

The two ate dinner and watched the movie on Brand's laptop as the evening began to fall. As the movie ended and both men were laughing, there was a light rap on the door.

Brand called out. "Welcome and come in, Miss Watson."

The door swung in and she entered. "Thank you, good sir." She gave a slight curtsey. "And good evening, Chief."

"Perfect timing. We just finished watching your favorite movie. Team America." Prim chuckled.

"Oh, you're a randy one." She stated, shaking her head at him. Looking to Brand, she questioned. "Are you ready?"

Brand was already dressed to run. Slipping on his Five Fingers running shoes, he looked to Prim. "Don't wait up late."

Looking at Watson, Prim quipped, "Don't be too dedicated."

She grinned and snarled back. "Oh, you have no idea."

Prim followed them out from the room and down to the courtyard to lite a smoke as the two disappeared. He waited, enjoying the silence as the last call to prayer sounded across the installation. He'd grown used to the calls to prayer and it was almost soothing.

Out of the corner of his eye he saw the bald headed middle-eastern man enter the courtyard heading for a trashcan in one corner of the open area. The man emptied the trashcan into a larger bin on wheels he was pushing and moved towards another can across the courtyard.

"Better you than me." Prim chuckled, standing up to put out his cigarette and head back into his room.

He took the stairs up to the second floor. Behind him, Kumar watched with anticipation and quietly followed. At the bottom of the stairs, he removed his shoes and placed them to the side, quietly padding up the steps.

Across the base, Fergus had finished dinner with Churchill and returned to the gym to practice the forms he had learned from Brand. The young Scot wrapped a towel around his neck and walked through the exit of the hardshell gymnasium. He patted his pockets and sought his phone, yet could not find it. As he walked out, Private Wilson approached him in a rush.

The young black enlisted man spoke to him in hushed, frantic tones. "Are you one of the British agents? With the Major?"

Fergus hesitated before replying, "I'm with Major Valko, yes."

"Weirdest thing. One of the TCN said he had some information you might be interested in. Something about … shape shifters and animals. He's really scared."

Fergus stood up attentive and looked around. Looking back to the soldier, he spoke one word, "Where?"

The soldier motioned, "Come on. I can point you to where I last saw him. He's just outside the fence line so we'll have to go outside."

Fergus followed as the soldier led on.

....

A short walk took them across the base and out through the side gate into the desert. The soldier on the gate nodded to the Army soldier as he led Fergus through. They had just rounded a short dune, taking them out of sight of the base and the gate watch, when the soldier pointed to a young teenager, squatting in the sand.

"That's him." The soldier stated, pointing. "I'm heading back in. Good luck."

Fergus hesitated. "Wait. I don't have my phone on me. I need to let the rest of my team know."

Private Wilson responded. "I can go tell them. I know where your team works."

Fergus nodded and watched the soldier head back towards the gate. As he approached the young teen, the boy looked up, his face anxious and afraid.

"Sir? Can you help me?"

Fergus squatted in front of the boy. "Maybe. Tell me what's bothering you?"

"I have to show you. Can you come? Hurry please."

Fergus again hesitated. Standing, he looked back towards the base. "I should wait for my team to show up."

"No time." The boy cried, standing up and moving across the sand towards another dune. "My family!"

Fergus shook his head and followed, topping the dune in tow of the boy and seeing a housing district. The houses were low-to-middle income housing, clustered fairly close together with narrow streets and no yards.

The teen looked back to Fergus for a moment before heading into the neighborhood. Fergus followed, gaining ground on the boy as they neared one of the houses. The boy walked up to the door, reaching for the nob and calling back over his shoulder. "I am sorry. My family is in dire need."

As he turned the nob, Fergus heard the click and hiss right before the door and front of the building exploded outward in a wave of flame and debris. The large man was sent flying backwards as he saw the young boy torn apart by the blast, his torso and limbs arching in different directions.

Fergus rolled, dazed and confused as he attempted to get to his hands and knees. Pain seared through his mind as he realized his left arm was mangled and broken and his kneecap was shattered. He was vaguely aware of dark forms racing in from all sides before he felt sharp teeth tearing in his arms and legs, and talons raking along his back and neck.

In a rage, the large man pushed himself to his feet, shaking the attackers off and starting to transform. As his body shifted, the initial injuries he had suffered began to heal at a rapid rate, a byproduct of the body taking on the lycan form. He was still in mid-change when a large, black lycan drove into him, and they went rolling in the dirt.

Fergus tore at the new aggressor as he felt more bearing down on him, snapping and swiping at him. Teeth and nails tore into him and he felt strong hands grabbing his limbs. Several hands on each wrist and others on his ankles attempted to hold him in place, yet he struggled on.

With one last, herculean effort, he tried to rise. Strong jaws snapped on his neck and again pushed him down, while other jaws and claws tore at his limbs and held him in place. He fell as the incredibly powerful jaws tightened and then began to tear, holding him in place and closing off the air to his lungs.

He tried to fight as his eyes began to go black and felt the burning pain in his throat and neck. Panic filled him and he again tried to rise. He failed and slowly the darkness closed in.

The lycan on his chest stayed in place long minutes after the large werewolf stopped struggling. After a while, the one on his chest began to savage his neck, tearing into it until with a crack and a pop, the head tore free and flipped away from the body.

The black lycan rose, glaring around at the other ten who continued to hold the massive body in place. He lifted his head and let out a long, deep howl.

....

Kumar gained the top step noiselessly and followed the trail of Prim to the door of his room. The door was still ajar and Kumar stopped a moment, smiling to himself. Placing a hand against the door, he pushed it inward and the creak of the hinges alerted Prim as he stood there, watching the Chief's back across the room while starting to shift into lycan form.

Prim chuckled, still not turning. "You know. TCNs don't ever clean this building. We take our own trash out. As a matter of fact, they stay as far away as possible. Apparently they think these buildings are haunted. That was your first give away. Now . . . do you know what the fatal funnel of fire is?" He turned with his M-4 in hand, smiling in the face of the beast. "Besides, I remember your face . . . ugly as you are. You were on the cameras the night of the boat attack."

Kumar's eyes went wide as he continued to change, moving forward even as he shifted. Prim triggered his weapon fully automatic and tore through the lycanthrope's chest and neck in a tight pattern, not allowing the weapon to run off target.

Kumar staggered and the Chief emptied the clip into him, deftly dropping the empty magazine and sliding a new, fully loaded magazine into place before slapping the slide forward and firing three round bursts at the assailant's head and neck.

As Kumar attempted to stand, he heard a booming echo and felt a shotgun round penetrate his back between the shoulder blades at close range. Staggering, he spun to see Chief Timmons bearing down on him, racking a new round in the chamber.

The bloodied lycan scrambled even as Prim fired three more rounds into his side and the shotgun roared again, peppering the side of his neck and face. He pushed to the railing and threw himself over to the courtyard below.

Prim came to the railing and took careful aim. As Kumar rolled over to look up, Prim triggered a round and hit him squarely between the eyes. In shock and dismay, the lycan shuddered upon impact and fell back limp.

"Fuck this shit. I'm going to pump a few more rounds into that mother." Prim stated, moving down the stairs towards the body.

Timmons followed, reloading his Mossberg shotgun as he did. When the two men were within feet of Kumar, they both opened up, tearing the hybrid lycan-man to shreds as they continued to rain rounds into him.

As they emptied their weapons, Prim took a deep breath and let it out. "This can't be good. We have to warn the others."

"Do you think there are more coming?" The larger Chief questioned.

"I do, but not for us. My officer is outside the fence line like a babe in the woods. Without me to protect him, he's a lamb led to the slaughter. And we need to hide this body. The whole base heard these rounds."

"I'll get a sheet. I think we did enough damage they won't know what that was." Timmons ran back up towards Prim's room.

"I'm calling the Brits and NCIS. We need them here pronto." He pulled out his phone. "They might be able to help us cover this up."

"And why are we covering this up?" Timmons called back from the room above.

"I don't know; probably the werewolf thing. Just go with it."

....

As Brand and Watson crawled out beneath the fence, she spied around and noted they were alone. With a wicked grin she slammed herself against him, wrapping her arms around him and clawing at his neck and back while kissing him. He pulled her in, one arm wrapped around her waist and one hand gripping her seat tightly while kissing her savagely in return. As she pulled apart, she staggered into him and whispered in a husky voice. "I've been aching to be near you again. This day seemed to take forever."

Brand reached out to touch her cheek and smiled. "Yes, it did. But now we're here. I want you, so get running."

She shrieked and turned, running into the desert. He watched her race, letting her gain a head start before starting out after her.

Just out of sight a single Middle-Eastern man knelt with binoculars watching the fence line and the gap through which they crawled. As they exited the base, he flipped a phone open and sent a text message.

Brand followed close behind, keeping an easy pace behind Watson as they crossed the sands. There were plenty of stars above and a calming breeze kept the evening cool in comparison to the earlier afternoon.

As Brand closed on her, he saw her glance over her shoulder and turn forward to sprint. He extended his gate and continued to gain on her when suddenly he felt something new and then heard the explosion.

He slowed and turned, glancing back to the base. He felt something in the air. Raw emotions struck him of rage, pain and fear.

Ahead of him, Watson slowed and looked back. She returned to him, sniffing at the air and looked to him with concern. "Williams. He's in trouble."

Brand felt the hairs on the back of his neck rise as a feeling of dread shot through him. Absolute fear welled within him, yet it was not his. And then he saw the black lycans approaching.

Watson saw them as well. Kicking off her shoes, she pulled her shirt and sports bra off in one move, growling at him. "Run!" Already the savage growl of the wolf tore through her chest as she transformed into hybrid form, a lycan wearing running shorts.

Brand shook his head as he saw the five Sons approaching. They were at a full run, and although in hybrid form, were running on all fours. He kicked off the Five Fingers and stripped of his shirt, rolling his head in a tight circle as he began to change.

In seconds, the silver lycan stood ready next to the white and blond Watson as he let out a long, aggressive howl. He waited for the approach and sunk down, coiling into his legs tightly as Watson knelt behind him.

As the five antagonists approached, he launched himself towards them catching them off guard and unprepared for his counter attack. He struck at the lead and central attacker, arcing over his head and swiping down as he passed.

Both his right and left forepaws struck along the back of the black lycan's head and neck, tearing flesh and muscle.

The lycan fell forward and Watson dove down upon it, snapping her jaws on its exposed and bloody neck while driving her claws into it's exposed back and shoulders. She tore, growling and savaging.

After the initial strike, Brand rolled forward and came up between the next two attackers, sliding in under their swiping paws. As he rolled to his knees, he swiped out with both claws to either side, raking the two as they raced past and tearing their knees and lower thighs. One tumbled to the ground as the knee gave way while the second spun off, his thigh lacerated yet healing.

The final two were still approaching when Brand rolled forward over his right shoulder outside the lycan to his left, placing the one between him self and the other. As he rolled he reached out with first his left hind paw and then his right, tearing through the closest lycan's abdomen underneath its poorly aimed swiping attack. As he continued up, he rose and delivered a right lacerating strike that tore through the lycan's throat and splashed blood across the sand in a wide, spraying fountain. As the creature spun away, Brand slid up behind it and grabbed the head by chin and forehead and twisted, hearing the loud pop as the neck severed.

He dropped the dead lycan and saw the fifth and final attacker turn tail and run. Brand spun back to the remaining assailants and saw Watson facing the two remaining, having killed the first. Of the two, both were healing although one was still limping horribly from the first blow Brand had dealt it.

He approached rapidly from behind and caught the second from its blindside, thrusting his sharp talons through its back to grab it by the spine and twist. The creature howled as he crushed the spine in his grip and then grabbed it by the chin and twisted, breaking its neck. One last swipe of his paw tore out its throat and left it dead in the sand.

With the one remaining unable to move well, Watson tore into it, driving in to close her jaws on its throat. She received a few cuts from its talons as it attempted to defend itself, but she drove it down and pounced her weight into its chest and stomach. She tore into its throat, ripping into the jugular and finally tightening down until she heard bone break. She waited until the death throws had subsided before letting go and raising her head to howl in triumph.

Looking around she saw the silver lycan looking down upon her, blood across his chest and arms. For a brief moment, his eyes narrowed on her and she felt he was about to tackle her, and then he lifted his snout and sniffed at the air.

Shifting, he became his human form, and ran to pick up both his and her shirts and shoes. "We've got to get to Fergus!" He declared, heading across the sand.

She began to change back, her fur disappearing as she ran in just her shorts. He threw a shirt back and she pulled it on, only realizing it was his after it pulled down past her head.

"Do you have a phone?" He queried as they ran. "I didn't bring mine."

"Nor did I, but Churchill and Major Valko should have felt him too."

They aimed for the small village of houses off base and then the raw emotions Brand had been feeling simply stopped.

"Fergus!" He roared, pushing himself into a sprint and starting to leave Watson behind. He fought every urge to shift into lycan form.

He arrived as Churchill and Valko arrived on the scene. The building entrance was in rubble with blood everywhere and the body parts of a young boy mixed in the bricks. The torn body of young Williams lay in the middle, his head in lycan form removed and sitting atop his shredded chest. Both arms had legs had been torn through, his lower legs thrown about the rubble zone.

Churchill growled and began to change, starting to enlarge into a massive black lycan.

Valko moved to his side and whispered, "Calm down, man. We cannot have this."

Churchill was beyond consoling and turned blood red eyes on the Major, growling angrily. He continued to change and uttered one word. "Death!"

Brand felt all. He felt Valko attempting to calm the massive Churchill. He felt Churchill turning his rage towards hunting the offenders. And he felt Watson torn between rage and attempting to remain calm and in human form.

Slipping between Valko and Churchill, he grabbed the huge man by the chin and held him eye to eye. "Not now! Keep it in check." He growled.

For a split second, Churchill seemed to ignore him and continued to shift. And then Brand asserted himself and growled from deeper. "I said not now. We will do this, but not now. It is not time."

The larger man struggled for a moment and then his transformation reversed and he returned to his human form. Rage gave way to anguish and then grief. He howled and fell beside the younger man's body.

Turning to Valko, Brand directed. "We need to cover this up. He's in lycan form. Will he change back?"

Watson moved to his side. "No, sir. He'll remain in hybrid form."

"Search out this house." He waved towards the ruined building they stood in front of. "Find something we can wrap him in." She nodded and raced into the building, while Brand looked to Valko. "Pull his parts together and place them on his corpse. And do your best to find anyone else. There was another victim here." He bent to grab a forearm at his feet. Looking to Churchill, he called, "When Watson returns, please wrap Fergus up. Do not let anyone near him until we get him back to the base."

As Valko searched the immediate area, Brand called over. "I don't have my phone. Dial up Chief Prim and tell him to bring our vehicle. We need to transport Fergus before the Army arrives."

"How long do you think we have?"Valko asked, flipping out his phone and punching quick dial.

Brand shook his head. "Minutes at best. We can only hope Prim gets here first. And if you don't have the number for Huang or Wong, tell Prim to get them here immediately. Huang is the only one who can keep Shaker at bay, and Shaker will be showing up."

Valko nodded and lifted the receiver to his ear.

"Chief Prim. Major Valko. We need you outside the fence immediately. Follow the explosion and bring your vehicle."

He listened for a moment and then hung up, turning a concerned look to Brand. "There was another attack on the base. He'll be here in minutes. Apparently he's already armed and was trying to reach you and I. I missed his calls as I was rushing here."

"It's ok. Who got hit?" He grabbed one of Williams' lower legs as he sought out other body parts.

Valko shook his head. "He didn't say. Just that a quote werewolf attacked your building. He said he and Timmons were on their way."

"Thanks. Call Huang or Wong. Get them here."

Again the Major nodded and dialed as Brand found each part of young Williams. He brought them to the torso, where Churchill stood vigil. As he gathered the last body part, Watson returned with a blanket, sheets and pillowcases.

"We should use the pillowcases to wrap his extremities and then cover them all with the sheets and blanket." Looking to the Major, she spoke directly. "Sir, if the U.S. security forces arrive before NCIS, you'll have to intervene and take command of the scene. Commander Brand can support your position and we can cordon off the immediate area around Williams. With the sheets covering him, we can keep him somewhat distant from the Yanks. But if the Colonel wants to view the body, you'll need to keep him away."

Major Valko nodded as he continued arranging the body. Churchill gently wrapped his young friend in the sheets and covers.

Both Chief Prim and Chief Timmons arrived first, pulling up in Chief Timmons HUMMVEE. They stepped out, armed and armored.

Prim took one look and shook his head. "Damn. Good kid."

Churchill looked up from where he squatted, his face torn with pain and anguish. Prim nodded to him attempting to pass silent condolences.

Timmons moved towards Brand, eyeing the buildings and houses. "What's the score, sir?" He held his M-16 gripped tight with his finger near the trigger.

"IED tore through the building and Fergus. He was injured by the blast but he was torn apart by lycans. They were just here. Left maybe a few minutes before we showed up. He didn't stand a chance."

"Any other victims, sir?"

Brand sighed solemnly. "One. Looks like a teenager. We need to secure the area. We've wrapped up Fergus," Prim joined the two. "We'll need to keep everyone away from his body. He was in lycan form when they killed him."

"Does he change back?" Prim asked, lighting a cigarette while his M-4 hung slung from his shoulder. He kept his eyes on the surrounding buildings.

Watson approached and shook her head. "No. He'll remain in the form he died in."

"What happened back at the base? Major Valko mentioned another attack." Brand questioned the two chiefs.

Timmons shrugged and spoke first. "Nothing a good Chief with a shotgun couldn't handle."

"Bull." Prim quipped. "A little fucker tried to go all rabid dog on me in my room. I saw him in our courtyard and thought something was odd as in they never come in our courtyard. Plus when I saw his face, I knew he was one of those fuckers from the boat attack. So we shot him full of holes. We pretty much fucked him up beyond all recognition, so I doubt we'll have to explain ourselves. Before he could go all full Monty, we'd lit him up so he just looks like a very hairy man with a massive hole in his face. We did cover him up as best we could to minimize the questions."

"We received your call shortly after we killed it." Timmons added. "Base MPs swung by in force and we left the body with one of the Master Sergeants. I know him. He'll tow the party line and he's keeping it low profile until we return."

"Considering our proximity to the installation, I'm guessing we have another few minutes before the Army shows up. We've done the best we could. Help Churchill load Fergus' body in our vehicle. If we get lucky, we can have him out of here before they show up. Then we can turn this over to CID and it will become a local matter considering the only other victim is a host national."

"Roger, sir." Prim snapped to, spinning on heal and heading towards Churchill. Timmons followed him.

The two gave the huge man another moment to greave and then the smaller Chief knelt next to him. "I'm sorry, buddy. We've got to get him in the vehicle."

Without looking up, Cedric let out a low growl, shaking his head. He kept his eyes on the wrapped body, almost as if to will his young friend to rise.

After another few moments, Prim placed a hand on Churchill's shoulder gently. "I'm sorry. We have got to go."

The giant's shoulders sagged under the weight and he nodded. Prim looked back to Timmons and the two moved in to gather the remains. They gently lifted the wrapped body and carried it towards the vehicle. As they arrived, Valko rushed to open the back door.

They had barely loaded the vehicle when they heard the approach of Army HUMVEEs. As the door slammed shut, Prim and Timmons saluted towards Brand and mounted up, returning to the front seats.

Looking over at Churchill, Brand called out. "Cedric: Stay with Fergus. Go back with the vehicle."

Churchill glanced up, first to Brand and then to Valko, before returning his vacant gaze to Brand. Brand nodded at him and the larger man stood and followed to the HUMVEE. "Aye, sir. I'll be with Fergus."

Brand looked to Prim. "I'll see you back at the courtyard as soon as we're done here, Chief. Keep an eye out . . . for anything."

Prim shook his head solemnly for once empty of jest. "Roger, sir. You be careful too."

As the Army arrived, Prim turned the wheel and the vehicle slowly drove past them. Brand looked to the remaining British and called them in closer.

"Without Fergus here, this will be easier to control; but now we have to explain why we're here."

"I'll cover this one. We made it here first. We don't answer to the Army." Valko stated. "You were with us when we responded to the noise. And hopefully the Colonel doesn't show up tonight."

"One can always hope." Brand attempted to smile as they settled in for the next few hours. "Let me borrow your phone. I'll contact Huang before they get here. I'll wave them off for now and maybe they can look into something for me instead."

Valko passed his phone and Brand stepped away from the group as the Army disembarked their vehicles. Watson stood by Valko initially but as the evening wore on and they answered the questions, Watson moved closer to Brand until she was at his side.

Chapter 16

Setting the Trap

By early morning, the Army finished as much of their investigation as they could and local Kuwaiti law enforcement showed up to take their reports. As the first call to prayer started across the city, the small band began their short walk back to the base. As they arrived, the three separated with Brand heading towards his building and both Valko and Watson heading away.

"Grab your gear and meet me back in my building. And bring Cedric." Brand called. "I know it's late, or early, but we need to speak."

He returned to find both Prim and Timmons waiting in the courtyard, still armed and armored. Brand caught them up as to what had occurred to himself and Watson as well as the little bit from the rest of his evening. Brand and Prim pulled up folding chairs while Timmons pulled up a milk crate to sit down.

They were waiting in the courtyard when Valko lead his remaining team members in. Huang and Wong arrived shortly thereafter.

Churchill continued to seethe with rage, pacing around the courtyard like a trapped beast. Brand watched him for a moment.

Siovhan pulled up a folding chair and sat beside Brand, leaning in against him. He could feel how sad she was to her core as if she had lost a close relative.

Major Valko sat opposite Brand, his head hanging low and dejected. He looked to Brand for guidance and direction, attempting to keep a slight smile and false bravado.

As Huang sat, he looked to the others. "I am truly sorry for your loss. Your young friend was . . . a good man." He chose his words carefully as if emotions were elusive to him.

For a brief moment, Valko looked up as if he was about to contest the sympathies, and then he sank back into his chair. He nodded and mumbled, "Thank you."

"What did you find out?" Brand asked, pulling the attention to their immediate task.

"My assistant was fortunate. She followed up on your lead." Looking to her, he gave a short nod. "Agent Wong."

She looked at Brand and for a brief moment he saw true empathy and sorrow in her eyes. And then she shook it off and began her report. "I inquired into the moments prior to Mr. Williams demise. He departed the gymnasium and two witnesses did in fact see the Army enlisted Wilson approach him."

"We found soldiers at one of the gates who confirmed Williams depart the base. He was following a local Middle Eastern: A young teenager by accounts. It appears an Army enlisted matching Wilson's appearance led him out the gate to the teenager. That was the last anyone saw of him."

"And what about Private Wilson?"

Wong looked back at Churchill, who had stopped pacing and sunk his massive frame to squat on all fours, his fury coiling within. His skin seemed to ripple as if he were about to shift. She returned her eyes to Brand. "He's been hanging out in the Army watch office. Since the attacks, he hasn't left."

Prim grunted and gave a knowing nod. "Makes sense. He's probably listening for reports. And buying his alibi."

Churchill stood, his muscles tensing as he ground his teeth angrily. Even the muscles on his jaw were corded and popping out.

Brand stood and moved to the larger man, standing right before him. Reaching up, he took the massive man by both shoulders and held him at arms length. Looking up, he was dwarfed by the giant.

"Patience, Cedric. We need you for this. We will hunt them down: All of them. But we can't do this publicly. There are too many innocents who might get in the way."

Churchill glowered down at the Commander, his muscles tensing. After a moment, he nodded and closed his eyes. Brand released him and the larger man moved to the side to squat.

"What are you thinking?" Huang called out from across the courtyard, watching Brand from the side. "I can see your mind is alive with thoughts."

Brand returned to his chair. "We need to draw them out and away from innocents. They attacked the base yesterday but I don't see them repeating that one tonight. They know security will be high. Besides, their attack on the base was more a direct yet covert attempt to kill Prim alone. I doubt they'll consider that one again."

"Ok. So what do you have in mind?"

Brand glanced at Prim. "Lure them out. Give them something they apparently want: Me."

"Scuse me, sir?" Prim shook his head. "Uh-uhh. No way."

"I agree with the Chief." Watson snapped, standing and putting her hands on her hips.

Even Wong seemed about to interject when Brand responded. "Hear me out. They've been eyeing us all but it's apparent I'm on the list. They know I run outside the lines. We just need to use that to our advantage."

"Ok. I'm listening." Prim spoke. "But that doesn't mean I agree yet."

Before Watson could argue, Brand continued. "Someone needs to visit the Army ops center. I need them to drop a few words in front of the Army, especially Wilson." He looked directly at Prim. "I'm thinking you go, Chief. Ask them to keep an eye on me since I'm going to go running and the Brits are all staying in tonight or going somewhere else. Remember – no one knows Fergus was killed, so make it generic. Come up with some story as to why they're gone. Let them know you're going to be going up to Doha with NCIS later this evening so I'll be alone."

"Alright. I'm tracking you. And we keep an eye on Wilson?"

Brand nodded. "But let him make a call if he decides to. We might get lucky and he might call Abdulla. Once he does and we're certain they take the bait, we need to make it look real. I want you all to depart the base." Looking to Watson, he stated emphatically. "You'll take Valko and Churchill and leave the base back to your hotel." She winced and opened her mouth as if to protest and Brand cut her off. "You need rest, so do it. I want it to be obvious, so drive through the gate."

Turning to Huang, he continued. "I'll need you to show up at Doha. It's a short drive away. Once Prim visits the Ops Center, I'll need him to catch some sleep, but late afternoon he can take you and Special Agent Wong up North. You should have plenty of time to get there and make an appearance."

"And what will you be doing?" Wong asked almost as if to argue the plan. For a brief moment, it seemed as if she joined the line of Watson and Prim opposing Brand.

"I'll be getting ready for a run. We might consider calling Major Mohammed. Let him know to keep an eye on Abdulla and what to expect before you head to the Army Ops Center. If he can confirm Abdulla receives the call, that's one more leg of the cell we can follow."

"It might work." Huang commented, nodding. "How do we know that enough of them will follow you if they do come out?"

Brand shrugged and smiled. "I believe they'll want to definitely finish me if given the opportunity. Considering how many times they've tried and failed, I'm guessing at this point they'll send everything they've got." Turning to Churchill, he asked, "How many lycans do you think were at the site where Fergus was attacked?"

Churchill snapped from his anger and shook his head, trying to focus on the conversation. After a moment, he replied, "A good number: Maybe half a dozen or a dozen. It was hard to tell. I wasn't . . ." His voice trailed off.

"And how many times have they tried to finish you?" Wong queried, her face growing stern and scolding.

"Why Special Agent: I didn't know you cared." Prim quipped, chuckling.

Brand dismissed the jest and simply responded. "A few times and counting. Tonight they sent five to hunt Watson and me. The time before that, I think there were three outside the fence line. And I've felt I've been under surveillance for some time."

"Interesting. You failed to mention these events earlier." Huang noted, as both he and Wong glanced from Brand to Watson and back.

Again, Brand seemed to dismiss the comment. "It didn't seem opportune at the time to mention it nor did I understand what I was feeling. Bygones: and in the past. We have a little more planning to do and then we all need to get rest. Tonight will be long and exhausting, no matter what happens."

"I concur, Commander. What else needs to be discussed?" The Senior Agent asked.

....

Wong walked with Prim across the installation to the Army operations center. The center was a hard shell construction with a double door entering into small quarterdeck area where the enlisted gathered to watch news on a widescreen television against the wall. Another set of double doors across the quarterdeck entered the operations center heart, where a few desks around the room were manned by enlisted and officers, tracking the operations of the Kuwait Navy Base Army personnel.

When the two entered the operations center, Prim immediately caught sight of Wilson but casually let his gaze continue around the space. He recognized Wilson from noticing him stalking around their building. Wilson caught sight of Prim and immediately sat up.

Prim smiled as his gaze passed each member of the operations center, keeping his eyes from staying on Wilson too long. He took note of an Army Captain who sat at the desk close to Wilson.

Wong followed as they approached the desk. The young Captain lifted his eyes from a logbook he was writing in, looking to the Chief and then smiling at Wong and addressing her. "May I help you?"

Prim looked over his should at Special Agent Wong and then back to the Captain. "Hey! Don't you see me standing here? I mean, yeah; she's a cute Asian chick . . ." He felt Wong gasp and felt the heat at his back. "But I am still standing right here. We're together here."

"I'm sorry . . . sir? I'm sorry. I don't quite get the whole Navy rank there. Are you an officer or enlisted? What do anchors mean?"

"Yeah, I'm a Chief Petty Officer. Which means I'm pretty much called a Chief. Something the Army sorely needs." Before the Captain could protest, Prim continued, "I wanted to ask a huge favor, so before this conversation goes anywhere south, I was hoping you could do me that favor."

A Master Sergeant approached from a desk across the room. "Hey, Prim. Why didn't you just come to me? I'm sitting right here."

"Sorry, Bertrum. I thought I'd give your O's a shot at doing some service-to-service support. A little joint training." He chuckled. "You know my O right?"

The Master Sergeant nodded. "Yeah. We hear good things. He's a good egg for an O-4. What does he need?"

"It's what I need. I'm normally his battle buddy, or we have some visiting Brits who've been hanging out with him. But tonight they've got to run some errands so they're leaving the base. And I'm . . ."

"Taking NCIS to Doha." Wong finished for him as she stepped forward. "I'm Special Agent Wong, from NCIS. We have to run up to Doha to question a witness, and Chief Prim is our driver." She glanced around the room.

Prim looked at her and shook his head. "Yeah. As I was saying, I'll be heading out later this afternoon to take them to Doha. My officer has a tendency to take runs in the evening. I was wondering if whoever is on watch over near our building could keep an eye on him. Make sure he gets back safe. Maybe even dial me up if you see him sneaking out." Without looking he could feel Wilson paying close attention.

The young Captain spoke up. "We've had a FRAGO regarding weather the last week. Recommendation is to limit travel as we could have pop-up sand storms the next few days."

Prim glanced at Wong and noted her perplexed expression. "Fragmentary Orders: updates from higher authority. I'll explain later." Turning back to the Captain, he shrugged. "I doubt we can wait for this interview, so keep an eye on my boss. Master Sergeant knows where he is."

"If it helps, we can contact your cell here when we depart and again when we reach our destination." Wong offered.

The Captain started to respond yet froze when the Master Sergeant shook his head curtly towards him. "That would be great. Go on, Chief. We'll keep an eye on him. Just call when you're hitting the road and when you arrive. We'll log it."

As they turned, Prim noted the Wilson was already at the double doors and exiting the operations center. Wong had turned to follow subtly, her eyes panning the room and taking in the rest of the center.

By the time they reached the first double doors, Wilson was already through the second set of doors and outside. With a quick nod to those sitting in the outside vestibule, Prim and Wong rushed to catch up.

As they opened the door, Wong glanced to the left and swept right, catching sight of Wilson as he disappeared around the edge of a trailer of portable bathrooms. She moved discreetly towards the trailer followed by Prim and hugged the corner as they approached.

Wilson was a few feet ahead around the corner and intent on dialing his cellphone as they listened. His call was brief.

"This evening; maybe tonight. The Commander will be alone." He paused as if listening and then responded. "I'm certain. The others are all going off base. I heard it directly from his Chief." Again there was another pause. "Thank you, sir. Thank you. When do I get what you promised?" He listened intently and then snapped the phone shut.

Prim grabbed Wong and pulled her back around the mobile trailer. Slinging open the door, he pulled her into the men's side and let the door shut.

Pointing towards an open stall, he nodded and went towards a urinal. She slid into the stall and shut it, waiting. After a few minutes, Prim whispered. "I'll check outside to make sure he's not around. Then we can run back and let my boss know."

"Quick thinking. Thank you Chief." She opened the stall. Glancing around she seemed just slightly awkward.

"First time in the men's room?" He quipped.

She shook her head. "Not something I typically do. But . . . again quick thinking."

Prim popped his head out and glanced around. "Cool, no one in sight. Let's rock."

As they started to move, his phone dinged and he reached into his pocket, still moving through the door. He flipped the phone open and glanced as he moved across the installation. He slowed to a stop and grinned, looking to Wong.

"Major Mohammed just texted. Apparently, the Colonel's nephew, Abdulla, just received a phone call and immediately left the Colonel's house."

"I'll let my Senior Agent know."

Prim chuckled. "A little too close to be coincidence. Abdulla is definitely our boy. But the question is: who's he going to tell? Who is next up the chain?"

Chapter 17

The Trap Is Sprung

Brand waited until the sun had set and clouds were covering the moon and stars before he slipped out from his room. The final prayer of the day had already been called as warm gusts of wind danced across the desert. He chose to wear only shorts and a t-shirt and was cautious as he moved from shadow to shadow until he reached the fence line and his escape. Slipping under the gap in the fence, he stripped off the t-shirt and left it on the ground before heading out at a brisk pace, bare feet treading across the sand.

He was uncertain as to when or even if he might be followed, but kept his pace even and his eyes forward, following a path he set in his mind. Sighing internally, he wasn't certain whether he would find himself running alone or would suddenly find himself in chase.

An hour into the run, he felt the winds begin to pick up and with them, the sand kicked up. Some gusts brought about a blast of sand that stung his skin and caused him to squint his eyes to avoid the grit.

As he ran, he felt it: the coming storm. Against the dark backdrop of night, he felt a wave of sand approaching from the distance as a darker cloud rolled, inking out the stars. He shook his head and turned to start heading back to the base.

The sight behind him stopped him in his tracks. It was hard to count the number of dark shadows rapidly approaching the short distance away, but dozens by initial guess. Where he thought he should have felt a wave of fear, instead he felt a hot desire to charge and meet them. The urge was strong as he fought down the instinct and forced him self to stand down and stick to his original plan. He felt the deep desire to shift into lycan form, yet held back, staying human as long as possible.

Spinning on heal, he broke into a run and from behind heard the baying of one of the lycans as the Sons of Anubis gave chase in earnest. His plans continued to fray and fall apart as the storm began picking up and the wave of sand closed in from the North.

Brand cut west, glancing over his shoulder and watching as the massive pack cut across the sand to follow. He lengthened his stride, trying to stay ahead of both the chasing pack as well as the massive wall of sand rolling across the desert. Both nature and enemy threatened to overtake him as the pack ran in hybrid form, some shifting into full wolf in order to run faster and the sandstorm picked up intensity.

The chase continued on for several miles, with some of the faster sons nipping at his heals forcing him to burst just ahead and out of reach. Leaning forward and stretching out, he started running on all fours, extending his arms and running like a wolf. As he did, he glanced under his armpit to see several of the wolves almost upon him. Looking forward, he saw a rim of dunes directly ahead.

He extended his senses as Ulric taught him, trying to ascertain how many possibly followed him. Within the group behind he felt one lycan of incredible strength: a female

In mid-stride he began to shift into hybrid form and leaped up, spinning and swiping out with his left hind leg and his left hand, both with elongating nails that tore through the side and throat of the nearest lycan in pursuit and followed by a sweeping right paw. The creature started to yelp and gurgled instead as it's head caved in and it fell aside. The next closest attempted to bowl into Brand, who stood tall against their numbers and spun into them, swiping with claws and snapping. He tore into those nearest and caught a second with a throw across his hip. He fought into them, his rage catching them off guard. As he did, they fell aside and attempted to encircle him as the remaining numbers were still catching up.

He heard the pump and hiss as the 40-millimeter explosive round was chambered and fired towards them. He trusted his Chief's aim and knew the round would be directed towards those immediately pursuing him and he was rewarded with the explosion behind. It was followed by intense gunfire.

From the dune tops, both Prim and Timmons opened fire. Prim launched two rounds of 40-millimeter high explosive while Timmons went fully automatic with his M-240. Both men fired weapons that seemed to belch fire as they had loaded their machine guns entirely with tracer rounds. While Timmons lay down a blaze of 7.62 rounds from the mighty machine gun he shouldered, Prim took a moment to reload the M-204 on the under belly of his M-4, launching more explosive rounds before selectively firing three-round bursts into individual lycans as they swirled around Brand.

When the tracer rounds hit their target, the incendiary burned into the lycans skin and flesh. The burning tore into them as heavily as the explosive impact.

Timmons fed the belt of 7.62 rounds through his machine gun until he ran dry and then knelt to pull a second belt of rounds from a duffel bag slung across his back. As he did, Prim stood over-watch, laying down suppressive fire and launching another explosive round.

Dzigeleski and Parker moved into place on either side of the chiefs with M-16 rifles. The two selected targets and burped rounds into individual lycans on the perimeter.

The wind began to wail as the sand drove down upon them and Brand tried to call out, howling against the storm. From the top of the hill, Valko, Cedric and Watson leaped down and tore into the confused lycans.

The massive Cedric with his dark black fur was a shadow against the wall of sand. He tore into the sons of

Anubis, raging and howling. The normally calm giant was beyond control as he raked his mighty paws into the first lycan he fell upon, rending flesh and snapping bones.

In his growls and thoughts, Brand conveyed that more were coming as he drove his long talons through the throat of the nearest pursuant. He tore his fingers loose and with his free hand he twisted the head and snapped the neck back, leaving it as dead.

Watson moved to his side, leaping on the nearest lycan to him and snapping her jaws on its neck. All four limbs tore into it while driving it down, shredding flesh and crushing it into the sand.

Valko moved around to the side and was immediately set upon by two. He fought back but a third and fourth leapt upon him. One snapped powerful jaws upon his arm and he yelped, feeling teeth rend against bone.

Two rounds erupted through the creature's torso and it rolled off to the side. Short bursts of automatic fire ripped into the remaining werewolves and Valko felt himself pulled away with a powerful grip on the back of his neck. He looked up to see Huang dragging him to safety while Wong fired twin MP-5s in either hand. She stayed close to the Senior Agent; firing short bursts into individual creatures and driving them back.

The massive Cedric drove into the remaining creatures while Huang and Wong pulled the injured Valko from the mix. Wong watched as more of the sons began appearing from the wall of sand and piling onto the giant werewolf.

She attempted to fire into the bunch and her twin guns emptied. Two of the new lycans turned on her and gave chase.

She heard the roar of the M-4 as Prim slid past her and went fully automatic on the two, emptying his clip before pumping a round from his M204 and launching an explosive round. It hit the nearest lycan.

"Fuck." He whispered, and turned to launch himself on Wong as the round exploded in the lycan's chest a few feet away.

Sand was spinning all around and the Chief rolled over, ejecting the magazine from his weapon and attempting to reload by slapping a new magazine into place. Parker stepped over him, shouldering his M-16 and firing short bursts into the increasing numbers of lycans.

From the growing throng of enemies, three burst forward, toppling Parker and savaging the young Petty Officer. He screamed, attempting to maneuver his weapon against them and instead firing rounds in a spinning circle.

Prim felt the impact as one of the 5.56 rounds slammed into his Kevlar vest and shattered the plate. He grunted and fell back, his breath hissing from his lungs as he attempted to gasp to recapture his air. He struggled to his knees, lifting his weapon as Wong grabbed him by the arm with one hand while firing one MP-5 with the other. Wong helped Prim to his feet and both continued backing up.

Prim shouted, "Heads!" And triggered the M-204, lobbing a 40 millimeter grenade into the group that had descended upon Parker.

The grenade exploded, sending lycans and body parts in a wide dispersal. Some died while other howled and rolled away, singed and injured but recovering.

They briefly saw Cedric stand in the midst of a dozen lycans before their sheer number weighed him down. Wong stood behind both Chiefs and reloaded her weapons.

Brand and Watson tore into the pack on top of Cedric, and the massive black werewolf erupted from beneath the weight of their numbers. The three pulled back and moved towards the dune, where Prim and Wong were backing slowly.

A few yards away, Timmons and Dzigeleski were busy firing into groups of lycans as they continued to appear from the wall of sand. The fury of the storm overshadowed the chaos of battle as sand pelted all the combatants. In the roar and confusion, one lycan slipped past the barrage of bullets and snapped his jaws around Dzigeleski's forearm and twisted savagely.

The Petty Officer shrieked as he lost his grip on the rifle and a second lycan followed the first, snapping his jaws on the sailor's throat and wrestling him to the ground.

Chief Timmons swung his heavy machine gun towards the two and laid into them fully automatic, ripping through the two lycans who hung over the dying Petty Officer. He emptied the last belt into them, tearing through them and leaving them dead upon the body of Dzigeleski.

Throwing the heavy machine gun aside, he picked up Dzigeleski's M-16 and checked the rounds remaining. The weapon was low on ammunition.

Prim passed the torn bodies of several lycans as they moved up the sand. Looking up the dune, he saw Huang standing over Valko, poised and ready: a quiet moment in the raging storm. The Asian man held his hands out to either side, blood dripping from the tips of his fingers and a slight smile on his thin lips. The visual was surreal.

Already Valko was beginning to heal and pushed himself up to his knees. Within the surrounding wall of sand, they could see dozens more of the sons of Anubis gathering.

The small group gathered close. Prim, Timmons and Wong checked their ammunition and loaded what they could. Valko pushed himself to his feet and Huang steadied him. Brand stood in the forefront of them, facing down the dune with Cedric to his left and Watson just behind and to his right.

Across the short distance, the throngs of dark lycans began to mass. Brand could just make out three central figures, around which the others circled. One of the two knelt before the second and even from a distance, Brand could make the second out to be female. He felt her strength above the others. The third stood just behind her, waiting for her orders.

Cedric growled beneath the wind. "That's the one who killed Fergus." His snout gestured towards the kneeling Hassem. "I can sense him from here." He shifted forward coiling to leap.

Brand snapped out at him, sensing his thoughts and giving his own. "Stay put. They will come to us soon. Remain in a tight formation."

"If it's the last thing I do, I'll tear out his spine." The giant snarled.

Lifting his head high, Brand barked and his howl drowned the cries of the storm. For a brief moment, the pursuing pack fell silent, all looking to him and then turning their eyes towards the leaders in the center of their pack.

Um Ghar lifted a long, taloned digit and pointed to him, barking sharply. As if in response the storm intensified and the sand stung harder. Brand found he had to cover his eyes and squint in order to see. He knew her orders were to kill and he braced himself for the impending assault but the storm raged harder and they all hunkered down, digging into the sand.

Brand felt Siohvan press against him and he wrapped an arm around her, pulling her down. The storm struck in full force, pulling sand up and around for what felt like hours.

The storm continued to pass and as suddenly as it rolled in upon them, the sand fell to the dunes and was gone. Brand stood, throwing sand off in every direction. Watson and Cedric stood next, as the others dug themselves out of the sand.

Looking down the dune, the sons of Anubis were already gathering again while digging themselves out. Um Ghar stood barking and sending out her orders as her pack moved forward and began to encircle the small team.

Brand realized their numbers were considerably larger than any of them had assumed. The pack surrounding them, now assembled together, numbered close to one hundred. Looking to either side, he realized they would be cut off and surrounded by a number to large to counter.

He sent out a calling to the others and they understood. Stay tight and make them pay as best they could.

Looking over his shoulder at Huang and Valko, he nodded and turned back to Cedric. He gave another curt nod. As the two stepped forward to meet the surge, a long, deep howl sounded from behind the dunes, its sheer power sweeping across the sands. The entire pack froze and looked back to Um Ghar. Even Um Ghar seemed to be taken off guard as she spun her snout from side to side, looking from dune to dune.

Brand looked up to the top of their dune and felt Ulric arriving. The great silver lycan suddenly appeared, landing on top and squatting down to hands and knees. As he stood, a number of the sons of Anubis turned and began running.

Valko took one look at Ulric and instantly fell to the ground, barking at Cedric and Watson. The larger werewolf fell prone, keeping his eyes down, while Watson scampered to Brand's side, falling behind his legs and wrapping an arm around his ankle.

Prim saw the great lycan stalking down the dune and dropped his M-16, allowing it to sling around his shoulder as he grabbed both Timmons and Wong, pulling them to the ground as he squatted. "Trust me. Stay down. And don't fucking touch your guns."

Timmons hesitated for a brief moment before dropping to one knee and placing his machine gun in the sand. Wong knelt faster as she glanced around and saw Huang standing quite still, hands at his sides and his eyes down. Her eyes shifted to Brand who stood facing the ancient lycan with Watson hugging his leg and she shifted across the sand to brace against the British agent's back, leaving her guns with the Chiefs.

The great silver lycan approached Huang and stood before him a brief second. It appeared he held a smile across his wide maw and then he moved on. Prim kept his eyes averted as he felt it stalking towards him and then saw the massive paws in his field of vision as it stopped to stand above him.

Taking in a deep breath, Prim glanced up and saw the great beast staring down. It shook its head and seemed to laugh a throaty, course laugh before winking at him. He then moved on.

As Ulric stalked down the dune, the sons of Anubis who remained closest fell, their eyes averted before the ancient. The three further down the dune, Um Ghar, Hassem, and Udei, turned and began to run.

Ulric turned towards Brand who had remained standing. He shook his long snout towards the escaping three and yipped. Brand lit out, leaping down the dune to give chase.

He passed through the prone lycans and raced after the three.

Glancing around the others, Ulric felt Churchill yearning to give chase. The ancient lycan stalked over to him and knelt. Churchill lifted his eyes and felt the ancient let him go.

Leaping across the sand, Churchill gave chase, rushing after Brand and letting out a long, deep growl.

Ahead Um Ghar stole a moment to glance over her shoulder as they distanced themselves from the ancient Ulric. She saw Brand gaining on them and shook her head. With a curt yip towards the brothers, she extended herself launching into a full run on all fours and extending her stride as she shifted further into full wolf form.

Hassem and Udei trailed behind, turning to look back. Already they were just out of sight of the others and they only saw Brand. Hassem took one last look at Um Ghar and then slid to a stop and turned, standing tall and extending his long talons to either side. Udei stepped out to one side, starting to circle in an attempt to catch the American between them.

Brand slowed as he approached, snarling at the Sons of Anubis. Before he could engage them, the massive form of Churchill launched past him and tore into Hassem, his paws tearing into flesh as he snapped his jaws towards Hassem's throat.

Hassem staggered under the larger lycan's attack and his blood erupted across the sand. He fell back just beyond reach of the first snap of Churchill's powerful jaws and tried to respond with frantic swipes of his own talons.

Churchill drove into him, accepting a few scratches across his chest and abdomen but tearing into the smaller lycan with both claws and his teeth. His maw closed upon Hassem's throat and he started tearing into flesh and bone, shaking his head back and forth and shredding into the smaller lycan's chest with his talons. In seconds Hassem lay dead beneath the continuing assault by the giant Churchill.

Brand watched the scene a moment and then looked to find Udei launching upon him. He stepped aside and swiped a paw but missed as Udei twisted his body in mid air.

When Udei landed, he spun and struck out with the talons of his right paw in knife hand. As he did, Brand swiped his paws in a flurry, right paw followed by left paw followed by right, each raking down Udei's forearm and shredding the flesh to the bone while drawing him in closer. The second paw tore into the arm near the elbow, raking down the forearm, and the third paw tore into the bicep, shredding down through the elbow joint. As he did, he launched his right hind leg forward, raking his talons across Udei's abdomen and hip. Udei winced and sunk, and Brand swiped his left paw across the lycan's throat, lacerating through flesh to the bone.

Udei gurgled and stumbled to his knees, clutching his long fingers to his torn throat. As he did, Brand slid past and behind, snaking one paw over his shoulder and across his jaw, while sliding the second up behind his head. With a savage twist, he snapped the head in a circle, breaking the neck.

The lycan went limp and flopped down upon the sands, his blood continuing to stream out as his arms fell aside.

Looking out from the scene, Brand sought Um Ghar. The sands were empty as she was nowhere to be seen. He lifted his snout to sniff, but the winds and whipping sands, although abated, continued to play havoc on sensing anything.

He turned back to the scene of Churchill continuing to rend the corpse of Hassem and gave him another moment. Finally he barked and the giant ceased his attack. Brand knelt and lifted Udei with both hands, throwing him over his shoulder.

Standing, Churchill looked back at Brand, blood dripping from his jaws and talons. He shifted from lycan back to human form and stood there, naked. In his deep baritone voice, he spoke in an unusual calm. "That was for Fergus, you ball-bag."

Brand moved closer to place a large paw upon Churchill's shoulder and look down upon the torn, dead body of Hassem. Lingering in the air within the mix of blood was the slight smell of jasmine and lavender, and even less the smell of sandalwood.

Brand nodded back towards where they had left the others and looked back down upon the corpse of Hassem. Churchill knelt and grabbed the limp body like a ragdoll in one hand, shifting back into lycan form as his long talons tore into the dead lycan's flesh. He stood and set off following Brand.

A short trot brought them back within sight of their band. Ulric stood tall and majestic above the group, with the remaining Sons of Anubis kneeling in prostration before him. Even Major Valko and Watson kept their distance and stayed low.

The bodies of the dead littered the sands. As Brand stalked through the corpses, he saw one and knew it to be Abdulla, the nephew of the Colonel, in hybrid lycan form.

Chief Prim and Chief Timmons has gathered the remains of the two Petty Officers and were standing closer to Huang and Wong. Of the party, only Huang seemed indifferent to the presence of the ancient lycan, yet he seemed intent upon keeping his distance and both eyes on the silver lycan.

Brand approached his maker directly and stopped in front of the prostrating group. Of the numbers that attacked them, less than two-dozen remained. The immediate desert sands were littered with the bodies of the dead. He dropped Udei's corpse to join the others.

Watson moved quickly to join Brand, standing just behind him. Ulric stared at Brand and then looked to Watson and finally massive Cedric. Lifting his snout and shaking his head, he suddenly shifted back into human form. Brand felt himself shifting as if his body was of its own volition, and as if on queue, all lycans immediately transformed back to human form.

From behind, he heard Prim quip, "Now we have a party." And Brand couldn't help but laugh.

Ulric placed a hand on his shoulder and smiled. "How is your pack, Hvelpr?"

Brand looked across the sand and shook his head. "We lost two Petty Officers. Everyone else seems to be recovering." He looked to both Chiefs and to Major Valko.

"I see you caught the younger two. The elder escaped?"

Brand nodded. "Yes. She sent them back to detain us. In the short time it took Cedric and I to finish them, she was gone."

The elder took in a deep breath and sighed. "We shall find her. I must deal with these young ones first." He gestured towards the group kneeling before him. "I shall have them help me with the dead." He looked at the dozens of corpses littering the sand. "You did well, young Hvelpr."

"I think I know where I can find her." Brand stated. "I've smelled a unique scent of perfume a few times. Colonel Khalil's wife makes a perfume from jasmine and lavender. When I found her trail, I smelled specific sandalwood cologne with it. Only one person I know wears that sandalwood, although his cologne usually smells more like schwarma and sweat. And I've smelled that perfume near his schwarma shop before. It just took me a moment to realize."

Ulric considered it a moment and shrugged. "Find her if you can. She is much older than those two." He pointed to Hassem and Udei. "Be careful. She will be considerably stronger and more experienced."

Brand nodded. "Yes, sir. I'll have my team with me when I go." He motioned towards the others.

"When you are done, come back to my home. We have more training to do." He stopped and seemed to hang his head. "I am sorry for your loss, Liam. I felt when you lost your friend."

Brand stood solemn. "Thank you, sir. He was a good man."

Ulric looked at those who knelt and called out in Arabic. They all rose and gathered closer to him. "I'll take them home with me. They will stay with me for a while." He shifted and as one they all began to shift.

He yipped and pointed a long talon towards the corpses. As the Sons of Anubis spread out and began grabbing corpses, each taking one or two and collecting most of the dead, he lifted Udei. He stalked towards Cedric, accepting the corpse of Hassem from the larger man. He hefted the bodies as if they were ragdolls, each in one hand, and then turned back up the dune.

As they disappeared over the sand dune, Brand looked to others. "He'll return with them to collect the rest of the dead. We can head back. We need to take our own with us." His eyes settled on the remains of the Petty Officers.

"What do we say about our two Petty Officers?" Prim questioned. He and Chief Timmons started walking towards where the Petty Officers fell.

Huang spoke up. "Perhaps I can help with that. It will take some effort and a few phone calls, but we can report the two were targets of improvised explosive devices."

Prim chuckled and shook his head. "Where have I heard that before?"

The Asian Special Agent shrugged. "It is believable considering where we are? And there are very few questions asked. Do the best you can to gather them up. I recommend we bring our vehicles from over the dune and load up. When we return to the Naval Base, we will find a few body bags and take care of the remains."

"Agreed." Brand replied.

"Hey, sir." Prim called from where he knelt near the remains. "Why don't you and the others go find your clothes in the HUMVEE first? I wouldn't want you to catch a cold." Both Chiefs laughed.

Valko stood and approached Brand. "He has a point. We brought our clothes in our vehicle. Watson grabbed a set for you."

The lycans moved up the dune first, followed by Huang and Wong.

They dressed and brought the vehicles back to where the two Chiefs stood watch over the fallen. As efficiently as they could, they loaded the remains into the HUMVEE and covered them with tarps.

Huang looked to the others. "We shall take the lead. Follow us back to your building and I'll coordinate to obtain the body bags. Special Agent Wong will coordinate the appropriate reports."

Brand concurred with a nod. "We'll follow to the Navy Base. Once onboard, take the Chiefs with you. I'll take Major Valko, Churchill and Watson. We have a short visit to the schwarma shop first."

Wong moved closer. "Do you think you'll find her at the food court? It's barely past midnight."

Brand shook his head. "Don't know. But if we don't find her, we can question the shop owner in the morning."

Huang agreed from the side of his vehicle. "It's a solid direction. Let's all head back. We need to clean up as well."

....

Chief Prim drove the first vehicle, with Chief Timmons in the front passenger seat and the two NCIS in the center seats. The bodies of the Petty Officers lay covered in the back.

Churchill drove the second vehicle, with Brand sitting in the front passenger seat and Valko with Watson in the back seat. The two vehicles drove straight back towards the Naval Base, staying close and stacked one behind the other.

When they approached the gate, Huang held out his credentials and the Army soldiers waved them through. As the British team's vehicle pulled through, Churchill took a turn towards the food court and the schwarma shop.

They pulled up close to the food court and all four climbed out. Brand led the way towards the schwarma shop, the other three following and starting to fan out.

As they approached, Brand shook his head. "The scent is dead. She hasn't returned here. I can sense the perfume as well as the shop owner's cologne. I'll have to ask him who she is in the morning."

The shop was closed and locked shut. Even with the wooden door in place, they were able to detect each of the different smells emanating from the shop. They mostly smelled the seasoned chicken, lamb and beef with the musky scent of the sandalwood cologne barely discernable beneath the odors of food. And as they stood there and focused, they were able to finally make out the undertone of lavender and jasmine.

Churchill spoke first. "I can taste the perfume in the air. But I cannot determine her smell." He moved as close to the wooden door as possible. "I smell the sweaty shop owner. But . . . not the female."

The others concurred. Looking to Brand, Major Valko asked, "What shall we do?"

He looked at the shop door a moment before responding. "Go get some rest. I'll check with our NCIS agents but will probably catch a few hours of sleep. We can swing back by in the morning and see what he has to say about the female he has working there."

"We all come back as a team?" Watson stated more than asked.

Brand nodded. "Of course. Best to play it safe."

The team returned to their vehicle.

....

In the morning, Brand woke to find both Prim and Timmons waiting in the courtyard for him. As he greeted them in the courtyard, Wong entered, carrying two coffees.

She approached the three men and offered one to Brand. "Good morning, Commander."

"Hey! Where's the love?" Prim protested, looking from Wong to the two coffees and then held up his empty hands as Timmons laughed.

Wong shrugged and offered a smile in return. "I know how the Commander takes his coffee."

Looking sternly at Brand, Prim shook his head. "I'm not even going to ask."

Wong returned to her normal business visage. "Huang asked that I visit you and bring you up to speed. We've submitted the initial reports on what happened last night. He already has approval for the cover story and we will be coordinating the repatriation of the two soldiers back to the states." Looking to Chief Timmons, she added, "I hope it offers some consolation that my Senior Agent is coordinating medals for their valor."

Chief Timmons nodded. "Thanks. It does. I'm sure their families will appreciate the effort. Although I'm certain they'll never hear the full story."

She shook her head. "I'm afraid not. But the official report will reflect that they sacrificed themselves in a heated engagement against a known terrorist cell of extremists operating in Kuwait. Although that much is true, we just won't go into any more detail."

"Yeah. Best not." Prim agreed.

Brand enjoyed a sip of coffee and nodded. "Thanks, Agent Wong: great cup of coffee. And just the right amount of sugar and cream."

At that moment, the British team entered the courtyard. Watson led both Churchill and Valko.

"Good morning, all." She spoke, glancing at Wong and then the two Chiefs. "Early rise?"

Wong shook her head. "No more than normal. I was sharing our official report on the events of last night. I had best head back to Senior Agent Huang. We have more reports to finish before we depart."

"And we have a visit to our schwarma shop." Brand stated, sipping his coffee. "We'll be back."

Prim called as they were walking across the courtyard. "Don't destroy my favorite shop. Just ask a few questions. I'm planning on eating there for lunch today."

"Heaven forbid we should let a terrorist cell interfere with your lunch." Churchill laughed uncharacteristically loud.

"Hey. It's my Commander's favorite place, too." Prim retorted.

At the schwarma shop, they found Abdullah wiping the tables and shaking his portly head. He saw their approach and gave an anxious gasp. "My friends. Please forgive me, but it will take me a moment to fill your order."

"What's up, Abdullah?"

The portly shop owner wrung his hands nervously. "My cook and his sister disappeared. They left last night and I haven't heard from them since."

"The sister: did she wear perfume?"

Abdullah nodded. "Yes. It was very unique. It made my shop smell better."

Watson spoke up. "What was their relationship like? The brother and sister?"

Abdullah thought for a moment and clicked his tong. "Not very usual. She was smaller and younger by appearance, but he did whatever she said."

"How long did you know them?" Churchill asked. "How long have they worked here? And how did you meet them?"

Abdullah shrugged. "I needed help as my old cook disappeared and I was advertising for a cook. This young Kuwaiti soldier visited. He said he was related to the Colonel. He asked if I would hire family members as a favor to the Colonel. I needed the help and it would bring favor from the Colonel. He is related to the Sheik." He grinned sheepishly.

"This soldier." Brand commented. "Do you recall if he was the nephew of the Colonel?"

Abdullah thought for a moment and then nodded. "Yes. I believe nephew. And although I didn't need both a cook and a waitress, I found I could use them both and they were not expensive."

"What were their names?" Brand questioned.

Abdullah replied. "Udei. And his sister was Aemilia."

Brand looked at the others and sighed. "Doubt it was his sister." Looking back to the portly shop owner, he followed up with another question, "Have they ever been late to work?"

Abdullah shook his head. "Never. They were the perfect employees. I have no way of calling them now. The numbers I have no longer work."

Turning back to the team, Brand stood silent before finally stating. "She's gone. I don't know if she's out of the country, but I doubt she'll be coming back."

"Concur." Major Valko agreed. "Do we have anything else to work on?"

"I'll have NCIS work the data they can find. They must have completed some paperwork. But I doubt it will lead anywhere. Chances are the Colonel's nephew pulled some strings and had them brought onboard without a thorough vetting. We should check with Major Mohammed."

"I'll take care of that." Churchill offered. "I can swing by immediately."

"We might as well tie up as many lose ends as possible." Major Valko said. "If you find what you can from NCIS and the installation, we can follow up with Major Mohammed. If we have any leads that might indicate whether we can find her, we will contact you."

"Thanks. And I'll pass on whatever I find with the base." Brand responded. "I think tonight should be a safe night to sleep. We should all try to get rest."

Watson moved closer to Brand. "Mind if I follow you while they go to the Major?" She looked up to him with hopeful eyes.

Brand smiled. "Please. I'd enjoy the company."

"We can all have dinner this evening." Churchill offered. "Maybe here."

They had forgotten Abdullah was still standing nearby as he laughed. "I would welcome you all. I'll make sure we have plenty ready for your dinner tonight. And I'll expect my favorite customer Chief with you."

Chapter 18

Homeward Bound

B rand had finished packing his bags when he heard the knock on his door. He turned and saw Special Agent Wong standing in khaki pants and a blue polo shirt.

"Special Agent Huang asked me to pass you his well wishes. He is encumbered with contact back to the states. We'll be heading back shortly."

He approached and extended a hand. "Travel safe, Special Agent Wong."

She broke a smile and took his hand, replying. "Bai. As in - my name is Bai."

"You're right, Bai. Thanks. And mine?"

"Liam. I remember." She shook her head. "Huang saw that you're out of the Washington DC area. Our offices are located there." She reached into her pocket and pulled out a business card. "My Senior Agent mentioned that perhaps when you're back in the states, you might consider visiting our offices. I'm certain I could find some coffee." She passed him the card.

They both laughed. "I'll look you up. If you're offering coffee, I'll be there." He looked at the card and found it was blank except for a phone number. "Nice. Cryptic."

She turned to leave and he felt Watson approaching. The two women passed each other in the door, casually giving each other the eye and a nod.

"May I ask what she was interested in?" Siovhan questioned as she stopped for a brief moment to watch her disappear before moving close and pressing her forehead against his chest.

Brand wrapped her in a tight embrace and laughed. "Saying goodbye. She and her Senior Agent are flying out soon. They'll be gone before I return."

"Enjoy your time with your maker. I wish I could come."

"I know." He said. "I'd enjoy having you along, but I understand."

"We're flying home with Fergus." She stated. "Once we land in London, we're all heading to Scotland to return him to his family. I also wish you could come with us."

"I do too. I'd like to be there when the team returns Fergus home. But I need to return to Ulric."

"What will you do after you visit?"

"Head home. My orders will end soon and I'll demobilize."

She wrapped her arms around him and squeezed. "May I come visit? It may take us a bit and we'll have reports to write. But . . ." She trailed off.

He squeezed her tighter in return. "I'd be offended if you didn't. Email me when you can."

"Enjoy your time with your maker. Learn as much as he can teach you. And maybe, if he doesn't mind, share with me what you can." She looked up smiling.

He responded with a gentle smile. "Of course. Travel safe and wish the rest of the team well. Tell them they can come visit the U.S. whenever they wish."

She pulled away and walked towards the door. Stopping, she kicked it shut and locked it. She turned, grinning wolfishly. "One for the road. I can't go that long without . . . well."

....

Brand swung by Prim's room later in the day with a large green duffel bag slung over his shoulder. His Chief sat in a chair smiling as his officer knocked and entered the room.

"I'll be heading out shortly. I'll have my phone on me so call if you need. I'll text you daily with updates."

"You sure you're up to travelling, sir? You must be kind of tired after your two visits." He chuckled.

"The first was all business, although she seems to be warming up to us finally." Brand responded with a shake of his head.

"Yeah, well that one didn't last that long. Second visit was considerably longer. And the door was shut. She gets a bit loud there, just saying."

"Thanks mom. Glad you were paying attention." He waited a moment while Prim laughed. "The Brits will be off soon. Do we have our return flight home set up?"

Prim nodded. "Yep, sir. You've got four weeks. I'll call you if things change. Otherwise, we're heading home to demob and become citizens again."

"I'll aim to be back a day early so we can grab dinner one last time at our schwarma shop." He extended a hand and his Chief took it in a firm grip. "Stay safe while I'm gone."

"You too, sir. I've got Timmons to catch my six. I'll see you in four weeks."

Author's Biography

Anthony M. Clark is a native of Virginia and a graduate of the United States Merchant Marine Academy. He has a Masters in National Security from the Naval War College and spent the past three decades adventuring the world for the Navy. He enjoys outdoor activities, running Spartan races, attending Renaissance Fairs, reading and writing, and teaching martial arts. *The Sons of Anubis* is his first published novel.